PENGUIN BOOKS

# VANARA

Anand Neelakantan is the author of the Bahubali trilogy, the prequel to S.S. Rajamouli's movie. The first book in the series, *The Rise of Sivagami*, was released in 2017 and continues to be the no. 1 bestseller across charts. The book was on Amazon's list of top five bestsellers for 2017. Neelakantan is also the author of *Asura: Tale of the Vanquished*, which told the Ramayana from Ravana's point of view. He followed it up with the tremendously successful Ajaya series. Neelakantan's books have been translated into more than nine languages, including Indonesian.

S.S. Rajamouli has announced a mini-series based on Neelakantan's books, on the lines of *Game of Thrones*. Neelakantan has also written scripts/screenplays for popular TV series like *Siya Ke Ram*, *Ashoka*, *Mahabali Hanuman*, among others. He writes columns for *The Hindu*, *Indian Express*, *Pioneer*, *Washington Post* and other newspapers. He also writes a fortnightly column called 'Acute Angle' for *Sunday Express*. He has upcoming series planned with Discovery, Star TV, Netflix and Amazon. Neelakantan is also a prolific writer in Malayalam and regularly publishes stories in the prestigious *Malayalam* magazine. He is also a cartoonist.

He lives in Mumbai with his wife Aparna, daughter Ananya, son Abhinav and pet dog, Jackie the Blackie. You can look him up on Facebook, Twitter and Instagram using the handle: @itsanandneel.

# CELEBRITY SPEAKS ABOUT *VANARA*

'Anand is one of those people who has adopted the neutral storytelling style, leaving the perception to the readers. He creates the characters and lets the audience discover them. While he excels in displaying inflated heroism always, it is interesting to witness how he has put Hanuman and Baali in his book, *Vanara*.'—S. S. Rajamouli, film-maker

'Like always, a very engrossing perspective on our mythology. Anand Neelakantan's writing makes you question everything you were taught. He researches his characters and goes to a great extent to bring detail into the narrative. For me Anand now, is what Amar Chitra Katha was as a child.'—Nagarjuna Akkineni, actor

'The grey shades are as real as they can get. You cannot put down *Vanara*. Anand Neelakantan makes you feel it's all happening now and here.' —Rakyesh Omprakash Mehra, film-maker

'*Vanara* is a politically relevant tale and should be boldly applauded. With a captivating narrative, Anand Neelakantan brings back his suave style of storytelling. A must read!'—Ram, director

'Very rarely does one come across books that shake the very foundation of one's beliefs, thought-processes and understanding of hero and villain. Following *Asura*, Anand Neelakantan delivers yet another perspective shift in his thoroughly engrossing *Vanara*. I am a fan.'—Dhanush, actor

'*Vanara* by Anand Neelakantan is almost like a Shakespearean tragedy, a story of love, loss and valour. Baali's uncompromising principles and his relentless fight for the dignity and the pride of the Vanaras is inspirational and relevant even today. Read this book and learn about one of the greatest heroes of the Ramayana.'—Emraan Hashmi, author and actor

'Anand Neelakantan has always been one of my favourite authors . . . And he has been an integral part of my book club, SBC. His style of writing is fascinating and gripping and gives a new perspective to the mythology we've all grown up with. *Vanara* explores a love triangle of sorts and one that I've not really heard of before—between Baali, Sugreeva and Tara. I'm really looking forward to it and I wish him all the very best.'—Sonali Bendre, author and actor

# VANARA

## THE LEGEND OF
## BAALI, SUGREEVA AND TARA

# ANAND
# NEELAKANTAN

PENGUIN BOOKS

An imprint of Penguin Random House

PENGUIN BOOKS

USA | Canada | UK | Ireland | Australia
New Zealand | India | South Africa | China

Penguin Books is part of the Penguin Random House group of companies
whose addresses can be found at global.penguinrandomhouse.com

Published by Penguin Random House India Pvt. Ltd
7th Floor, Infinity Tower C, DLF Cyber City,
Gurgaon 122 002, Haryana, India

First published in Penguin Books by Penguin Random House India 2018

ISBN 9780143442837

Typeset in Adobe Caslon Pro by Manipal Digital Systems, Manipal
Printed at Thomson Press India Ltd, New Delhi

www.penguin.co.in

*Dedicated to my elder brothers Lokanathan and Rajendran*

# Contents

*Glossary*                          ix

*Cast of characters*                xiii

*Acknowledgements*                  xv

*Introduction*                      xix

# Glossary

Amma:       Mother

Ayya:       A term for someone elder or superior, like Swami in Hindi.

Ayyan:      A primitive form of Shiva. Many tribal communities call their God Ayyan. A forest God. The lord of the beasts and all creatures. The God who protects.

Ashrama:    Hermitage, a place where spiritual knowledge is imparted.

Rishi:      The one who sees beyond, spiritual guru, seer.

Maharishi:  The great seer, a superior guru.

Muni:       The one who has taken the vow of mounam or silence. A mendicant.

Tapasya:    Penance for a purpose. Also used as a term for supreme concentrated effort to achieve an aim.

Yata:       Ancient Sanskrit for sister-in-law. Sugreeva doesn't want to call Tara by her name as it would be against convention as long as she is Baali's wife. So he uses the unfamiliar term for his tribe while addressing her in public.

Bhrata:     Brother in Sanskrit

Anna:       Elder brother

Dharma:      Roughly translated as righteousness, morality
             though it has many layers of meaning and requires
             many books to explain (not to be confused with the
             Hindi meaning of the word, which is religion).

Brahmachari: The one who seeks Brahmam or ultimate truth.
             Also, students in an ashram.

Samskrit:    Sanskrit, what is refined, polished as against
             Prakrut which is unrefined or natural.

Prakrut:     What is natural or unrefined as against Samskrit or
             what is refined, artificial, polished.

Moksha:      Roughly translated as salvation, though moksha
             has much deeper meaning which requires a separate
             book to elaborate.

Kishkinda:   The capital of the Vanara kingdom. Believed to
             be the present-day Hampi, the medieval capital of
             the classical Hindu Vijayanagara kingdom which
             was founded by two brothers Hakka and Bukka
             to fight against the Islamic invasion from the
             north of the Vindhyas. It is in Bellary district of
             Karnataka, roughly 250 km from Bangalore. It's a
             world heritage site, where one can find many of the
             hills and rivers mentioned in this book. Hanuman
             is believed to have born in Anjanadri hills across
             the river, though a few other places in India also
             claim to be the birthplace of Hanuman.

Gada:        Indian mace

Parvata:     Mountain

Vana:        Forest

Nara:        Man

Vana Nara:   Man of the forest

| | |
|---|---|
| Vanara: | Monkey |
| Yaksha: | The tree-dweller tribe in this novel. They are tree spirits in mythology. |
| Kinnara: | A cast of travelling musicians among tribal people in this novel. They are celestial musicians with half horse, half human body in the Puranas. |
| Gandharva: | The Deva musician tribe in this novel. They are the musicians and dancers in Indra's court in the Puranas. |
| Apsaras: | Beautiful woman in this novel. They are the consorts of Gandharvas in the Puranas. |
| Rakshasa: | A wild Asura tribe in this novel, who were cannibals. In the Puranas, they are maneating creatures. |
| Asura: | A tribe in this novel. In the Puranas, Asura strictly means the chiefs. In earlier scriptures, there were good Asuras called Adityas and in this, Varuna, Agni, Indra etc., were included. The evil Asuras were called Daityas in which Vrita, Hiranya etc., were included. Ravana is the Asura King in this novel. |
| Mrudangam: | A percussion instrument |
| Para drum: | A tribal drum. Sometimes it is used during funerals in south India, though it is used in auspicious occasions also. We can see them in Tamil Nadu more. |
| Chenda: | Another kind of drum, now mainly found in Kerala and coastal Karnataka. |
| Nagaswaram: | A wind instrument, usually used in south Indian marriages for auspicious music. |

# Cast of characters

- Baali: Also pronounced as Vali, Valin, Bali etc., was the leader of the Vana Naras or Vanaras.

- Sugreeva: Baali's younger brother

- Tara: Daughter of the tribal physician Sushena. Loved by both Baali and Sugreeva.

- Swayamprabha or Prabha: Friend of Tara

- Sushena: The Vaidya or physicians of the Vana Naras or Vanaras

- Riksarajas: Adoptive father of Baali and Sugreeva, an eunuch.

- Indra: Indra is the king or chief of the Deva clan. Indra is not a person but a position like governor or prime minister or king. There were many Indras.

- Ahalya: Young wife of the mendicant Gautama

- Gautama: A mendicant

- Jatayu and Sambati: Giant eagles, considered representative of gods by the Vana Naras.

- Kesari: Adoptive father of Hanuman and one of the elders

- Rishabha: One of the elders among the Vanaras. One among the three in the council. The other two being Kesari and Jambavan.

- Jambavan: A tribe elder, the third member in the council. Because of his shaggy appearance and huge body, often mocked as a bear behind his back.

- Angada: Son of Baali and Tara

- Karthy Veerarjuna: A pirate king in this novel. He ruled from the mythical Mahishmathi (not to be confused with the Mahishmathi of the Bahubali world) on the banks of the Narmada. He is said to be a Vidhyadhara in some Puranas. He conquered many kingdoms and looted them. He is also said to be an avatar of Sudarshana Chakra as per some Puranas (Narada Purana). He is also known as Sahsra Bahu Arjuna or the Arjuna with a thousand arms. He defeated Ravana and imprisoned him. He was beheaded by Parashurama.

- Nala: The sculptor and builder among the Vana Naras

- Hanuman: A learned Vana Nara, minister of Sugreeva, a wise man

- Chemba: The tamed wolf of Baali

- Ravana: the Asura emperor who ruled the prosperous kingdom of Lanka

- Vibhishana: The sly brother of Ravana

- Dundubhi: A giant untamed bull, often thought of as the demon bull or Rakshasa

- Mayavi: An Asura chief who owned many fighter bulls like Dundubhi.

- Vijaya: A young Vanara warrior

- Rama: The prince of Ayodhya

- Lakshmana: Rama's brother

- Sita: Rama's wife who was abducted by Ravana

- Soorpanakha: Ravana's sister who was mutilated by Lakshmana

# Acknowledgements

This book is a tribute to the great storytelling tradition of India. From Valmiki, to Vyasa, to Kambar, to Ezhutachan, to Kritivasa, to modern-day masters: I owe everything I know to your works of genius. Your works tower before me like the Himalayas and I am a child standing in awe, wondering when I will be able to climb those peaks. I bow before the countless oral storytellers and masters who have taught the world how to tell stories.

I was writing the second book in the Bahubali series when the first book was picked up for a Netflix show and the book was pushed to be released the next year. I was writing the screenplay, but I was toying with the idea of writing a short story on Tara. I had already written short stories about Sita, Soorpanakha and Shanta, sister of Rama, and published them on Kindle. This would have been another short story in the series had I not met the ever-smiling, charming Milee Ashwarya of Penguin Random House. She encouraged me to turn this into a novel. I was scared whether I would be able to do justice to such a novel. It had taken me six years to write *Asura* and almost the same time for my *Ajaya* series. She pointed out that I had written *The Rise of Sivagami* in 109-odd days. Even then, I was scared to take up the work as I was working on screenplays of TV shows.

Milee stood behind me like a rock, chiding me, scolding me, pleading with me and prodding me to give my best. I will never forgive her for the many sleepless nights I spent punching furiously at my keyboard. I will never forget the encouragement she gave. No wonder the lady is heading the country's largest and

most respectable publishing group, Penguin Random House.
Take a bow, Milee, for without your support *Vanara* would have
just been a short story.

I should thank my copy editors, Pritsikha Anil and Saksham
Garg, for the outstanding effort they put in to edit the book in
such a short time. I salute their patience for dealing with a writer
who kept harassing them every hour with a new rewrite. I thank
my proofreader for doing the daunting task of sieving through
almost 100,000 words and Ishani Bhattacharya for correcting the
same in record time.

The stunning cover is a masterpiece. I thank the talented artist
Mihir Joglekar, and designer Neelima Aryan. This one is a classic,
lady, and I only hope my writing does justice to your art. I thank
you, Mihir, for the illustrations.

Preeti Chaturvedi and Twinkle Yadav deserve a special
mention for all the public relationship work they have done for
me and arranged for some fascinating interviews. I am grateful
to the press and TV journalists too for the extensive covering of
the book.

Priyanka Sabarwal and her team, who handled the social
media campaigns, deserve special thanks.

I am thankful to ace directors S.S. Rajamouli, Karan Johar,
Vetrimaran, Ram and Rakyesh Omprakash Mehra for reading
the book and talking about it. I am thankful to my friend and
superstar actor Dhanush for his words of encouragement after
reading the book. I thank my friend Sonali Bendra for taking out
time to encourage me in not only this book but for my previous
works too. I am proud to be a member of Sonali's book club. I am
thankful to Emraan Hashmi for his kind words of encouragement.

To you, my love, Aparna. What have I done to deserve you.
You will soon get that Nobel prize for patience that my friends keep
promising you for tolerating a cranky life partner for sixteen long
years and counting. Thanks for being my first reader. My daughter
Ananya, my greatest critic, avid reader, editor who always finds

fault with my Malayali-accented English and teaches me diction, and my son Abhinav who loves football and who I hope will one day read some of my books. To my Jackie, the blackie, from whom the character Chemba was inspired. One day, I will learn to love the world as much as you love me.

My extended family have always stood with me, even when I wrote books that challenged their beliefs and convictions. They have been my source of inspiration since childhood. My siblings Lokanathan, Rajendran and Chandrika, my brother- and sisters-in-law, Parameswaran, Meenakshi and Radhika and my niece and nephews, Divya, Dileep and Rakhi, have always made our family get-togethers lively with many debates about the Ramayana and the Mahabharata.

My neighbour Niteen Jakka and his daughter, Rucha Jakka, who gave the first feedback and criticism and made me rewrite a few chapters; Laksmi Nair, who was one of the first readers for *Asura* and now *Vanara*; my friends for more than three decades, Rajesh Rajan, Santosh Prabhu and Sujith Krishnan; other friends like Sidharth Bharatan and Anubhooti Panda, who were my beta readers for various drafts—all of you deserve special thanks for keeping me inspired. My Government Engineering College, Trichur batchmates of EEE 1996, especially Cina, Gayatri, Ganesh, Malathi, Maya and Balamurali who have read some of my works, and Mathew, Anjali, Brinda and Habeebulla Khan, who have never read and are never going to read any of my works but still encourage me to write, all deserve my heartfelt gratitude.

My special thanks to all the readers of my last four books. Your words of criticism, praise and suggestions have been my inspiration and the reason why I continue to write.

# Introduction

One of the most fascinating characters in the Ramayana is Baali, also known as Vali (Valmiki Ramayana) or Baalin, Valin etc. Unarguably, he was the strongest man in the Ramayana and had defeated even Ravana in a duel. I have always been fascinated with Indian epics and folk tales. The Ramayana and the Mahabharata played a major part in my growing up. I was seeped in the stories of the Puranas from my childhood. Most of my writings have their base in our epics and the Puranas. My first three books were on Ravana and Duryodhana and I had explored the familiar stories from the antagonists' perspective. Except for my last book, *The Rise of Sivagami*, where I based my story in the Bahubali world, most of my works, whether for television, short stories or novels have been based on the Puranas. I had also written a few episodes of the legal thriller *Adalat* for Sony TV and the story of *Battle of Saragarhi* for Discovery Jeet. However, my first love and fascination has always been our Puranas.

In my first book, *Asura*, I had written the Ramayana from the, perspective of the antihero, Ravana, and Bhadra, a common Asura. I had explored the Ramayana from Sita's point of view in the series, *Siya Ke Ram*, and explored Hanuman's heroics in the series, *Mahabali Hanuman*. Most of the readers will be more familiar with Hanuman. He is our God and perhaps the first superhero in the world.

The Ramayana has a fascinating story-world. One of the most intriguing stories is that of the Vanaras. As per Brahma's orders, Devas started parenting children in various races. In this, the Vanaras resembling monkeys, were born. All Vanaras had the traits of the Deva father who parented them. There are many stories about how Baali and Sugreeva were born. As per Brahmanda Purana, the story goes like this.

Once, there was a virtuous wife (*pativruta*) called Sheelavati who was married to Ugratapas, a leper. Ugratapas wanted to visit a brothel and the virtuous wife Sheelavati carried him on her shoulders. On the way to the brothel, a mendicant named Agnimandavya lay impaled by the king. Agnimandavya, who was in the throes of death, saw Sheelavati carrying her leper husband to a brothel. The uncontrolled passion of the lecherous Ugratapas angered Agnimandavya and he cursed that Ugratapas would die before sunrise the next day. Sheelavati used all the power she had gained through unconditional surrender and service of her lecherous husband to stop the sun from rising. Due to her virtuosity, the sun could not rise in the morning.

Aruna, the charioteer of the Sun God, arrived for duty on time, but was surprised to find that his master was still asleep. Aruna tried his best to awaken the Sun God Suryadeva, but the power of Sheelavati's virtue prevented the sun from rising. A bored Aruna wandered around and stumbled into heaven. Indra, the king of Devas, was enjoying the dance of the celestial maidens Urvashi, Ramba, Menaka and Tilothamma, and he had banned the entry of any other male into his harem. Aruna pleaded with the guards but he was thrown out from heaven. Aruna was desperate to see the dance. He turned into a beautiful damsel with his magical powers and reached the gates of heaven to try his luck again. This time he was allowed without a question. He enjoyed the dance of the celestial beauties, but as he was about to return, he was summoned by Indra. The king of gods, Indra, had fallen in love with the female Aruna. In their union, a boy was born, and he was Baali.

Meanwhile, Agnimandavya had withdrawn his curse, and Sheelavati took her husband to the brothel so that he could enjoy with his mistress. She also withdrew her curse and the Sun God woke up. When Aruna came back to Surya after assuming his own form, the Sun God was livid for making him wait. Aruna pleaded with him, but Surya wanted to dismiss Aruna from his service. Cornered, Aurna confessed what happened in heaven. Surya was curious to see the female form of Aruna. There was no way Aruna could object to his master's wish without jeopardizing his job. He turned into a woman and Surya was smitten by the lovely lady. In their union, Sugreeva was born.

Indra, Surya and Aruna were ashamed at what had happened. They didn't know what to do with the two baby boys. Indra took the boys to Sage Gautama and his young wife Ahalya, and asked them to take care of the babies. Indra saw the beautiful Ahalya and fell in love with her. The affair of Ahalya and Indra is another story, told differently in various Puranas and Ramayanas. Baali and Sugreeva were brought up by Ahalya and Gautama, but after Ahalya was cursed by her husband, they were adopted by Riksarajas, a Vanara chief. This is the *Brahmanda Purana* version, Chapter 42.

*Uthara Ramayana* has a different take on how Baali and Sugreeva were born. *Kamba Ramayana*, *Poorva Kanda*, has some variation, but it is more or less the same. Riksarajas was born out of Brahma's tears. He was an ugly but strong monkey. Brahma asked him to fight the Asuras and destroy them and Riksarajas roamed around the forests of the world, killing Rakshasas and Asuras. Once, he happened to see his own reflection in a lake. Mistaking his reflection to be another Rakshasa, he jumped into the lake to fight his foe. The moment he jumped, the water was disturbed and he thought the Rakshasa had run away. He climbed back and sat on a rock to dry himself. By that time, the water was still and he could see his reflection again. He roared and jumped into the water to vanquish the foe. This continued till the sun set and he understood his folly. But by that time, a strange thing had happened. He had lost his manhood and had become a beautiful woman. As the sun had set, the Sun God Suryadeva and Indra, the king of gods, had to come to take a bath in the lake. They saw this beautiful woman and became passionate. The woman Riksarajas ran from the passionate gods, but they caught her. From Indra's semen that fell on Riksarajas' hair, Baali was born. From Surya's semen that fell on Riksarajas' neck (greeva), Sugreeva was born. Riksarajas went to Brahma to complain and Brahma gave Riksarajas the boon of being a man and woman at the same time. Later, Riksarajas became the King of Vanaras with the help of his sons.

Similarly, Tara is mentioned as an Apsara who came out of the ocean of milk during the churning as per *Kamba Ramayana Yudha Kanda*. Along with Tara, Ruma also emerged. Other precious things that emerged during the churning of the ocean (Samudra Manthan) were Airavata, Uchaishravas, Kalapavriksha, Chintamani, Kaustubha, the Moon, other Apsaras, Mahalakshmi etc. However, in *Valmiki Ramayana*, *Kishkinda Kanda*, verse 22, it is said that Tara is the daughter of the Vaidya Sushena of Vanara Kula. Tara is said to be the wisest of all in *Valmiki Ramayana*. She is a true leader and was respected by her husband and other Vanaras. Hanuman considered her a friend and sister. Tara is one of the five great ladies of Indian Puranas, the Pancha Kanyas. The other four are Ahalya, Mandodari, Sita and Draupadi. Please note that all these women were strong-willed and had an independent mind. Neither Sheelavati nor Savitri, who are considered to be docile, virtuous wives who consider their husbands as God, is in the Pancha Kanyas.

I have mentioned these stories to give a background of what the various Puranas and Ramayanas say about the Vanara race. However, if you have read my previous works, you might have observed that I try to tell the stories in a rational fashion. There are usually no gods, demons, magic, fantasy etc., in my novels. It is not because I hate fantasies. Our Puranas are full of fantastical elements, magical creatures, flying superheroes, gods, avatars, etc. They served a great purpose, and I love hearing stories that way. When I write stories by eliminating all such elements, it is not because I mean any disrespect. In my TV shows, I use the fantasy elements to the hilt as they work superbly in a visual medium.

There are many ways to approach our rich literary tradition. One way is to see them as religious books. Bhakti or devotion is the main emotion associated with such an approach. This is tempered with some entertainment. This is the method adopted by storytellers in temples and villages. Another approach is the general entertainment television approach. Here, the stories are changed to fit present-day morality. It is a sanitized version. The plot loses the rich layering, and characters become unidimensional cardboard puppets, but it is compensated by gaudy sets and costumes, predictable but dramatic dialogues, and pop philosophy with entertaining visuals. This is the Amar Chitra Katha template on steroids. Asuras are depicted as black-skinned, thick-lipped, fat, curly haired barbarians wearing gaudy jewellery and horned crowns. They laugh uncontrollably. The Devas are handsome, tall and fair dudes, preferably with a six-pack abdomen.

Another approach is to add fantasy elements resembling a Marvel adventure template, pepper the same with patriotism and imagine a world more advanced than ours. A Brahmaastra becomes a nuclear missile and chariots become fighter jets. This instils a pride about our country in the readers. It also addresses the hidden insecurity complex that every Indian carries as we have lost out on the last two centuries of scientific revolution due to historical reasons. It is comforting to think that the Mahabharata involved a nuclear warfare. It is easy to forget that the warriors were riding chariots and horses in the war, and yet they had the technology to make nuclear warheads. Stories need not always be rational. They must be entertaining, emotional, should quench human curiosity and validate our prejudices. All these approaches have their place, and all are equally relevant. So many storytellers are experimenting in expanding and interpreting our heritage in so many varied ways and keeping our traditions alive, and it is something we should be proud of.

So why is my *Asura*—the Ravana's Ramayana, *Ajaya* series—
the Duryodhana Mahabharata, and now *Vanara*—the legend of
Baali, Sugreeva and Tara, written like a historical fiction? I believe
the Puranas and our two great epics are our way of telling history.
This is how India recorded history. Typical to our fashion, our
rich imagination added many fantasy elements. My attempt is to
remove these layers and peep into what it could have been. So,
Devas and Asuras become two tribes fighting for dominance in
some remote era. What if the Vanaras are a mixed tribe? Is that
why it is told that Devas parented Vanaras in Asura women?
However, one cannot completely take away the fantasy elements
either. Many tribal Ramayanas, especially of central India, say
Pushpaka Vimana, the mythical aircraft of Ravana, was an
ass-drawn cart. If the same is used in a story, it will look ridiculous.
I tried to solve it by imagining the flying machine as one quirky
invention, totally different from modern aeroplanes. Something
that would fly with the help of sails, like the pictures seen in
some sculptures in temples. It is a choice the author taking the
quasi-historical fiction route while interpreting our epics must
make.

All my books are point-of-view literature. The reader
must keep in mind that the thoughts expressed are those of the
characters. There will be some elements of my thoughts. No author
can escape that. However, when I am writing about Baali, I am
inside Baali's mind. When I am writing about Ravana, I am inside
Ravana's mind. For these characters, the conventional heroes are
their enemies. If Duryodhana also considers Krishna as the God
and avatar, there is no story left in the Mahabharata. There would
have been no war. The greatest criticism of Krishna comes from
the mouth of Gandhari after the war in the Mahabharata. The
greatest criticism of Rama comes from Sita's and Tara's mouth
in the Ramayana. When Valmiki or Vyasa wrote them, they were
inside the minds of the characters.

My attempt is to stitch together a proto-historical narrative through the Puranas and the epics. If a youngster reads the Puranas, he is bound to be confused. It is a good thing, but it may also make him averse to our stories. Many translations available are horrendous. Sanskrit, classical Tamil, etc., are dying languages. My humble attempts are to make the stories available to the masses. I am sure there will be many portions that a learned reader may not agree with. I have narrated the story of Baali's and Sugreeva's origin from two different sources to show how they differ in various Puranas and versions of epics. Please bear in mind that this book is a rational explanation, my explanation, of how things might have happened. I am sure there could be different interpretations, understandings and inferences. I would be worried if there aren't any. A book should not be read and forgotten. It must be argued over, debated and, if possible, imbibed.

Our Puranas are like a gigantic Chinese whisper spread over many thousands of years. One can imagine how much distortions and additions could have creeped in or deliberately been put in to serve the agenda of the dominant classes. The greatness of Indian literature is its diversity. There is no one authentic holy book, nor a church or religious clergy insisting on one point of view. This is a tradition we should preserve with utmost care.

Baali's, Sugreeva's and Tara's legend is arguably the world's first triangular love story. Please do let me know your opinion and suggestions. I am reachable through:

E-mail: mail@asura.co.in
Facebook, Twitter, Instagram: @itsanandneel

# Chapter 1

His mother was in the hands of a man who was not his father. He was dressed like his adoptive father, wore the sacred ashes like him, but this man was younger. The eight-year-old could not control his tears. She was kissing him when he stumbled into his mother's room with a sparrow-nest he had found. There were three sparrow-chicks in it and they were twittering sweetly. His brother had climbed high up the palmyra tree for the nest when he had insisted that he wanted it. He wanted to show it to his mother and ask her for some millet to feed the chicks.

The boy stood transfixed at the doorstep—blushing, embarrassed, afraid and angry. He was old enough to know that his mother was cheating on his father. They still weren't even aware that he was there. He wanted to run away, yet he stood there transfixed. He needed to scream, but no voice would come out of his throat. He gulped, and his mouth felt dry. Hot tears streamed down his cheeks. Unwittingly perhaps, he must have let out a sound. The man turned his face towards him. Their eyes met for a moment and the man scowled. The boy felt scared and looked at his mother. His mother hadn't opened her eyes. Her face was filled with a beauty and pleasure that the boy had never seen before. She stood, wrapped in the man's arms, her lovely face thrown back and her lustrous black tresses falling down like coiled snakes, kissing her waist.

'Run, monkey.' The man's bark made him shudder.

His mother opened her eyes, looked at the man and followed his gaze. The boy saw his mother's eyes widening in surprise and

1

then blood draining from her face. The boy's thumb went into his mouth. The sparrow's nest he had been carrying carefully so far, fell from his hand. He saw his mother hurriedly prising away the man's hands from her waist and rushing towards him. The boy removed his thumb quickly. He knew his mother was angry. She was going to scold him for sure. He was too old a boy to suck his thumb.

'I'm sorry, Amma,' he mumbled.

'Sugreeva.' She stood before him, her face flushed red.

The man chuckled from behind and tightened his dhoti. 'Tell me, Ahalya, is this brat my son or his?'

His mother didn't reply. She was now leaning before him. She placed a warm damp hand on his shoulders. *Poor sparrows*, the boy thought, looking at the nest that lay scattered on the mud floor. He should not have brought it here. He should not have come here at all. The birds were chattering in fright. His mother lifted his chin and for a moment he stared deep into her eyes, which were brimming with tears. Sugreeva was aware of her misplaced clothes and her untied hair. He turned his face away to look outside. His skin burned with shame. His vision turned hazy and the Tungabhadra river that simmered in the summer sun faraway appeared as if it had dissolved into the sky. His brother might be swimming there. He wanted to see his brother. He would know what to do.

'Son, don't tell anyone.' He heard his mother's voice crack.

'Oh, why should he tell the old man, dear.' The man walked towards them. He stepped on the nest carelessly and crushed the chicks. The boy turned away, horrified at the dying squeaks of the birds. The man cursed and kicked the nest away from his way. As he approached, he leaned before the boy and glared at him. Sugreeva was watching the sparrow-chicks twitching in their death throes.

'Keep your mouth shut, boy,' the man hissed. Sugreeva kept looking at the chicks that lay lifeless now. A breeze that wafted from without flurried the feathers and a few loose ones flitted in circles, a finger breadth above the floor.

'Look here when I speak.' The man slapped Sugreeva hard. His mother held the man's wrists. Sugreeva glared back defiantly.

'You're scaring me, boy,' the man chuckled. His mother tried to say something, but the man raised his palm and she fell quiet. She tied her hair into a bun, stood up and walked away from them. Sugreeva wanted to get away. He tried to run, but the man held his wrist tight.

'Listen, you are not to speak a word about this to anyone. It does not concern you, so why are you bothered?'

'Indra, please,' his mother cried from the corner. She was not facing them. She was arranging the manuscripts of his adoptive father, Sage Gautama, in a neat pile in the corner. But Sugreeva could sense that she was tense.

'This monkey needs to know that he can't squeal. Not that I'm scared of your old man, that impotent fool, Gautama, but I don't want him to spread the word and make our meetings difficult.' He turned back to Sugreeva. 'Boy, she fed you and many urchins like you when you were hungry. She is the mother of the ashram. She will do what she pleases. So you will keep your mouth shut, understand? If she wants to sleep with anyone, that is her business.' Indra shook his shoulders. Sugreeva looked at the dead sparrows. A teardrop traced its way down to his chin.

'Please, don't make it worse. He is just a child. Let the boy go. He won't tell anyone,' he heard his mother say.

'He daren't. No one crosses the King of Devas. I have a doubt that this brat is one among my many sons. I don't know how many women I would have bedded so far and this monkey-faced brat might be one of them,' Indra chuckled.

'That's enough.' Ahalya rushed to them and freed Sugreeva. She dragged him out and slammed the door shut. Sugreeva heard Indra laugh from inside. Ahalya took him aside. His mind was still with those dead sparrows. He had made a mistake. What

would he tell his brother Baali now? Baali hated to see anybody
get hurt. Sugreeva had promised Baali that he would take care of
the sparrows before he had agreed to get him the nest. Now that
he had got the chicks killed, Baali would be mad at him.

'Were you even listening to what I said?'

Sugreeva was startled by his mother's words. He nodded,
though he hadn't heard a word.

'Sparrows,' he mumbled.

'Sparrows? What are you blabbering?' Ahalya asked. 'Never
ever breathe a word. Not to your brother, not to my husband. I fed
you and your brother when you were this little.' Sugreeva stared at
her hands showing how little they were when she had found them.
Were he and Baali as small as the chicks?

'You're too small to understand. Now don't bother about what
grown up people do. Be a good boy and play. Go for a swim.
Hunt. Climb trees. Do whatever you Vanara boys do,' she smiled
at him. He nodded.

He wanted to argue with her. He didn't belong to the Vanara
tribe. There was nothing called the Vanara tribe, his brother had
told him. Their tribe was Vana Nara, the jungle men, a name given
to them by the Deva Brahmins. Forest was their home. Vanara
was a slur, an insult used by all higher castes. It meant monkey
men. But even his adoptive mother used it. He looked at her with
empty eyes.

'So what are you waiting for?' she asked as she washed her
hands. She had touched a Vanara and had to purify herself. She
smiled at him.

'Ahalya,' Sugreeva heard the King of Devas' voice booming.
Indra, his mother's lover and killer of sparrows, was calling from
inside. His mother was getting impatient.

'Sparrows,' he muttered.

The door flung open, startling Sugreeva. He saw Indra
standing at the doorstep, glowering at him. Sugreeva gulped hard.
Indra hurled something at him, grabbed Ahalya's hands and went

inside. The door slammed shut in his face. Sugreeva saw what lay down at his feet and his heart sank. The nest and the dead chicks lay scattered around him looking grotesque, twisted and broken. He picked them up gently, not wanting to hurt them anymore. He gently caressed the lifeless birds, trying not to cry. Sugreeva wanted to see his brother Baali. At once. He jumped to the courtyard and ran, calling out his brother's name aloud. Somewhere on the way, the dead birds slipped from his hand and were forgotten forever.

# Chapter 2

Baali was perched on a rock overhanging a cliff. He wiped the sweat off his forehead with the back of his hand and went back to what he was doing. The sun was beating down on his bare back with a vindictive intensity. A hot breeze blew, covering Baali in dust, and then everything became still again. Rivulets of sweat traced their path over his black skin and pooled under his cracked feet. Baali tried to spin the Arani twig once again. He had seen the mendicants doing that in the Ashram. They spun the pointed Arani twig on a hole dug into a wooden plank and chanted mantras for hours. Baali had seen the twig smoulder at first and burst into flame. That was how holy fire was made. Baali was not sure whether it was the magic of the mantras or the spinning of the twig that made the fire. He knew no mantras and he was never allowed near the sacrificial altar where the Brahmin mendicants performed their rituals, but he was always fascinated with fire. He had got a discarded Arani twig and had rushed to the rock to conduct his experiment. He had spent some time in the morning to get the sparrow-nest for his twin, Sugreeva. The thought of Sugreeva made him smile. Though they were of the same age, Sugreeva always considered Baali his elder brother. Baali had no one else in the world, except Sugreeva. *The boy is a dreamer and trusts everyone blindly. he needs to be protected*, thought Baali. He wiped sweat from his brow with the back of his hand and went back to spinning the twig.

A whiff of smoke rose from the tip of the twig. Baali paused to smile. He whistled a long-forgotten tune and resumed his work rigorously. He pushed some dry leaves into the stone depression and blew hard as he continued to twirl the twig. Baali paused to catch his breath. His palms had grown red with exertion but he looked at his handiwork with satisfaction. The thin waft of smoke had dissolved into the air, but he was feeling elated. Sage Gautama, the head of the Ashram, had barked at him when he had asked how fire was made. The sage had lectured Baali that fire was sacred, and it was not something Vanara boys should even think about, let alone learn how to make. Fire hid in the trees and in the sky, the sage had said, and it was the mantras that set the fire free. The world was made of five elements—fire, water, earth, air and sky, and the fire was the most important among the five. Those who controlled fire, controlled the world.

The fire burst with a snap and licked the dry leaves. The fire needed no magical chants to appear. It had come to him, a low-caste forest dweller, just by rubbing a few twigs. It needed only effort and perseverance. That he had in plenty. Baali watched the flames consuming the leaves and pushed more of them into the fire. The fire cackled, and Baali slapped his thigh hard in satisfaction and laughed out loud. Agni, the fire God, didn't discriminate between the Brahmins who knew Vedic chants and a poor Vanara child. Did he think himself as Vanara? He paused. He always hated the slur, but had no power to protest against it. His desperate attempts to correct other children in the Ashram had always ended in disaster.

But one incident amused him still. It had happened during last summer, just before the monsoon clouds had arrived across the western mountains. Baali chuckled to himself as he remembered it. A Brahmachari had called Sugreeva a monkey, a Vanara, and his brother had come to him crying. Baali decided to give the high-born boy a taste of his own words. Baali and Sugreeva had climbed up the Banyan tree and hid behind its branches. They lay in wait for the Brahmin students to appear. Baali had carried a reed basket full of ripe mangoes. Sugreeva was scared that they were committing a sin by acting against Brahmins, but Baali assured him that they were just making the words of Brahmins come true. They would show what monkeys could do. The two brothers sat sucking the ripe mangoes. Baali carefully collected the mango seeds after they had sucked the last strands of their juice. The sweet smell of mangoes attracted bees and birds who flocked around them. Baali amused Sugreeva by allowing sparrows and crows to eat ripe mangoes from his hands. They weren't afraid of him. When Sugreeva asked how they could be so trusting of him, Baali replied, 'They return the trust you give them. You trust them not to peck you and they trust you not to catch them.' Before Sugreeva could reply, the students of the Ashram had arrived for the lessons. The brothers watched them sitting cross-legged and chanting mantras in Sanskrit. They were waiting for the sages to arrive. Baali chuckled at their chants, and the boys paused and looked up at the tree fearfully.

A carefully aimed throw of sucked mango seed splashed on the face of the Brahmachari who had called Sugreeva a monkey. There was an uproar from the Brahmin students. Baali grinned at them and scratched his dark body like a monkey. Then he threw his next seed. That too found the mark.

'Don't worry,' he cried as he threw another sucked seed, 'they're just mango seeds.'

A boy cried indignantly, 'Vanara, it's disgusting.'

The boy yelled as a half-eaten mango hit his mouth and splashed all over his face.

'We have licked them clean, Swami,' Baali shouted.

'Apacharam, Apacharam!' the boys screamed in horror.

Sugreeva joined his brother in the celebration, and the brothers threw the mango seeds and ripe mangoes they had collected at the Brahmin boys who were screaming and shouting from below. One of the boys attempted to climb the tree but slipped and fell down.

'Go and croak your mantras like a frog, you wimp,' Baali shouted as the boy lay down sobbing. Some boys resorted to throwing stones at the two Vana Nara boys, but none of them reached even half the height. Baali mocked their poor aim and strength.

'Enchant some blades of grass and make them the mighty Brahmastra. If you've not learned that trick, try cursing and making us real monkeys, Swami,' Baali taunted. Sugreeva was laughing so much that he was clutching his belly.

Soon, the sages in the Ashram assembled around the tree. They were furious. They asked Baali and Sugreeva to come down and Baali climbed further up the tree in reply.

'We're monkeys, and we live up in the tree,' Baali said dangling dangerously from a branch that swayed in the wind. 'You're the ones who seek Brahma or whatever, the ones who know magical chants. Bring us down using your mantras and prove you're Brahmajnanis, holy ones.'

No number of curses brought them down. As the night fell, the two monkey boys were still perched high on the tree and the entire Ashram lay in wait for them to come down. The Brahmins knew that their magical chants may have been useless in capturing the monkey boys, but they had a more potent weapon. What holy mantras could not achieve, hunger could. The boys would have to eventually come down to quench their hunger and thirst. They waited under the tree with sticks and stones, ready to pounce upon the monkey brothers the moment they came down.

The brothers spent a defiant night on the branches and Baali told Sugreeva the tales of their Vana Nara tribe, the tales of valour and the tales of the jungle. From the swaying branches, they watched a full moon rising over the Gandamadana hills and painting the valley silver. They saw the gushing Tungabhadra afar and reminisced of their frolicking when they took the cows to bathe. From afar, a night bird sang a melodious note and it triggered the primordial urge in the monkey boys to sing. Sugreeva sang with a sweet innocence. After a pause, Baali joined him smilingly. Baali's voice that had started to break added a rugged flavour to a song that was as old as the hills. The Brahmin boys who were keeping vigil, frowned at the odd rhythms and tunes of the wild that refused to obey the narrow straits of their canned music. The monkey song reverberated in the air, as free as the breeze and as fragrant as wild honey. It fell on them like rain, gentle, soothing and sweet. The forest responded with a vigour that the men of books could scarcely fathom, and a thousand crickets and fowls of the night joined the symphony. Far away, across the brooding hills, from the deep jungles, someone sang back. They were the men of the forest, the Vana Nara, to whom the forest belonged. Their songs merged and rose to the heaven, as a plea, as an admonition, as an accusation of betrayal. Their songs melted in the air and dissolved forever.

Baali woke up first. It was yet to be dawn but he was used to waking up early. His brother was sleeping in his arms. He looked down and saw that their pursuers were still waiting for them to come down. In the Ashram, the sages had started their rituals of pouring ghee and assorted twigs into an altar of fire. They chanted in an unnatural language which they called refined or Sanskrit. Baali resented that they called the language of the monkey tribe Prakrut, the natural or unrefined. It was natural for the invaders to see anything of the vanquished as inferior. The sages, who denied reality for the sake of the unknowable, invoked strange gods who they had brought from their arid cold lands. They continued to invoke them in the steaming tropical jungle where their fire altar looked ludicrous. They had forcefully taken over the land of the Vana Nara and many of their tribesmen had withdrawn deeper into the forest, fearful of the civilization that was marching at them with an unrelenting pace. Baali and Sugreeva were orphans left out of some forgotten war, raised in the Ashram as service hands. Their position was well defined. They had to wake up before anyone and clean up the place. They had to carry the night soil away. They were not to be seen when the sages and their disciples woke up, for the Vana Naras were impure. They were not to touch anyone and had to carry a broom on their back, so that the sacred Ashram wouldn't be defiled by their footmarks. They had to hew the wood and bathe the cattle. They had to clean the beasts that were sacrificed for pleasing the unforgiving gods who had marched along with the trespassers.

Baali resented every moment of his life in the Ashram. He might have run away long ago, but for his fragile brother. Baali ran his palm over his brother's forehead and frowned. The boy had developed a fever. He gently kissed his forehead. There was cold sweat that lined Sugreeva's brow. He mumbled something. Baali shook him awake. Sugreeva half-opened his eyes and blabbered. He was getting delirious. Baali knew they had to get down. He was scared of the forest-fever which had affected many of his people. The fever never discriminated based on whether the skin colour was golden or black or whether the tongue spoken was refined or not. It had carried away many to the abode of eternal silence.

'Sugreeva,' Baali shook him again. The boy was developing rashes over his body. Baali hugged him tight, trying to push back his own mortal fear of contagion. The lynch mob looked up. There were hushed whispers among them.

'Come down, you monkey!' a fat sage shouted.

'My brother . . . my brother has forest fever,' Baali cried in desperation. There was a shocked silence.

'Let me come down,' Baali said as he raised his brother to his shoulders. The branch swayed dangerously. A few dry leaves swirled down. The mob stepped away from the leaves, scared and angry.

'Stay there, you fool,' a sage cried.

'Die there.'

Baali was now jumping from branch to branch, balancing precariously and carrying the weight of his brother on his shoulders. As he came in their range, a few boys hurled stones at him. A few found their mark, but he continued to come down, not even bothering to wipe off the blood that was almost blinding him. As he landed down with a thud, the boys scattered and the few junior sages who were leading them stood fearfully away.

'Run away, you monkey!' a mendicant screamed. Soon it grew into a frenzied chant.

'Help him,' Baali cried as more stones rained on them. He covered his brother from the shower of stones. They were cursing them.

'Help,' he cried again as a stone smashed on his face and broke his lips. He had had enough. He hurled himself into the nearest Brahmachari. The boy screamed. Baali scratched his face and bit his cheeks. A few hurried to help their fallen mate but backed out when they saw Baali's face. He roared with all his strength and the forest stood still. The trees above exploded with frightened birds. The boys and Ashram inmates circled him, with sticks in their hands. Baali roared again and thumped his chest. A stone hit his chest, but he kept advancing at them. They backed up. Someone stealthily approached him and tried to hit him from behind. Baali caught hold of the stick that came down on his head and snatched it from the attacker. He smashed and broke the stick across his assailant's face and bellowed, 'Coward, attacking from behind?'

The man lay whimpering on the floor. Baali roared again, 'I want help, my brother is dying.'

'Die, you monkey boy,' cried someone. With a rage and strength that Baali never knew he possessed, he attacked the Ashram inmates. They scattered, running in fear and indignation.

'The world is going to end. The untouchable Vanara is hitting us,' a sage cried. Soon, the entire Ashram was in uproar. Baali knew they would turn against them as one. He had done the unthinkable. He, an untouchable, had dared to raise his hand against the upper castes. He had mocked them by throwing half-eaten mangoes and made them impure and instead of submitting to their punishments as per their sacred texts, he had dared to question them. He and his brother were sure to be killed. He had been a fool.

He hurriedly picked up his brother, who was now unconscious, and ran. He could hear the shouts of the lynch mob. A few stones bounced past him. He forded through the knee-length water of the river. It was a miracle that he did not slip and break his head on the sharp rocks. He made it safely to the other side. He put his brother on a bed of damp grass and collapsed on his knees, panting and puffing. He could see the angry mob still hurtling curses and stones. He was too far to be affected by either, but both created ripples, the stones in the river and curses in his mind. Why were they hated so much?

When the sun rode to the high skies and the breeze stopped blowing, Baali dragged Sugreeva to the relative coolness of a tree shade. Sugreeva was still feverish. He was not talking. Baali tried every trick he knew to try and wake him up. He carried water in the cusp of his palm from the river and poured it over his brother's face. He dipped his dirty dhoti in water and put that over the forehead of Sugreeva. He tried to revive him with jokes they had shared, and promises about the travel they had planned to the great city of Trikota that the Asura King Ravana was building in the pearl island, across the southern seas. He prayed to the God of the mountains and the God of the beast, Ayyan, who the invaders had usurped and called Shiva. The fever continued to be unabated even when the sun had begun disappearing behind the western mountains.

Baali wanted to go to the distant jungle villages of his tribe to find an oracle who knew chants in the old tongue, who knew the heart of the plants and the mind of the moon and who could work a miracle. However, he didn't want to leave his brother alone. He cried holding Sugreeva's limp body which was turning cold. The night that was hiding in the shadows crept out like death and slowly embraced the two forlorn figures. Trees started dripping dew. An owl hooted nearby and flew away with a noisy flapping of wings, startling Baali. Centipedes crawled over fallen leaves around his feet. Baali pleaded to Ayyan fervently, to save his brother or if he was powerless to do that, to make him sick too along with his brother. *Wouldn't my poor brother be afraid to go alone into the dark cave of death? Take me too, the Lord of the Beasts,* he prayed to Ayyan.

By midnight, Baali too had developed a fever. He knew they were going to die. Nobody would miss them. Nobody would even care. They were urchins of a forgotten tribe, not important in the world where mighty Devas and Asuras fought for dominance. He wished he would die first so that he would be spared the agony of witnessing his beloved brother's death. He could see eyes twinkling in the darkness. Jackals had come, sensing an imminent feast. Some time before dawn, he woke up with a start. A cold palm was pressed against his forehead. A shiver went down his spine. He was sure it was Death. He took one last breath and was surprised at the fragrance of sandalwood paste.

Baali opened his eyes and saw a beautiful face looking down at him. It took a moment for him to recognize the face as that of Ahalya, the young wife of Maharishi Gautama, the head of the Ashram. She forced him to drink some hideous concoction. He spat it out. His first thought was that she was trying to poison him. Yet, she forced him to drink it. He slipped out of consciousness soon.

When he woke up, he was lying on a mattress of hay. The pungent smell of cow urine and dung made him feel at home. *Sugreeva . . . where is Sugreeva . . .* he looked frantically for his brother. He was sitting in a corner, on his haunches. He smiled at him.

'You slept for two days,' Sugreeva said with a tired smile. He had grown thin. Baali tried to sit up but his head spun. He collapsed back onto the hay mattress. The cow mooed loudly and splattered a stream of urine on the floor. Baali watched it snake its way towards him. He didn't care. He was alive and more importantly, his brother was too. Nothing else mattered. They had beaten the forest fever together. They felt strong and invincible. A spider was stealthily moving towards a fly it had trapped in its web. Baali lay watching the drama without a word.

A boy called out his name from without. Baali and Sugreeva looked at each other. They had forgotten about the punishment they were sure to receive. Sugreeva helped Baali get up. They had to go through the indignity. That was their fate, to be oppressed, kicked around and considered lesser than the beasts of the jungle. They were Vanaras, mere monkey men. They walked out of the cow pen, swatting straws from their hair. The brightness of the sun dazzled their eyes. A crow hopped around in the courtyard. The smell of boiling rice made Baali realise that he was hungry.

They waited for the big men of the Ashram to arrive and read out their punishments. Baali looked at Sugreeva to see whether he was scared. The boy seemed to be resigned to his fate. When Ahalya came to them, carrying an earthen pot with steaming kanji, Baali was more suspicious than surprised. He thought she was giving them their last meal, like how they feed the goats before they're ritually sacrificed. She gestured to them to dig a hole in the ground. They were aware of the ritualistic purity involved in the gesture. The nobles didn't want their utensils to be polluted by a low-caste eating out from it. Who would clean the vessels that a Vanara touched? Baali eyed Sugreeva warily digging the ground with his bare hands. He sighed and started digging a hole in the ground. When they had made a mound of mud, Ahalya came near them, careful to keep the ritualistic distance. She put two banana leaves that she had brought on the ground. Baali picked one up, made it into a round bowl and placed it in the hole. Sugreeva imitated him. She poured steaming kanji into it. The boys waited for the water to drain away so that they could eat the rice. Ahalya poured a watery curry made of buttermilk, cucumber and turmeric into the hole in the ground. She stepped back and waited for the boys to eat. Baali and Sugreeva looked at each other for a moment. Sugreeva looked down as if in guilt, and started eating the boiled rice, licking his fingers once in a while to prevent them from being

scalded by the hot rice. Baali kept staring at the steam rising from
the hole and the yellowish curry settling down to give a pale colour
of stools to the rice. He didn't feel like eating but his stomach
protested with a grumble. He closed his eyes and started eating.

'Why're you two so naughty?' Baali heard Ahalya asking.
He continued to eat without answering. An ant came to enquire
and sniffed the lone rice grain that had fallen on the sand. Baali
watched it carry away the grain, staggering yet managing to take it
back to its nest. There was a quiet dignity to this tiny creature. A
dignity which they lacked, the monkey people.

'They mock us as monkeys, Amma,' Baali heard his brother
answer. Ahalya laughed, 'But you two look like monkeys.'

Baali's eyes flashed in anger. The rice she served seemed to
have stuck in his throat. He stood up.

'Eat son,' Ahalya said, but Baali had walked away to the cow
pen, to lie down on the hay mat. Sugreeva watched his brother go
and looked longingly at the rice. Baali wanted him to follow, but
he saw Ahalaya serving him another round of rice. Baali shook his
head in sadness. *The boy has no control over his hunger*, he thought.
Then he remembered that he too was hungry. He would die
hungry but wouldn't stand the taunt of that Deva woman, he told
himself. She came inside the cow pen.

'So much anger isn't good in monkey boys,' she said. He
looked at her in surprise and wondered how someone could
speak like that. He understood that she had no malice. She was
parroting what had been taught to her, but she was kind. Uneasily,
he remembered that he and his brother owed their lives to this
woman. She was barely a few years older than them, maybe in her
late teens. She was beautiful to look at. Baali averted his eyes. How
could she consent to marry Rishi Gautama, who was more than
seventy years old? The customs of Deva people were unfathomable
to him.

Ahalya pushed the bowl of rice she had brought with her to
Baali. 'Eat. You're recovering from fever and you should not go

hungry.' Baali took it reluctantly. He should not be rude to the woman who saved his life. He swallowed his pride and started eating. She watched him eat, sitting a few feet away.

Sugreeva entered the cow pen. He fell on Ahalya's feet, 'Amma, you saved our lives,' he sobbed. Baali saw Ahalya hurriedly moving back, lest Sugreeva's polluting hands touch her feet. Baali watched her smile, enjoying the respect she was getting. She looked at Baali, as if expecting him to imitate his brother. Baali continued to eat.

'You can keep the pot,' Ahalya said as she turned and walked away. Suddenly the cow pen felt empty. The lone cow in it continued to chew cud. Flies buzzed around.

Sugreeva said, 'Such a nice woman, isn't she, Brother?'

Baali didn't reply. He didn't want to tell his innocent brother why Ahlaya had generously gifted them the vessel he was eating from. Baali licked the last of the rice clean and smashed it on the floor.

'Why?' Sugreeva asked in horror. Baali went out without a word. Baali had decided that day to leave the Ashram, but his brother would hear nothing of it. They continued to live in the Ashram as if nothing had happened. Obviously, Ahalya had instructed the Brahmacharis not to disturb them. The taunting continued nevertheless, but never in the open. The two boys grew indifferent to it, or acted as if they didn't care, but it still hurt. They were neither treated as humans nor respected as monkeys. But Sugreeva was scared to venture out of the security of the Ashram. This was where they had grown up. He had started calling Ahalya mother and Baali didn't have the heart to stop it. For Baali, the jungle was his mother and father. He kept his distance from Ahalya and her old husband, the chief of the Ashram, Sage Gautama. He tried his best to wean Sugreeva off from his slave-like loyalty towards the masters but was unsuccessful. He gritted his teeth and stayed on.

So when Sugreeva spoke about what he had seen Ahalya doing, Baali's first reaction was to scoff at it. He was wise enough to know what it meant. Sugreeva was worried. Baali advised Sugreeva to keep his mouth shut. What Deva men and women did was their concern and Vana Naras need not interfere in them. Sugreeva nodded in agreement, but Baali was sure that it was tearing his brother apart. Though Sage Gautama was often indifferent to the brothers, he was the head of the Ashram and any misdoings of any member of the Ashram were to be reported to him. Baali himself was confused about what he should do. He cursed and wished that Sugreeva hadn't witnessed Ahalya with her lover. His fool of a brother had jeopardised everything. His ecstasy in discovering the method of making fire had evaporated.

'Shall we run away?' Baali asked, pleased at the thought of killing two birds with one stone. He had always wanted to escape the slavish existence in the Ashram and was ready to face the wild. Maybe, this would convince his reluctant brother to come with him. Sugreeva shook his head slowly. Baali cursed.

'It isn't right. I should tell father!'

Baali grabbed Sugreeva's shoulders and shook him hard. 'Father? Whose father? That sage isn't our father. Neither is that Brahmin lady our mother.'

Sugreeva gulped. His eyes were filling up. Baali averted his gaze.

'But . . . but . . . it isn't right. They fed us, clothed us and we should not be—'

'Fool, if you need to show any loyalty, you should show it to that lady and not to that old man. Has he ever bothered to speak to you, even look at you? For him, we're mere monkey boys,' Baali spat.

'Hmm . . . but what she is doing is wrong. She can't—'

'Why can't she? Are you a small kid? You're twelve. Grow up. Men do such things and so do women. She is young and beautiful and he is old and shrivelled like an old coconut.'

'But she is his wife. She is supposed to be loyal—'

'Says who?' Baali bellowed. Sugreeva's shoulders stooped and he looked down. 'Says who, you fool? These are rules made by a few selfish men. Who are they to decide who should be loyal to whom, who should bow to whom, who should rule over whom? A few men are manipulating everyone. Open your eyes and see. In the forest, does any animal obey such a rule? There, might is strength. What is true for a beast should be true for a man too. If the old man finds his wife is taken by a younger man, let the two men fight it out with each other. What has that got to do with us?'

'But there are rules—'

'No, there aren't. Not for us. For us, the rules aren't set by any books written by some old croak under the influence of Soma. They call us Vanaras, the monkey men. So be it. As far as Vanaras are concerned, Ahalya did no wrong. So you keep your mouth shut.'

Sugreeva didn't raise his head. Baali stared at him with contempt. He loved his brother, but it was exasperating the way he trusted people and developed a dog-like loyalty to anyone who behaved half-decently with him. *The poor boy yearns for love and affection*, thought Baali. He put his hands over Sugreeva's shoulders and pulled him close.

'I have made fire,' Baali whispered with a conspiring smile. Sugreeva's eyes widened in surprise.

Baali stepped back and threw his arms wide. He howled, 'I have made fire. The God of fire answered my call. They're all liars. Agni Deva doesn't care for the mantras or the caste of the caller. He comes to all, if we follow the method. I have a feeling that it's true about everything. There is a method, there is a process for everything. We can achieve anything. There are no magical chants that bring miracles. We can create our own miracles.'

Baali took a smouldering firewood from the Arani pit and waved it in a circle. With a swoosh, it caught fire. Baali waved it and the fire burned bright. Sugreeva started laughing. Baali pulled another flaming firewood and threw it at Sugreeva. The boy caught it mid-air. Together, they started waving the fire, making circles and ovals, drawing patterns in the air as they laughed and howled in delight.

'We have made fire. We can make anything now!' the brothers screamed, standing on the edge of the cliff. The valley echoed their cries back, as if challenging them. Far away, from the deep forests, drums started rolling. Maybe it was other Vanara men who were in hiding, or maybe they were Asuras thinking of this as a warning signal. It didn't matter to the two boys. They had lit the fire.

# Chapter 3

Baali was hewing wood when he heard the commotion from the main Ashram. He threw the axe down and ran towards Sage Gautama's hut. Most of the Ashram inmates were already assembled there. Some were jostling to find an advantageous place on the rock that stood before the hut. The sage was sitting on the veranda. His cragged face was grim. Without the customary toothless grin, he looked grotesque. He was pale like a ghost and seemed agitated. Baali searched for Sugreeva but his brother was nowhere to be seen. More and more Sanyasis and Brahmacharis were assembling in the courtyard of the Sage Gautama. Four Sanyasis brought a struggling man outside. The crowd gasped when it saw that the man was naked. 'Indra—the King of Devas . . .' the Sanyasis whispered to each other. The man was struggling to break free but the Sanyasis held him firmly. Another Sanyasi brought Ahalya, dragging her by her hair. He threw Ahalya at the feet of Sage Gautama. Everyone expected her to beg for forgiveness, but she remained quiet. Her clothes were in disarray, as if she had hurriedly put them on. Her hair was undone.

'Leave him!' she screamed at the Sanyasis who were holding Indra. Gautama sat without a word, looking far away. Only his trembling lips betrayed the emotion he felt. There were sniggers and chuckles among the Sanyasis. Some looked ashamed, some angry.

'Leave him alone. It's my fault, my fault,' Ahalya broke down. She covered her face in shame.

22

'No, it's my fault,' Indra said. A Sanyasi smacked the King of Devas across his face. Indra spat the blood and said, 'I . . . I had disguised as her husband. She mistook me for Gautama.'

There was an astonished silence for a moment. Then the crowd roared in laughter. The difference between the tall, fair and handsome Indra in the prime of his life and the old, frail and shrunken Gautama in his late seventies could not have been more apparent.

'No, I invited him to my bed,' Ahalya said with her head erect, 'Why should not I? I was married against my wish. This old man never wanted a wife but a maid to look after him. I have done that well. I have looked after him, fed him, bathed him, nursed him. But I have my needs too—'

'Enough, you whore.' Gautama stood up. He staggered and almost fell down. He steadied himself and pointed his trembling hands at his wife. Ahalya glared back defiantly. The Sanyasis and Brahmacharis drew their breath. A few chuckles could be heard.

'I curse you,' Sage Gautama's voice was shrill. 'You're stone-hearted. I curse you to be a stone.' People waited with bated breath. Nothing happened. Ahalya scoffed.

'Chain her!' Gautama roared. A few Sanyasis rushed to Ahalaya and grabbed her. They dragged her to the rock. The crowd pushed and shoved to get a view. A few howled and taunted. 'Whore, whore, whore,' the words rose like a chant. As Ahalya was being dragged, her gaze met that of Baali.

'You cheat. You unfaithful dog. I saved your life and you repay by betraying me, monkey,' she cried. Baali was shocked. He didn't understand what she was saying. He watched the Sanyasis drag her and put chains on her. They hammered iron pegs to fasten the chain to the rock. Indra managed to break loose from his captors and rushed to Ahalya. However, the mob soon caught him. He struggled to break free, but they started pummelling him and kicking him. They brought him bleeding and battered to Gautama. Ahalya was already chained to the rock. The crowd waited for Sage Gautama to pass judgement.

'Castrate him,' Gautama said. Indra screamed and tried to escape. The crowd had him spread-eagled on the floor. The crowd surged forward, baying for blood.

'Let all the castes remember that this is the punishment for violating a Brahmin woman. Let everyone know that not even the King of Devas is exempt from the rule of Varna.' Gautama's shaky voice rose over the din. Baali was carried by the crowd. *Where was Sugreeva?* His eyes searched for his brother but he could not see him anywhere. A blood-chilling scream rose from Indra and blood spurted up. A Sanyasi danced with something in his hand as Indra rolled on the floor, writhing in pain. The crowd was in a frenzy. Baali looked at Ahalya who was quietly weeping.

'Sew the balls of a billy goat on Indra. Let the world know the punishment for immorality,' Gautama said and the crowd cheered. A billy goat, that was brought for ritual sacrifice, was dragged by a few Brahmacharis. It bleated in fear. The air carried the rusty smell of blood. Dust rose high in the sky. The goat was pressed down by many Sanyasis. It bleated in pain and fear and another cheer went up the sky. A frightened leather worker came with a rusted needle half a foot long. Indra had lost consciousness and was lying on his face in a pool of blood. The Sanyasis kicked him to make him lie on his back. He didn't move. The shoesmith started sewing the balls of the goat to the king of Devas. The wrath of the Sanyasis was fearsome.

Baali moved to Ahalya. She didn't raise her head when he reached her.

'Mother,' he called her. He had never called her 'mother' before. His brother used to call her that. Baali didn't know why he had addressed her like that. She raised her head and a wave of hatred passed through her face.

'Why did you do it?'

'I . . . I didn't do anything,' Baali stammered.

'It could be only you. Your brother is an innocent boy. Only you would be so heartless to inform my husband. Didn't I feed you? Didn't I save your life? This is how you repay me?'

'I . . . I never informed anyone,' Baali said, trying to hide his frustration. It was unfair of her to accuse him.

'Get lost. I don't want to see your face. Get lost, you monkey. Take your accursed brother and go. Only he knew and he would have confided in you. You evil monkey, you took revenge on us. I know. I know.'

'Lady, I don't know why're you accusing me . . . I never—'

'Get lost. Get lost. I curse you. Let your brother be the cause of your death. I curse you. Let you die as an animal.'

Baali didn't wait to hear any further. He hurried away. He had to find his brother. He wanted to know how the Sage Gautama knew. He hadn't told anything to anyone.

Baali found Sugreeva hiding in a cave, not far away from the Ashram. When Baali called out to him, he refused to come out.

'Come out, you fool!' Baali bellowed. There was no response. Baali entered into the damp darkness of the cave, calling out his brother's name. A bat flapped its wings and flew past dangerously close to his head. His voice echoed in the cave. The cave smelt of pigeon-shit, stale urine and moss. Water dripped somewhere inside and the floor was damp and slippery. Baali's voice echoed in the cave. His eyes were getting adjusted to the greyness of the closed space. A rat scurried away. Baali could see Sugreeva crouching in the corner.

'There will be snakes, you idiot. Come here,' Baali's voice had lost its edge when he saw his cowering brother. Sugreeva slowly got up. He ambled towards Baali but never raised his face. He stood like a chastised child. Baali found his anger melt away. He sighed.

'I thought it was the right thing to do,' Sugreeva's voice was a little louder than a whisper. Baali didn't reply. They stood without talking, each brother understanding the other without any words exchanged, for a long time. Baali had a hundred questions to ask. He wanted to chastise the foolishness of his younger brother, but he understood this was neither the time nor the place. *The boy is worried sick*, thought Baali.

'We have no place here anymore. We have to leave,' Baali said softly. Sugreeva nodded. Baali turned and walked out. It was already dark. He paused for Sugreeva to catch-up with him. He heard his brother stand still a few feet behind. Without a word, Baali started walking towards the river. Night had already fallen in the jungle.

# Chapter 4

Baali and Sugreeva continued to walk through the thick jungle. Sugreeva wished the moon was brighter. He was scared of the forest. He saw his brother walking confidently and wished he had the same assurance, the same raw courage. The forest looked gloomy and brooding around him. It seemed as if unknown and unthinkable perils hid in the shadows. *They were waiting for a chance*, Sugreeva thought. Even the sound of dry leaves crunching under their own feet made him jittery.

'Brother, Brother, where are we going?' Sugreeva asked.

'To freedom,' Baali replied and continued to walk.

How will they eat? Who will look after them? What if some Asuras or Rakshasa attacked? What if they met a hungry tiger? Sugreeva was full of fear and doubts. Maybe his brother was taking him to some unknown relatives among the Vanara tribe. 'Vana Nara', he corrected himself. He was feeling tired and hungry. He should have listened to his brother, he thought ruefully. His brother was angry with him. Though he didn't say any harsh words, Sugreeva could sense the anger. He had betrayed his brother. He had betrayed his trust. He felt guilty.

'I'm sorry,' Sugreeva whispered. His brother seemed not to hear. He was peering at something on the ground. The dull moonlight had drawn curious patterns on the forest floor. The ground was carpeted with rotten leaves. There could be snakes. Every hair on Sugreeva's body stood up. He grabbed Baali's hand.

'Did you say something?' Baali asked.

Sugreeva shook his head. Baali knelt down and scooped
something from the forest floor. He smelt it. Sugreeva watched
Baali's face lining with worry and felt fear creeping up his toes
from the damp ground.

'Wh . . . what is it?'

Baali gestured him to be silent. He started retracing his path,
making Sugreeva turn and walk ahead of him. Sugreeva felt his
mouth going dry. Baali was shoving him to walk faster. A twig
snapped under his feet. They froze. Something rustled up in the
trees. Baali looked up. Sugreeva could not see anything. Vines
the size of a full-grown man's body entwined the branches and
vanished into the thick-leafed branches. Moon light filtered
through the canopy and made the branches look scaled like the
body of a python. Was something hiding there?

'Run!' Baali screamed and shoved Sugreeva. The forest
exploded with a flutter of wings. Sugreeva took off, tripping
against the undergrowth, getting up, smashing against trees and
falling back. He didn't understand what was happening. A whoosh
of air almost knocked him down. Then he saw it. Snapping the
branches of trees and sending leaves swirling down, a huge eagle
arose in the sky. In its talon, it had Baali and it was flying away
with his brother. As it rose higher, Sugreeva broke into a clearing.
He saw Baali flailing his limbs, trying to get free. The size of the
bird shocked Sugreeva. He ran behind it, screaming in terror.
By the time he could gather his wits, the eagle was a speck in
the sky. He picked up rocks and tried throwing them at the bird
which was speeding away, but his projectiles fell woefully short.
He watched helplessly as the eagle and his struggling brother
appeared frozen against the dull moon for a moment. Then the
bird took off, vanishing beyond the western mountains. Sugreeva
fell on his knees and wept. He had brought this fate to his brother.
He should not have informed his foster father Sage Gautama of
his wife's infidelity. He should have listened to his brother. He
had struggled with his conscience and had decided that he should

tell Sage Gautama about Ahalya and Indra. He had thought the
Sage would reward him. Instead, the sage ordered his disciples
to kill him. He had run away and hid in the cave. He hadn't had
enough time to even inform his brother.

Until now, he was afraid the Sanyasis would catch him and
kill him. When his brother said they should run away, he had
agreed thinking they would be safe away from the Ashram. He
was always scared of the jungle for he had heard about the fantastic
beasts, Rakshasa and Asuras who were rumoured to be living in
it. His worst fear had come true today. He had to find his brother
somehow. He might already be dead, might have become food to
the giant eagle. He had to do something. Sugreeva ran, calling out
his brother's name through the meadow. He didn't know in which
direction he had to go. The mountain where the eagle had taken
Baali loomed to his west. There was a thick jungle and perhaps a
few mountain streams to cross. If at all he managed to reach there,
Sugreeva realised it would be too late. *I have lost my brother for ever.
It's my fault. He was the only friend and relative I had in the world.
Now I'm truly an orphan.*

There was a distant rumbling of thunder. A wave of cold
breeze swept the grassland and made Sugreeva shiver. *I have to
do something. My brother might be dead by now.* Sugreeva started
running towards the mountain where the bird had taken his
brother. He tried to brush away the thoughts of poisonous snakes
that might be lurking in the grass behind. He told himself that the
distant roar of the tiger that he heard was not really that. 'That is
just thunder, that is just thunder,' he whispered to himself as he
continued to run. A bolt of lightning cracked a few feet before
him, blinding him. He fell down as the splitting thunder boomed.
He picked himself up and ran. The grass had caught fire. He
ran diagonally, away from the spreading grass fire. Another bolt
of lightning struck somewhere behind him followed by another
loud crack of thunder. Wind carried the smell of burning grass.
Without any warning, it started to rain.

Sugreeva ran through the grassland. Rain pelted on his face. In the next flash of lightning, he saw it clearly. The bird was back again. After killing his brother, it was coming for him. It was swooping down fast. In the lightning, its talons shone like daggers. He ran for his life, jumping over puddles, slipping in the mushy grass, getting up and sliding half the way. He reached the heavily wooded area and heard the bird screeching high in the air. He stood leaning on a tree, panting and puffing, trying to catch his breath. The forest was brooding and silent around him. Lightning lit up the thickly wooded forest in an eerie blue light. 'The bird can't reach here. The bird can't reach here,' he realised that he was saying this out loud. He cried in relief. 'I'm safe. I'm alive.' Then he remembered that the bird had caught his brother from just such a wooded area. He looked up fearfully. Nothing. He sighed. The bird had gone.

Sugreeva stood drenched in rain, looking at the sky swirling with dark clouds. Should he go in search of his brother? Why had the bird come back for him? Did it mean Baali had escaped or had the bird eaten his brother and come back for more food? Sugreeva sat down and sobbed. *I'm all alone in the world. My fault, my fault.* Somewhere deep inside, he was feeling happy that it was Baali and not him who had died. He fought the thought with all his might. He was supposed to feel sad. His brother was dead. 'My fault, my fault,' he kept mumbling.

Sugreeva was thrown aback by a loud crash. A branch had broken and fallen down. It had missed him by a whisker. He stared at it with dull fear. A blood-curdling screech reverberated in the air and he froze in terror. The bird dove in, with its talons pointing at him. Its wings caught in a branch and for a moment, it stood hanging in the air, his cruel eyes looking at the boy. The branch snapped and it fell down with a crash. Sugreeva took off, not waiting to see whether the bird was following him. He didn't know how long he ran. The screech of the bird from the sky urged him on. The bird tried to attack him whenever there was a small gap in the forest canopy. Before he knew, he was blinded by searing pain. He thought that the bird had caught him, but the bird was still flying low, above the unusually thin canopy of the bush. Then he understood the cause of his pain. He was running through a jungle of thorny shrubs. The pain was excruciating but the fear could overcome any pain at this point. The bird was keeping away respecting the sharpness of the thorns.

Sugreeva thought he saw some men huddled ahead, crouched under the bush. He was not sure whether he was hallucinating. He had lost too much blood. It was an unending nightmare. He fell down before a huge man.

'My . . . my brother is dead,' Sugreeva said, his voice breaking in terror and exhaustion. The bird circled above, screeching and flapping its huge wings.

He saw there were hundreds of black men, rugged and wild-looking. They looked at the boy and the bird circling above the thorny jungle.

'Jatayu . . . the boy survived Jatayu's attack.'

Sugreeva heard them whispering. He saw more people crawling towards him. They were speaking his tongue. The Vana Nara tongue. He had reached his people. He had cheated death. He was safe. And his brother was dead. He started crying inconsolably as the people surrounded him. He was expecting them to help him. Instead they started yelling at him. They wanted him dead. A couple of men grabbed him and started dragging him out of the protective bush.

# Chapter 5

As Baali was being carried away, he saw his brother chasing the eagle. He had screamed, asking him to run away. He didn't want his brother to be in any danger. As he was struggling high in the sky, he had seen his brother stopping his chase in the grasslands. He had seen him like a dot amid the swaying grass when the lightning stuck. He had seen him safe and Baali felt relieved. Sugreeva would survive. His sacrifice wouldn't go to waste. Then, sinking all hopes, he had seen the second bird. As big as the one that was carrying him, it flew past them. It seemed both the birds exchanged some communication. There was a pattern to their screeching. Baali saw the bird was flying towards where his brother was standing. He could not afford to die. He had to fight back, kill this bird and go back to save his younger brother. He didn't know how, but he had to do it.

The bird landed on a cliff and the stink of decaying flesh hit him like a jolt. In the flash of lightning, he saw there were carcasses of many animals and men strewn around. Rats nibbled flesh from the broken rib cages. It was a sight from hell.

The bird had pinned him down on the rock. At any moment it would tear him apart with its sharp beak. His frantic hands searched to grab a rock, a sharp bone, anything that could be used to hit the legs of the bird. He found a rotten rib bone of some beast the bird had devoured. With all his strength, Baali thrust the bone into the foot of the bird. There was a loud screech and the bird pulled its leg. Baali rolled away and stood on his feet. The bird turned towards him and tried to peck him with its sharp beaks.

Baali side stepped it and attempted to pierce the eagle's eyes. The bird caught the bone and snapped it into two. Baali staggered. In panic, he didn't know where to run. The bird pounced on him, knocking him down. It pecked his shoulders and a searing pain shot through his body. The flowing water carried him to the edge of the cliff. He somehow managed to hold on to a cleft in the rock. The bird hopped to the rock and snapped to rip off his head. The slippery rock spoilt its aim. Baali saw the rock he was holding break into splinters. He screamed in terror, imagining his head splintering like that. The water was pushing him down and his hands were slipping away. In the lightning, he saw that he was a few feet away from the precipitous drop of the cliff. Water flowed over him, chocking him, drowning him. It disappeared with a roar into the darkness beyond the cliff. He struggled to stand up but lost balance. The eagle's next peck missed him by a hair's breadth. He fell down and was carried towards the precipice. He gripped a protruding rock and leaned on it. Something prodded his waist— the Arani twigs. He was not sure what he would do with them. In the rain, it was impossible to use them. The only way he could hope to survive was with fire. He needed fire, now. A blinding lightning strike was followed by thunder.

Baali saw that the lightning had struck a tree at the top end of the hill. After momentary darkness, the tree burst into flames. The eagle that was coming towards him was blinded for a moment when the lightning struck so close. That was his only chance. He left the safety of the rock that he was leaning on and ran up the hill. The bird screeched and turned towards him. He had to fight the rain falling in sheets, the water hurtling down the cliff and beat the bird in the race. The bird hesitated as he ran towards the burning tree. He somehow made it in time before the bird decided to attack him again. As the bird came to him, he picked up a burning branch that had fallen on the ground and struck the bird. The bird had anticipated the move and it deftly jumped sideways. He waved the flaming branch at the bird and

yelled at it to go away. The bird screeched in reply and waved its
wings. Baali stared at his hand in shock. The flame had gone off.
The eagle came at him for the final charge. Baali dove to the tree
that was still burning and with all his might he pushed it towards
the charging bird. The tree crashed on the bird and the eagle was
engulfed in fire. It tried to escape as the tree pinned it down. Its
wing had caught fire. Baali screamed with relief and thumped
his chest. It was then he noticed that his hands were on fire. He
hadn't even felt the pain. He dipped his hands in flowing water
and fell down exhausted. Near him, the bird was trying to wriggle
out from under the tree. Its cries had become pitiful and Baali felt
sorry for the bird.

Just then he remembered that his brother's life was in danger.
The second bird had gone to hunt him. He had to somehow get
down and find his brother. He tried to get up on his hands, but
the searing pain of his burned palms took away his consciousness.
He started hallucinating that he and his brother were fighting the
birds together. The faces of the birds turned to those of demons,
then they changed to an unknown man having features of the
Deva race which again morphed to become an Asura with ten
faces. Suddenly, his brother started fighting him instead of the
attacking the birds. Nothing made sense. He was only aware of the
pain. Baali continued to scream, his limbs writhing in pain. *Why
was my brother fighting me?* 'I want him to be safe, I want him to be
happy,' he kept on murmuring between his screams.

Between his nightmare, he had a strange feeling that the
injured bird had started crawling towards him. *I have no strength
left to fight*, he thought warily, before the nightmare possessed
him again and took him back to a more painful world where his
brother wanted him dead.

# Chapter 6

Sugreeva tried to dig the floor. The men were trying to drag him out. It was straight out of his worst nightmare. He could hear the bird screeching above. Why were they trying to feed him to the bird? They were his own people who his brother always talked about, who he wanted to join and they were about to feed him to the giant bird. He tried telling that he too was a Vana Nara, but his cries were of no avail. He was too weak to fight the two men who were dragging him out. There was no hope left. He was going to die like his brother. He closed his eyes tight and resigned himself to his fate.

'Leave the boy.'

Sugreeva heard a gruff voice. There was an angry cry from the men. The men dropped him and he hit his head on the hard ground. He opened his eyes and saw a woman standing between him and the rest of the tribe. Her back was turned towards him, but he could see that everyone else was angry with her. They started yelling at her.

'No one escapes Jatayu.'

'It's a sin.'

'Once the great one eyes a prey, the prey belongs to the great one.'

'Defying the great one will bring misfortune to the entire tribe.'

The woman raised her hand. 'Enough.'

Her voice was like that of a man. There was an angry silence. Sugreeva watched the woman with surprise. Though he could not see her face, he observed that she had strong limbs like that of a man.

'Those who still want to follow the old ways, can leave now. They can go back to Jambavan,' she said.

'We didn't follow you to lose our religion, our beliefs,' a voice rose from among the men.

'Who said that?' the woman roared. The men looked down. No one dared to talk. The bird screeched above the thorn jungle, as if angry at the silence.

'Cowards!' the woman shouted.

'It . . . it's our law, our forefathers won't forgive us . . .' an old man said in a low voice.

'What law? We don't live for our forefathers' sake. If your faith says that we have to sacrifice someone who took asylum, it's time to burn your faith.'

There were angry murmurs from the crowd.

'We have sacrificed enough. We have lived like beasts in the forest for long. I'm ashamed of you. That bird is not God and it isn't our fate to be devoured by it or its twin. I thought you came with me, defying Jambavan, because you were disgusted with the way we lived and died . . . because you wanted a better life for your family, your children. You've proved that you deserve to be nothing but slaves.'

There was silence. The woman turned towards Sugreeva.

'Get up, son.'

Sugreeva stared at the woman. She was no woman, but a man. She had a beard.

'What are you staring at? Never seen a eunuch?' the man asked. His voice was rough, but Sugreeva could sense the kindness in it. Sugreeva stood up slowly.

'Riksarajas, the man who's also a woman. The monkey who's also a man. Ha, I'm the leader of the rebel Vana Naras. The so-called leader of these fools, these cowards who are chained to the past.' Riksarajas picked Sugreeva up. There were angry murmurs among the group.

'It's a sin. It will invite misfortune,' the old man muttered again.

'I want your help, friends. I want to end this all. I want that bird Jatayu and its twin, Sambati, chased away from the forests of Kishkinda. Better, I want them dead!' Riksarajas addressed the group.

There was a collective intake of breath. The old man came forward.

'Riksarajas, no one talks about the great ones, the divine eagles like that.'

'I will,' Riksarajas said. 'I will talk because I don't want our people to die like rats. And this boy, let Ayyan bless him, he has proved that one can escape from the clutches of the great one. If a boy can escape, so can we. Perhaps we can capture those birds, perhaps even kill them.'

The men cried, 'Sin, sin.'

The eunuch said, 'Sin? Ha, you fools!'

'I have no power to stop you, eunuch. I'm old and feeble,' the old man stepped forward. 'I followed you for my silly son's sake. I thought you would be the answer to the tyranny of Jambavan and his minister Kesari. But you've proved to be a headless rebel. You've proved to be having the virtue of neither a man nor a woman. Woe to us who trusted an eunuch. You're asking us to defy our beliefs.'

'You want to watch this poor child die?'

'You want our race to be cursed for the sake of a child who we don't even know? Curse be upon you, eunuch. I don't fear for my life. I spit on your face, eunuch, for you've betrayed our faith, our traditions. I can't fight you, but still I can defeat you. I offer myself to the great one.'

The old man rushed out of the thorn bush before anyone could stop him. Riskarajas ran behind him, trying to stop him, but before he could reach him, the giant eagle snapped the man in its beak. Before their eyes, it tore the man into pieces. Sugreeva watched the gory scene in horror. A young man, probably the son of the old man, was screaming and sobbing, trying to leave the, safety of the thorn bush. Risksarajas held him back, firmly, yet kindly.

The bird finished its meal, pecked its feathers and stared at them. One by one, all the men except Riksarajas fell on their knees and bowed. The man who had lost his father was asking for forgiveness from the bird. Riksarajas stood defiant and angry. The bird let out a loud screech and in answer, Riksarajas roared back. It was feeble compared to the ear-splitting screech of the monster bird, yet it had the power of defiance that made the bird stop its screech. The bird took off, flapping its huge wings. The bush shook like it had been hit by a typhoon. Sugreeva saw the bird do a tight circle around the bush as if measuring them, warning them. It gave a final triumphant call and flew away. The men lay prostrate on the ground. Riksarajas, the eunuch, stood screaming at the bird until it disappeared among the dark clouds. Thunder continued to rumble and it rained heavily.

Riksarajas turned to Sugreeva. 'Thank you,' he said kneeling before the young monkey boy, 'thank you for proving to me that one can escape from the clutches of the great one.'

Sugreeva's lips trembled, 'I . . . I was lucky . . . but my brother . . .'

'What happened to your brother?'

Sugreeva pointed at the distant mountain and started weeping.

# Chapter 7

When Baali opened his eyes, the bird had crawled near him. Another couple of feet and it would be able to peck him to death. He tried crawling away. The bird let out a screech. It had lost its previous power. The cry sounded pitiful. Both its wings were broken and charred. The feathers on its head had been burned and it resembled a vulture more than an eagle now. Yet, it hadn't lost its will to kill him. He crawled away and moaned in pain. His hands had swollen up. Water flowing over the rock had narrowed to small rivulets. Patches of water in the crevices reflected the sun like shards of broken mirror. The sky was azure, cloudless and clear. Dragonflies flitted above the rock. The bird continued to drag its half-burned body towards him. Baali had to keep clear of the bird, for now. He hoped he would recover faster than the bird. He didn't have any more strength to fight. The eagle continued to make croaking sounds but Baali was getting used to it. In the daylight, the bird didn't seem half as frightening as it was in the dark, stormy night. It looked like an overgrown pet seeking attention from its master. Baali looked at the bird and smiled. The sinuous eyes of the bird had nothing but malice. *It wants to kill me*, Baali thought. Maybe, the poor bird was very hungry.

The bird became alert before him. It turned its head and started crawling towards the cliff in great urgency. Baali strained to lift his head and saw a woman coming with someone. Sugreeva. He was alive. Baali wanted to get up but could not. The woman paused when she saw the giant eagle. The bird screeched but it was a sound more morose than threatening. The woman kept a fair distance between herself and the giant eagle and approached Baali. Baali saw Sugreeva looking at the bird with fear. Baali wanted to cry out that he had slain the bird, but his voice came out more as a whimper.

The woman knelt before him. He was blinded by the dazzling sunlight. He saw a woman huddled above him. Something was wrong. Baali found that the woman had stubble on her cheek; her shoulders were strong like that of a man. He was not sure whether he was still dreaming or he had woken up to a different reality. He was not even sure whether he was alive or dead. He blinked, trying to make sense of things. Sugreeva rushed to Baali and hugged him tight. Baali winced and to hide the pain he was feeling, he laughed. Relief swept over him like a wave. His brother was safe. He started sobbing.

The man-woman was looking at the brothers with affection. The bird had reached the edge of the cliff. It tried to flap its burned wings and fly. With great difficulty it lifted itself a few feet from the ground, but collapsed in a moment. It cried in pain.

'Riksarajas, a eunuch,' the man-woman introduced himself to Baali. 'You and your brother are remarkable. Your brother escaped from the attack of Jatayu and you've almost slain Sambati. I wish the fools who worship these birds as gods were here to see this.'

Baali didn't understand what this strange eunuch was talking about, but when he saw the shine of knife in his hand, he shouted, 'No, no, don't kill it.'

The eunuch paused, 'Why not?'

Baali had no answer. The bird had tried its best to kill him a few hours ago, yet he didn't want it dead. It felt wrong to kill an injured bird. Riksarajas was walking towards the bird and as if it sensed its imminent death, the bird tried to fly away.

'It's wrong to kill anything when it's helpless.'

Riksarajas paused. He had an amused smile when he turned to Baali. 'Who taught you such things, son? Life doesn't give many chances against the enemy. The best time to kill an enemy is when he is least expecting it, when he is most vulnerable. This bird and its twin have claimed many Vana Nara lives.'

'How about the other bird?' Sugreeva asked. The eunuch hesitated.

'You've a point, boy. I think I should spare the life of this evil bird for some more time. My people consider the two giant eagles the brothers of Garuda. You boys know who Garuda is?'

'The eagle of Deva God Vishnu,' Sugreeva volunteered.

The eunuch laughed, 'Yes, and these birds are considered to be his brothers. Even more reason I want them dead. But I want my people to see that these are just giant eagles—some quirk of nature that has made them so gigantic. They're perhaps the last of their species, but I'm sure they've no divine powers. They can be hunted and killed like any other beast. But I'm going to spare its life for now. I want my people to see it being killed, to prove that it isn't the God. Such are the stories propagated by the Brahmins to keep us in slavery. This has to end.'

Riksarajas hurried towards the hill top, leaving the boys alone. The bird gave another cry and tried to flap its charred wings. Sugreeva sat near Baali and held his hands.

'I feared you were dead,' Baali said softly.

'I was sure you were,' Sugreeva smiled.

Riksarajas came back with thick vines from the forest. He tied the bird with the vines after a brief struggle.

'Time to go, boys,' the eunuch said as he lifted up Baali on his shoulders. They started climbing down the cliff carefully.

# Chapter 8

Sugreeva sat on the floor watching Baali sleep on the reed mat spread on the mud floor. The eunuch had carried his brother to the hut of Vaidya Sushena. He didn't know what to make of the eunuch. He was repulsed by a man who dressed like a woman. Sugreeva hadn't seen anyone like that before. But he was the only one who was kind to him when he had met the tribe. Without Riksarajas, he would have been gobbled up by the giant bird. The thought of the giant eagle, Jatayu, sent shivers down his spine. His brother had fought a bird, more ferocious and stronger than Jatayu and won. Sugreeva didn't know how his brother could do such admirable things. Baali was his hero. But somewhere deep inside, he felt resentment. He had seen the disbelief in the eyes of the Vana Nara tribe when they saw that he had escaped from the clutches of Jatayu. That was a momentary glory. Now with his brother almost killing the larger bird, Sambati, his achievement paled. *No, I should not be having such thoughts*, Sugreeva told himself. His brother had almost died for him. It was sin to be jealous of his brother. Sugreeva caressed Baali's forehead. Baali opened his eyes and smiled weakly.

'Sleep,' Sugreeva said.

'Get up, enough of sleeping.'

Sugreeva was startled by the sudden command. He turned to see a girl of his age standing at the doorstop with a bowl in her hand. As daylight was shining behind her, he could not see her face, but his heartbeat increased.

'Who's that?'

Sugreeva heard Baali's annoyed voice, but before he could say anything the girl had come inside. She sat on her knees near Baali. In the slanting light that fell through the windows, Sugreeva saw that she was breathtakingly beautiful. His heart skipped a beat. She tried to lift Baali and his brother pushed her hand away. Sugreeva wished it was he who was lying on the mat instead of his brother.

'Get up and eat this,' her voice was stern.

'Who are you to command me?' Baali was irritated. Was his brother such a big fool? Was he not seeing how beautiful she was?

'This is the Vaidya's order,' she said and tried to lift Baali up. Baali pushed her hands away and sat up leaning on the mud wall, scowling at her.

'Drink or my father will be angry with me. Don't you want your wounds to be healed? Or is it—' she put a wooden ladle filled with oozy greenish paste to his lips.

'What is this? Cow dung paste?' Baali asked.

'Drink,' she pushed it to his lips. He refused to open his mouth.

'Who are you, Devi?' Sugreeva asked politely. His heart was beating like a caged bird.

'Hmm, Devi?' she cackled. 'Devi . . . am I, a Deva girl, to be called Devi? Where did you learn such strange manners?'

'I . . . I don't know your name,' Sugreeva said.

'I never told you my name. So how will you know it?' she laughed. Sugreeva smiled awkwardly. Baali scowled at both of them.

'I need to sleep. I'm tired,' he growled.

'Drink and sleep then. You want me to sing you a lullaby?' the girl said with a smile and pushed the ladle again to Baali's mouth. Baali turned his head away. The girl stared at him for a moment. Sugreeva was keenly watching her. He saw her gaze settling on Baali's shoulders, where there was a gash. Some dark paste had been applied over it, but the skin around it was still swollen. Without warning, the girl poked the gash. Baali screamed in pain and in a flash, the girl emptied the medicine into his open mouth.

She closed his mouth and nose with her hands before he could spit it out. She left him only after he had swallowed the hideous paste. She then stood up with a victorious smile. Sugreeva started laughing.

'You may be the giant bird slayer, but don't mess with Tara,' the girl laughed, patted Baali's cheeks and ran out.

Baali flung the empty pot to the farthest corner of the room in great anger. He roared, 'How dare you?'

'The cost of the broken pot will be charged from your foster-father, Riksarajas,' Tara cried from outside.

'He isn't my foster-father,' Baali screamed.

Tara peeped in through the window, 'Ok, foster mother, if you choose. He is both, you know.' Before Baali could answer, she had gone, leaving only her laughter reverberating behind. Baali cursed and shouted while Sugreeva sat caressing his cheek. Tara's hair had brushed against his right cheek when she ran out. Her hair smelled of champaka flowers. Sugreeva sighed as Baali continued to curse under his breath.

# Chapter 9

Having been confined to his bed and room, Baali was always in a morose mood. Sugreeva was his shadow, catering to his brother's whims and managing his temper tantrums. Despite Baali's displeasure, Tara diligently visited him and ensured that he took his medicines on time. Sugreeva used to look forward to her visits. He would sit dreaming about her, recalling her every gesture, trying to find meaning in pauses of her conversation, her taunting, and the way she played with her hair or her eyes. He could not discuss her with Baali, since his quick-tempered brother might get upset. However, Sugreeva observed that in her presence, Baali was silent and obeyed her instructions without much effort on her part. She brought the sunshine and laughter with her into the room whenever she came. Sugreeva would relish the fragrance of champaka flowers that lingered on for hours after she had gone.

Riksarajas kept visiting them often. Sugreeva learned that a lot had happened in the eunuch's life. The Vanara tribe had expelled him. They had set the bird Sambati free. It was rumoured that Jatayu had carried the wingless Sambati to some forest deep in the south. The absence of the two birds that had preyed on the Vana Naras should have made the eunuch a hero. Instead, he was blamed for the divine birds abandoning the tribe. The tribal leaders, Jambavan and his deputy, Kesari, had declared that the two boys had brought bad luck to the tribe and the eunuch had brought shame. The divine birds had been disrespected. One of the birds had almost been killed. The eunuch had tied up the holy bird, the brother of the divine eagle, Garuda. Gods would be angry with the Vana Naras, they decreed. They also held Riksarajas responsible for the death of the old man who was killed by Jatayu.

The council of tribal elders had met and had decided to expel Riksarajas from the Vana Nara tribe. They also decided not to accept Baali and Sugreeva into the tribe. They had even wanted the boys to be expelled from the Vaidya's home. But Sushena had said that as a physician, his doors were open to all. The elders had left unhappy. Riksarajas was invited by the Vaidya to stay in his humble hut, but the proud eunuch had declined. He was a loner, living by hunting and collecting forest produce, and would often come to visit them with curious presents from deep inside the forest. There would be other members of Vana Nara tribe or from other tribes like Yakshas who were tree dwellers who depended on Sushena's skills in treating ailments. Initially, all had been reluctant to talk to an expelled man, but he soon won them over with his amiable nature.

Riksarajas would come and sit with the boys, sharing his dream of making the Vana Nara tribe as civilized as that of Devas or Asuras. He didn't want to leave his beloved forest, but he wanted his people not to be slaves to anyone, not to live in ignorance and poverty. He wanted to stop the raids of Deva kings and Asura kings which took Vana Nara as Dasas, a polite term for slaves. 'We're caught between two aggressive people. We neither have the self-respect of Nagas who would fight to the last man than be slaves, nor the skills of Gandharvas who are respected for their musical skills and are employed in the palace as entertainers.'

Sitting on the narrow veranda and sipping gooseberry wine, Riksarajas would say to whoever he could find as a listener, 'We're just slave material. We're ignorant, superstitious, forest dwellers. They want our land, our forests to build their cities. They want our children to be their slaves for perpetuity. And they treat us as untouchables. They call us Vanaras, monkeys. They treat us worse than they treat their cows. For Devas, cow was holy, for Asuras cow was food, and in each and everything Devas and Asuras differed, except in one matter. For both the warring races, we're just monkey men. Crude, black-skinned, forest dwellers. And we stand before their ruffian, barbarian kings and sly priests with our arms crossed in reverence, our spine bent, a palm over our mouth. They make us carry brooms on our back when we visit their towns because the monkeys' footprints are polluting. They make us carry a pot on our neck, so that our saliva doesn't fall on the path their holy feet treads. And we call them Swamis, Ayyas. Asuras talk about equality, but do they practise it? Ha! Go and see any Asura town. Are they any better than those of Devas? They too treat us the same way. We're monkeys for everyone. Vanaras.'

Riksarajas would add colourful expletives after this rant, each of them addressed to some king or another. He didn't discriminate between Deva kings or Asura kings, or the priests on either side. He reserved a special place for the Asura emperor of Lanka and would say that that man had fooled his people. He had promised the rule of Mahabali, but now he was busy playing the Brahmin gentlemen. He plays veena, he claims he is a pundit in Vedas of Devas. And he came to power claiming he is the saviour of Asuras.

Vaidya Sushena didn't bother to reply to such rants of Riksarajas, but it left a great impact on Baali and Sugreeva. Sugreeva felt Riksarajas said whatever Baali used to say, but with more clarity and force. Baali's eyes would glitter with anger whenever Riksarajas explained how Vana Naras have been treated over centuries. 'We're monkeys, good for nothing,' he would often end his ranting and Baali would argue with him vociferously. Except for Baali and Sugreeva, no one paid any heed to the outbursts of the drunken eunuch. Riksarajas would continue to drink the gooseberry wine and the tirade would continue till midnight. Tara would giggle and provoke him by saying something good about Asuras or Devas. It was a source of entertainment for her. It provoked Baali to no end. He would pick a fight with her. Sugreeva was amazed that whatever the provocation, Tara would never lose her cool. She was not intimidated by Baali's temper. She would often leave Baali speechless with her arguments. Sugreeva's admiration of Tara kept growing as the days passed.

By the time Baali recovered and was able to walk, it was time for the rains. The jungle had blossomed in myriad colours and the brooks were gushing with joy, like never before. That day the creepers had acquired an abundance of flowers and buds. It was one of those rare days when the sun shone for a few hours, giving a well-deserved break to the monsoon. After many weeks of sullen silence, Baali decided he had had enough of Tara's proscriptions. He was sick of being told what to do, what to eat, when to sleep and when to wake up.

Tara was gathering herbs for her father Sushena. Sugreeva was struggling to have a conversation with her. He often found himself tongue-tied in her presence and this day was no different. She chatted incessantly like the monsoon rain, and he was happy to be soaked in its sweetness. Sushena was squatting on the rock that bulged over the falls where River Pampa plunged down before rushing off to the distant sea. A couple of old Vanara women sat on their haunches, waiting patiently for the Vaidya to prepare a balm for knee pain. Baali burst out of the hut and jumped into the courtyard.

'Sugreeva, let us wrestle,' Baali shouted. Riksaraja, who was sleeping in the mud veranda, from the previous night's hangover sat upright. He blinked a few times, not comprehending what was happening. Tara giggled. Sushena looked back, smiled and went back to tending to his patients. Baali scowled at everyone.

'Sugreeva!' Baali screamed.

Tara yelled from the far end of the herb garden, 'Go to sleep.'

Riksarajas joined, 'Come, sleep here near me. You get good breeze here, come, come and sleep.'

Even from the distance, Sugreeva could see Baali was angry. 'Sugreeva!' Baali yelled again. Sugreeva ran towards Baali. Tara shouted at him to stop, but when she found he paid no heed to her, she followed him.

'Hey, why're you yelling at him? You're sick. You should rest. Come and sleep here,' Riksaraja said from the veranda.

'Yes, Brother,' Sugreeva reached Baali before he could say something rude to Riksaraja. The eunuch saw Sugreeva and said, 'Ask your brother to rest. Bring him here. Come boy, sleep here near your father. Good breeze here.'

Baali exploded with anger, 'Stop babysitting me. You're not my father. I'm not sick. I want to wrestle. I want to flex my muscles.'

'Wrestle?' Riksaraja stood up in surprise.

'Muscles?' Tara asked in mock surprise. Baali muttered some expletives under his breath. Tara closed her ears with both her hands and laughed. Tara's laughter got under Baali's nerves. Sugreeva tried to pacify him, but Baali pushed away his hands.

'Fight me, you fool. You coward. Wrestle me,' Baali bellowed.

'You're not well, Brother,' Sugreeva said softly. Without warning, Baali punched Sugreeva in his stomach. Sugreeva doubled up and fell back on the floor, holding his belly and cringing with pain. Baali danced around on his toes, shouting, 'Get up, you coward. Fight with me.'

'You're crazy,' Tara said, running to pick up Sugreeva.

'Stay away, girl,' Baali jumped in her way and blocked her. Sugreeva gestured her to move away. Riksarajas also had come near them to pick up Sugreeva.

'It's between us brothers, all of you stay away,' Baali roared. Vaidya and his patients hurried towards the courtyard. Sugreeva had managed to stand up. He gestured Riksarajas and Tara to move away. Riksarajas went back to the veranda and poured another helping of gooseberry wine.

'Fight and die, you fools. You want some swords to swing, boys? Cut off each others' heads for fun? How about some stones to throw at each other? Bows? Arrows? Spear? Mace?' Riksarajas took another swig of wine and spat it out. He wiped his lips with the back of his palm and sneered, 'No wonder everyone calls us monkeys. Vanaras.'

Sugreeva saw that Tara had moved to stand near her father.
The Vaidya said to her, 'Make the paste for treating bruise. You
know how to mix the herbs, right?'

Tara glared at her father. 'I thought you would stop them.'
Her father smiled at her. Sugreeva too wished someone would
intervene and stop his brother. They were circling in the mud
courtyard like two fighter cocks. The patients of the Vaidya had
taken comfortable positions in the veranda to watch the wrestling
match between the brothers.

Baali attacked Sugreeva unexpectedly. Before Sugreeva could
comprehend what was happening, Baali's arms were wrapped
around his waist. Sugreeva was thrown on his back and a jolt
of pain shot through his spine. He was blinded for a moment.
Baali released his grip and bounced back. Sugreeva could hear his
brother's laughter. Everything was black for a moment. Sugreeva
got up, wobbling from the impact. His back had gone stiff.
Baali danced around him. The strength in his brother's arm was
incredible, even when he was resuscitating from such a serious
injury. Next time, when Baali attacked, Sugreeva was prepared.
He sidestepped him and put his leg across as Baali charged,
tripping his brother. Baali lost his balance but before he could
steady himself, Sugreeva grabbed him and flipped him over his
head. Baali fell on his face. Sugreeva jumped on his chest while
Baali was still turning to face Sugreeva and locked him in a pincer-
like movement. Sugreeva knew he would have been no match had
Baali been in good health. This might be the only occasion where
he could beat him. He felt bad that he was taking advantage of the
situation. But one look at Tara's face settled this dilemma quite
decisively for him. He could not afford to lose face before the girl.
He held a struggling Baali to the ground. But it was difficult to
hold his brother down for long. He saw that there was a pebble
embedded in the beaten mud courtyard, a hand width away from
Baali's head. If he thought too much, he knew he wouldn't do
what he was planning. He hoped no one was looking. He loosened

one of his arms from the pincer lock and Baali tried to wriggle out. He slammed Baali's head on the embedded pebble. For a moment, his brother stared at him. Sugreeva watched his brother's eyes glaze over and roll back. Sugreeva stood up and dusted off his hands. He felt proud that he had beaten his brother for the first time. But as he watched his brother lying still, an unknown fear gripped his heart.

'Brother, Brother,' he cried, leaning down and shaking Baali's shoulders. 'Someone please help. He isn't moving,' Sugreeva cried. Vaidya Sushena and Riksarajas came running and others followed. Vaidya checked Baali's pulse and asked for water. Tara ran to fetch it. Sugreeva stood with his head hanging in guilt.

'Nothing, son. Nothing will happen to your brother. He was weak and was yet to recover from his injury. Don't cry,' Sushena pacified Sugreeva but his words only helped break the dam of Sugreeva's grief. He started sobbing unconsolably. Tara hurried with herbs and water and the Vaidya applied them with a calm urgency. After a few minutes, Baali opened his eyes.

'Sugreeva . . .' Baali mumbled and his brother fell upon his chest. Sugreeva hugged him tight and cried, 'I'm sorry, Brother,'

In a weak voice, Baali said, 'There, there. Such things happen in wrestling. Why should you cry? You won for the first time. You should be happy.'

Sugreeva smiled through his tears, 'You were weak and I . . . I . . .'

'Warriors do not cry. Neither in victory nor in loss.' Baali patted Sugreeva's cheeks. He held Sugreeva's hand and got up. 'Take me to the bed. I feel tired,' Baali said, leaning on his brother's shoulders. Ignoring Riksarajas' scolding for wrestling and his lamenting Baali's health, Sugreeva walked Baali to the hut. He gently helped Baali onto the cot and covered him with a blanket. He sat at his brother's feet and watched Baali slipping into a tired sleep. Sugreeva sat for a long time, trying to dissolve his guilt and justifying his act in his mind. He felt someone was in the room beside him and his brother. When he turned, he saw Tara was standing behind him, staring at them. Their gaze locked. He tried to smile.

Tara said, 'I saw what you did.' Before Sugreeva could answer, she walked away, slamming the door shut. Sugreeva sat down, devastated that Tara had seen it. He thought of running behind her and pleading his innocence. He searched for some explanation that would convince her.

'You could've beaten me otherwise too, brother,' Sugreeva heard Baali whisper.

That broke Sugreeva. He hugged his brother and wept, 'I'm sorry, I'm sorry.' It was disconcerting to know that his brother knew. Sugreeva felt a wave of hatred coming up like undigested food. He should not have done it. A mistake, but something which couldn't be corrected now. There was no point dwelling over it.

Baali's weak hands ran through his curly hair, 'Promise me that you will always play fair, to your friends, to your enemies, to everyone.'

Sugreeva continued to sob on Baali's chest. To pacify his brother, Baali started telling old tales of honour and valour of the Vana Nara tribe. The tales of the forgotten heroes and the useless battles that they had lost. The tales of naïve people who had been overrun by the civilized. The tales were as old as the mountains and as deep as the forests. Rains, which had taken a break since morning, started falling with a vengeance. The thatched roof protested as rain pounded on it. The smell of herbs and medicine, disease and death hung heavily inside. Baali continued to drone out the stories, not aware that his brother was not listening. Sugreeva was thinking about how he would convince Tara that he was not evil.

# Chapter 10

They didn't have time for goodbyes, thought Sugreeva ruefully. It was getting darker and the forest was alive with the chatter of birds coming to roost. They had been walking for many hours, following the course of the river. A cool evening breeze, carrying the fragrance of Saptaparni flowers, dried the beads of sweat from his back. His legs were aching. His brother hadn't spoken a word since they had left the hut of Sushena. What was the hurry to leave so soon? It was true that his brother had recovered, yet they could've hung around for some more days. He had never gotten a chance to express his feelings to Tara. He had seen her rushing from the river bank when they were saying their goodbyes to Sushena. Sugreeva wanted to talk to her, but she was only looking at Baali. A blob of distaste came up his throat. What wrong had he done for her to avoid him like this? He saw Riksaraja pat Tara's cheeks, but he was sure he hadn't told her anything. She kept looking at Baali, who walked as if he was relieved to be going away, as if Tara didn't exist. Sugreeva walked past her, without speaking a word, trying not to look at her. He was angry. He didn't deserve this. They had spent many delightful evenings together. Was it not he who had shown her the nest of the weaver bird? Was it not he who had climbed the topmost branch of the jamun tree to collect ripe fruits for her? Was it not they who sat on the veranda and exchanged many a tales of the ghosts and yakhshis? Yet she had stopped speaking to him for no reason. Since the last four months, they had barely exchanged a few words. Sugreeva felt a numbing weight in his chest.

'How long do we have to walk?' Sugreeva asked aloud.

'As long as it takes,' came the reply of Riksarajas from behind. He had forgotten about the eunuch so far. He wished his brother would say something. Was he thinking about Tara? Sugreeva felt a pang of jealousy. Darkness crept from the shadows and embraced the forest. Memories of the fight with the giant bird made him restless. Didn't his brother even think about such things? *He doesn't have the imagination, he is a fool*, Sugreeva thought. He looked around fearfully. He felt as if the giant trees that towered over him had eyes—a thousand of them—and they were watching them, judging them. He hurried to Baali and held his wrist.

'I can't walk anymore,' Sugreeva said. Baali smiled at him and nodded.

'Let us rest here,' Baali said. Ignoring Sugreeva's protests, he sat down on the roots of a giant Banyan tree.

'There could be ghosts living in the tree. They would be happy to know that their dinner has arrived', Riksarajas said, looking up the huge tree which had many prop roots that hung like monster hands stretching to strangle them. Sugreeva's heart skipped a beat. He could imagine ghosts—all species of them—vetalas, pisachas, raktarakshas, brahmarakshas, hanging invisibly from the branches of the tree. They would come alive once the darkness gripped the topmost leaf of the tree. They would start their hunt and would find that their dinner had walked to them. Had his brother got no sense? He regretted that he had requested they rest.

'I think we should climb up. Sugreeva, don't you find those thick branches inviting?' Baali said, stretching his limbs

*No, I don't*, Sugreeva wanted to scream. Riksarajas muttered some swearwords and took out his customary pot of gooseberry arrack. He took a swig of it and settled on a thick root. Baali was climbing up the tree like a monkey. Sugreeva hesitated. The forest looked ominous and the drone of the crickets and the distant hoot of owls added to the eeriness. Riksarajas was busy with his drink and was humming some song about some beautiful Vana Nara girl who had skin as luminescent as the blackberry. When she smiled, it was like a full moon rising in a cloudy sky. Memories of Tara came like waves and Sugreeva felt despondent. Would he ever see her again? His brother was calling him up. Sugreeva could see his silhouette over a thick branch and with a sigh, he started climbing. There was moss over the tree trunks and it was slippery. Sugreeva cursed and fretted, as he scrambled up. His brother lent a helping hand and made him sit atop a branch. The branch swayed and when he looked down, Sugreeva felt dizzy. He balanced himself gingerly and carefully placed himself. Baali smiled at his discomfort and said, 'They call us monkeys and it's a shame if we can't even climb trees.'

Sugreeva was watching a leech that was crawling towards him. He extended his fingers to flick it away, but before he could, Baali picked it and casually put it on a nearby branch. For some inexplicable reason, it made Sugreeva angry. *Should he be so irritatingly good?*

'Do you know where our father is taking us?' Baali asked with a distant look, a smile playing on his lips.

*Father? Who's our father?* Sugreeva wanted to ask. As if in reply, the song of Riksarajas rose in the air. Through the cracks in the canopy, moonlight fell like butter oozing out of a sieve. Sugreeva didn't want a father, nor a mother now. He wanted Tara. He was already missing her laughter, her smell when she came near and her playful talk. The last thing he wanted was to consider the fat, ugly eunuch as his father.

'Riksarajas wants us to study,' Baali said in a conspirational tone.

*Study? Study what?* They knew all about tending cows, hewing wood, drawing water, carrying the night soil discreetly and burying it away, sheering sheep and watering plants. What else did they need to study?

'He is taking us to Mahabali,' Baali said and Sugreeva saw he was excited. *Mahabali who?* Sugreeva was least interested.

He never wanted to go away from Tara. He had to make her understand that he was not an evil boy. He had to make her speak to him again. It was unbearable that for five months she hadn't spoken a word to him. He was her best friend. How could she do that to him? That too for nothing. Was it such a big crime?

'Mahabali is the Asura emperor. Sorry, he was the Asura emperor, who ruled from the great city of Muzuris,' Baali said. From below, Riksarajas started singing some folk songs about the golden age of Mahabali where everyone was considered equal and there was no discrimination based on caste or gender, and where no children died. Baali waited for him to finish his song and laughed when the eunuch ended with some choice expletives about some dwarf Brahmin who ended Mahabali's rule. History had always bored Sugreeva. He had seen Baali trying to pick up whatever knowledge he could between the household chores in the ashram of Sage Gautama. For Sugreeva, the constant arguments about Atma, Moksha and many such weird words that the Ashram inmates flung at each other made no sense.

'Are you even listening to what I have been saying,' Baali asked with a trace of irritation. Sugreeva scrambled for a response. He didn't want to hear his brother's tirade against his carelessness and lack of attention.

'Why're we going to an Asura? We're Vana Naras and Asuras hate us,' Sugreeva said. He wanted to say they should have stayed back at Sushena's place and he could've made up with Tara.

'You speak the truth, Sugreeva. Both Asuras and Devas have hated us. We're crude, black, good for nothing, forest dwellers. We're as low in caste as it could get for them. For either of them, we're no better than monkeys and hence they call us Vanaras. But why did we become like this? From many folk singers I have heard that there was a time when we roamed as free as tigers, from the roaring seas of the south to the cold snowy mountains in the North. We belonged to this soil and this soil belonged to us. When did we lose it all, first to Asuras and then to the Devas?

When did we become slaves? How long will we remain like this—to be oppressed, to be ruled over, to be treated like animals? We need to learn their ways, we need to understand how they rule us. We don't want to rule over them or anyone else. We just want to be left alone. For that, we need to know how they became so powerful,' Baali said excitedly.

From below, Riksarajas cried, 'Baali, I have been telling this to our people but they blame the fate, they blame the wrath of the great God Ayyan, they blame the displeasure of the giant birds and the mountains, but they never blame themselves. You're too wise for your age. How many rains would you have seen? Thirteen, fourteen? Your enthusiasm is giving me hope, my son. My boy. I have been telling, you ask Ayyan for little things, he gives us little things. You ask Ayyan for big things, he will give *big* things. Baali, you're asking him the freedom of our people. Believe this eunuch, if you're ready to work for what you believe, Ayyan will give you that and more than that. No one believes this eunuch when I say this,'

Baali cried, 'I believe you, father.'

Sugreeva watched the eunuch trembling with ecstasy, his eyes shining with wetness. Riksarajas saw the teenagers looking at him and turned away hurriedly. He started reciting some old chants that made no sense to Sugreeva. There was a small clearing a few feet away where a branch of the giant Banyan tree had collapsed. Riksarajas swaggered to the clearing and looked up at the sky.

'What are you staring at, father?' Baali laughed.

'Hush,' Riksarajas's said. 'If Ayyan believes in me, he will send a signal.'

'If you believe in Ayyan is what you mean,' Baali shouted from the tree branch.

'No, fool. Of course I believe in Ayyan. It's he who needs to believe in this eunuch,' Riksarajas cried and Baali laughed. Riksarajas stared at the distant sky and sprinkled his arrack in a circle around him. He started chanting again.

'What is he doing?' Sugreeva asked with rising distaste. This man was becoming an embarrassment. He and Tara used to laugh at his antics behind his back. The memories of Tara shredded his mind.

'There, there,' Riksarajas' sudden cry startled Sugreeva. The fat eunuch was jumping up and down and pointing to the western sky.

'Ayyan has spoken, Ayya . . . Ayyaa . . .' Like a mad man, he rushed towards the west and crashed into the bushes. They could hear swear words but could not see him.

'He is drunk,' Sugreeva said and Baali laughed.

'Yes, he is. And happy,' Baali chuckled. He pointed to the sky, 'Sugreeva, see that shooting star. It's believed Ayyan gives signals like that to say he will fulfil our wishes. Ayyan is smiling at us. Let us pray.'

Baali closed his eyes and started swaying from side to side. The branch shook and Sugreeva feared they would lose balance and tumble down. He had nothing to pray for. The face of Tara flashed in his mind and he angrily pushed it away. He looked around. Far away, from some remote Vana Nara village, floated the rumblings of drum beats.

From the bush, Riksarajas croaked, choking with emotion, 'Oh, Ayyan, oh the God of the mountains, at last, you're showing this accursed race some mercy. You've given us a boy who's wise beyond his years and brave enough to fight the giant bird. Finally, you're lifting your curse, the Lord of the Jungle. I believe, you're saying to us, one day we would be free. Let the great Asura not deny him the knowledge. Bless us, for one among us may one day grow worthy of your worship.'

Sugreeva was thankful that there was no one else to watch this spectacle. Had Tara been there, he would have been embarrassed. Why the hell was he thinking about that girl? *She is no one to me*, he asserted himself and his heart felt heavy. He sighed. He heard the roll of distant drums. Maybe there are Vana Nara villages

deep inside the forest. The tribe might be hiding from the raids
of Devas and Asuras who often came to pick them up as slaves.
Their number was fast dwindling and by drumming so loudly the
fools were sending invitation to slavers to capture them. Perhaps,
a festival might be going on, perhaps a wedding, a birth of a
girl child, or even a funeral. For Vana Naras, everything was a
celebration. Birth was when Ayyan decided to let his spirit, *Uyyir*,
dwell in the form of a Vana Nara. Death was when he decided
*Uyyir* should come back to him. Both were Ayyan, so was the life
in between. Ayyan's *Uyyir* dwelled in the trees, in the worms, in
the birds or the beasts, in the rocks or in the river. Every moment
had an *Uyyir*, a spirit that changed form before one could blink.
Vana Naras and countless creatures that made up the universe,
everything had the same *Uyyir* of Ayyan. There was nothing that
had no *Uyyir*, the earth, the mountains, the trees, the stones, the
stars, the sky, the sun, the moon, everything lived and throbbed
with the spirit of Ayyan. Riksarajas had told them of the glory of
Ayyan many times. But Sugreeva didn't know what to pray for or
how to pray.

The forest was washed in the dull silvery moonlight. To his
east, the Tungabhadra river snaked its path to the distant sea.
Bats skirted above the hills far away. Countless stars blinked in
unison as he looked up. A gentle breeze tingled his skin. It was
getting cold. The cicadas, with their unceasing symphony from
the bushes, filled his ears. He looked at his brother mumbling
prayers and listened to the murmuring of his adoptive father.
What were they praying for? If everything was Ayyan's will, why
should one pray? He looked around and smiled at the fireflies
dancing above the jungle. Were they drawing some pattern?
Were they telling him something? He smiled at his folly. The
air had the sweet stinging smell of Saptaparni flowers. He took a
deep breath and chilled air traced a path to his chest, making him
shiver. Sugreeva wished he could capture the ethereal beauty of
the forest, the giddy fragrance of Saptaparni flowers, the dance

of the fireflies and the coldness of the distant stars and preserve the moment for eternity.

The prayer to Ayyan continued in fervour. The eunuch had transformed his brother, Sugreeva thought ruefully. Suddenly, he paused his rumination. Did he hear something odd in Baali's prayers? Every nerve of his body became taut. Anger had started raising its ugly fangs, so had jealousy. He listened to confirm whether he had heard it right. His brother was praying for the countless Vana Naras who were slaves to Devas or Asuras. His brother was praying for the few free Vana Naras who ecked out a living and hid deep inside the forest, fearing the raid of Devas or Asuras. Sugreeva didn't care for either of them. But he had heard a familiar word which made the hair on the back of his neck stand up. He waited impatiently for his brother to finish his prayers or repeat the word that alarmed him. To his dismay, Baali went silent and stood with his eyes closed. Sugreeva fidgeted with the corners of his dhoti, twiddled with his fingers and waited, gritting his teeth.

'Sugreeva,' his brother's soft voice startled him. Baali appeared to be in a trance.

'Ayyan spoke to me, brother.'

From below, Riksarajas cried in ecstasy, 'Ayya . . . Ayyaaa . . .'

A strong breeze rustled the leaves, sending a wave of chill down Sugreeva's spine. Baali closed his eyes and said, 'He spoke to me about a great tomorrow. Ayyan said we're the chosen ones. Together, we shall free our people.'

Sugreeva stared at his brother in silence. He was not bothered about tomorrow. He was worried about today, about the words his brother had uttered in his prayers.

Baali opened his eyes and pointed his fingers towards the river. 'Mark that place brother. If Ayyan wills, we will make a city by the river, for Vana Naras. See those Kishka trees by the river. Seven of them. They're the mark. That is where Ayyan's spirit will be the strongest. By the side of that holy grove, we shall build our dwelling place. We will call it Kishkinda, a city for our people. The black-skinned, broken, monkey people. Ayyan asked me, why do I get angry when someone calls us Vanara? Monkeys too are my sons, so are all of you—he told me, brother, and he opened my eyes. Be proud of who you are, Ayyan told me.'

Riksarajas cried in ecstasy, 'Ayyaa . . . my Ayyaaa . . .He is right. We're Vanaras. We're monkeys. We're anything that Ayyan wants us to be. We're everything what we want to be.'

Baali started thumping his chest with both his hands. He stretched himself, threw his head back and let out a wild howl, 'I'm a Vanara!' After a moment's pause, the valley echoed back its reply many times, 'I'm a Vanara.' It amused Baali and he repeated his scream. Each time, the forest replied with vigour. He and the forest were one. They were Ayyan, one and the same.

After some time, Baali got tired of his screams. His voice had an unusual strain that made it appear comical. He put his hand over Sugreeva's shoulders and said, 'Tomorrow, we will reach the Asura Emperor, Mahabali, and perhaps stay there for another five years. By the time we return, we will no longer be teenagers. We will be young and strong enough to lead our people and make them free. We shall—'

Sugreeva cut short Baali. He didn't want to stand through another rant on how oppressed his tribe was or what Baali was going to do about it. He was dying to clear his doubt. Gathering courage, he asked, 'Brother, I heard you mention that girl's name in your prayers.'

Baali stared at him for a moment and Sugreeva waited with a throbbing heart. Baali's face broke into an impish smile, 'Oh, you heard that. I had always wanted to tell you, Sugreeva, but somehow I felt awkward. I . . . I . . . I prayed to Ayyan that when we come back and win a place where our Vanaras can no longer be slaves, Tara shall be my wife.'

# Chapter 11

Tara waited excitedly at the river bank. It was almost noon and the summer heat was unbearable. The forest had lost its lushness and the river flowed lean. If not for the dry dusty breeze that blew from the north, it would have been impossible to stand in the scorching sun. There were a few old men and women scattered by the river bank, chatting with each other. She could sense the excitement in them. They had travelled from deep inside the forest, from the caves where they dwelled, from the little huts to the Vaidya's home. They had come to see the first men from the Vana Nara tribe who had gone far away from the forest to study and were returning home. There was a sense of achievement among all members of the tribe. Tara felt proud that she had known them from childhood. Though it had been six long years since they had left the forest, she had fond memories of her childhood friends.

'Why isn't this girl married yet?'

Tara heard one of the old women say loudly. She ignored her and continued to stare at the far river bank. They should be here any moment and she felt she could not wait any longer. Many pleasant memories about the days the brothers had spent in the hut made her smile.

'The Vaidya is giving the girl too much freedom. Girls of her age have at least a couple of kids,' another old woman prattled.

'These days, girls have become too irresponsible. In our times, would our father allow us such liberty? I hadn't even seen my husband's face. Elders decided and before I could blink, I was married and had half a dozen kids tugging at my dress.'

'I can't believe she is eighteen and still single.'

'Who knows, maybe the girl has someone in mind.'

Tara moved away from the chattering old women. She had taught herself to go numb to such complaints and comments about her continuing spinsterhood. The old aunties would be shocked if they knew her father had never even broached the subject with her. She knew the reason and felt sorry for him. He had little money for dowry and the marriage expenses that he would have to incur were far beyond his means. He had to invite every Vana Nara family. Marriages were one occasion where slaves working in faraway lands would get a few days of freedom. There would be thousands turning up for the wedding. People would come at least a week before the wedding and it was the bride's family that had to feed them and entertain them.

Her father was someone who refused to take even the little gifts his impoverished patients brought in lieu of fees. After more than thirty years of serving as the only Vaidya of Vana Naras, his possessions were two faded dhotis, a few clay utensils and the hut with a leaking roof. Even the land where the hut stood belonged to the Vana Nara council. Since he was the only Vaidya, they allowed him to stay on the land. Some time ago, Tara had seen some silver ornaments tied in a bundle. Those were her mother's ornaments, the only thing that connected her to her mother who she had never seen. One day, that too disappeared. She was shattered when she found that the bundle was empty and questioned her father. He sat without a word as she cried and accused him of being heartless. She slept with the empty bundle under her cheeks, but a little after midnight, she felt her father's loving fingers running through her hair affectionately. She hadn't opened her eyes. She was still angry with him and waited him to go away and leave her alone to cry for her mother. Her father never loved her mother, she thought bitterly. It was after a couple of days that she came to know what had happened to her mother's ornaments. A man had come with a small boy and fallen at Sushena's feet. He thanked him for loaning him the amount for freeing his son from slavery. The child's mother had died, and the Deva master was a kind-hearted man who accepted the money and gave back the boy to his father. Tara then knew where her father had got the money to gift the man. When the man and his boy had gone, it was Tara's turn to fall at her father's feet to beg for forgiveness. Sushena kissed her on her forehead and went back to his work.

Tara was startled by a sudden slap on her shoulders. She turned and found herself in the arms of her friend, Swayamprabha. Swayamprabha was brought to her father's care four years ago by Kinnara tribesmen who had seen her wandering about in the forests bordering the Asura kingdom of Ravana in the deep south. When the Kinnara had found her, the girl was unable to talk and had burn marks all over her body. Someone had left her for dead. The travelling Kinnara tribe had taken the half-dead girl with them and brought her to Sushena's hut. It had taken almost two years of rigorous treatment to bring the girl back to normal life. She never talked about her past and no one knew what her tribe was, except that she too was a slave. For Tara, who was badly missing the brothers, she had become a dear friend. Swayamprabha appeared to be the same age as Tara, though she herself was not sure. She had been abused as a child slave in a Yaksha nobleman's household, but when the Asura army under Ravana overran Lanka and the south of the subcontinent, the Yakshas had run away to the north under the leadership of Kubera. Most of the slaves were butchered before they left and Swayamprabha's parents might have been among the thousands who were killed by their masters. Those slaves who managed to survive were captured by Asura noblemen and put to use along with the bulls and cows they had captured from the Yakshas. It was a miracle that the girl had survived. Since no one knew what her tribe was, the Vana Nara tribe never truly accepted her. She grew up in Sushena's household as a dear friend and sister to Tara, who called her Prabha.

'I can sense the anticipation,' Prabha said pinching Tara's cheeks. Tara pushed her away.

'Everyone is waiting for them, not just me,' Tara said, walking towards the edge of the river. The waterfall was just a narrow ribbon of water, reluctantly flowing down the grey rocks. A myna was bathing in the little water that had pooled in a rock crevice.

Prabha caught up with her. 'Both of them look alike?'

Tara blushed but hid it with a smile. Then she chided herself. She was not sure how the brothers would behave with her. They were the first ones to get some education from the tribe. Why should they care about a poor Vaidya's daughter?

'You choose which of the brothers you want. Whoever you don't choose, I would take. Is it a deal?' Prabha put out her hand. Tara slapped it away, 'Fool, why should they care for us?'

'Hmmm, let me think. Why should those two boys care for us? For one, we're beautiful. Though you're not as beautiful as me, you may pass muster if they see you alone. Two, we're intelligent and smart. Though you're not as intelligent and smart as me, you may . . .'

'Enough—smart, intelligent, beautiful . . . Tell me, how are you going to feed the multitudes who are going to attend the marriage feast? And what dowry would they be asking? Who would pay for all these? My father?'

Prabha hushed, 'Why marry? We will elope with the brothers. We will go into deep jungle and live like animals. Hunt, eat and make love, and think about nothing else.'

'Shut up,' Tara smiled, 'You think dirty all the time.'

'Dirty?' Prabha poked Tara's cheeks. 'Who talked about sex, dirty girl? I talked about love—the divine love of gods. And some lusty love of Asuras; hey that too is needed. And our father would have saved some money too.'

Tara blushed, 'Oh, what a pure soul and how noble-minded.'

'Thank you. At last, you've divined my genius and nobility.'

'It isn't that we're the last women on earth. They would have plenty to choose from. The council of elders will be standing in queue to offer them their daughters, nieces and sisters. And—' Tara was interrupted by a loud commotion.

'It seems you've guessed right, Tara. The council of elders are here.' Prabha said. The commotion grew in volume and people hurried towards the hut. For a moment, dark thoughts possessed Tara and she was scared for her father. She ran towards the hut, praying that her father was alright. She sighed in relief when she saw Sushena standing in the courtyard. He was pleading with the elders. The elders, Kesari, Jambavan and Rishabha were shouting at the same time.

'You can't allow them here, Sushena,' Kesari's voice was stern.

'How can you think of arranging a welcome to those who have been ex-communicated from the tribe?' Rishabha raised his voice. There were angry murmurs among the crowd.

'Everyone is welcome to a Vaidya's home,' Sushena's voice was serene.

'Not those who are thrown out of the tribe,' Jambavan said.

'They've come after gaining knowledge. A first among our people. We should celebrate the achievement of our boys,' an old man cried from the crowd.

'Who dares to question the council?' Rishabha raised a clenched fist and roared. 'Fools, listen to this. That eunuch and his two boys aren't to be allowed to set their foot in Vana Nara land. They went to our enemies to learn.'

'Mahabali is no one's enemy. Had treated everyone as equal when he ruled. There were no Dasas or slaves during his time,' Sushena said.

'It's sad that you're talking like a common man, Vaidya,' Jambavan said. 'We have our traditions, we have our honour, we have our beliefs. When someone in our tribe goes astray, it's our duty to protect the rest of the members from their evil influence.

Besides, those boys had assaulted the holy birds. The council has decided that we don't want them.'

'Nor do we want that drunkard eunuch,' Rishabha said, and in the next moment, he had fallen flat on the floor.

'Your father is the drunkard, whoreson,' Riksarajas stood with his fists on his waist. There was a collective intake of breath. No one had seen Riksarajas arrive with Baali and Sugreeva.

Prabha nudged Tara. 'Both of them look alike. I'm game for any of them. You choose fast,'

'You kicked me? You kicked me?' Rishabha was trembling with rage.

'You needed not repeat everything. I'm not deaf,' Riksarajas said and there was a smattering of laughter from the crowd.

'Guards, teach these expelled criminals a lesson,' Kesari cried.

'Boys, teach them what you've learned,' Riksarajas said and Baali and Sugreeva bowed. Prabha saw Sugreeva smile at Tara and nudged her, but Tara's gaze was on Baali. Baali was standing with his legs spread, flexing his huge arms. Riksarajas offered his hand to Rishabha. 'Come, let us sit in the veranda and watch how your guards are going to get bashed up.'

Rishabha ignored him and got up, grunting.

'I have excellent Arrack that I have brought from the Asura land. Care to share a drink?' Riksarajas called out, fishing out a leather carrier from his bundle. He opened it and smelled it. 'Ah . . . brewed with cloves and cardamom of the Asura land. You don't know what you're missing, Rishabha. Alright, if you don't want, you go and jump into the river. Kesari, Jambavan, why are all of you glaring at me? Come, let us watch the boys bash up your guards. Guess, I must drink alone today. Bloody monkey men . . .' Riksarajas walked towards the hut and paused before Tara. 'Ah, you've grown beautiful, daughter. You're Tara, right? You're apt for my son.'

Tara blushed. Prabha waited expectantly, but Riksarajas hummed a song and walked past them. 'Which son, uncle?' Prabha called out, but the eunuch went away without answering. 'Which son, my friend?' Prabha teased Tara.

A loud cheer arose from the crowd. A guard was flying in the air. Baali and Sugreeva stood back to back, crouching like tigers. From the hut, Riksarajas's voice rose over the din, 'Show them, boys. Teach the monkeys how to fight.'

Tara watched with baited breath as the guards attacked the brothers. Baali and Sugreeva fought in a co-ordinated fashion, each anticipating the other's move. Together, they were a formidable combination. Sugreeva gambolled with an amazing grace, while Baali surprised with his power. They were showing the prowess in the ancient Asura martial art of Kalari and the Vana Nara guards were no match for them. When it ended so one-sided and quick, there was a disappointed reaction from the crowd.

'You almost peeled the skin off my hand,' Prabha said, showing her hand that had nail marks where Tara had gripped. Tara mumbled an apology and turned away, not wanting to show her embarrassed face to her friend. She cursed herself for blushing for no reason.

Riksarajas ran past them, howling and shouting, and embraced Baali and Sugreeva. He raised their hands and shouted, 'Who dares to stop us from stepping here? Is this land your father's property? See, I have stepped here before,' Riksarajas stamped down. 'I'm stepping now and will step again and again. Let me see which monkey stops me.'

People laughed at his antics. Jambavan stepped forward. Riksarajas bowed to him. 'I have good Arrack from the Asura land. Care to share . . .'

Jambavan smacked Riksarajas across his face and screamed, 'Enough of your antics, monkey!'

Baali rushed to Jambavan with clenched fist, but Riksarajas stopped him, 'Oh, no son. He is an old monkey. Respect his age and spare him. If you still feel the itch to beat someone up, beat Rishabha. That monkey deserves all the beating.'

Jambavan roared, 'Enough. Riksarajas, I'm warning you for the last time. I order you and your louts to go away. I had argued in the council to be lenient to your boys, but they've proved to be hooligans of the first order. We don't want them here.'

Riksarajas exploded with rage, 'You don't want them here, old monkey? Does this forest belong to your father? We're only a few free Vana Naras left. Majority of our people are slaves or Dasas, slogging like donkeys in the homes of Devas or Asuras. You've any idea of how your brethren live in their mansions? Even animals are treated better than them. People think seeing Vanaras is a sin. I got the two boys who showed some intelligence to study. Do you think I did it for my personal gain? Do you think it was easy for us in Asura land? Mahabali might talk about equality, but he is no longer the ruler. When it comes to treating us like worms, Asuras are no different from Devas. Every moment was a humiliation. My boys had to work like slaves after the study hours. I have seen them being made to sit at the far end of the class, so far that other students aren't polluted. They had to wash everyone's clothes, do odd jobs for them and be the errand boys. I slogged, carrying the night soil on my head, cleaning the drains, mopping floors and such menial things, but what kept me going was the thought that my boys were studying. Do you think it was fun for me to be ordered around, whipped, kicked and screamed at? Do you think it was easy on my boys? I'm proud of them, for they're better than anyone else. Mahabali himself told me so, when we were leaving. He said my boys are as good as his best students so far and do you monkeys have any idea who he was referring to? Ravana, you foolish monkeys, Mahabali said my boys are as good as the Asura emperor. And when we come here, hoping everyone would be happy to have some learned boys among our group, you come armed with your stupid tradition. Burn your tradition that has kept all of us slaves, untouchables. Burn those traditions that make people calls us monkeys.'

'Have you finished your rant, eunuch?' Kesari interjected. Riksarajas turned towards him, but Baali restrained his father.

Baali joined his palms in salutation and the crowd listened in awe to his commanding speech. 'We didn't come here to fight. We have no intention of staying in rickety huts inside the jungle. I'm going to build a new city that will rival those of Asuras and Devas. A city for Vanaras. A city by the river Pampa where seven palmyras stand guard. We have come to invite everyone to the city of Kishkinda that we're going to build.'

Tara had tears in her eyes. This was not the boy who she had teased and played with. Here was a man, who could be a King. Nay, here was a man who acted as if he had conquered the world. His confidence was unsettling. He towered over everyone. Tara wished she had the courage to rush forward and hug him.

Kesari said, 'My dear Vana Nara people, you've heard the arrogant voice of the newcomers. They're demanding that we change our age-old traditions. They're inviting us to a city that doesn't exist. We aren't Asuras to live in majestic cities; we aren't Devas to live in luxurious homes. We're Vana Naras. We're low-castes, Dasas and God has decreed how we're supposed to live. If we defy what has been decreed by God, his wrath will fall on us.'

'God appeared and told you that you remain a monkey forever. Eh? You fool!' Riksarajas was straining to get free from the clutches of Sugreeva who was restraining him.

Jambavan said, 'The council's decision is final. The eunuch and his two arrogant sons can't enter Vana Nara territory. No one will give any help in whatever they plan to build. No one will even talk to them. And Vaidya Sushena will pay a fine of hundred cowries for allowing the outcastes to step on his land.'

Tara could not believe her ears. How was her father at fault? Her father hadn't invited them, nor had he arranged a welcome party. People had come on their own accord and most of them were his father's patients at some point of time. Her father's doors were always open to anyone, irrespective of their caste, creed and social status. How dare they treat him like a criminal?

She rushed to the courtyard, but before she could say something, she saw Sugreeva flipping a fist-sized cloth bundle at Rishabha.

'Take them and swallow them, you greedy pigs,' Riksarajas cried, still struggling to break free from Sugreeva's grip, 'That was the money my boys had saved working their backs off.'

Baali started walking away and Sugreeva dragged a screaming, cursing Riskarajas towards the river. People had begun disbursing. Tara stood watching them go away. She hadn't even spoken a word to her friends. She pursed her lips tight, lest she cry, but her eyes welled up. She hated her people from the bottom of her heart. She was sick of the traditions that strangled the aspirations of all. Prabha came and stood near her, without speaking a word.

'I don't know how I'm going to pay back that boy.'

Tara heard her father's worried voice and that broke her restraint. She would have finished her entire race, had she had the power to do so at that time.

# Chapter 12

It was back-breaking work and when the initial enthusiasm had worn off, Sugreeva started resenting the grind. No one had followed them after Baali's grand announcement. Undeterred, Baali had started clearing the undergrowth and levelling the land by himself. Riksarajas sat under the banyan tree, sampled toddy, arrack and gooseberry wine, and gave advice on how a great city had to be built. He knew as much about city-building as he knew about the sacred books of the Brahmins—almost nothing. However, that did not deter him from forming an opinion on everything.

It fell on Sugreeva to break the rocks and tug them away. They had learned the basics of building in Mahabali's ashram in Patala, but Sugreeva soon found out that bookish knowledge was not of much practical use. He hinted at this to his brother, but Baali was adamant. After a few lectures by his brother on how one must believe in the strength and skill of one's arms, Sugreeva gave up asking his brother for help. He resented doing the hard labour. He had not spent six years of his life poring over books to work like a common slave. He had travelled with his brother to many towns and cities of both Asura and Deva land and had stood in awe of their size and beauty. Asuras swore by the school of Mayan and Devas had Vishwakarma's disciples who designed and nurtured majestic cities in their lands. The biggest structure Vana Naras had built was the thatched hut of Kesari, which had two rooms instead of the standard one room huts of common Vana Naras. And here was his brother wanting to build a city rivalling that of Ravana's Lanka or Karthya Veerarjuna's Mahishmathi. Here, in the middle of nowhere, where jackals and mongoose wandered, he wanted to build a city for slave people. The monkey city of Kishkinda. His tribe members would sit on the other side of the river and watch them slog. They would smoke cannabis and mock the foolishness of the three expelled men. Sugreeva's skin would scald with shame. He was working like an uneducated labour, a Dasa and his people were making fun of his fate.

Baali spent more time nurturing the seven palmyra trees that stood by the river. When asked, he would say he was making a sacred grove. They had seen such groves in Asura lands and for some reason, it had caught Baali's fancy. Sugreeva thought them to be too dark and sinister. For Asuras, living in cities, groves gave a feel of the forest. Vana Naras were a forest tribe and Sugreeva could not understand the need for a special forest. But once Baali was determined to get something done, no one could stop him. Sugreeva wanted Baali to help him break the stones and lay the foundation, but Baali was busy planting flowering plants and trees, and watering them in the sizzling summer heat. The grove that had started deepening stood incongruous with the surrounding with the patch of greenery in the otherwise arid surroundings. The forest was yearning for rains and the river had shrunk to a small stream. The breeze carried the rusty heat of rocks rather than the fragrance of flowers and dust swirled across brown grass.

Had it not been for Tara, Sugreeva would have preferred not to come back to this godforsaken forest. *Our people are fit to be slaves and nothing else*, Sugreeva thought as he slammed the hammer upon an obdurate rock for the umpteenth time. The head of the hammer broke loose from the wooden handle and was thrown away. Sugreeva cursed and was rewarded with another bout of advice from his brother on the virtue of hard work and why one should never give up. He could stand the scorching sun that baked his back, but he was sure he wouldn't be able to stand another piece of advice from his brother. He hadn't even talked to Tara yet. Why the hell did he come here? Riksarajas's off tune song rose in the air and Sugreeva strained to contain his rising temper. Baali asked him why he was not fixing the hammer and returning to work. *Why did God create elder brothers?* Sugreeva groaned as he picked up the hammer handle.

She had grown so beautiful and he had not even talked to her. When he had followed Baali, after his brother's grand declaration of founding a city, he had expected that she would follow them. Every day he had waited impatiently for Tara to appear. He had dreamed of working together, sharing jokes, making fun of his elder brother and talking sweet nothings. As the days passed, his hopes started wilting.

'Enough of daydreaming. Get back to work,' Baali said.

'One can't build a city all alone,' Sugreeva said.

'We are three of us,' Baali said as he lifted a huge boulder on his powerful shoulders.

'Three? That eunuch is good for nothing. He sits and drinks. It is we –'

The boulder fell from Baali's shoulder with a crash and broke into two pieces. He rushed to Sugreeva and shook his shoulders, 'That eunuch? That eunuch? He is our father.'

'He is not my father.'

Baali slapped him hard across his face, 'That man slogged –'

'He is no man.'

'He is a better man than both of us. That man slogged as a slave for our sake. Six years he spent–'

'For what? For this? For us to work like slaves? Under this scorching sun? See my hands . . . see these lesions –'

'Get out,' Baali's voice was dangerously cold.

'What?'

'Out of my city. NOW!'

Sugreeva glared at his brother and threw the hammer down. He turned in a huff and walked away. Riksarajas was singing about the celestial maidens who had breasts like melons. The eunuch called him to sit by his side and share a drink. The eunuch and his brother were mad. He was going away. He would run away to some place in Deva land and find work. He paused when he reached the proposed city boundary, half-expecting his brother to call him. Baali was busy carrying boulders. He was never coming back. He had had enough of monkey people. Barbarians, all of them. Sugreeva turned and came face to face with Tara and another girl.

'You are going to someone's wedding?' the girl asked.

'Devi, I don't understand,' Sugreeva said.

'Devi,' the girls giggled. Sugreeva smiled. Memories of how Tara had reacted when he had first called her Devi came rushing back. He was relieved. Tara was laughing and that meant she had forgotten about the wrestling incident six years ago. His throat felt dry. He had to ask her something but couldn't find the appropriate words.

'I asked, are you going for a wedding? You seem to be finely dressed,' the girl said with a sly smile.

Sugreeva blinked, not comprehending what the attractive girl was saying. Slowly it dawned on him and he wished the ground would split open and swallow him. He was just wearing a loincloth and was covered in dust. In his anger, he had not bothered to tie his dhoti and had walked away in what he was working in.

'If you aren't in a hurry for the wedding feast, show us around your great city,' the girl said with a deadpan expression. Tara burst out laughing. Sugreeva didn't know where to run.

'If you're wondering who this beautiful girl is,' the girl said pointing to herself, 'you're talking to Swayamprabha.'

Sugreeva joined his palms in greeting. Prabha returned the greeting and pointed to Tara, 'And this not so pretty girl is Vaidya Sushena's daughter.'

'How are you, Tara?' Sugreeva asked.

'Oh, you know each other?' Prabha asked in mock surprise.

'I know him since when he was this small,' Tara laughed.

'Was this his preferred outfit since childhood or did he grow up in his loincloth and never bothered to change?'

Sugreeva stood tongue-tied, embarrassed at his nudity.

'Show us your new city, Sugreeva,' Tara said. Sugreeva grabbed the lifeline and turned enthusiastically. Thankfully the topic had changed from his dressing style. It was a mistake and he realised it too late. The loincloth hardly covered his rear and he could hear the girls giggling. He did not want to face them and hurried back to the 'city', with the two girls whispering and tittering behind him. His only relief was the thought that his brother would be similarly dressed, but when he reached the place where he had been working, Baali was nowhere to be seen. He stood at the middle of the 'city' and the girls waited for him to say something.

'Here will come up the city market,' Sugreeva said, feeling stupid the moment the words left his mouth. The 'market' was a dirt track with a few cactus sprouts on either side.

'And this would be the place for the palace?' Prabha said pointing to a rock that had patches of bird droppings splattered over it.

'No, that is the public bath,' Baali said from behind. To Sugreeva's dismay, his brother was wearing a proper dhoti. He seemed to have had a bath and looked smart and handsome.

'You're back? Is this the way to be dressed before ladies?' Baali asked Sugreeva. He saw the girls smiling and felt his rage returning. He shouldn't have come back.

'What are you gaping at? Go and have bath,' Baali said, 'Let me show the ladies our city.'

Baali grabbed Tara's palm, 'Come Tara, we have a lot to catch up on. And let me show you the city of Kishkinda.'

Sugreeva saw Tara blushing at Baali's touch and that sent a pang of jealousy deep into his heart. He watched them going away with a sinking feeling.

'Do you want me to wait? Or you can show me around your . . .
er . . . city. I do not mind your fashion a bit,' Prabha smiled.

Sugreeva had forgotten about the girl. 'Devi, apologies. I have
a city to build for the monkeys. Why don't you join them?'

Prabha shrugged and hurried to catch up with Baali and Tara.
At least, his brother won't be alone with Tara, thought Sugreeva
with grim satisfaction. Someone touched his shoulders and he
turned. It was Riksarajas. He shoved the hammer at Sugreeva.

'I have repaired this. Now you can work without getting
frustrated. I will be under the tree. I should hear the sound of
the hammer striking the stone there,' Riksarajas sauntered away,
complaining about the heat.

Sugreeva stared at the hammer for a moment. He could hear
his brother's confident voice and the laughter of the two girls as he
showed them his dream city. Sugreeva started smashing the rock
with all the anger he could muster. He ignored the comment of
the eunuch that he was building a city and not demolishing one.
Right now he could break stones till the end of the world.

# Chapter 13

It was after a few days that Sugreeva learned the reason for Tara's visit. She had come to give back the money he had lent to her father. He felt bitter that she had handed it over to Riksarajas rather than him. It was his hard-earned money and the eunuch would spend it all on palmyra toddy and cannabis. She could have thanked him. He had made a fool of himself, standing in a loincloth, covered in dust and grime and breaking stones under a hot sun. Baali had acted as if everything was normal. Neither Riksarajas nor Baali mentioned anything about the fight. Baali had walked till Sushena's hut along with the girls and had come back with some foul-smelling paste given by the Vaidya. He had insisted on applying it on Sugreeva's cracked hands and when Sugreeva protested, his brother had scolded him. Sugreeva knew that was Baali's way of apologizing. That was how his brother loved him. It was stifling and touching at the same time. Sugreeva felt that he was in a trap from which he could never escape. His fate was to be under the protection of his domineering brother and he resented it. The way Tara blushed when Baali touched her made him bitter and he replayed the scene repeatedly in his mind, trying to convince himself that it meant nothing.

Sugreeva was now convinced that the city was never going to be built, not anytime soon, not with two of them slaving it out. They needed some labour and they needed someone who knew how to plan the city. His brother would never understand such a simple thing and he did not want to have another round of argument with his brother. Baali believed in magic, not the kind where one would sacrifice a goat to some unknown God and the God would bring miracles, but the magic of dreams. Baali was sure that if they kept working hard, everything would happen by itself. Sugreeva had no such delusions. He tried to recollect the names of the famous sculptors that he had met during his travels. Not that anyone would allow a Vana Nara to interact with sculptors who were higher in the caste hierarchy. But he had heard about many names and had seen a few from a distance. Who would work for the untouchable Vana Naras? Even if he could convince someone, either from Asura land or from Deva countries that lay beyond the river Narmada, he had no idea how he could pay them. He felt he was chained to his fate, like Ahalya, his adoptive mother who he heard was still chained to a rock for her crime of adultery. The thought of Ahalya tasted bitter in his mouth. He should not have betrayed her trust, but was she not betraying the trust her husband had in her. There was no point thinking about the past. Had he not seen Ahalya and Indra that day, he and Baali would have been living in the Ashram as house slaves. There would have been a stable roof over their head and some gruel to eat.

The money they had earned had run out and other tribesmen like Kinnaras or Gandharvas had stopped giving them provisions. No Vana Nara would sell them anything as long the ban existed. For a few days, they had survived by trapping small animals that came near, but the animals soon grew wiser and avoided those parts of the forest. Besides, Baali was against hunting animals as he said it was a primitive way of living. He wanted to do agriculture the way Asuras and Devas did, but the river had totally dried out. The grove that Baali had nurtured had wilted, with only the seven palmyra trees standing strong. Dust-laden winds blew from the north and the sky remained a sizzling blue, naked without clouds. The only thing that appeared to thrive were mosquitoes. Sugreeva had heard of many starvation deaths in the distant Vana Nara villages. There were some slave raids by Devas and some had voluntarily surrendered to become Dasas with the hope that they would be fed at least once a day. Baali was always in a morose mood and snapped for silly reasons. Sugreeva avoided talking to him. Riksarajas had stopped singing. That was the only consolation for Sugreeva in those bleak days.

One day, when Baali had gone to the forest to get some saplings for his grove, Sugreeva decided to leave the 'city' and visit Sushena's hut. His excuse was that he had a severe stomach ache which warranted a visit to the Vaidya. Riksarajas wanted to tag along as he wanted to enquire why he was unable to drink as much arrack as he had been used to, but Sugreeva dissuaded him somehow.

When he reached the hut, the Vaidya had gone out, but the two girls were there. Sugreeva was annoyed by the presence of Prabha. The girl chattered without a break and he struggled to start a conversation with Tara. He was trying to gauge her mind and her reticence worried him. She was polite, but distant and the warmth he thought he had rediscovered when they had visited the 'city' was missing. Was she dreaming about his brother? To further the conversation, he talked about his troubles with the building of the 'city'. He was self-depreciating and tried his best to be humorous. Prabha laughed at the slightest provocation, while his half-hearted humour was lost on Tara. She appeared to be in a dream-like state and he had to often repeat his questions to her.

Sugreeva mentioned his need for an architect who could design a real 'city' but got no reaction from Tara. They were strolling by the river. It irritated him that Tara had not paid any attention to him. He tried flirting with Prabha and regretted it soon. The girl was enthused by his encouragement and bored him with stories of her difficult childhood and how she was rescued. He answered in grunts and nods, while trying to read Tara's face. He didn't even notice Prabha had stopped chatting. The silence was embarrassing and for the sake of courtesy, he repeated his need for an architect who would work for free.

Tara said, 'Prabha, won't Nala be the right man?'

Prabha, who was sulking, nodded indifferently. Tara said, 'The boy was a slave in the home of Vishwakarma the architect. His father bought him back and he is wasting his life relaying thatch over the huts. I will send for him.'

Sugreeva nodded and when the silence became unbearable, he thanked them and walked back. His mind was heavy. He should not have gone to Sushena's home. Tara's demeanour worried him, and he juggled with various possibilities and arrived at absurd conclusions, only to rejig the same and start all over again. He toyed with the idea of asking for Tara's hand. He was a nobody, had no money, had no land and was an expelled member. Why should she bother to marry him? He felt a deep sense of inferiority. *I have an ugly face, am poor and broken. What is the point in living further?* He strayed towards the waterfall and stood at the edge for some time. Perhaps his death will make her realise how much he loved her and what a grave mistake she had committed by ignoring his love. His death would be a lesson to all girls who broke the hearts of men. When he looked down at the rock below and imagined his body lying prone, with blood splattered over the zigzag rock at the bottom of the fall, the idea of suicide lost its appeal. Slowly, despondency gave way to anger. He wanted Tara. He vowed that he would do anything to get her. He sat at the edge of the rock, reminiscing about each gesture and conversation of his past few hours. He had once again made a fool of himself, he concluded, and vowed that he would never give up. He decided he would never be intimidated by her or be tongue-tied. He was far more sensible and caring than his brother and there was no reason for her to choose Baali over him.

When he reached the 'city', a lean dark man was waiting for him. Riksarajas wobbled towards Sugreeva and said, 'Where have you been loitering around? This boy has been waiting for quite some time.'

The man bowed and said, 'The Vaidya's daughter has sent me here. I am Nala.'

At first glance, Nala didn't seem impressive. He looked unwashed, wearing a dhothi that was torn in a few places and his hair and beard were matted. He looked too young to be a city builder. What would a Vanara know about building cities? Without waiting for Sugreeva to respond, Nala started inspecting the work done so far. Sugreeva saw him shake his head in dismay several times.

'Have You made any model? In clay or in wood? Any plan for the city?'

Sugreeva blinked as if Nala was talking a different language. Riksarajas said, 'Son, we don't plan anything. Things just happen.'

Sugreeva was not sure whether the eunuch was mocking them or saying the same in earnest. Nala stared at Riksarajas and said, 'You'll aren't going to get anything built this way.'

'I know how my city should be.'

Sugreeva hadn't seen Baali coming. His brother had his arms crossed against his broad chest and was frowning at Nala.

'You are Baali, right? Brother, this is stupid.'

*Not a right way to start a conversation*, Sugreeva thought. No one called Baali stupid, not to his face. This man was either crazy or foolish. Baali's face had grown dark.

'Who the hell are you?'

'I am Nala. I am a builder and I want to say you seem to have no clue . . .'

'Who invited you?'

'Tara, the daughter of Vaidya said you guys are looking for a builder . . .'

Sugreeva saw Baali's face ease to a smile. 'Oh, Tara has sent you? That is great. Come, let us plan how we can build Kishkinda.'

Sugreeva watched them go away, without bothering to talk to him. Riksarajas returned to his resting place under the Banyan tree. Baali's sudden transformation on hearing Tara's name bothered Sugreeva. He had disliked Nala at first glance and the way Nala went without even acknowledging him made him bitter. The next few weeks were hell for Sugreeva. Baali and Nala would discuss plans for the city for hours, while he was ordered around to fetch something or the other. A clay model, three-feet high and twenty feet in radius was built by Nala. Sugreeva had constant arguments with Nala and Baali over how the city should be.

Nala made the city move away from the place they had initially chosen. The grove was left as the outer part of city, which moved further south where there were many caves. The idea of using caves as dwelling place with gardens and groves in plains appealed to Baali, but not to Sugreeva. Baali wanted the city to be secure and Sugreeva wanted it to be beautiful. He had admired cities of Asuras by the seaside and wanted to model Kishkinda the same way. Nala said the sea made for a natural barrier against attacks, but a mountain city should use the caves and rocks effectively.

Nala soon came with a group of his men and a few women to assist him. Baali was happy ordering everyone around and he had developed a kind of camaraderie with the workers. People had come with their own provisions. The building space looked like a massive picnic camp, with open hearths for cooking, and arrack being brewed surreptitiously in the nearby jungle under the expert leadership of Riksarajas and hundreds of people milling around, each shouting orders to others and offering opinions on how things should be done. The wages were never discussed, but Sugreeva was sure they would have to deal with this issue sooner or later.

Sugreeva's suggestions were brushed away with a scorn or a laugh and that made him hate the city they were planning to build even more. The labourers treated him like an eccentric, who had innocuous but crazy ideas like having a fountain at the centre of the city. Who wanted a fountain when the mighty Pampa river flowed a few hundred feet away? Who wanted a jasmine garden, when the whole jungle around was filled with fragrant flowers? His suggestions were met with headshakes and smiles. Nala would laugh aloud and go back to fortifying the city walls with huge boulders. He would ask with a deadpan expression whether Sugreeva needed some sculptures at the top of the fort gate, like some dancing elephants or smiling porcupines, and his people would laugh aloud. If he complained to his elder brother, Baali would ask him to stay away and leave the city-building to experts. If Sugreeva wanted to help, he could break a few boulders to pave stones. Baali would offer to have a competition in breaking stones and force Sugreeva to compete before a cheering, bawdy labour gang. Invariably, Sugreeva would lose. He felt humiliated and worthless.

Baali made it worse by trying to make up for his harshness when they sat down to drink after the day's work. His brother's declaration of his affection for his foolish, yet lovable, younger brother made Sugreeva cringe. He did not want Baali's affection, but his respect as an equal, which Baali never bothered to give. He was sick of playing the clumsy little brother. He was desperate for a word of praise from Baali.

The worst times were when Tara and Prabha visited them to see how the city was progressing. Baali would order Sugreeva around, ask him to fetch water, fruits or flowers for Tara. Sugreeva couldn't stand the sense of ownership Baali showed towards him and Tara. He rarely got time to talk with Tara and hated every moment he was forced to spend with Prabha who chattered away without a pause. The love and lust for Tara and the thought that his brother would perhaps take the girl away from him forever, made him fear that he would start hating his brother. He felt guilty for the murderous thoughts he often felt towards Baali and tried to assuage his guilt by obeying his brother diligently for a few days. Invariably, Baali would notice this and would ask him whether he was sulking. Baali would try to be nicer to Sugreeva and that irritated him more. Sugreeva felt he was unwanted—by Baali, by Tara, by everyone. Riksarajas made it unbearable by often commenting how heavenly the pair of Baali and Tara looked and insisted on getting Sugreeva's opinion every time. And when Sugreeva lost his cool, as was the case often, Riksarajas would offer his choicest brews that could cool the temper and ease the nerves.

To add to his frustration, the city was taking shape in front of his eyes and he thought of it as a monstrosity. The city that was being built looked bland and utilitarian, something like prisons that Devas and Asuras build to incarcerate the slaves who erred. Sugreeva was worried, for he knew the enthusiasm would not last for long. Motivating speeches and a pat on the back by Baali was not going to keep people working forever without proper wages. The people had defied the council to work for the brothers. The council of elders were biding their time, too. Sugreeva could sense a crisis was looming and his brother was blind to it.

It came sooner than he had expected.

# Chapter 14

Tara was waiting for Prabha to get ready. It was the first sunshine after weeks of rain and the earth was as fresh as a newborn. The sun glittered from the puddles in the courtyard and the roar of the waterfall could be heard from afar. Even the rocks and the dark barks of trees had turned slimy green. Tara was feeling excited, for Baali had sent for her. It thrilled her that he had thought of her at the time of crisis. Prabha came, adjusting her hair and smoothening her dress. She waited a moment for Tara to compliment her.

'Looks like you are determined to impress someone,' Tara laughed.

'As if he cares,' Prabha said, looking away.

Tara did not want to dwell on it further. It was comical and tragic at once that the more Prabha tried to impress Sugreeva, the more he was indifferent to her. Tara wished Sugreeva would fall for Prabha. The girl desperately needed him. She knew why Sugreeva was not attracted by Prabha and it made her uncomfortable. Tara had seen it in his eyes, the way he fumbled when he talked, the way he looked at her. She was flattered by the attention and sometimes she flirted with him to see whether Baali would get jealous. It made her guilty later, more so, because Baali did not even seem to notice it. She was giving false hope to Sugreeva and she was hurting Prabha, too. Every time she would vow that she would make it clear to Sugreeva of her feelings towards Baali. However, she could never bring herself to do it as she herself was not sure about Baali's love for her.

The two friends walked in silence through the forest path to the city. Tara tried to bring the customary joviality, but Prabha replied in monosyllables. When her friend talked, Tara could feel it was forced. The conversation lingered on the beauty of the wild hibiscus flowers that had bloomed on the bushes by the side of the path, about how they missed mangoes in the monsoon and such trivialities with blocks of uncomfortable silences in between.

Tara was aware that she had been called because there was a crisis in the city. Nala and his people had stopped the work as they had not been paid and the provisions for food had run out. The flood was worse in the forests up the river and many tribal villages were inundated or washed away. An epidemic had started taking its toll and her father had left to treat people in the faraway villages. There were rumours about slave merchants coming to take advantage of the situation. There was no need to slave hunt. Vana Naras were surrendering voluntarily to work as Dasas in exchange for food for their family. Some had started selling their children for as little as a bowl of rice. The labourers wanted to be paid for the work they had done so far as they had hungry families to feed in their village. Some had lost family members in their distant villages and needed money for the burials. The council chiefs took advantage of the crisis and spread a rumour that the gods had become angry at Vana Naras for their arrogance. Vana Naras' life purpose was to be Dasas to others and to build one's own city was challenging the gods who had sent flood and famine to the Vana Naras to show them their place on Earth. This had led many to leave the city and beg forgiveness from the council chiefs. The construction of the city had come to a grinding halt.

Tara should have accompanied her father, but she had chosen to stay back. In the hour of such a crisis, Tara should have felt her problems were trivial and though she had pangs of guilt occasionally, she had learned to replace such uncomfortable thoughts with daydreams. Love had made her selfish and self-centred. The unrequited love and the anticipation of a sweet conclusion made her life dreamlike, as if she was floating in air.

When they reached the half-built city gates, she could sense the tense air. The labourers were huddled at the gate. They glared at Tara and Prabha with hostile eyes. Someone passed a lewd comment and Tara's ears burned with anger and shame. She itched to reply but there was no time. She had to see Baali.

When she entered Kishkinda, Sugreeva was arguing with Nala. They were standing by the side of a massive half-built pillar. Sugreeva paused his argument and stared at her. His expression softened.

'Tara?'

'Where is Baali?' Tara asked. Sugreeva's face fell. He pointed to the cave that was being carved out of the hill to the west and she started walking without saying a word. She could feel Sugreeva's gaze on her back. She walked fast. The argument picked up heat and the harshness of it disturbed her even as she climbed up the stone steps. Her heartbeat accelerated as she was climbing up. Cold moisture-laden breeze rustled in her hair. A parijatha tree that clung on a protruding rock showered her with flowers. *I feel like a bride entering her new home*, she thought and blushed.

Her eyes adjusted for the darkness inside the cave. It was huge and only a part of it was lit by the filtered sunlight that came from the mouth of the cave. *This place looks like the mouth of a monster*, thought Tara as she stepped into it. She felt she was being swallowed by a giant and any moment the monster would close its mouth, trapping her forever. The floor was damp and there was an earthy smell that hung in the stale air. *Who builds a city like this?* Though she had seen labourers chipping the stone from the hillside, it was the first time she was entering the cave.

She called his name and the cave startled her by echoing 'Baali' many times. There would be no secrets in this cave. Every little conversation would be amplified and repeated, and the thought scared her. What are we without secrets that we hold close to our hearts?

'Tara', the cave boomed with Baali's voice and it was surreal to hear her name repeated by the cave, in his voice. When the echo died down, she walked to Baali who was sitting at the farthest end on an incomplete rock cot. She went near him. She could smell him better than she could see him.

'Tara.' He said in a soft voice and her heart melted. There was a childlike helplessness in his sound. The way he called out to her made her shiver. There was no mistaking the want in his voice. She wished he would pull her to his chest and embrace her tight. For a moment, she thought he would grab her and devour her. Her thighs went weak and her laboured breathing was amplified in the hollow cave. She waited for him to say something, do something.

'They are destroying my city,' Baali said, and Tara felt betrayed. She was relieved the darkness hid her face. She tried to ignore the musky smell of his body, tried hard to suppress the wild desire in her heart that scared her. He needed her, more as a friend than anything else. He needed sympathy, an ear to hear his complaints. She sat near him and took his hand in hers. When his fingers intertwined with hers, she felt she would lose herself and would kiss him unabashedly.

'Tell me,' Tara whispered.

Baali pulled her up and for a moment, her heart stopped in anticipation. He hurried towards the cave mouth, dragging her along. They stood at the edge of the cave mouth, a few inches from where the hill dropped into a precipice.

'Behold my city of Kishkinda,' Baali said.

The view was spectacular. The forest lay in an arc, as far as the eyes could see. River Pampa, which the Devas called Tungabhadra, rushed through the verdant plains like molten silver. A rainbow arched in the horizon. Tara watched a flock of birds lazily sailing through the azure sky. She could even see the waterfall near her home and like a toy, her hut. Wind howled in her ears, played with her tresses and misplaced her Uthariya from her shoulders. Her skin tingled and she was abashed with the thought that he might be looking at her bare shoulders and the promise that her breasts held.

'Here, look down, Tara,' Baali whispered in her ears. His breath was hot, and she gripped his fingers tight, wanting to keep him close forever.

'I am building the most beautiful city in the world, Tara. A haven for our people, where they would be safe from the enemies. A place where every Vanara would be an equal and no one would ever have to sell themselves or their kin as slaves. Kishkinda would be a place for all the oppressed people of the world. But our people are fools. They cannot see the future. They are protesting for petty things like a bowl of rice. I want you to talk to them, Tara. You talk sweet, you talk well. I lose my temper if I hear people talking without sense. Why can't we starve today for a greater tomorrow? Only you can make them understand, Tara. Talk to them.'

Tara was flattered and flabbergasted at the same time. She was excited that he trusted her with such a task about something that was so close to his heart. She was surprised by his naïvety. How did he expect people to dream about cities when their loved ones were starving? Baali was staring at her face and he might have sensed the uncertainty. He grabbed her wrist again and dragged her in.

'Where are you taking me?' she laughed. Tara loved his childlike enthusiasm, the way his face lit up when he talked about his dream. He took her to another corner of the cave. He let go of her wrist and knelt, facing the wall. He was fumbling, looking for something.

'What?' she asked impatiently. With a whoosh, a fire lit up in the corner. Baali turned, grinning from ear to ear. A beautiful fire danced behind him. Tara looked around in astonishment. The cave, that looked gloomy and damp earlier, had metamorphosed into something enchanting. The walls were pearlescent with the light. Behind her, on the rugged wall and the roof of the cave, their shadows intermingled, and appeared they had merged into each other. Her eyes were wide with surprise.

'The holy fire,' Baali whispered. His husky voice dissolved in the air. Her breath became shallow. He moved towards her and she closed her eyes. Fire danced behind them, the golden hue of flames caressing her face. Light touched the beads of sweat on her brows and glittered. His musky smell made her giddy, her knees went week. He was so near, his hot breath on the tip of her earlobes made her breathless.

'I have brought fire, Tara. The fire that was always denied to our people. I want this to burn at the centre of our city eternally. The fire to be shared by all.'

She turned and kissed him full on his lips, unabashed, hungry. Tara tensed up when she felt a moment of hesitation in him. Then he swept her off her feet and carried her to the stone cot. She buried her face in his broad chest, drinking him in.

Later, when the fire had died down and when she had woken up, she saw him standing at the entrance of the cave. She sat up for a moment, relishing her guilt. She adjusted her hair and dress and walked to him.

'Sugreeva seems to be angry' Tara said, standing by his side.

'He is just a boy, Tara. He doesn't understand. He is sulking because I didn't allow him to put decorative statues—what do you call that—er . . . sculptures? I want my city to be safe from Asuras and Devas. He wants a toy city, in which he can paint weird colours and make grotesque figures or make fountains where people must walk. He is a kid. Talk to our people, Tara. Please.'

When she looked into his eyes, she saw a touching earnestness. She nodded her head. His face lit up with a smile and he squeezed her palm. It sent rivulets of fire through her nerves. The magic was never-ending, the enchantment of the cave. She leaned towards him, with a faint hope that he would lean down and kiss her lips, at least peck her cheeks. She felt his fingers loosen up and leave hers. Before she could react, he had left her, feeling unfulfilled, empty. She sighed and relished every moment she had spent with him. His smell still lingered in the air. She looked longingly at the cave he had vanished into and for a moment, wished she stayed in his arms, in his lap, in the rough half-carved stone cot in the dark corner of the cave. Just her and him till the end of the world.

Tara descended the steps, feeling light-footed and heavy-headed at the same time. She had no idea how she was going to help Baali achieve his dream. When she reached down, she saw Prabha sitting like a stone in the shade of an overhanging rock. Tara had forgotten her and felt guilty. She went near her and spoke to her but Prabha stared at her with a stony face and looked away. Tara attempted to kindle some conversation. She wanted Prabha to make fun of her about the time she had spent with Baali inside the cave. She wanted to share the moment with her friend and relive the possibilities. She wanted to deny there was anything between her and Baali, while giving her just a hint to tease her about her love. Prabha was in no mood to talk and Tara had a big task to do. She left her friend alone and walked to the city gate.

The labourers were still huddled together, but the crowd had thinned down. An idea started forming in her head. She searched for Sugreeva but could not find him. She saw him standing by the river in the grove that had started to thicken with wild plants and flowers. She hurried to Sugreeva. He saw her coming but made no attempt to move. When she reached him, he stood with his arms crossed over his broad shoulders. She did not like the frown on his face, the suggestion of jealousy and the suppressed anger.

'Devi.' He bowed stiffly. This was going to be difficult, she thought as she put on her best smile.

'Sugreeva, your brother needs help.'

'Oh? I didn't know that. I wonder why he needed you to tell me that?'

'He . . .' Tara wasn't prepared for this. She fumbled.

'He considers me a good-for-nothing child, to be pampered, to be sheltered from all worries, to be scolded and to be controlled.'

'Not at all, Sugreeva. He respects you a lot.'

'Respect!' Sugreeva scoffed, 'Tell me that he loves me a lot—and that I *can* believe. Perhaps. But, he has no respect for me. I am just a child to him. I will remain a child to him even if we both live up to our eighties.'

'Elder brothers are like that everywhere,' Tara laughed, trying to ease the difficult situation.

'Why are you taking his side, Devi? Is there something you want me to do for him?'

The formality of his tone was unsettling. Tara braced herself and plunged in. She said they must solve the crisis. The city was every Vanara's dream, but the labourers were also right. One can't expect them to work on empty stomachs. Provision for food and clothing had to be arranged but no one would lend anything to an untouchable caste like Vanaras.

'What are you suggesting, Devi?' Sugreeva asked peering into her eyes.

'Why don't you call me Tara,' she laughed, desperate to lighten the mood. He remained stiff and formal.

'Am I to understand that you are asking me to somehow arrange for food for the labourers?'

'Only you can do it, Sugreeva,' Tara smiled with relief.

'How?'

'I . . . I don't know. You will find a way.'

'This city that is being built is monstrous. There are no aesthetics, no art, no plan—it is an insult to call this a city. This looks like what Riksarajas would have made after getting high on cannabis on his worst day.'

'It is your brother's dream.'

'Why should I do it for my brother?'

Tara swallowed. He waited for her answer. She looked away and said, 'Do it for me.'

Sugreeva bowed and walked away. She stood still, the silence of the grove enveloping her, pondering whether she had told him the right thing. Had she given any hint to him unknowingly? Or did she give the hint deliberately, though she was not ready to admit it to herself? She was not sure. She could hear him negotiating with the labourers and some excited shouting. She stood watching the river flow, without a care to its distant destination. Crows cawed in the trees, breaking the spell of silence. Two crows were fighting for a slice of fish and she shooed them away. They flew away, still fighting with each other.

When she returned to the city gate, only Prabha was waiting for her. Her face was dark, and it seemed she had cried. When Tara reached her, she forced herself to smile.

'Where are the others?' Tara asked.

'He has left with the labourers,' Prabha said. Tara felt heavy. They walked back in silence. When they reached the hut, Prabha held Tara's hand.

'I am going away, Tara,'

Tara was shocked. 'Why . . . why should you go away? What happened?'

'Nothing,' Prabha shrugged, 'I am going to my mother's village. Thanks for everything you did. Tell father that I will come and visit him.'

'Are you crazy, Prabha?' Tara shook her friend's shoulders. 'Tell me, what happened?'

'I am a fool, Tara,' Prabha said with a teary smile, 'I did what no girl should do. I shamelessly proposed to Sugreeva.'

'And?' Tara asked, dreading the answer.

'He said he can love only one woman,' Prabha said, looking away. 'And that is you, Tara.'

# Chapter 15

Sugreeva was lying flat on his chest, waiting for the right moment to attack. He looked around to see whether his followers had taken the positions as he had instructed. To his left was Suhotra, a lad of sixteen. He was the most enthusiastic of all when Sugreeva told them the plan. He gestured to Suhotra to keep his head down. On his right, a few feet above him and hidden behind the bush, was Gaja, a man in his late forties and a father of three grown-up sons. Vijaya was stationed at the edge of the cliff where River Narmada entered the gorge. They were all Vanara men whom he had chosen carefully from the labourers. Nala had accompanied Sugreeva but had refused to participate in this mission, which he called robbery. Sugreeva knew there was no point arguing with the mad architect and left him to wait in the cave they had slept in the previous day. He had forty men, armed with clubs and crude spears. He hoped that would be enough.

Sugreeva had set the ambush point carefully. They had travelled for almost two months to the north, crossing raging rivers and hiking difficult mountain paths. He had not said goodbye to his brother. He was sure Baali wouldn't have let him free. He had left a message with a shepherd boy to convey to Baali that he had gone to find some funds to pay the wages. The freedom he felt after leaving the oppressive love of his brother was exhilarating. He was doing something on his own, without Baali instructing him at every step. For a fleeting second, his thoughts went to Tara and he smiled. It was the first time Tara had asked him something and he was determined to do it. He was sure his brother would stop considering him a child and understand his worth once he arranged for funds.

Building a city was an expensive affair. The cities of Asuras or Devas were built by kings who had huge armies, treasuries with gold and silver, granaries overflowing with grain. If they ran out of money, they had the option of raising their taxes and if that failed, looting the neighbouring country. They were in constant war and the huge tracts of irrigated lands, busy ports and trade routes gave them deep pockets and manpower to build majestic cities. The Asuras, who held the southern coastal towns, had the added advantage of ports and forests that yielded spices, valued by the barbarians of the west. Baali was trying to build a city in wilderness. Vanaras had neither a kingdom, nor any trade route. This was a fact that his brother refused to acknowledge. Sugreeva concluded that the only way one could raise funds quickly was to rob those who had money.

There was a reason he had travelled so far to the banks of Narmada. The Dandaka forests where Vanaras lived ended at the southern banks of Narmada and beyond the mighty river lay the city of Mahishmathi. It was ruled by the robber king, Karthya Veerarjuna. He was neither a Deva or Asura, but of mixed-race. Arjuna, as he was called by many, had built a dazzling city with the loot his gang of five hundred, which he called his hands, had acquired. Once the city was built, trade ships frequented the city, adding to the wealth. Arjuna had conquered the ancient village of Nagas and hanged the king of Nagas, Karkotaka. He had butchered most of the male inhabitants and made the women and children slaves. He served as a buffer between the Deva kingdoms of the north and the Asura kingdoms of the south. He was feared by all and in his cruelty he did not discriminate between Devas and Asuras. He entertained himself by stoning rishis to death or by feeding them to his pet tigers.

Sugreeva wanted to ambush one of the trade ships that left from Mahishmathi to the distant eastern sea. He had marked his hiding places in the deep forests of Vindhyas where he could lay holed up if Arjuna's men came after him. He had even found a few merchants who were ready to buy the loot. It was a risky proposition and Sugreeva lay in wait, relishing the thought of how he would impress Tara by the tales of his valour. He was going to contribute to the creation of Kishkinda in an effective manner. When he returned, he would demand to have a say in the city-building. He could have those fountains, the arched gateways, the elaborately carved balconies and sculptures. He could lay out gardens that would rival those of Ravana's Lanka. He could even think of having a golden temple for Ayyan. He could get the choicest Apasaras from Deva Kingdoms who would entertain the Vanaras with their sensuous dances. In the street corners, he would place musicians who would play the Nagaswaras. He would get Kinnaras who could play their Veena by the river ghat. He would get a carved stone Mandap built at the middle of the Pampa river, a place where he could sit with Tara and enjoy the sunset. The more he thought about the future, the more exciting it seemed.

Vijaya gestured with his hand and suddenly the entire Vanara gang became alert. Sugreeva let out a deep breath, but that did nothing to calm his frenzied heartbeat. The tip of the ship's sail was visible above the rock where Vijaya perched and soon, the ship came to view. Sugreeva counted twenty oars. The ship was loaded with goods. He whistled softly and on cue, Vijaya jumped and caught the sail. He slid down and landed on the deck. The captain of the ship was surprised, and before he could react Vijaya brought down his club on the Captain's head. He missed, and the club smashed the captain's shoulders instead. Captain collapsed on the deck, screaming. The guards in the ship were too shocked to react for a moment. Vijaya brought his club down again, but the captain caught it with his uninjured hand and prised it away from the Vanara. Sugreeva cursed. More guards were rushing to the deck. They surrounded Vijaya, who was shivering with fear now.

The ship was drifting in the water. The oarsmen had left their positions and had rushed to the deck, waving their heavy oars.

Sugreeva gave orders to attack. He jumped first and almost missed the ship. He was fortunate not to have fallen between the ship and the jarred rocks. He waved his club and roared. Why were his people not following him? The guards attacked him, and he swung his club like one possessed. He was putting the Kalari training he had received at Patala to good use. The first two guards who attacked him were dead before they had hurled their spear. An arrow pierced Sugreeva's shoulders. The ship hit the cliff side and screeched. The rudder might have hit a rock and got stuck. The ship started turning and soon got stuck in the narrow cliff. It got grounded and it squeaked and shivered as the roaring river tried to escape through the small gaps it left in the gorge.

Sugreeva's show of valour inspired his men. The stationary ship might also have helped in assuaging their falling courage. His two score men soon joined him in the battle. Before long, Sugreeva's men had killed half the men and flung them into the river. About twenty men surrendered. Sugreeva ordered his men to strip the ship of all valuable possessions. The merchants watched helplessly as Vanaras carried away all the valuables from the ship. When the last of the boxes was transported, Sugreeva ordered his men to butcher those who had surrendered. It was too much of a risk to leave them alive. He climbed back to the cliff and counted the number of boxes which had valuable silk clothes, gems, fresh water pearls, lapiz lazuli and other precious things. The hunt was worth the life of six men from his side. He ignored the pleas of the merchants who were being clubbed to death. His boys wanted to avenge the death of their gang members and a true leader should never stand in the way of their anger, he reasoned. Besides, he had a city to build and a woman to impress. What were a few deaths for a great cause?

By the evening, his men had completed taking the inventory and Sugreeva was proud of his achievement. He never knew

earning a fortune was easy. His brother was a fool. Baali never
knew what Sugreeva was capable of. He ordered his men to carry
the loot on their back and they started towards their hiding place.
Sugreeva wanted to see Nala's face when he showed him what
he had brought back. The city-builder must listen to him from
now on. He was funding the city and it would be built as per his
wish. The train of robbers hiked through thick forest, weaving
their difficult path through thorny shrubs and thick undergrowth.
Some Vanaras were humming. Some were speculating how rich
they had become with just a day's work. Birds had started roosting
in the trees and the breeze had cooled down. Sugreeva walked like
a king, leading his gang of adoring men, past the meadows that
had deer grazing, over the hills that had streams gurgling, cutting
across the paths of elephants and bison. Someone started a song
and soon, Sugreeva found himself singing along. The moon rose
over the mountains, washing the forest with a silver paint. The air
became cool and rich with the fragrance of Nishagandhi.

When they reached the cave, the air was almost freezing, and
they longed to huddle around a fire, have a steamy gruel and share
some old tales. They found that the cave was lit, but Nala was
standing outside.

When Sugreeva's gang reached near the cave mouth, Nala
gestured them to be silent. Sugreeva was bursting to tell him
how much they had earned. Nala said in a voice filled with awe,
'Hanuman, son of Kesari, has come.'

Sugreeva knew trouble had come seeking him.

# Chapter 16

'Why should we be worried?' Sugreeva was getting irritated. They had spent the entire night listening to Hanuman. The son of Kesari had left home in his childhood. He had travelled far and wide and was returning from the Himalayas after spending many years in the ashram of different saints. Sugreeva looked at the sacred ashes on his forehead, the Rudraksha chain on his neck and the sacred thread across his body. What was this Vanara thinking of himself? *Is he a Brahmin to wear the thread?*

'There is nothing to worry, *if we act wisely*,' Hanuman said with a smile. That did not ease the tension in the room. If Hanuman was telling the truth, they were trapped.

'What you did was wrong, Sugreeva. One should not covet what is not ours. You should give your plunder back to Karthy Veerarjuna . . .'

'It is not wrong to rob a robber . . .' Sugreeva replied.

'Then what is the difference between you and him, Sugreeva?' Hanuman asked with a smile.

Sugreeva felt irritated. He could sense his companions were wavering in their resolution to continue the life he had encouraged them to lead.

'The difference is, Arjuna has built a great city. He is a king and he lives in luxury, while I am an untouchable tribe, lowest of the lowly caste and starving.'

'Do you think if you built Kishkinda on a foundation of Adharma, it would last? Nothing built on sin lasts, my son.'

Sugreeva slapped his thighs and sprung up. The last thing he wanted was unsolicited advice. The Vanara had come uninvited to create trouble.

'Nala, call the merchants and ask them to buy these goods. Hurry and take the money to my brother. The city will be built as per my wish too. We will have to discuss this before you go. Assure my brother that more will be coming and not to spare any expenses to build the city of Kishkinda. It is high time the Vanaras too live in dignity and not as slaves.'

'You are–.' Hanuman tried to say something, but Sugreeva cut him off.

'We have to find ways to escape, friends. There is no time to discuss what is right and what is wrong. Nothing is wrong if we are doing it for the greater good. I did not rob a robber king for myself. I did it for the benefit of our race. Let's have no discussion on this.'

'The city is being built on weak foundations, son,' Hanuman said with a sad smile.

'Enough, son of Kesari. Your father never liked us, and you too are here to create trouble and discourage my brave friends. What Dharma are you talking about? The Dharma that kept us as slaves of Asuras and Devas? Is being Dasas forever our dharma or our cowardice? Where was Dharma when Karthya Veerarjuna plundered both Devas and Asuras, murdered sages and enslaved women? See Mahishmathi? It is standing tall and glorious. Was not that city built on Adharma? Whatever the strongman does, that is called Dharma.'

'The ways of Dharma are mysterious,' Hanuman said.

'You are wearing a sacred thread like a Brahmin and attempting to talk like one. You are a pretender. No dharma saved us when we were enslaved, bought and sold like cattle.'

'I am no pretender, Sugreeva. The learned men say, those who seek the Truth, only they are Brahmins. I believe I am one.'

'Ah, you believe . . . But does that change the reality of life? You are still an untouchable Vana Nara and if some slavers see you,

they would capture you and make you a Dasa. Your pretension of
being a Brahmin is not going to help. You become a Dasa the
moment you are born in a Vanara womb. Nobody would think for
a moment that you have become a Brahmin just because you wear
a thread and chant.'

'How does what others think matter to me? I know who I am.'
Hanuman smiled.

'Who are you?'

'I am who I am.'

'You are exasperating. I don't care who you are.'

'You don't even care who you are and who you could be.'

'So be it. Tell me, where did you see the army of the Asura
king, Ravana?' Sugreeva asked.

Hanuman started drawing a map with his index finger on the
dirt floor of the cave. Sugreeva and his men huddled together. As
Hanuman drew the position of Ravana's army, who had secretly
moved to take on Karthy Veerarjuna, Sugreeva understood his
position was tenuous. He was trapped between the Asura army
that was marching towards Mahishmathi on one side and the
Mahishmathi army, which must be combing the jungle in search
of the robbers.

'What do we do now?' Vijaya asked. Sugreeva didn't have any
answers. A cold fear descended on the Vanaras. Hanuman went
back to his meditation. The rest of the gang huddled together in
twos or threes to discuss their perilous situation. They spent three
miserable days, not knowing what to do or what the future held.
The man who had gone in search of the merchants never came
back, nor did the merchants turn up. The loot, that was bundled
and kept at the corner of the cave, was not touched by anyone. It
was becoming a liability. The scouts that Sugreeva had sent to find
out about the enemy positions, came with the disturbing news that
Arjuna's elite army of five hundred was combing the forest for the
robbers. They had no clue about the army of Ravana which was
stealthily moving through the forest to attack Mahishmathi.

'Ravana is caught in the circle of Maya, Sugreeva. He is doomed. His Adharma will catch up with him,' Hanuman said to Sugreeva.

'When would it catch up with him?'

'That, I don't know. But one day . . .'

'Thank you.'

Hanuman was getting on Sugreeva's wound-up nerves. Whatever be the provocation, Hanuman never lost his temper. Arguing with Hanuman was like banging one's head against a hard rock. As the days passed and the provisions in the cave ran out, arguments broke out between the gang members. Some went out to hunt and never returned. Some came back with deer or fruits and fought like mad dogs for every morsel of food. Amid the chaos, Hanuman sat meditating. If someone gave him some fruits, he accepted with a smile. If no one cared for him and forgot to feed him, the smile never waned.

As the days progressed, more alarming news came in. Ravana's army had taken a detour and had used the forest path to travel further south east of Mahishmathi. It was camped now down river, by a jungle clearing. It surprised Sugreeva why Ravana had not attacked Mahishmathi and wondered what he was waiting for. He decided to investigate it himself. It was a risky proposition, but he had to do it. He took Vijaya with him and proceeded on a full moon night.

The forest path was bathed in a buttery moonlight. It helped him avoid the use of torches. He and Vijaya kept to the shadows, and treaded carefully, not rustling the dry leaves, careful not to break any twigs. It was almost dawn when they walked past the gorge where they had ambushed Arjuna's ship. Sugreeva was immersed in thought and didn't see that Vijaya had stopped. He continued walking until a small pebble hit his back. He turned, gripping his club in alarm. Vijaya was gesticulating wildly. Sugreeva looked at what he was trying to show. He could not believe his eyes. The ship they had ambushed had not drifted away. It was wedged in the narrow gorge and the small gap between the ship's hull and the rocks on either side had been filled with slit and mud. Water trickled out from one side, while it swelled on the other and rose continuously, almost reaching the top of the cliffs. An idea was forming in his head.

'How far is Ravana's camp?' Sugreeva asked.

'Maybe three or four songs away,' Vijaya said. Vana Nara people measured distance in the number of songs one could sing while walking before reaching the place. Sugreeva stood gazing at the swelling river. He sighed. He had no other choice.

'Vijaya, can you climb down and move the ship?'

Vijaya gulped as the risks of the task slowly sunk in. He looked fearfully at Sugreeva.

'Brother–'

'Fine, if you value your life more than the future of our jati, it's fine. You go back and sleep in the cave. I'm going down.'

'I . . . . . . I don't understand Brother . . .'

Sugreeva started climbing down the cliff on the drier side of the ship. He watched Vijaya carefully. He had no intention of climbing the whole way down. It was getting slippery and he was struggling to cling on, let alone climb down, but he had to pretend he was until Vijaya followed him. He saw the Vanara getting down gingerly. He encouraged him and praised his sincerity. Egged by Sugreeva, Vijaya climbed down. Sugreeva was at the same place where he had perched himself, a few feet from the top when Vijaya reached down.

'Here, use this, son,' Sugreeva flung his club down. It bounced on the rock with a clang and rolled away. Vijaya picked it up gingerly.

'Go to the front of the ship or the rear, wherever it is narrow. Good. A little more to the corner.'

Vijaya went to the front corner. Water was trickling through the narrow wedge between the ship's prow and the rock.

'Let me see how strong you are, son. Give it a mighty blow!'

Vijaya swung the club and hit the wooden hull with great force.

'Not good enough.'

Vijaya hit the hull with renewed vigour. The ship shuddered. Sugreeva started climbing up, mouthing encouraging words. He said songs would be sung in all Vanara villages of the bravery of Vijaya. He said that in every slave colony, in every village of Vanaras, a *veerakal*—a hero stone in his name would be raised. 'Hit, Vijaya, hit, for your race, for your people, for your freedom, for your leaders, for Ayyan the great God and for all the forest gods, hit till the ship breaks and frees the river,' Sugreeva kept shouting from the top of the cliff. Every word of Sugreeva energized Vijaya. Water had started gushing from the edges and Vijaya was drenched completely. The ship was groaning and shuddering and the river was straining to break free. Sugreeva took a few steps back, while shouting slogans about Vanara glory and the promise of a great tomorrow to Vanara people.

With a loud crack and a boom, the river broke free, moving the ship off its path and splintering it into many pieces. It rushed down, swallowing everything in its path and grabbing whatever it could from either bank. Sugreeva said a silent prayer for Vijaya as he watched the fury of the river. 'Our sacrifice for you, mother Narmada,' Sugreeva said. 'We have nothing else to give other than our lives and we have sacrificed the life of our brave son, Vijaya. Now go forth and destroy Ravana's camp.' Sugreeva laughed aloud, above the roar of the river. He was feeling ecstatic. For a moment, the thought that he was responsible for the death of Vijaya stung his conscience. He pushed such useless thoughts away. Everything was for a great cause. He would keep the promise to the poor boy. He would raise hero stones in a few villages in his name. He would pay the bards some money and ask them to make some songs about the boy. He would tell them how Sugreeva and Vijaya had together made the river free and bid her to swallow Ravana. He would tell the bards how mother Narmada had appeared in her divine glory and said, 'I am taking Vijaya, my beloved son to my bosom. But I am gifting Sugreeva to mother earth, for he has many glorious deeds to do on earth.'

Sugreeva wanted to dance. He wanted to swirl his club and do a wild Vanara dance. He searched for the club and remembered he had given it to Vijaya. The river had carried it away along with the boy. Sugreeva discarded the grief of losing his club and started dancing. The sun was rising above the hills and he could see that even the city of Mahishmathi was inundated and muddy water rippled in the streets. His dance became more vigorous. It would have been nice to have drummers who could keep rhythm with his dancing feet, but it didn't matter. He had rhythm in his mind. He was an artist, a musician, a sculptor—he was whatever he wanted to be. Hell, he should have had his club. He could have swirled it and twisted it, smashed a few stones with it, hurled it high and caught it mid-air or flung it at a tree. Some losses are tough to accept. He would get a new club. He would take some money from the loot and get a club of gold made with it. It was his money, earned by his intelligence and hard work. He could even have a few diamonds embedded in it. *Aha, Aha, Aha*, Sugreeva danced, covered in sweat and laughing like a mad man.

His dance stopped when his eyes caught the glint of steal by his side. He stood panting, staring in shock and surprise at the two dozen Mahismathi warriors pointing their swords and spears at him. The river roared in laughter and rushed to the distant sea.

# Chapter 17

Tara was helping her father dress the wound of an eight-year-old boy, when she heard the news. People were rushing towards the city. The Vanara warriors who had gone north in search of money to build their city had come back. She excused herself from her father and hurried to the city. She was excited and happy, but as she neared the city, it appeared gloomy. She could hear the screams and shouts of Baali. She ran through the gates and saw Baali holding Nala two feet off the ground. His fingers were around Nala's throat and the builder was thrashing his legs, struggling to get off Baali's grip. People were trying to calm down Baali. Riksarajas was struggling to free Baali's vice-like grip on Nala's throat.

'Baali,' Tara cried, and Baali froze. He slowly turned his head and Tara saw his eyes were red and swollen. He looked haggard.

'Leave him,' Tara said. Baali threw Nala and people rushed to attend to the semi-conscious builder. Baali staggered, as if in a daze. Tara tried to touch him, but he walked away. He stumbled on the heap of copper and silver coins strewn on the ground without a care and dragged himself towards his cave. Tara ran behind him.

'Baali, Baali . . .' She caught up with him and grabbed his hand. He didn't pause. He was walking, as if drunk, dragging her along. She ran to stand on his way. He was mumbling something, but didn't appear as if he had seen her. He sidestepped with a faraway look and kept walking. He staggered through the steps, unaware of the presence of Tara near him. He stumbled on the uneven steps, got up and continued to climb. As he entered the cave, the emptiness caught Baali's despair and amplified it many times and Tara heard what he was murmuring, 'Sugreeva . . . my brother . . .'

'What . . . What happened to Sugreeva?'

Tara dreaded the answer. Baali continued to stumble through the damp, musty cave. A bat flitted past their heads. She tried to hold him, prevent him from falling and breaking his head. He shrugged her away.

'Baali . . . Baali,' she cried.

'Sugreeva . . . Sugreeva,' he mumbled.

The cave caught their sounds and echoed them back. He tripped at the edge of the stone cot and fell. 'Baali,' she screamed. The cave screamed back, and the echoes died down in a whimper. He coiled into himself, keeping his cheek on the cold stone. She stood at his feet, not knowing what to do. In the dim light that pervaded the oppressive air, she could see him. He was shivering, sobbing and talking gibberish. She sat near him and touched his shoulders.

'Baali . . . please . . . what happened?'

Baali turned and held her hand, 'They say Sugreeva is dead, Tara.'

'Wh . . . what are you . . .?'

Tara's head was swimming. *Sugreeva dead?* Her heart was heavy as a mountain. *It can't be. Must be a cruel joke.*

'He went away without even saying goodbye. I didn't even see his face one last time. Someone misguided my boy.'

Tara turned her face away. She no longer wanted to be in the cave. Her head was bursting.

'Tara, Tara, tell me, it isn't true. You are wise. Sugreeva can't die, not so young, not while his brother Baali is alive.'

Tara couldn't control her tears. She covered her face with her palms and cried.

Baali jumped up from the cot. 'Where is my mace? I want to break that bastard's head. That fool. That Nala, he took my boy away from me and brought him dead. I want to break his head. Where is my mace? My mace?' Baali stumbled on the mace which fell with a clang. He picked it up and roared. The cave roared back many times.

'Baali, my son . . .'

Tara heard the voice echoing from the entrance. Riksarajas. She ran to him. The eunuch ignored her and ran to his son. She rushed behind Riksarajas.

'Put it down, you fool,' Riksarajas ordered.

'Where is that fool, that Nala? Who wants his wealth? He has brought immense wealth to build a city after sacrificing my Sugreeva. Who wants to build a city where my brother won't live? The fool has killed my brother. I want to crack open his head.'

'Put that mace down. *Now!*'

'Move away,' Baali cried and swung the mace. Tara screamed. Riskarajas stood dazed as Baali pushed him out the way and ran out.

'Stop him, Tara, before that fool kills someone.'

'Baali, I sent Sugreeva,' Tara cried. Baali stopped as if he was caught in a lasso. Her words died down slowly in the cave. Baali turned towards her. Her knees went weak. He walked towards her and she was ready to die in his hands. He walked past her and his mace fell down with a clang. He went to his cot and sat on it, like a stone.

'Baali . . .' Her voice trembled. The stony silence sent a chill down her spine. She sat near him, without speaking a word. She heard Riksarajas walk away. The silence thickened. She waited for him to come out of his grief. He didn't speak. It grew darker in the cave. The bats returned. The sound of water dripping down somewhere gave rhythm to the silence. When the heaviness of the crushing silence became unbearable, Tara fell at Baali's feet.

'Forgive me,' she sobbed.

His trembling hands lifted her up. 'What is your fault, Tara?' his words didn't soothe her guilt. She had made the man she loved lose what he loved the most.

'I . . . I sent Sugreeva to find money for our city.'

'He would do anything for me, Tara. It wasn't your fault. And I have been listening to my heart. I can hear him. He is alive. I can feel it in every part of my body. He is in danger, but alive. He is calling for my help. I must hurry.'

Baali stood up. Tara grabbed his wrist, 'Please . . .' she was scared.

'Leave me, Tara. I must go. I must find my brother. He can't be dead.'

'People say there is a war out there between Ravana and Arjuna's men,' Tara said, fear gripping her voice.

'All the more reason I should go, Tara. My boy is in danger. I have to go.'

'Baali, please . . . What if he is already . . .'

'No!' Baali yelled, shocking Tara, 'If he is dead, where is his body? How can I sleep here, when my brother is in peril? I must go, Tara. Don't stop me.'

Baali rushed to his mace and put it on his shoulders. He walked out with deliberate steps. Tara ran after him and hugged him from behind. Baali stopped and lifted her chin. 'I thought you were brave. Why are you crying?' Baali tried to lighten the moment.

When she turned her face away, he said, 'Tara, look after my father. I will be back soon with Sugreeva.'

Tara nodded. She heard him keep the mace down. He pulled her closer and kissed her forehead, 'If I come back, I will come to your home. I will ask the Vaidya whether he would give the hand of his daughter in marriage to a monkey.'

Before she could reply, his lips were on hers. She stood forgetting everything, unmindful of the tears flowing down her cheeks. She had been waiting to hear these words, but when they were said, she felt fear more than ecstasy. Was she the right woman for Baali? Could she make him happy? She pushed such thoughts away. He was hers and nothing else mattered.

When she opened her eyes, he was gone. She climbed down the steps with a light head and a heavy heart. At the last step, a dark thought came from nowhere. Baali had said, if he came back. What if he didn't?

# Chapter 18

It was past midnight, but the argument that had started the moment Baali had left the unfinished city was refusing to die down. The council members had come and were insisting that the money that Nala brought be handed over to them. The money belonged to Vana Nara tribe and was not to be wasted on building cities. They were not Devas or Asuras to live in any cities. They were Vana Naras and were supposed to live in tiny huts in the forest, or perhaps in caves. That was what Ayyan wanted. That was what the scriptures of Devas said. Devas would be angry if Dasa Jatis like Vana Naras built cities. A Dasa should wear only one cloth, should walk bare feet, and sleep on a dirt floor. Those were the rules. Besides, the council had come to know that the money was looted by Nala. The revelation shocked Tara. Did Baali know about it?

Riksarajas was abusing the three council elders, Kesari, Jambavan and Rishabha, in the choicest of words. He was standing near the pile of the silver coins, swinging his club and daring anyone to come near him. Nala and the labourers were huddled in a corner, waiting for the outcome of the argument. Tara knew what was happening. The council was scared. Until now, they had tried their best to scuttle the city building and were sure that without labour, Baali's city would never be built. But with the news of the money spreading like wildfire, more people had started arriving from distant villages. In a city built by Baali, the council didn't expect anyone to obey them. Tara knew the three men were desperate to keep their hold and she was determined to protect Baali's dream at any cost.

'When men are talking, how dare you interrupt, girl?' Rishabha asked Tara as soon as she attempted to calm them down. Riksarajas came forward swinging his club.

Tara stopped him with a gesture and said, 'I respect all the elders, but the work on the city will go on.'

'Says who? While we are alive not a stone will be lifted here. We will excommunicate everyone,' Rishabha threatened. Kesari and Jambavan were frowning at her.

'You have already excommunicated everyone. Go jump into Pampa now,' Riksarajas said. Tara pleaded with him to keep quiet and let her handle the issue. The eunuch grunted and took another swig from his toddy pot.

'Daughter, this is sin,' Kesari said to her. 'This is looted money. My son told me.'

Tara searched for the famous son of Kesari, but he was nowhere to be seen. She wanted to know the truth.

'It is our money,' Nala cried and the gang of Vanaras who had gone with him agreed loudly.

'These three are trying to loot these boys. There is only one treatment for such greed.' Riksarajas swung the club and moved forward. Rishabha swung his mace.

Jambavan shoved them back and said, 'Enough. There is nothing to discuss. We don't want any city. For thousands of years, we have lived as per our customs. The two upstarts and this eunuch want to change everything. Fortunately, one of the upstarts is dead and the other will die soon.'

That provoked Tara. She said, 'This can't be decided by three people. Whether Vana Naras need a city or not should be decided by Vana Naras.'

'We are the chiefs. We are the council,' Rishabha growled.

Tara ignored them and turned to the crowd. 'Those who think we deserve a city like those of Asuras and Devas move forward to me. Those who think they want to continue living in tiny huts or in the open, in remote caves deep inside the jungle or as slaves in the homes and cities of others may move behind the three chiefs.'

Not a single person moved, either to Tara or to the council. Kesari said, 'See daughter. Everyone fears the great Ayyan. The traditions are for a reason. They are divine decrees. We are Dasas and we should not aspire more in life. Baali . . .'

Tara raised her hand, 'We will have a decision soon. No one wants to defy you three openly. If they didn't want the city, they would have come behind you.'

'Ah, the Vaidya's daughter is speculating. Kesari, why should we talk to this chit of a girl? Women should not open their mouth and like fools, we are listening to her girlish prattle,' Rishabha scoffed.

Tara flushed with anger. She restrained Riksarajas who had jumped forward again, swirling his club and shouting expletives at the three chiefs.

'Those who support the three chiefs may bring one pebble each and pile it under the first palmyra tree in the grove,' Tara said, pointing to the sacred grove by the river. 'And those support Baali should pile their pebbles under the seventh palmyra tree.'

'What is this? A girl's game of hopscotch?' Rishabha laughed.

'To ensure that you will take your decision without any fear, the three chiefs and myself will come there to count only after the last of Vana Naras present here has put his pebble.' Tara said.

Rishabha was about to protest, but the labourers had started walking towards the grove. The three chiefs huddled in an intense discussion. Riksarajas took another gulp from his pot of toddy and walked to the grove, singing a loud limerick. Tara stood alone, tense about the outcome of the voting. No one had done anything like this before in the Vana Nara tribe. What if the majority rejected Baali's city? Would she have betrayed Baali? What answer would she give him? And there was the pesky issue of the money coming from a loot. It was well past midnight and her father would be awake, worried. She hoped her father would understand and be secretly proud. She was doing this for Baali. She prayed Ayyan

would not be angry and make her lose the city. Nala called out to
them to count the pebbles.

Tara was sweating by the time she reached the grove. She
had developed a severe bout of headache. A cold breeze blew
from the river, rustling dry leaves in the grove. Countless stars
blinked from the sky. She nodded when Nala asked permission to
count hers and the chiefs'. She didn't want to go near the palmyra
trees and see how she stood. What if she had lost and there was
only one pebble in her side, the one of Riksarajas. She stood at
the border of the grove, staring at the river hurrying towards
the distant sea. She thought about Baali and wondered whether
he would be sleeping under the stars. The same stars that were
winking at her would be winking at him too. She smiled at the
thought. She thought about that day in the cave when they woke
up in each other's arms and blushed. She was shocked by the
sudden commotion.

'This is unacceptable,' Rishabha was shouting.

'Jump into Pampa and drown,' Riksarajas cried.

Tara rushed to the palmyra trees. She couldn't believe her
eyes. There were hardly a dozen pebbles in favour of the council
chiefs. The city has been saved. She had saved the city for Baali.
She fell on her knees and cried.

'Get lost old monkeys,' Riksarajas screamed, waving his club.
'You have lost. Bury your old traditions forever, Ayyan is with us.
Ayyan wants us to be free and not to remain Dasas forever. We
are building a city. We are building Kishkinda. You can rot in the
jungle.'

'We don't accept this, eunuch,' Rishabha screamed. 'These
young monkeys were enticed by her charms.'

Blood drained from Tara's face. When they had lost, they
were blaming her character, shaming her, trying to bully her, just
because she was a girl. Not a man was supporting her. Not even
those who voted for her cause. They were sniggering, enjoying her
being shamed.

Encouraged by the response, Rishabha continued, 'See this Vaidya's daughter. See how she dresses. To seduce, to tempt all young blood and these fools . . .'

There was a loud crack and Rishabha staggered down, holding his ear.

'Next time you talk like that to any woman, I will make you like me—a eunuch,' Riksarajas kicked Rishabha in his face.

'You hit me? How dare you? I am excommunicating you, I am expelling this girl,' Rishabha cried.

Riksarajas had his mace in his hand and he swung it menacingly, 'Another word, and I will expel you from this world,' He brought down the mace with great force and smashed it near Rishabha's head. The chief screamed in fear and stumbled backwards. Riksarajas cursed him loudly. He asked Rishabha to stay still so that his next hit with the mace would not miss his head. Kesari and Jambavan rushed to pick up their friend.

'I will show who we are eunuch, will show you,' Rishabha threatened as Kesari picked him up. Tara held Riskarajas's wrist.

'This city is built on sin. Let this city perish. You all will pay a big price, monkeys. You were blinded by this shameless girl's youthful charms. Fools,' Rishabha cursed as he was being dragged away by his two friends. A few people, mostly old men, followed the chiefs out of the city gate. Tara stood numb, shaken by the events. She had not expected a victory, nor had she anticipated so much hostility. The way Rishabha shamed her for being a woman riled her. Except for the eunuch, no man came for her rescue. They were enjoying her discomfort, grinning from ear to ear when Rishabha was talking about how she dressed or how she talked. Tara felt sick and angry. She couldn't control her tears. She felt everyone was staring at her dress; every man was stripping her in their mind.

'Don't worry, daughter. Weak men fear intelligent women like you. They will try to break your spirit by shaming you about your dress. They will find lust in everything. But no one will dare to talk to you as long as I am alive.' Riksarajas smiled at her.

Tara struggled to control her tears, 'I want to save Kishkinda for my Baali.'

When Riksarajas smiled, she bit her tongue. She had uttered 'my Baali' unwittingly. She turned her face away.

'You did it admirably. Now build his city for him. Only you can do that. When my son comes back, gift him his Kishkinda, Tara.'

'I . . . I am but a girl. How can I manage so many men?'

'You speak your mind, Tara and give instructions to your people.'

'They won't take orders from a girl,' she smiled sadly.

'I will hurt anyone who dares to disobey you, girl.'

Tara laughed through her tears. She knew Riksarajas would do that and more if she asked. The eunuch was the only man in Kishkinda now. Yet, she knew hurting those who resented a girl ordering them around was no way to build a city. She had to be practical. She was not doing it for herself. She was doing it for her Baali. She clapped her hands and summoned everyone. They formed a circle around her.

'I sincerely thank you for your support. We are building a city for every Vana Nara. This is the dream of Baali. The doors of Kishkinda will be open for all, irrespective of their race, tribe, caste, language or gender, but on one condition. We will treat everyone as equal. There will be no priests, no noble men, no one superior or inferior. This is the city of equals, this is the city of Baali.' A huge cheer went up from the men. 'Spread the word far and wide. Let our brethren who live in the deep forests reach here if they want. They will be paid for their work and given a place to live. There will be an eternal fire . . .'

A sudden hush fell on the crowd. Tara watched the shock and awe among her people. She continued, 'Yes, you heard it right. Our leader Baali has discovered the secret of fire. There is nothing holy about the fire. They had kept it a secret from us, saying it is holy, divine, not to be sullied by the dirty hands of Dasas like us.

They had conspired to keep us ignorant. The fire is like water and air. It belongs to all. It belongs to Vana Naras, too. The city will have eternal fire and each member will be entitled to a share of the flame. There will be no darkness in night. We shall start cooking food and not eat raw food like animals.'

There were excited whispers.

'Isn't it a sin?' a voice piped up from the rear.

'Ignorance is sin. Slavery is sin. Knowledge is not. Fire is knowledge. Spread word that it is the will of Baali to have all the brethren of Vana Nara and other enslaved tribes to live together and live freely in Kishkinda. We shall start farming soon and not just survive on fruits and game. We will have granaries so that during the rains we do not die of starvation. This is my Baali's will.'

Tara cursed herself. Her people were grinning. She had said 'my Baali' again.

'Girl,' a middle-aged man addressed her, 'But who will lead us? The chiefs have gone.'

Riksarajas smacked his mace on his palm, 'Address her by her name, you fool.'

Tara stopped Riksrajas, 'It is alright, father. You are right. We need a new chief.'

Tara waited for that to sink in. She could see the confusion among people. She saw Nala coming forward. She had to act now.

'And Baali had told me the name of our chief,' Tara saw Nala smiling. She continued, 'And the new chief is . . .' Tara raised Riksarajas's hand in the air. There was a shocked silence. Riksarajas was the one who was most shocked.

'This eunuch?' Nala scoffed.

'That is Baali's choice. If anyone has any problem they can talk to Baali when he comes back,' Tara said, smiling at Nala.

Nala laughed. 'Speak with Baali? Eh? When he comes back. Ha ha! Are you sure he will come back?'

Riksarjas sprang at Nala, but Tara restrained him. 'I am as sure as the sun will rise in the east.' She said eyeing him straight. Nala dropped his gaze and withdrew. Tara sighed in relief.

'Tomorrow, we will resume the work on our city. That is our gift to our chief Baali. We obey Riksarajas without any questions. Any doubts, difference of opinion or suggestions can be discussed after sunset. There is only one leader for us and that is our chief. We will put the eternal fire at the centre first and let the free city of Kishkinda rise as a beacon for all the poor, oppressed, slaves of the world.'

The Vana Naras cheered. Some called out her name, but she stopped them. 'Riksarajas is our chief. Hail him. Hail Baali,' Tara said. After a moment's hesitation, she added, 'Hail Sugreeva, for Baali will bring him back.' The crowd cheered. Tara turned to Nala, 'Nala, I want you to build the fountain that Sugreeva always wanted. Let it be near the eternal fire. Like the brothers, let fire and water be close. Let them be eternal. Can you do it?'

Nala stared at her. Tara smiled at him without any malice, 'Nala, let the world know Vana Naras can build a city that can rival Trikota of Ravana, Mahishmathi of Hehayas or Amaravati of Devas. Let the world know Nala as the greatest builder. It is for Vana Nara pride. We have to prove those who kept us as slaves that, given half a chance, we can compete with any Deva or Asura and perhaps better them too.'

Tara knew by the look on his face that Nala had not expected he would be trusted after his altercation with her. He was silent for some time. Tara waited for him to reply. Finally he said, 'I shall build the greatest of cities. I shall build forts that cannot be impregnated, a grand temple for Ayyan, decorate the cave with sculptors, paint gorgeous scenes over the walls. I shall create magic.'

Tara nodded. The crowd cheered. Nala turned to them and commanded, 'All for Kishkinda'. The Vana Naras marched to the city of future with Nala leading them. Tara was alone again.

She had taken many decisions without consulting anyone. It was exhilarating. It was frightening too. Would Baali love what she did or would he feel she had usurped his power? She tried to push away such apprehensions. She would gift Baali a great city. She heard someone crying. She turned and saw Riksarajas was sobbing. She rushed to him.

'Girl, you made me cry. You have been too kind to me. I have been scorned as neither man nor woman since childhood. I was always an *it*, a thing to be scorned and you made me the chief.'

Tara took his palms, 'There is no one who deserves to be chief other than you. People who scorned you would now bow before you.'

'I . . . I am a drunkard. I am no good.' Riksarajas said.

'You are soberer than many who are drunk on tradition and prejudice. Besides, you are Baali's father. He had asked me to make you the chief,' Tara smiled.

'Oh, did he?' Riksarajas's eyes glinted. 'That is my boy. That is my Baali.'

Baali had said no such thing, but she was sure he would approve of what she did. Tara laughed, 'Yes, he admires you the most. He is your son.' She put his palm on her head, 'Now bless your future daughter-in-law,' she said blushing.

'I knew it, I knew it,' the eunuch cried and laughed. He lifted her chin and she looked abashed, 'Bless you, daughter. He is a lucky man.'

The sun had risen over the eastern mountains. The grove was alive with birds welcoming the dawn. From afar, they could hear the Vana Naras striving to build their dream city. The breeze was fragrant, and the river sparkled like gold. The seven palmyra trees swayed their heads in rhythm as the wind whooshed past the groove. The new chief of Vana Naras and the girl who made him the chief watched a peacock coming out of a bush and spread its plume. The silence was sweet, and their thoughts were sweeter. Both of them were thinking about the same man.

# Chapter 19

Sugreeva hated the man from the day he had set eyes on him. They had brought him to the dungeons in chains. He was sick of thinking about ways to escape his captivity and he had a new companion in the smelly dungeon. For a few weeks, the man kept to himself, morose, always in deep thought. He had a haughty air about him which put off Sugreeva completely. All his attempts to strike up a conversation ended in grunts or being ignored. He walked and acted as if he was born a king. It took many weeks for him to be open and when he revealed who he was, it took Sugreeva's breath away. The dungeon may be infested with rats, the air might be foul, the floor might be damp and stinking with rats the size of cats scurrying around, but Sugreeva felt proud that he was sharing the dungeon with the emperor of Asuras—Ravana.

Ravana complained about how he was cheated by a flood that swept away half his army. He worried about his toddler daughter who was in the camp and what happened to her. Sugreeva wondered which idiot carries his toddler to a war field, but daren't say anything to Ravana. Later, Ravana told him that he had carried the Asura princess with him wherever he went because astrologers had pronounced that she would be the reason for the destruction of the Asura empire. There were many among his own people who wanted the little girl dead. Ravana often expressed hope that his servant Bhadra would protect his little daughter from his superstitious ministers. It amused Sugreeva that the so-called civilized Asuras were equally superstitious like Vana Naras. It was also touching and naïve for the king to depend on some lowly servant. Ravana talked about his wife Mandodari and later, about his love Vedavathi. He worried about his people a lot.

When Ravana had asked who he was, Sugreeva had given a fake name. Not that Ravana would have recognised his name or the name of an insignificant monkey man would have mattered to the once mighty emperor of Asuras. Sugreeva was cautious by nature and thought it would be foolish to be frank with strangers, or with friends for that matter. Sugreeva was impressed by Ravana's vast knowledge. He was also aware of how, despite all the talks about Asura pride, Ravana still kept him at an arm's distance. In the dim light that filtered through the sky holes in the roof, Sugreeva had seen that Ravana still wore the sacred thread across his body. Sugreeva had heard Ravana's father was a Brahmin and the emperor took pride in his lineage. Even in the shared misery, the gap between the Dasa Sugreeva and Brahmin Ravana was too wide to bridge. He may talk for hours but took care that he didn't accidentally touch Sugreeva.

Sugreeva bid his time like an animal, making and remaking plans of his escape. Dull, monotonous time went by in the dungeon where it was always dark. Time had no meaning. Sugreeva was worried about Baali and Tara. He had planned a grand arrival at Kishkinda with money which Baali could have never acquired. With payment in real money, there would be no dearth of workers. Money held no value in Vana Nara society except for buying the freedom of loved ones. The Devas and Asuras freed slaves if they got a good price. The slavers may catch them again, but every Vana Nara had a slim chance of being free for a brief period. Some lucky ones could hide in the forest forever, from the prying eyes of slave merchants. With his money, Baali would have been forced to accept his ideas. He could have built Kishkinda the way he wanted, with magnificent palaces and beautiful streets. He could have asked for Tara's hand in marriage. Everything was lost in a moment of carelessness. He should have seen it coming.

What surprised Sugreeva was Arjuna not using him as a slave. Why had he put him in a dungeon with the king of Asuras? It dawned on him one day and he laughed aloud. Karthya Veerarjuna wanted to insult Ravana by making him share a dingy room with an untouchable, low-caste monkey man. The wily robber king Arjuna might be negotiating a king's ransom to free the Asura king from his predicament. Sugreeva was afraid what would happen to him once Ravana was set free.

One day, the guards took away Ravana and Sugreeva spent a tense afternoon wondering about what happened to his dungeon mate. By evening, the guards came for Sugreeva. He was scared and didn't want to go. He clung to the bars and they had to drag him. He was sure they were going to hang him or worse, make him a slave of some Heheya official. When the guards dragged him past the palace, he was sure they were going to execute him. Sugreeva started screaming and thrashing his legs around. The guard chief punched his face and ordered him to keep quiet. They reached the fort gate and Sugreeva watched helplessly as a small opening in the massive gate creaked open. Sugreeva struggled to free himself.

'Monkey, you want to go back to the dungeon again? Fool, we are freeing you. The Asura king paid for your release too.'

Sugreeva couldn't believe what he had heard. Why should Ravana pay his ransom? Before he could think any further, they had flung him out of the fort and the gate crashed shut behind him. He stood confused in the darkness. The massive fort of Mahishmathi towered behind him. The few torches that were burning from the fort wall accentuated the darkness around. The drone of crickets and the deep forest that lay a few hundred feet away from the fort gate gave an eerie feeling. The earth had a muddy smell, as if a sudden summer shower had cooled the soil. Sugreeva didn't want to stay there for long. What if Arjuna's men changed their mind? He looked up, trying to recall the lessons on finding direction using sky as a map. The star positions confused him. He had no idea which month of year it was or how many years had passed since he was jailed.

He decided to follow the course of Narmada. That would take him to the west, towards the sea. If he could cross the river somewhere, he could proceed south and reach Kishkinda. He walked all through the night, putting maximum distance between him and the accursed Mahishmathi. By dawn, he had reached an unknown town. There was a small temple near the river. People had already woken up and were on their way to their farms. They were of mixed race, with both Deva and Asura features, nothing unusual in the countries around river Narmada. They looked at him suspiciously. No one stopped him from going near the temple. It was a village of low-castes and the caste laws were not strictly implemented, he assumed. The temple was dedicated to the buffalo Goddess, Mahishi, and there were traces of blood around the sacrificial stone. He waited for the priest to come out, half-expecting to be chased away.

The priest saw him and went inside. He came back with a banana leaf full of rice and freshly cooked lamb and placed it before him. This was a tantric temple which followed no caste rules, thought Sugreeva gratefully. He identified himself as an Asura noble man and the Asura language he had learned under Mahabali came to good use. The priest was friendly and talked about Ravana's capture by Mahishmathi king Arjuna. Sugreeva feigned surprise and the priest became talkative. He talked about the rumour of Ravana's daughter having gone missing. Sugreeva felt sad for his former jail mate. Perhaps as Ravana feared, the superstitious ministers might have killed the toddler. The priest whispered in hushed tones that the girl was not dead but abandoned by Bhadra, one of the servants of Ravana as per ministers' instruction, and the girl was adopted by a Deva king called Janaka. Sugreeva smiled at the irony of an Asura princess growing up in a Deva land. Who knows, perhaps the prediction may come true and the girl may return to Lanka as its nemesis.

Then the priest talked about an alarming news. The Brahmin army under the leadership of mad warrior Parashurama was moving towards Mahishmathi. Parashurama had vowed to kill all Kings who didn't respect Brahmins. He had killed sixty-three kings so far and his army of axe-wielding warriors were feared by all Kings irrespective of whether they were Devas or Asuras. The priest advised him to stay clear of them. Sugreeva lost his appetite. He said a hurried good bye and rushed out of the town. He had to take care to stay in the forests. He was determined to reach Kishkinda. He hoped his gang would have safely reached the city with the loot. He worried about how monstrous the city would look by the time he reached Kishkinda. As he travelled, he started hearing the rumour of a monkey man enquiring about him and travelling towards Mahishmathi in search of him. The more he heard about this mysterious man, the more he was convinced it was his brother Baali. He was moved to tears when he thought Baali had come in search of him. As days passed and he continued to travel south, he heard of the large-scale butchering that had happened in Mahishmathi. Parasurama's army had broken into Mahishmathi and annihilated Karthya Veerarjuna and his five hundred elite warriors. The news sent shivers down the spine of all Kings. No king would dare to defy a Brahmin now. Sugreeva knew the lives of Dasas were going to be more miserable now onwards. When the news got confirmed, Sugreeva decided he had to go back and find his brother. He was worried his brother would fall into the hands of Parasurama's men or the Mahishmathi soldiers. Sugreeva started walking back to Mahishmathi.

The brothers met at the banks of Narmada twenty-one days later at the same temple where Sugreeva had had his meal. Baali was sitting at the temple steps, conversing with the priest when Sugreeva stumbled upon him. For a moment, the brothers looked at each other, overwhelmed with relief. Then they ran to each other's arms. They hugged and punched each other, laughing, teasing, wrestling. They were relieved about each other's safety.

After thanking the priest, they started their long journey home. Baali said how worried he was for his brother's safety. Sugreeva said how he had walked back, when he became sure Baali was looking for him. Sugreeva was relieved to know that the money had reached safely. He never told Baali how he had got the money. When Baali asked, Sugreeva said with a wry smile, 'We got a little help from Heheya king Karthya Veerarjuna.'

Baali lamented the fate of the slain Heheya king and praised the late king's generosity even to monkey men. Sugreeva indulged his brother with a smile. They both found the little strain and distance that had crept in their relationship had melted away. They laughed at each other's jokes and shared the dream of Kishkinda. They argued over many things and wrestled in river banks and valleys to flex their muscles. When they crossed river Pampa, Baali turned to Vaidya Sushena's home.

'You seem to have lost the way to your own city, brother,' Sugreeva laughed, 'Kishkinda is this way to the right.'

'Ah,' Baali laughed, 'I was waiting to give you a surprise. Do you remember the vow I had made when we were children? The day has come to fulfil that vow. Brother, we are going to Vaidya Sushena's home. I am going to introduce you to your future sister-in-law, Tara.'

Baali beamed in happiness and Sugreeva stood, struggling to bring a smile to his face.

# Chapter 20

'Sushena, will you offer your daughter's hand to me in marriage?' Baali asked. Her knees went weak and eyes misty. This was not happening. *This is just a stupid dream*, she thought. And she saw her father bow down. Never in her wildest dreams had she imagined Baali would come to her home and ask for her hand in marriage. She heard her father's voice crack with emotion while saying, 'Baali, it's a great honour but we're just poor forest folks.'

'Swami, I'm just a dreamer with a half-built city. Can I marry your daughter?'

Tara wanted to say it is no longer a half-built city. She had waited every moment for his arrival to show him the beautiful city she had built for him. She had imagined meeting him in Kishkinda.

Her father came forward and kept his trembling palm over theirs. 'I have limited means, but I have brought her up like a princess. Keep my daughter happy forever.' Sushena broke down as he said this.

'She shall remain my queen till my last breath,' Baali said softly. Tara looked at him with foggy eyes. She couldn't believe that in her small kitchen paved with beaten cow dung, sooty and cramped, amid broken utensils, in a place so incongruous to the ecstasy she was feeling, she would be stepping into a married life she had always dreamed about. She wished her mother was alive to see her happiness. She felt sad for her father, who she would be soon leaving alone in the broken hut. She wriggled out of Baali's hands and touched her father's feet. Sushena lifted her up by her shoulders and kept his wrinkled palm over her forehead.

'May you have a hundred sons,' he prayed, and his cataract-thick eyes shone with unshed tears. She hugged him tight. Her father went stiff and then awkwardly hugged her back. She could feel his bare ribs and the cracked skin of his back. He would be left with her and her mother's memories in this dilapidated hut soon. For a fleeting moment, she thought whether it was worth growing up. She sobbed on his frail shoulders. He had lost his inhibitions and now he was crying with her, patting her back and whispering that she was going to be happy in her new home. Somehow, that made her sad and happy at the same time.

She looked at Baali, loving him from all her heart for the life he was offering and hating him for parting her from her father. She wanted her father to come to Kishkinda, a city she too played a major part in building, but she knew that her father's place was here. He was never going to leave his poor patients. Tara promised herself that she would visit Sushena often. Baali was watching them with an enchanting smile. His eyes shone with kindness and understanding. She felt proud of him.

Tara's eyes met that of Sugreeva and she was startled. When had he come? When Baali had entered the hut and surprised her, she had not seen him. She had forgotten about him. Did she see envy in his eyes? He was teasing his brother, cracking jokes and talking to the curious patients who were peeping in, saying that the Vaidya's daughter is going to be the Queen of Kishkinda. But every time Tara's eyes met his, he looked away. There was pain of a forlorn hope in them, a slice of jealousy that he tried hard to hide with his forced merriness. She knew he loved her. She knew he could have construed her words when he left for his adventure as a hint for loving him. She regretted not having made her intentions clear. She had done it for Baali. She had never meant to manipulate him, she told herself repeatedly, but her mind was heavy with guilt.

Tara felt pity for Sugreeva. She was horrified that somewhere deep inside her heart, she felt a strange pride that both the brothers yearned for her. She chided herself; such thoughts were evil. Sugreeva would soon be a beloved brother-in-law. Nothing more than that. Never. She didn't want to peer into the darkness that lay coiled in the depths of her heart. She thought about Prabha and wished her dear friend was with her at this moment of happiness. If Sugreeva married Prabha, it would be perfect.

Before she could linger more on the pleasant wish, a few women, who she barely knew, but who were now acting as if they were her bosom friends came. Teasing her, they pulled her away from her father's embrace, and made lewd jokes. She didn't know how the news travelled so fast. The friend she wanted most to be with her at this time was far away. *How can she not attend my wedding?*

Things happened in a jiffy. Baali expressed his wish that the wedding should be held without delay and he wanted it to happen at Kishkinda, the city he was going to build. Tara suppressed a smile. Baali was yet to know what a wonderful city she had built for him. However, Sushena pleaded that the ceremony happen at his hut. If Baali wished, they could have a grander ceremony in Kishkinda. Baali agreed gracefully. Word was sent to Riksarajas and the eunuch arrived by afternoon, carrying honey and a basket full of black berries as wedding gifts. He was excited and emotional to see his adopted sons. He hugged Baali and Sugreeva and cried a lot. When he tried to talk about the great city, Tara winked at him to keep quiet. She wanted her gift to be a surprise for Baali.

By evening, the arrangements for the ceremony were complete. People came from far and wide to see the Vaidya's daughter getting married to Baali. Sushena had gone to the homes of the three chiefs and pleaded with them to attend the function and bless his daughter. Kesari and Jambavan arrived by late afternoon, grumpy and proud and started ordering people around. Rishabha had refused to speak to Sushena when he went to invite him and didn't turn up for the ceremony.

For the next four days, people came from villages Tara was unaware even existed. The path from the river to the Vaidya's hut was decorated with tender leaves of coconut palm and marigold and jasmine garlands. A pandal was raised by volunteers in the courtyard and women created intricate designs with powdered rice and turmeric in the beaten cow dung yard. Urchins ran around, screaming and laughing, with frustrated mothers chasing them. Old men sat by the river side, in the veranda, in the backyard, reminiscing the good old times and complaining how life was changing and values eroding. Old women teased each other with the stories of their youth and wondered how young women of these days were so bold. Some mothers sighed at the memories of their lost sons who were in faraway lands, slogging as slaves in some Deva or Asura household and wished they had the money to free them.

On the fifth day of their engagement, at dawn, a bashful Tara held the hand of Baali and went three times around the holy banyan tree as men threw jasmine and rice at them and women ululated. Before the mud statue of Ayyan and Ammal that stood under the Banyan tree, her father clasped Baali's and Tara's hands together and proclaimed them as man and wife. Old women sang wedding songs as old as the hills, about Ayyan's marriage to the daughter of the hills. They prayed to Ayyan to grant the newlyweds a son who would be as strong as Pillai, the elephant-faced son of Ammal.

Tara didn't know how her father arranged for the tasty, yet simple feast that followed. He might have borrowed and begged to ensure his only daughter's marriage to the prince of Kishkinda was conducted in a grand fashion. Even as the ceremony was going on, tribes from deep inside the forest were arriving for the marriage, carrying honey or fruits as presents. A portion of the feast was kept aside for the beasts and birds of the forest to eat. Monkeys came, followed by rabbits and hares, sparrows and crows and countless birds, which had no names, followed. Meat was kept for jackals and hyenas across the river. They all were family.

The next day of the marriage, Tara came to know that Sugreeva had left for somewhere after taking permission from his elder brother. She was relieved beyond words. Tara and Baali slept separately for seven days as per the custom. On the seventh day, they proceeded to Kishkinda. Tara was excited to show Baali the new city. She had left the city to Nala and Hanuman; the son of Kesari had volunteered to prepare for Baali's arrival. Tara had not gone to the city for the past one month and was equally curious about what arrangements Nala and Hanuman would have made. They had sent word that a grander ceremony of marriage awaited in the city and Tara was excited at the thought of it.

As the procession approached Kishkinda, Tara keenly observed Baali. She saw his eyes expand with surprise. Riksarajas was waiting at the newly-constructed ornamental gate to receive the bride and groom. He was wearing his best dress and had an exotic headgear. He announced pompously, 'The chief of Kishkinda welcomes the prince and princess.'

People laughed and Riksarajas forgot all his royal decorum. He abused everyone with colourful swearwords, leading to more laughter. Baali was amused by the new title and Tara was desperate to tell him all about it. She wished they were alone; there was so much to talk.

'Welcome to Kishkinda,' Nala swept his arm and two workers swung open the massive fort gate. The crowd gave a loud cheer. As they entered the gate, Tara watched with swelling pride at the way Baali was looking at the sprawling city.

'What marvellous work you have done, Nala,' Baali hugged the builder.

'My pleasure,' Nala said.

'But how did you arrange the expenses?' Baali wondered.

'Sugreeva provided the means, the workers their effort and I gave my skills,' Nala said, as they walked through the city streets that had beautiful fountains. Jasmine gardens lined the side streets. Granite slabs were paved on the street and there were stone pillars for keeping lamps. Baali forgot that he was a new groom. He followed Nala who was showing Baali the magnificent city of Kishkinda. Tara stood alone, trying hard to swallow the bitterness that was bobbing up her throat. She would have been happy had Nala said a word about her contribution.

'Don't worry, daughter. That is a man thing. No man is going to admit it was a woman's will and brain that made Kishkinda,' Riksarajas said. Tara smiled, but somewhere deep inside, it hurt. She didn't even get a chance to show Baali what she had done.

'What in the hell is that?' Riksarajas exclaimed and Tara followed his gaze. Hanuman was coming with a few Brahmins from the river ghat. When they reached the gate, Hanuman greeted Riksarajas.

Hanuman smiled at Tara. 'Priests for the marriage ceremony'. Tara had no idea why they needed Deva priests for the marriage. She nodded politely, restraining Riksarajas from saying something rude. They watched Hanuman leaving with the priests towards the eternal fire.

'The reforms of the Son of Kesari will ruin the Vanaras,' Riksarajas hissed. Tara didn't pay heed to his complaints. She desperately wanted to be with Baali, show him around the city she had built, and hated Nala for taking her place.

# Chapter 21

The wedding ceremony at Kishkinda was fixed for the next full moon day. Sushena had come with a few close friends to attend it. They watched wide-eyed the carved walls of the colossal cave where Baali would dwell with his aides. They felt the smoothness of the silk curtains and the cushions on the seats. Brahmins chanted mantras in some unknown tongue, and a fire was lit at an altar. The old men and women who came from the forest frowned at the new fashion and customs that was gripping the city dwellers of Kishkinda. Instead of circling the banyan tree that gave life and shade, they had to circle a blazing fire under an unforgiving sun and throw assorted things into the fire to please strange gods. Hanuman was directing things, teaching new ways to Vana Naras. The feast too was different. Instead of everyone eating together, the Brahmins were fed first and then people according to their social positions. Tara felt sad that her father and his few poor friends were among the last to be fed, but they did not complain. Tara was uneasy with what was happening to her city.

Except for a few street dogs and stray cows that fought for discarded banana leaves from the feast, no animals came near the city. Everything was new for her. She felt suffocated by the strictness of the new ways. She felt strange to be addressed as princess and flushed red every time someone double her age bowed before her. People were addressing Riksarajas as the king, despite his protests. The ceremonies and rituals dragged on for ever, sober, solemn and boring. There was no revelry. In her village, funerals were livelier than this wedding.

By evening, her father and his friends came to bid goodbye. Tara felt a pang of guilt when one of her father's friends, an old man who was bent double with age told her with a toothless grin how proud they felt Sushena's daughter had become the Maharani of Kishkinda. She was touched by their concern and love. She thrust some sweets and savouries in their hands. One of the old men joked that he couldn't even chew the savouries with his toothless gums. They wanted to bless the couple before they left but Baali was busy with the rituals. She tried to apologize for him and accepted their blessings alone, feeling guilty for it. Their wishes were heartfelt and that made it worse. Her father didn't utter a word. She could feel his sadness in parting with her. She knew if she spoke a word to him, he would cry and embarrass himself. Tara watched them go away, a group of old men with her father amid them, reminiscing their old times and their own weddings, distributing sweets and savouries to the urchins who had patiently waited at the gates of the palace, walking back to their simple lives. She stood watching them in silence, feeling a world and a way of life slipping away from her, fighting the void that was forming in her stomach.

Hanuman came and invited her to come near the eternal fire. Baali was waiting for her to seek the blessings of the Brahmins. She prostrated herself in front of strangers with her husband by her side. They blessed her in a language that she didn't understand by throwing rice and flower on her head. Tara wished Baali would enquire about her father, but he didn't say a word. When she got a chance, she told him that her father had left for the village. He nodded and turned to the next guest to enquire about his health while insisting that he should partake in the feast. She ignored the pain she felt; she had to learn to live with such small slights. Men are careless, they don't know who they hurt, she told herself. He loves me, and I love him, that is more important than anything else, she thought as she stood close to him. As the sun set, the ceremonies concluded, and Tara sighed in relief.

Just then, Tara heard a commotion at the gate. Hundreds of cows and buffaloes rushed through the city gate. Dust rose in puffy clouds and the air was filled with the moos of the cows and the excited screaming of people running beside them. Tara had never seen a domesticated cow. She had heard of the Asura tribe of Mahishas, who lived to the south east of Kishkinda, five hundred songs away, had thousands of cows and water buffaloes. The Deva villages in the faraway lands of North also had pastoral lands and cows.

People thronged to see the cows being led into the city. At the rear end, Sugreeva rode a cart drawn by a huge bull. The coming of a cart was an event in Kishkinda. Most of the Vana Naras who had never left the Dandakaranya forest had never seen a cart. The ones who had worked as Dasas in the lands of Asuras or Devas had seen carts, and some had even cleaned them for their masters, but it was unheard of for a Vana Nara to ride one and here was a Vana Nara riding the cart like a hero returning victorious from battle. Old women lamented that the end of the world was near for only Ayyan rode a bull. Sugreeva was committing a great sin by acting like Ayyan. The wrath of Ayyan would surely fall on the Vana Naras, the old women warned. People were too excited to listen to old women's words. Hundreds of children ran beside the cart, screaming with enthusiasm. The procession reached the centre of the street and stopped a few feet before the eternal fire where Baali and Tara were standing. The drummers who had come from the Kolli mountains danced before the cart, hitting their *parai* drums and swirling around in a frenzy. The crowd waved their hands and danced to the wild rhythm. The cart reached the eternal fire and Sugreeva jumped out and said, 'My wedding present to you and your new bride, brother. Behold the great bull Dundubhi.'

'Dundubhi', the crowd whispered in awe and fear. The strength of the bull was legendary. It was the most prized possession of the Asura King of Mahisha tribe. The bards used to sing many songs about its strength and power. In the Mahisha kingdom of Mayavi, the Asura who was the owner of countless cows and buffaloes held an annual fest during the month of the crocodile, when winter gives way to summer in the forest. The holy day, when the great God of Ayyan wed the daughter of mountain, Asura men who were farmers and cowherds assembled at the banks of Kaveri to fight the bulls. It was a mating festival of Asuras, for the man who tamed the bull would be courted by many damsels. Dundhubhi was the prized bull of the Asura king, Mayavi, a distant relative and vassal of Ravana. The bards used to sing that for Mayavi, the bull was like his brother and had promised hundreds of cows and buffaloes to anyone who could tame Dundubhi.

Baali came forward and admired the majestic bull, 'How did you get this wonderful creature?'

Sugreeva laughed, 'I won it.'

The crowd gasped. Sugreeva beamed with pride. 'That is the least I can do for my beloved sister-in-law,' he said, looking at Tara. Tara looked away. Something was wrong. She had a feeling that Sugreeva was lying. Baali caressed the forehead of the bull. The bull gave a grunt and the crowd let out a nervous laughter. Something was sinister about the bull. Its shoulders were five feet from the ground and the muscles rippled in its black body. Its curved horns, almost three feet long were as sharp as swords. The small eyes were cruel, and its nostrils flared in anger, as if it was about to charge. It stood, proud and erect, with untamed wilderness brimming from every inch of its chiselled body. It looked like the bull of Kala, the God of time and death. Tara didn't want Baali to stand so near the bull. She tried to call Baali and the bull stared at her with its bloodshot eyes. She shuddered with an unknown fear.

'And I have brought so many cows too,' Sugreeva said, pointing at the herd that filled the street till the fort gate.

'Cows?' Baali laughed, 'What will we do with cows?'

Nala, who was standing beside Baali, answered, 'Cow is the new money, Baali. For the Devas, cows are holy animals and they worship it like a God. For Asuras, it is a delicious food. The two keep fighting for cows, among other things. The Deva term for war is Gauvishti, the desire for cows.'

'Cows are the greatest gift one can give to Brahmins,' Hanuman added.

'We will need cows and bulls, if we start farming,' Nala added, 'and to sustain the city, we need farming. We have to become civilized.'

'A few may be gifted for virtue,' Hanuman smiled.

Riksarajas, who was holding his patience for so long, scoffed, 'The cows are shitting all over our beautiful city. Your gift is stinking, Sugreeva.'

Sugreeva glared at Riksarajas. He asked, 'Already drunk?'

Riksarajas gave him a derisive smile, 'Just started. I have saved a cask full of toddy for you.'

Before Sugreeva could retort and make things worse, Hanuman intervened, 'Let us continue the rituals.'

The brahmins started chanting their mantras in a language that no one was familiar with. The scene before Tara's eyes had an unreal quality, like the dream one vaguely remembers when one wakes up. The bull, that was tied in the grove of the seven palmyra trees, bothered her for no reason.

'Wedding functions are exciting only in dreams. In real life, they're dreary and boring, isn't it?' Sugreeva who was standing near Tara whispered in her ears. Despite herself, she chuckled, and Baali frowned at them. Sugreeva repeated his joke aloud, much to the chagrin of the priests, but Baali laughed loudly.

'Wait till you're married, Sugreeva. I'm looking for a good bride for you,' Baali said. Tara saw Sugreeva's face darken. It was only for a lightning second, but it sent shivers through her spine. The way he was looking at her was not right. She moved closed to Baali and intertwined her fingers with his. He looked at her in surprise, but thankfully, he gave her fingers a squeeze. That was reassuring. She didn't dare look at Sugreeva. From his forced laughter that boomed in her ears, she knew that Sugreeva hadn't missed the gesture.

Soon the Brahmins left, leading the cows they had received as a gift. Hanuman went to see them off after blessing the couple. He was not to return soon as he was entering a month-long penance. The moment the boat across River Pampa vanished from sight, the sober mood changed dramatically. Riksarajas gave orders for the celebrations to commence. It started with the beating of Mizhavu from the top of a nearby rock that towered over the Royal cave. A parai drum picked up the rhythm. Soon, the entire valley was reverberating with wild drumbeats. A huge campfire rose by the bank of the river. Some Vanaras rolled huge wooden barrels of palmyra toddy and started serving them. Wild, out of tune and raunchy songs were sung and soon it descended into a wild party as if to compensate for the rituals of the morning. Social barriers that were carefully constructed broke down and there was an easy camaraderie among the crowd.

Tara saw another facet of Baali that night. Gone was his stern demeanour. The toddy had loosened him up. He sang the most raucous songs and laughed the loudest. He matched wit for wit with his brother and the crowd roared in appreciation. For a change, Riksarajas was finding it difficult to keep up with the enthusiasm of his two boys. Baali danced with gay abandon and had a drumming competition with his brother. On the silky-smooth river bank, under a full moon that painted everything in buttery yellow, he wrestled with many men, beating them easily and pounding his chest to proclaim his victory every time he slammed his opponent on the ground and pressed his heavy feet on his chest. Tara was laughing her heart out, forgetting that she was a new bride. Sugreeva came to challenge his brother, much to the cheer of the crowd. She watched with bated breath as the two drunk brothers hurled colourful expletives that made her blush and the crowd roared with whistles and howls of laughter. Like two bison in the fight for a mate, they rammed into each other, trying to trip the other, catching each other's torso, grunting, falling, rolling on the sand, separating, and clashing again.

As the wrestling progressed, Baali got the upper hand and slammed Sugreeva on to the ground. He held him pressed to the ground and Tara clapped in appreciation. Sugreeva's eyes met hers and she saw his expression change to pain and then anger. She stopped clapping. With a grunt, he wriggled out of Baali's grip, grabbed his leg and tripped his elder brother down. Baali laughed and cursed as he got up. Sugreeva stared at Tara and she was scared. She watched him attacking Baali with full vigour. Baali continued to laugh and parred his younger brother's attacks playfully, but Tara could see that Sugreeva was dead serious. Somehow the crowd sensed that something was wrong. The drums died down and an uneasiness descended. Baali continued to laugh and fight but Sugreeva's face was contorted with rage. The image of Sugreeva slamming Baali's head when they were boys came rushing to Tara's mind. From the darkness of the city, Dundubhi bellowed, sending shivers down her spine. It was like a warning, a premonition that riled some dormant primeval fear in her mind.

Tara wanted to get between the two brothers and separate them, but they were like two elephants clashing. Soon, despite Sugreeva's spirited fight, Baali slammed him down and held him firm. He kept his feet on a panting Sugreeva's chest and beat his broad chest, proclaiming his victory. Baali extended his hand to Sugreeva with a smile. For a brief tense moment, Sugreeva didn't take his brother's hand. Baali abused his younger brother in colourful language that would have made Riksarajas proud and a few people laughed. Tara saw Sugreeva's face flush with anger. But what scared her more was how it changed to a smile in a flash. Sugreeva took Baali's hand and Baali yanked him up. The drums picked up in frenzy and the crowd cheered.

Sugreeva hugged his elder brother and patted his back. Tara saw that his eyes were searching for her. She tried to sneak away, to get lost in the crowd but he found her. For a moment, their eyes met, and he winked at her. It sent tremors down her spine. He left his brother's embrace and rushed to her. Before she could react, he grabbed her hand. Baali stood watching indulgently. To her dismay, she found herself blushing at Sugreeva's touch. She was scared whether Baali could understand the effect Sugreeva was having on her.

'Sister-in-law,' Sugreeva said with his charming smile. 'Why are you hiding here? My brother is waiting for you!' Before she could react, he lifted her off her feet and threw her to his brother. She would have fallen had Baali not caught her. The crowd burst into laughter again and there were a few bawdy comments. Baali lifted her off her feet and swirled her. She cried, half in fright, half in relief. Faces became a blur as he swirled her, and she grabbed him tight, burying her face in his broad chest. The rawness of his sweat made her giddy. When he placed her back on earth, the world was swimming before her eyes. Baali held her close and proclaimed to his subjects.

'Behold your Maharani Tara,' Baali said, and the crowd roared in approval.

'Tara, the best of the women, the most beautiful,' Sugreeva cried and the cheer was deafening this time. She kept her face down. She didn't want anyone to observe how flushed her face was. She hated herself for the effect Sugreeva was having on her. The rawness of Sugreeva's sexuality, his audacity and his obsession for her was arising the bitter sweetness of forbidden pleasures in her. She felt she was betraying Baali.

Baali swooped her off her feet and started walking. The drummers walked before them. She was surprised at what was happening. Sugreeva was hurrying beside them.

'Have you forgotten our ancient custom, Yata?' Sugreeva said, using the Northern tongue for sister-in-law. 'The marriage is to be consummated in the grove of palmyras. My brother is taking you there.'

She was horrified. Why was half the population of Kishkinda following them for something that needs to be done in private? The procession soon reached the grove. Seven towering palmyra trees stood in a line on a hill, like ghosts of a bygone era. As they neared, she saw that the place was breathtakingly beautiful. From the hill, they could see River Pampa taking a turn at a distance. The earth lay bathed in golden moonlight, but there were stars sprinkled in the sky too. Jasmine creepers had entwined the palmyra trees and the star shaped flowers gave a heady fragrance to the breeze. As Baali gently lay her down on the ground, the grass was deliciously soft. Dew had started falling. There air was thick with the smell of Nishagandhi flowers. She stared at Baali's eyes with all the love she could muster. For a moment, she forgot they weren't alone. Her lips parted, thirsty for a kiss from her beloved.

'Not so fast, Yata.'

She was startled when she heard Sugreeva's voice near her. He was standing behind Baali. She could not hide her shame. He had seen her desire and that was worse than seeing her naked. She hated him with all her heart and was afraid of the hate that was perhaps love in another form.

Tara saw that Sugreeva was passing pots of toddy again. Anger bubbled up in her mind. This was not right, she wanted to scream. Sugreeva came near her and offered a pot to her. She was livid.

'You're supposed to drink, Yata,' he said with a smile. She looked at Baali. He nodded in consent. She was confused. Were they playing a prank on her? Should she take it or refuse it? Sugreeva pressed the toddy pot to her lips and the pungent sweet smell of the white liquor assaulted her senses. She turned her face away. He turned her face towards his. He was so close to her that she could smell him. He smelt like his brother. She was afraid of him and herself. She grabbed the pot and gulped the content down. It burned its way to her stomach and she gagged. She pushed him away and ran to vomit the contents out. Laughter exploded behind her.

Soon a circle had formed. They were still passing on the toddy pots. Sugreeva was at the centre. His brother sat near him with an indulgent smile. She was confused and didn't know how she should react. She stood at the edge of the circle as Sugreeva started singing. His voice was rich and melodious. For a moment, she got lost in its fullness. It had the power to carry her away to forbidden lands. She was thankful for the ridiculous dance that Riksarajas did. The eunuch's dance lightened the mood, breaking the enchantment Sugreeva's mellifluous voice was weaving around her. She was grateful for the laughter he elicited from the crowd, for she could hide her feelings in smiles.

'I said I would tell a story about you, Yata,' Sugreeva repeated, bringing her back to reality. 'I am going to tell a story about how my brother won his beautiful wife,' Sugreeva said, raising his pitcher of toddy. The crowd cheered. Sugreeva cleared his throat, hummed a few tunes, snapped his fingers to get the rhythm right and started singing. The lyrics formed by itself and filled the grove. It merged with the mist that rose from the bushes and floated away to the river. The palmyra fronds swayed as if keeping rhythm with the song.

Sugreeva sang about how the gods and demons had once decided to churn the ocean of milk that lay beyond the seven worlds. The great Naga Vasuki was the rope, and Mandara Mountain, the churning rod. Holding the head of the great snake Vasuki were the Asuras under Mahabali and the tail of the snake was held by Devas under Indra. They kept churning the ocean of milk and from it, spectacular things emerged. Celestial nymphs emerged from the waves, the Apsaras like Rambha and Menaka. Devas and Asuras fought to appropriate the women, but when the most beautiful of them emerged, Devas and Asuras were stunned by her beauty. The woman with rounded breasts and narrow hips, fish-shaped eyes, hair so curled and thick like a colony of bees, skin so smooth and dark like ripe Jamun, was none other than Tara. Devas and Asuras fought for her hand, but when the great hero named Baali claimed her, there were none among Devas or Asuras who would dare to challenge. Thus Tara was married to Baali.

The absurd song was received with much appreciation and applause. Tara didn't know what to make of it. She remembered her humble hut and an old father who struggled to make his two ends meet, who thought serving people with his knowledge of medicine was more important than acquiring fame or money and chose never to leave the village. She remembered the mother she had never seen. She didn't want to be an Apsara, she was happy being herself. Baali came to her, unsteady on his legs. He smelt of toddy. He took her by her waist and pressed her to his body. He tried to kiss her, but she shoved him back.

'My Apsara,' Baali drooled as the crowd roared in laughter. Tara wanted to get away from all the ruckus. She saw Sugreeva smiling at her and knew that he was getting Baali drunk.

'Enough, please don't drink more,' she said and to her horror, Baali repeated it aloud. 'My bride says, not to drink.' That was received with more laughter.

'I'm the son of Indra, my Apsara. I'm the son of the King of Devas. That is the nonsense that the bards sing. And everyone knows, Devas are the greatest Surapanis, drunkards. They enjoy life,' Baali said, unsteady on his legs and lisping. People laughed again.

'And you know, my Apsara,' Baali went to Sugreeva and put his arm over his shoulders. 'This devil is the son of Surya, the sun God.'

Another bout of laughter followed. More toddy was passed around.

'I see doubt in your eyes, my Apsara,' Baali came lurching to her with an idiotic grin. He touched her nose with his index finger. 'You're ignorant, my Apsara. Brother, brother . . .' He went back to Sugreeva who hadn't had a drop of liquor.

'Brother, tell your story about how Indra and Surya made us,' Baali said and slapped his thighs. 'It's one hell of a story.'

The crowd roared in appreciation. 'Yes, tell us the story, tell us the story,' they demanded. Sugreeva raised his hands and pacified them.

'Once, Aruna, the charioteer of Surya, came early for his work. The sun God hadn't woken up and it was still dark. Aruna felt bored. He didn't want to wake up his master. He was pacing in the veranda of Surya's palace when he heard an enchanting music. He was confused. Who could be singing at this time? Who could be playing the Veena? He started moving towards the sound. He reached heaven, the Sabha of Indra. But the guards stopped Aruna. They said, 'You could be the charioteer of a big man, but in Indra's sabha, he is the only male who is allowed. The dance of the nymphs is going on, but you can't enter.' Aruna was not pleased with this. He walked back to his master's palace, but the thought that celebrated beauties like Rambha, Menaka and Thilothamma would be dancing in front of Indra made him restless. When he reached Surya's palace, he found his master was still asleep. An idea formed in Aruna's mind,' Sugreeva smiled.

'This is hilarious,' shouted Baali and howled with drunken laughter. Sugreeva waited for his brother to stop his laughter before continuing.

'Aruna decided to dress like a woman. He hurriedly shaved off his beard, and wore a woman's dress, in the most seductive fashion,' Sugreeva winked at Tara, and she recoiled. She was getting more and more uncomfortable. The crowd seemed to be deeply involved in the story. Sugreeva stood up and started walking in an exaggerated effeminate way, 'Aruna, now looking like the most ravishing of women, started walking towards Indra's court. The guards let him in, when he said he was the new nymph. Aruna entered and saw the celestial nymphs dancing. He was not impressed. He thought he could dance better. Not being a man who hesitated when a thought struck him, he ran to the centre of the sabha and started dancing. Indra was astounded by the talent of this new nymph. More than the dancing skills, it was the sheer

beauty of the new nymph that attracted the king of Gods. Like
Aruna, Indra too didn't believe in dilly-dallying once an idea stuck
him. He didn't wait for the dance to be over. He rushed from his
throne and lifted Aruna up. He carried her to his bedroom. And to
his chagrin, he found that instead of a nymph, he got a man who
had cross-dressed. He cursed Aruna to be pregnant and deliver a
child then and there. And before Aruna could blink, a baby was
born to him. And that baby is . . .'

Sugreeva paused and the crowd, though it knew the answer,
waited with bated breath. 'Yata, do you know who that baby is?'
Sugreeva asked. Tara was on the verge of tears.

'That baby is my brother, Baali,' he said and Baali bowed.

'You're insulting my husband,' Tara could not control her
anger.

'Tara, my Tara,' Baali came to her. 'This is just a game. You've
not heard how this idiot was born. Now, let me tell the story,' the
courtiers clapped in appreciation. More toddy was passed around.

'This Sugreeva is the son of Surya,' Baali said and Sugreeva
kept his palm on his chest and bowed to everyone. People laughed.

'Listen, listen. I'm going to tell the second part of the fantastic
story my brother narrated,' Baali cried and an anticipatory silence
descended. Some people had already started guffawing. *They might
have heard the story a hundred times*, thought Tara.

'Aruna rushed back to Surya,' Baali continued, 'He was already
late. The world was in darkness as the Sun hadn't risen. When
he reached his master's palace, Aruna found that Surya was in an
angry mood. He was walking up and down the veranda with his
hands clasped behind his back. When Aruna entered the palace
gate, Surya saw him and started shouting at him for being late.
Aruna apologised profusely. He had changed to his normal clothes
by this time. When he finally reached, Surya found something was
different about his charioteer. Surya started questioning him and
Aruna was forced to share the story of his misadventure. When
Surya heard the story, he started laughing. Aruna stood with a

sheepish grin, scratching his head. Surya, between his laughter demanded to see Aruna in his feminine avatar. Aruna was reluctant as already he had received a curse for his effort, but he was in no position to disobey his master. He requested Surya that he should not be cursed. Surya promised that he wouldn't curse Aruna and would rather bless him. Aruna changed to his feminine avatar and Surya was as stunned as Indra was by the ravishing beauty of Aruna. But Surya was true to his word. He didn't curse Aruna like Indra. Instead he blessed Aruna with a baby and that baby grew up to be Sugreeva.'

Sugreeva fell on his knees before his elder brother, showing exaggerated respect and Baali, laughing and mouthing expletives, blessed him by keeping the toddy pot on his brother's head. The drums started booming again and the Vanaras started dancing wildly. Riksarajas stood up, unsteady of his legs, dripping saliva and reeking of toddy. He tightened his Dhoti that was slipping down. He started abusing his sons. He said, 'Idiots, telling stupid stories about how you were born. If anyone wants to know how they were born, they should ask me.'

'How was my brother born?' Sugreeva asked the old man, laughing. The crowd howled with laughter.

'He was born from my hair ,' Riksarajas said, electing howls of merriment. Baali spat the toddy he was drinking, clutched his belly and laughed.

'And me?' Sugreeva asked.

'You . . . you were born from my . . .'

The crowd waited for some profanity, ready to burst out in laughter. Riksarajas stared at Sugreeva, 'How did you get that bull?'

Sugreeva laughed, but Tara saw he was getting restless. 'Tell me, how I was born?' Sugreeva laughed, scratching his beard.

'You were born from my neck,' Riksarajas said. He frowned and asked, 'Tell me, how did you get that bull . . . what's it name . . . dum dum dum . . . dumbi . . .Dhundubhi . . . ah Dundubhi? You stole it, right? You stole it from Mayavi . . .'

'Neck, ha ha,' Sugreeva laughed, 'I was born from this eunuch's neck.' The crowd didn't laugh. Tara was staring at Sugreeva. In the dim light of the moon, half his face was in the shadow. From afar, Dundubhi cried.

'I will tell a story,' Sugreeva laughed, 'I will tell how we were born of this eunuch.' The merriment had died down. An uneasy silence descended. Tara stood all alone, feeling angry and frustrated. Somewhere in the drunken melee, Baali passed out among the other vanaras. Tara wished Baali would wake up and put an end to this farce. 'Once Brahma, the God of Devas, shed a drop of tear. From that tear, a monkey was born. The monkey found a pot of Sura, the drink of Devas and got drunk. He started walking in the forest and saw a pond. When the monkey saw his reflection, he felt an ugly monkey was staring at him. He decided that such a monstrosity of God's creation should not be allowed to exist on earth. He jumped into the water to kill his own ugly reflection. Alas, the monkey had turned into a beautiful female. The pool was a magical pool,' Sugreeva sniggered.

Tara was feeling restless. Why was Sugreeva doing this? She had no doubt who he was taunting. Riksarajas stood on his unsteady legs, blinking, scowling at Sugreeva. People were shifting their feet, uneasy while Dundubhi let out a chilling bellow from the city.

Sugreeva took another gulp of toddy and continued, 'The sun God Surya and the King of Gods Indra were loitering in the mountains and they chanced upon this beautiful female monkey. The sexy woman arose a desire in them,' Sugreeva paused to look at Tara. Baali had passed out.

Sugreeva spat, cleared his throat and pressed on, 'Indra's semen ejaculated and fell on the beautiful woman's hair. From the hair, Baali was born. Surya ejaculated on the woman's neck and from the neck, this poor Sugreeva was born.' Sugreeva laughed, slapping his thighs. A few men joined in the laughter. The majority were silent. Riksarajas blinked many times, as if he didn't comprehend. Sugreeva went to Riksarajas and put his hands over the old eunuch's shoulders.

'Friends, do you know who that ugly monkey, who is neither male nor female is? Here he is, I mean, here she is,' Sugreeva pressed Riksarajas close to himself. 'Am I not right, eunuch?'

Riksarajas wriggled out of Sugreeva's grip and in a flash, tripped Sugreeva to the ground. Sugreeva had not expected it. The eunuch jumped to Sugreeva's chest. 'You want to know how I became a eunuch. I was born as a slave in Indra's household. My mother was a Dasi. I was castrated at the age of three. I was abused by Indra, by anyone who wanted to have fun with boys. And you make fun of me, bastard. I looked after you, treated you as my son and you mock my misfortune!' He punctuated each sentence with slaps across Sugreeva's face. Sugreeva lay scoffing, not bothering to wipe the blood flowing from his lips that were cut.

Riksarajas got up, unsteady, panting and puffing. Tara rushed to him, but he waved her away.

'Enough, stay away.' His wrinkled cheeks had a stream of tears flowing over them. 'I have no one. I am an ugly monkey, neither male, nor female.'

'Father . . .' Tara called, unable to bear the pain of Riksarajas.

He didn't bother to look at her. He walked away into the darkness, muttering, 'Thankless creatures. I've wasted my life.'

One by one, the crowd dispersed. Sugreeva was lying on his back. He started laughing. Tara turned towards him, 'Aren't you ashamed?'

'I am drunk, Yata,' he said, slamming his palm on the ground repeatedly and howling with laughter. 'Ah! The freedom of being drunk. One can speak one's mind. I had always wanted to tell that eunuch what I think of him . . . sorry . . . her . . . to hell with the correct word to address that creature. I told that monkey today the ugly truth and I'm so happy. I can sleep peacefully.'

Tara stood trembling in anger. She had never hated anyone more in her life. Sugreeva stood up and bowed in an exaggerated manner. He looked at Baali and said with a smile, 'The moon is beautiful, the night is sweet. Enjoy your first night.'

He bowed again to Tara and walked away. Tara felt his laughter hung heavy in the air, long after he had gone. She looked at Baali, snoring, drooling from the corner of his mouth, reeking of toddy and unaware of the most important day of his life. From the city, Dundubhi's haunting bellow rose. In response, the wolves howled from the hills. Tara sat near Baali, trying hard to suppress her tears.

# Chapter 22

When the group of two dozen Vana Nara women came to invite the new groom and bride to their dwelling, Tara was still awake in the grove. They found Baali sleeping in her lap. The women giggled, exchanged lewd jokes and secret smiles. They touched Tara and woke her from her dazed state. An old woman saw dried tears on her cheeks and cusped her chin in her shrivelled palms. She said with a toothless grin, 'It is painful the first time. Don't worry.'

Baali woke up gingerly. He stared at Tara's face, confused as to why he was there. Tara felt a surge of anger. Baali heard the women laugh and sprang up. Tara sat with her head bowed, angry and sad. The women's laughter was burning her ears. Baali offered his hand to her to get up. She took it after a moment's hesitation and lifted herself up. Baali embraced her and whispered in her ears, 'My queen is angry?'

She pushed him away, but he pulled her closer. The women were laughing and passing comments. He whispered in her ears, 'I am sorry, Tara. It won't happen again.' Tara's anger melted. He lifted her chin and gently pecked her on her cheeks. Blood rushed to her face and she wanted to be in his arms forever. She wanted the pesky women who were standing around to vanish. She wished the night was different than what it had turned out to be.

'Still not ready?'

Sugreeva stood behind them. She writhed free of Baali's embrace. 'Hope you had a nice sleep, Yata,' Sugreeva winked at Baali. Tara looked away.

'The cart is waiting for you,' Sugreeva said and turned on his heels. Baali took Tara's hand and started walking. The women walked behind them. Their hushed whispers and suppressed laughter irritated Tara. Baali and Sugreeva exchanged some jokes, each taunting the other. In the crowd, Tara felt alone, unwanted and unattended to. She froze when she saw the cart. Dundubhi was standing with its head erect and when it heard their footsteps, it snorted and swished its tail.

'What a fine creature,' Baali went to the front of the cart to admire the bull. Tara felt uneasy, standing near Sugreeva.

'I tamed it, brother. No one has ever done that before,' Sugreeva said.

Tara looked at Sugreeva. She had a feeling that he was lying. Such a bull can't be tamed so easily. There wasn't even a bruise on his body. She remembered Nala's words about how Sugreeva had earned the money for the city.

'One day, I will wrestle with it,' Baali said. The bull shook its head and the bell on its horns jingled ominously.

'I bet you would. Let me warn you, it isn't easy,' Sugreeva said.

'Ah, you think you can tame it, but I can't? You're forgetting, I am your elder brother,' Baali laughed and Sugreeva joined his palms in submission.

'I agree, big brother, but you should see how Asuras tame their bulls. They call it Jallikattu. They make the bull run through the narrow streets of their town and young men jump from all sides and try to tame the bull. No clubs, no swords, not even a stick is allowed, and one has to use one's bare hands to tame this magnificent bull.'

'Ah, that is the way it should be. Man against beast in its purest form. We should have this sport.'

'Why else did you think I brought this here?' Sugreeva smiled, 'I will make arrangements, brother.'

Baali continued to run his fingers through the contours of the bull's rippling muscles. Tara hated the challenge Sugreeva had so

smoothly thrown. Why did he steal the bull and bring it here?
There were countless other gifts he could have thought of. Why
this bull? The idea of Baali fighting the bull made her shudder.

'Tara.'

She grew tense. Sugreeva's face was so close that she could feel
the warmth of his breath.

'Tara,' he repeated in a hushed voice, as if relishing her name.
The honorific Yata was gone and somehow, Tara sounded wrong,
immoral and natural from his mouth.

'Can you be mine, Tara?' Sugreeva whispered.

Tara was speechless. She looked around to see whether anyone
had heard him. Baali was caressing the bull. The women were
standing a few feet away, gossiping.

'What are you saying, Sugreeva? I'm your elder brother's wife!'
Tara said.

'Can you be mine too, Tara?'

Tara was livid.

'Get lost, you . . .' she hissed. His face was full of agony. He
grabbed both her palms and pressed them to his chest.

'From the moment I set my eyes on you, I have yearned for
you from the bottom of my heart, Tara.'

She pulled her hands away from his grip and turned away
from him. Her heart was pounding in her chest. Did Baali see
them?

'I'm wedded to your brother, Sugreeva. You should not speak
like this to your sister-in-law.'

'From childhood, my brother has shared everything he had
with me, Tara.'

'And you repay his kindness like this? What a beast you are!'

'Be mine, Tara. Be mine. The marriage isn't consummated.
There is time still. I will beg him to share you with me. I will fall
at his feet and request him to relieve you. I know my brother. He
won't disappoint me. Say the word, Tara, say that you wouldn't
say *no* to me.'

'I married Baali because I love him. There is no man other than Baali in my heart. Go away, Sugreeva. I don't want to see your face again, get lost.' Tara closed her face with her palms and started sobbing. She prayed Baali wouldn't see them like this.

'Look at me, Tara. Face me and say it. Why are you not facing me?' He grabbed her palms and prised them open. Tara turned her face away. Her body trembled. She shut her eyes tight, scared that he could stare so deep into her.

'Somewhere in your heart, there is a little space for me. I can see it now. I'm so happy, Tara.'

'No, No–'

'I will request my brother. I will say that we love each other. My dear brother may be heartbroken. I know he loves you, but not as much as I do. No one can love you like me, Tara. I will beg my brother for you. And he will give you to me. I know him. There is no one who loves me more than him. He has given me everything I have asked for.' Sugreeva's tone had become frenzied.

Tara glared at him. She straightened her shoulders and faced him square. 'Go. Go and tell him. But by the time you're back, I will have left this world.'

Sugreeva slumped. 'You're so cruel, Tara. Women are so cruel.' Tears streamed from his eyes. He stood before her, heartbroken and pitiful. She felt angry that Baali had left her and was admiring the bull.

'Tara, Tara, don't judge my brother harshly, Tara,' Sugreeva said, startling her. *Could he read her mind?* 'My brother is a good man. He isn't irresponsible. I can't stand anyone thinking ill of my brother. Not even you, Tara. But I laced his drinks with seeds of poppy. I did it for you, Tara. I had never harmed my brother until yesterday because I couldn't imagine you sleeping with him. If that doesn't prove the depth of my love for you, I don't know what will. Please Tara–'

'You're so cruel. It was . . . it was our first night–'

'I want you, Tara. I want you pure, unsullied. You promised me, Tara that if I came with enough money to build the city, you will be mine.'

'I never did any such a thing,' Tara sobbed.

'You are beautiful even when you lie,' Sugreeva smiled.

Tara turned away and saw Baali standing behind her. Her heart skipped a beat. She looked down, as if she had done something wrong. Sugreeva said, 'I committed a grave mistake, brother.'

Tara felt she would faint. Sugreeva continued, 'I have to ask your pardon. I behaved like a cad.'

Tara felt giddy and she held the cart to steady herself. She didn't want to face Baali.

'I misbehaved with our father,' Sugreeva said. 'Yata was scolding me. I was drunk, Brother. I am sorry. I don't even remember how I behaved last night.'

Baali laughed and patted Sugreeva's shoulders, 'She did the right thing. You deserve all the scolding. Now go and ask for his forgiveness.'

'Sure, Brother. I am ashamed to face him.'

'Face him like a man and he will forgive you, whatever naughtiness you did, boy,' Baali said as he jumped onto the cart. He moved to the front and took the reins. 'What a magnificent creature. What are you waiting for? Jump in.' Baali cracked the whip in the air.

Tara tried to climb in, but the cart platform was too high for her. Sugreeva held her narrow waist and lifted her up. It happened so fast that she had no time to react. Blood rushed to her face. His unshaven chin had brushed against the back of her neck and it still prickled her. She sat on the rough seat, gripping the uneven edges tight, not lifting her head. The cart creaked as Sugreeva sat opposite her. She tried her best to avoid her legs brushing against Sugreeva. The cart started with a jerk and moved towards Kishkinda. The brothers cracked jokes and laughed. They sang together. The women walked behind the cart, talking loudly.

Before she knew it, Sugreeva had changed his seat and he was sitting between her and Baali, who was in the driver's seat. When the cart swayed, his thighs brushed against hers, however hard she tried to avoid it. Tara felt angry that she hadn't asserted herself with Sugreeva. *He is stalking me and he should be feeling guilty, not me, she told herself.* She should have cried out the first time. She decided she would not take such behaviour lying down. Her father had brought her up to think and act decisively. He had never taught her to behave only in a demure way, yet she had forgotten to assert herself when it mattered. She hadn't failed just herself, but also her father. She loved Baali and she would trust him to understand her. Tara decided she would tell Baali about Sugreeva's behaviour. She would also talk to him about getting rid of that evil beast Dundubhi, which she was sure, was a harbinger of misfortune. She had no clue at that time that Dundubhi was going to change the fate of Kishkinda forever.

# Chapter 23

Tara started climbing the steps leading to the cave, holding Baali's hands. She was relieved to have gotten rid of Sugreeva. She had got the cave painted with everyday scenes of the Vana Nara lives. She had got the stone cot carved with sculptors of animals, creepers and plants. In places where sunlight came through the gap in the roofs, she had planted ferns and flowering plants. She had made a small pond with lotus flowers in it and sat at its edge, watching its reflection on the roof. She was excited to show all this to Baali. Though they had reached Kishkinda almost ten days ago, they were supposed to enter the cave, which would be their home, only after their marriage.

At the entrance of the cave, where two stone lions stood in an eternal roaring position, the new bride and groom were welcomed by two women holding a lotus leaf filled with water. They poured the water on Baali's and Tara's feet. Nala came running. He was panting and puffing but was excited.

'Chief, I will show you—'

'Nala, you may go. I shall take my husband around,' Tara said with a smile. She saw Nala's face fall.

Little girls sprinkled sandalwood oil on them. The floor was strewn with petals of hibiscus flowers. She watched Baali's face brighten with surprise. The cave was breathtaking in its sublime beauty. Baali ran through the huge cave, excited like a child who had got his favourite toy. Tara felt proud and happy. He stopped to admire each sculpture. When they reached the stone cot, memories came rushing to Tara and coloured her cheeks red.

156

She felt her heart gushing with love for Baali. She looked at his broad shoulder and his narrow waist, his muscled thighs and thick hands and felt her throat going dry. Desire overwhelmed her. He was standing with his back turned to her, running his fingers over the carvings on the bed post. She was about to touch him when Sugreeva burst into the room.

'Brother, Nala is a wonderful man. He has started getting the street ready for Jalikattu. I had to just say the word about your wish and Nala had already started the work.'

Baali turned excitedly. 'That's wonderful. Let us have a look.'

Before Tara could react, Baali had left the room. She collapsed into the bed and sat like a stone. She had no idea for how long she sat there, feeling alone and helpless. She was determined to warn Baali, but it was frustrating that they were never alone for her to broach the topic. By evening, Baali came with Sugreeva to the chamber. Sugreeva's eyes met those of Tara and he winked. She turned her gaze away deliberately. Sugreeva put a reed mat on the floor and placed a pot of water by its side. Baali sat on the mat and Tara looked at him in surprise. She was about to ask him what he was doing, when Sugreeva held her wrist.

'He is in Vruta, the penance before the bullfight. The warrior must take the vow of celibacy and silence for twenty-one days. He must lie on the floor to sleep, wear only one piece of cloth and pray to the bull of Ayyan to give him strength'. Sugreeva's eyes twinkled with mischief.

'This is—'

Sugreeva didn't allow Tara to complete the sentence. Tara called out to Baali, but he was sitting in meditation and didn't respond. Sugreeva dragged Tara out of the cave.

'Yata, you may sleep with the women. It's only for twenty-one days. I will tend to my brother's needs. He shouldn't even see any woman during this time.'

'I am his wife,' Tara said, staring at Sugreeva.

'All the more reason you should stay away from him at this time, Yata. Who can resist your charms? You are an Apasara,' Sugreeva winked.

'Why are you doing this?' Tara said, feeling helpless and angry.

'You know the reason, Tara. I have told you. You are mine, Tara.'

'Devil,' Tara hissed.

'Tara, my Tara, we have twenty-one days and I have no vow of celibacy.'

Tara slapped Sugreeva across her face. He smiled and said, 'You have such soft hands Tara, like the petals of lotus. You are so fragrant that I am going mad with desire. Every moment, I think only of you Tara.'

Tara was horrified. She looked around to check if someone had seen them. There were many Vanaras arranging things inside the cave. Guards moved here and there, but no one was within earshot. She started walking down the steps.

'I will wait, Yata,' she heard him say. Tara half-expected him to follow. She walked through the streets that were milling with people. More and more Vana Naras were coming from afar and Nala was busy allocating homes to them. Asura merchants from the South had come with spices. She saw a boat anchored in the river. Her city was growing faster than she had imagined. She tried to push away her worry about Sugreeva by feeling happy about the dream she shared with Baali taking shape in such a grandiose way. People bowed to her as she walked the streets. There were workers putting up bamboo barricades on either side of the main street. A temporary gallery was coming up on the sides. Tara saw Nala instructing his workers and felt uneasy. The gallery might be for Jalikattu, the wild Asura game of taming the bull. Nala saw her and ran to her. She hurried as she didn't want to have any conversation with anyone now. She wanted to be alone, in the palmyra grove.

'Devi, I am sorry if I hurt you,' Nala said.

Tara stopped in her track. What was he sorry for?

Nala said, 'I thought you didn't trust me. I wanted to show Baali what I had built and was scared you would never acknowledge my work.'

'Why would I do that, Nala?' Tara was surprised. It was true she had felt uneasy when he was trying to corner all the credit.

'I saw it in your face, Devi,' Nala said. Was her face such that people can read her thoughts so easily? She was scared about Sugreeva now. Was she giving him some unconscious hint about liking him. *I hate him*, she told herself.

'I never—'

'I was a slave for two decades under Vishwakarma, the great Deva architect. I was the best worker and I did most of the work. But when it came to appreciation, I was a just a low-caste slave, a Vana Nara. So I was eager for a word of praise when Baali came. I am sorry if I intruded into your privacy.'

Tara grabbed the master builder's hand. 'Nala, you did a fantastic job. Everyone knows it, Baali knows it best. I have not seen Amaravati, Mahihsmathi or Trikota, but I am sure Kishkinda rivals all of them.'

She saw Nala's eyes fill up and she was touched. Genuine appreciation was the best way to get people to do great work. She was learning fast.

'I know, Devi. I was so happy when Sugreeva informed me about your instruction to build the gallery and track for bull-taming. I thought you would never trust me with another work.'

'I did what?'

Nala swept his hand and beamed. 'I will not fail you my lady. I will make you the best arena. I too am really eager to watch Baali tame the bull.'

Before she could react, Nala bowed and hurried away, shouting instructions at his workers. As she walked to the grove, dark thoughts possessed her. Why should Sugreeva take her name to build the Arena? She had to do something to stop this madness.

She was sure some danger lay hidden for Baali. Sugreeva's obsession for her was taking on sinister proportions.

Tara saw a figure by the river. He was standing up to his waist in water and praying to the rising sun. She walked aimlessly, trying to push away the premonitions. When she reached the river side, she saw it was Hanuman deep in prayer.

He seemed to have sensed her presence. He slowly opened his eyes and looked at her.

'Pranam, Hanuman. It's Baali's bride.'

Hanuman folded his palms respectfully to Tara and bowed. Then he returned to his prayers. Tara returned the greeting and waited for him to finish his prayers. She didn't know why she came here or what she was going to tell him. It felt good to be in his presence.

'Where is your husband, daughter?' Hanuman asked reverently.

'He . . . he is in penance.'

'Penance? Is this the time for . . .'

Tara's eyes filled up. She smiled to hide her agitation and said, 'He wants to tame the bull. They are going to play the Asura game of Jalikattu.'

Hanuman shook his head in dismay.

'Baali is behaving so irresponsibly. It's a shame. I heard he was drunk on his wedding night.' Hanuman said. Tara wanted to intervene and say that it was Sugreeva who made her husband drunk, who laced seeds of poppy in his drink. But she didn't want to answer unnecessary questions that it would give birth to. Hanuman started walking and she struggled to keep pace with his long strides.

'He is the chief of the Vanaras. Everyone knows Riksarajas is just a namesake chief. This isn't the way a leader should behave. Sometimes, I wonder whether you should have been the choice for Vanaras,' Hanuman said.

Tara didn't know what to say. She said, 'Swami, we didn't see you at the wedding feast.'

'Daughter, I don't go for such functions. I'm a Brahmachari. My time is spent in meditation.'

'I would be blessed if you could come with us to my home and accept our humble hospitality, Swami,' Tara pleaded.

'I don't step out of my Kadalivana, the grove of plantain I cultivate, daughter.'

Tara didn't reply. She didn't know whether she could confide in him. She gathered courage and pressed ahead. She didn't talk about Sugreeva or his passion for her. She talked about her worry about the bull-taming game. When she finished, Hanuman was watching her without any expression. His eyes pierced her soul and she looked down, unable to face him.

'You are worried that Baali will be hurt in the game?' Hanuman asked. Tara didn't reply.

'I am not worried about Baali. He is a great warrior and will tame the bull,' Hanuman said. She stood, debating whether she should tell him her fears.

'Daughter,' Hanuman called in a gentle voice and she looked up, 'taming the mind is more difficult.' Hanuman walked away.

Tara ran behind him and stopped him, 'Don't speak in riddles. What did you say now?'

Hanuman smiled, 'I said the mind is a beast. Untamed, it could destroy everything. Not clear? Don't worry. Just remember Baali and only Baali is your husband.'

Tara stood rooted, her mind in turmoil as Hanuman walked away.

# Chapter 24

*Tara loves me, but is scared to admit it*, thought Sugreeva and smiled. He was massaging his brother's feet. His brother was lying on his back on the reed mat spread on the floor and Sugreeva was sitting cross-legged beside him. When Sugreeva stretched to take the heated oil, his brother stretched and caressed Sugreeva's curly hair. Sugreeva felt a pang of guilt. He could feel his brother's affection in his every action. Even when Baali treated him like a kid and his taunts became unbearable, Sugreeva knew how much his brother loved him. Sugreeva tried his best to return the affection, but since childhood, Tara was an obsession for him. *If only Tara was mine, I could love my brother like no one else*, he thought.

'Sugreeva, did I make a mistake by taking the penance now?' Baali's question broke his chain of thoughts.

'Yes, you did Brother. But we are warriors and she is a warrior's wife. Yata will understand.'

Baali smiled without opening his eyes. 'Poor girl, she might have had so many dreams about married life.'

'Brother, it is only for twenty-one days. She will love you more once you show how brave and strong you are.'

'Fool, she knows I am brave and strong. Our union was decided in the heavens. We understand each other perfectly well.'

Sugreeva continued to massage Baali's legs. His mind was in turmoil.

'How did you win the Jalikattu?' Baali asked.

Sugreeva said sheepishly, 'I cheated.'

Baali sprang up, 'You did what?'

Sugreeva said, 'I bribed the caretaker of the bull. He laced opium in its feed. When it came to the arena, Dundubhi could barely stand. It fell on my first blow.'

'That was unfair.'

'I wanted to gift it to you, Anna. Besides, Mayavi and his Mahisha army had stolen the calf from Rishi Matanga, the Deva Brahmin, when he was doing Penance. So there was nothing wrong in using some trickery.'

Baali said, 'Maybe they had stolen it. They are Asuras. They have no values or morals, just like the Devas. We are Vana Naras. We cannot—'

'They rule us. We have been slaves always, the Dasas. The sooner we learn their ways, the sooner we can cease to be slaves.'

Baali stood up. 'I can't approve this. You have to return the bull to Mayavi.'

Sugreeva said, 'As you say, Anna. But the world would say that the great Baali was scared to tame the bull and sent his brother to steal Dundubhi. I agree, I acted in haste, Anna. Punish me, but if you don't demonstrate you are stronger than any Asura warrior, sooner or later they will raid us and take all of us as slaves. We need to send a message.'

Baali sat on the floor, deep in thought. He said, 'You made a grave mistake, brother. You acted unfairly. Both with the beast and with its owner. But you have a point about taming the bull. I shall fight the bull and tame it. Then I will go myself to Mayavi and beg his forgiveness for your shameful act.'

'I . . . I am sorry, Anna. I did it for . . .'

Baali kept his hand on Sugreeva's shoulders. 'Your youth makes you do such hasty things. My duty is to show you the right direction. Did you apologize to our father?'

Sugreeva stood with his head hanging in shame.

'Go, do that first,' Baali said. Sugreeva stood up, bowed and left. He walked to the cave door and stretched his limps. The work for the bull-taming arena was going on. He decided to visit Dundhubi.

When he reached the pen, Riksarajas was watching the bull from a distance, leaning on the stable fence. Dundubhi grunted and bellowed from the stable. The effect of cannabis was wearing off and the bull was getting stronger by the day. It could no longer be used to draw the cart. The bull was trying to break off the ropes and the stable shook when it struggled.

'That is a mean beast you have got,' Riksarajas scowled as Sugreeva approached him.

'I am sorry,' ' Sugreeva said without looking at him. Riksarajas stared at him for a moment. Dudubhi bellowed and tried to smash the pillar to which it was tied. The stable roof shook dangerously.

'You stay away from your brother's wife,' Riksarajas hissed.

'What?'

'You think I am blind? You scoundrel. I can see how much you lust after her.'

'You are drunk, eunuch.'

'You are a drunk, horny monkey. Strip naked and rub yourself on the bark of a coral tree. Its thorns are the only cure for your madness.'

'The time has come to chain you . . .' Sugreeva slammed his fist on the stable fence.

Riksarajas scoffed, 'You better chain me. I am going to expose your dirty plans. He would die for you, your fool of a brother and you are planning to kill him.'

'You have gone senile,' Sugreeva hissed.

'Ha, you think I don't know what you are up to. You stole this beast—'

'I didn't steal it. I won it.'

'Like hell you won it! My foot! You used some trickery and brought this demon here. You have put a challenge to your brother, appealed to his bloated ego and ensured he will take up the challenge like a fool, which he has. You want it to gore him to death.'

Sugreeva grabbed Riksarajas by his throat, 'Bloody eunuch. I will pull out your tongue if you talk nonsense. There is no one I love more than my brother. You understand that. You understand that, you fool.'

Sugreeva threw Riksarajas over the fence and hurried away. Dundhubhi bellowed from the stable and gave another hit to the pillar. The stable shuddered. Riksarajas pulled himself up and stood shivering by the stable fence, panting. He had to warn Baali. With unsteady steps, he dragged his tired body to meet his son.

# Chapter 25

Tara rotted in the chamber, sharing her room with countless other women who had taken up jobs in the cave. They called it the King's palace and addressed Tara as Maharani. All the egalitarian dreams of a society that had no hierarchy were slowly dissolving, but Tara was not in any state of mind to bother about them. She pined for Baali; she wanted to be in his arms, wanted to look at his eyes when he smiled. She wanted to cook for him, a skill she had learnt recently. The eternal fire at the city centre had ensured every Vanara household had a hearth. From eating raw tubers and flesh, they had started eating cooked food. For many, it brought memories of eating leftovers in the households where they had slaved in their childhoods. Some even thought about those days nostalgically and talked about the kindness of their masters who would beat them only lightly and feed them with leftovers to assuage their guilt. Many women burned their limbs, trying to master the fire, but it was a period of awakening. Tara tried to spend her time, trying to teach the women how to use fire, but nothing could quench the dull pain she felt whenever she thought about Baali. With a sinking feeling of helplessness, she saw the arena being built for the bull-taming festival. All attempts by her to meet Baali had failed as Baali had shut himself up in the bedroom chamber with Sugreeva taking care of all his needs. She was livid and sad but there was nothing much she could do.

As the time wore on, her frustration festered like a wound that refused to heal. Sugreeva served his elder brother like a slave. Sometimes, she wondered whether it was Sugreeva's possessiveness for his brother that made him behave the way he did rather than his professed love for her. Yet, there was something pitiful, something flattering in the way Sugreeva sought her. Whenever he found her alone, he whispered his love for her. He pleaded with her, abased himself, wept, raged and apologized to win her. All her efforts to stop him were in vain. Tongues had started wagging and she was scared how Baali would react when the rumours reached him. In certain dark moments, when she was lying alone in her bed, she wondered whether Baali loved her as much as Sugreeva. She didn't know the answer. She was afraid to know the answer. She wanted to be left alone to live her life with the man she loved. She told herself countless times a day that it was Baali who she loved. She tried to hate Sugreeva, tried to forget him, but like a cursed dream, Sugreeva found ways to return to her thoughts. There were curious gifts, often kept hidden in the chamber she slept. She found flowers under her pillows or some kids came and narrated some love songs, saying Sugreeva had taught them and had asked them to narrate them. There was no escaping from Sugreeva's stifling love. Tara felt she would go insane.

Tara felt she had to do something. Her life was becoming a living hell. She decided to take the help of the only man she could trust in Kishkinda. On the day before the bull-taming festival, she caught a glimpse of Baali when he was busy wrestling Sugreeva. She thought of confronting him then, but there was a crowd watching the brothers wrestle. She slipped away to seek the counsel of Hanuman. She met him in the plantain grove where Hanuman had built an Ashram. He was meditating when she reached there, and she patiently waited under a plantain tree with red bananas that were ripening. When he opened his eyes after sometime, the sun was already dipping westwards. He didn't look surprised when he saw her. It was as if he was anticipating her. She fell on her knees and started crying.

He understood without her speaking a word. He said in a soothing voice, 'Daughter, go home in peace. I will find a solution.'

And as an afterthought, he added, 'Nothing will happen to Baali, but . . .'

The incomplete sentence hung like a sword in the air. She waited for him to complete it, but he had gone back to meditation. She went back with a heavier heart than she had come with. She spent a sleepless night, tossing around on her reed mat, worrying. She could hear Dundubhi's enraged bellowing piercing the peace of the night. She cursed the beast with all her heart. She worried whether she would ever see Baali alive again. The beast had gone mad as per the servants and no one went near it to even tend it. The grass was thrown inside the stable from a hole in the roof. The servants whispered that the ropes that tied the demon bull were withering away and everyone feared it getting free. Tara hated Sugreeva for bringing Dundubhi to Kishkinda. The thought that Baali would be facing it barehanded in the arena made her sick. A horrible thought came to her mind. She wished it was Sugreeva who would be facing it instead of Baali. What if Sugreeva is gored to death? It was an unpalatable wish, but somehow, she found herself wishing it. She felt horrible for such an evil thought, yet she could not resist imagining the scene again and again in her mind.

Even before dawn, Kishkinda was brimming with people. As far as eyes could see, Vana Naras marched to their city. The word had spread far and wide that the chief of Vanara, Baali, was taking on the untamed bull Dundubhi, barehanded. The city brimmed with merchants selling wares. Dust rose into the air from the many thousands of feet treading in the area. The air was filled with cries of vendors shouting out about their wares. Nala had raised a huge flag with a totem of a monkey at the top of the hill that had Baali's palace cave. It fluttered in the wind, beckoning all black-skinned monkeys to their first free city. Even Asuras, Devas, Kinnaras, Gandharvas, Nagas, Kimpurushas and other tribes had arrived to see the spectacle. Other tribes felt jealous as Vanaras showed them the wonders of their new city. The proud citizens of Kishkinda boasted about how the new fountains that decorated the four corners of the shining arena were named after the four oceans and Devas sniggered when they heard such boisterous claims of the slave people. Asuras compared the city with their own famed cities like Muzuris or Trikota and were forced to admit that Kishkinda was much grander than anything they had seen. That an emancipated slave, Nala, had built a city better than what a Vishwakarma of Devas or Maya of Asuras could, was unpalatable to those who had always looked at the black-skinned monkey-faced forest people as uncivilized, uncouth people, fit enough only to be slaves. They secretly wished Baali would be killed in the arena and that would put an end to the new-found arrogance of these untouchables. Some spoke about the black magic of Baali, where unknown evil forces had helped him build a city. Hadn't the ancient scriptures spoken that the end of the world was nearing when such people rose to prominence? Some of the foreigners were spies, assessing how strong the fort was and how to destroy the city of the black people with a well-planned invasion.

Tara was seated in the front row, near the bamboo barricade. Riksarajas sat near her in a log chair made especially for him. His customary pot of toddy was kept near him. When two women came to fan them with a fan made of peacock feather, he rebuked them saying he was not the king of Devas or the emperor of Asuras. He was a monkey man and they should leave him to drink in peace. The women ran away laughing. Tara looked at the arena, a sea of black faces brimming with pride and joy. She was sweating despite the cold breeze that blew from the river. Riksarajas kept mumbling, 'the fool, the fool Baali' until she pleaded with him to keep quiet. The sound of Parai drums could be heard from the distance and the crowd stood up, cheering, screaming, and howling in excitement. First came the drummers, dancing with their drums, swirling round and round. Behind them came the peacock dancers with flower bows on their shoulders. They gave a vigorous performance before 'Maharani Tara'. The crowd cheered on Tara and she squirmed in embarrassment. She was just a vaidya's daughter, she wanted to tell them. When the crowd cheered for chief Riksarajas, he raised his toddy pot high. Someone called him eunuch maharaja from the crowd and people laughed. Riksarajas retorted he was the heckler's father and the crowd roared with merriment. Tara sat, gripping the hand rest of her bamboo chair tight. The announcement came that Baali and his brother would be entering the arena. The Parai drums rolled in a frenzy. Horns blared in incongruous tones. Amid screams and cheers, howls and whistles, Baali bowed before the eternal fire and walked through the street. Behind him, carrying a mace on his shoulders, Sugreeva walked, waving to the crowd.

Tara's eyes filled with tears. Baali was the epitome of manhood. He towered above everyone, with broad shoulders, chiselled muscles, rippled stomach. With skin as black as ebony, he looked as if a granite statue had come alive. Her gaze fell on Sugreeva. He was at his charming best. His smile had an impishness that could increase the heartbeat of any woman. He had grace in his every moment, as if he was performing the steps of some exotic dance. His gaze fell on Tara's face and she quickly averted her eyes. She wished Baali would look at her. When he went past her, she screamed his name, forgetting that she was the Maharani. He saw her and smiled. Her eyes went hazy with tears. She wanted to rush to his arms and stop him. *Would I ever hold him again*, she wondered.

Tara saw Sugreeva coming towards her. He took his seat by her side and smiled at her. She moved away from him, shrinking herself as much as possible, thankful for the armrest that separated them.

'I won't devour you. Relax,' Sugreeva said, looking straight ahead.

'I am relaxed. My husband has gone for a walk by the river, right?' Tara asked gritting her teeth.

'I don't know about your husband. My brother will beat that beast today,' Sugreeva said. Before Tara could retort, the

horn sounded, and a sudden hush fell on the crowd. Everyone was craning their necks towards the enclosure where the bull was constrained. Tara closed her eyes and prayed. She heard the creaky noise of the gates opening. For a moment, everything stood still. She opened her eyes with fear. Baali was standing at the centre of arena with his fists curled on his waist. From the other end, the gates were open, but nothing seemed to happen. Suddenly, the arena exploded with excited screams. Tara saw the enraged bull rushing at great speed towards Baali. It was as huge as a mountain but that didn't deter its speed. The earth shook as it thundered towards Baali, who was standing in a combat position, ready to grab the sword-like horns and slam the bull on the ground.

Tara saw the mountain of flesh and horns moving towards Baali, but in a blur, it turned its course and smashed the barricade. The crowd panicked as the bull, instead of rushing towards Baali, broke free and ran up the stadium, a few feet before it would reach Tara. Everyone was scrambling up. The sound of chairs being cracked under the weight of the bull, screams and frightened cries rent the air. Before she knew what was happening, the bull had turned towards them.

'Tara, run!' Riksarajas cried, struggling to get up from his seat. Tara saw him trying to tackle the enraged bull. Sugreeva had caught her wrist and was tugging her away. She saw the bull fling Riksarajas like a rag. He landed among the stampeding crowd. The bull snorted and charged at Tara. She lost her balance and fell on her back. She saw the bull a few feet away as it was coming towards her, with its head tilted, its sword like horns pointing at her. In panic she tried to get up, but she was slammed down. The bull aimed its horns at her and missed. She had escaped by a whisker. She screamed and tried to move away.

'Tara, run!' She was disoriented as she tried to stand up. When her head stopped reeling, she saw that Sugreeva was holding on to the horns of the bull and it was trying to shake him off.

'Run for God's sake!' Sugreeva screamed. She ran towards him, trying to free him of the demon bull's horns. She caught hold of his Angavastra, but the bull charged. She lost her balance and fell. The bull rumbled past her, carrying Sugreeva on its horn. The crowd was running hither and tither. She saw Sugreeva losing his grip and falling. The bull pierced his belly and lifted him in the air. She struggled to reach him against the panicked crowd rushing out. She saw the bull kicking him with its hoofs, slamming him down on the ground repeatedly and goring him with its horns. Then she saw Baali. She saw him catch the bull by its horn. She ran towards them.

'Take him away,' Baali screamed as he struggled to keep the bull away. Tara rushed to an unconscious Sugreeva. She dragged him away from the arena with great difficulty. Baali was fighting the deadly bull with all his might. With rising panic, she saw Sugreeva's entrails out of his belly and he was wheezing. He left a trail of blood as she dragged him away. She screamed for help. Everyone was running for their life and no one bothered to stop. She tripped a young man rushing out. When he fell, she slapped him hard across his face.

'Maharani Tara?' The young man asked, holding his stinging cheek.

'Help me carry him,' Tara said. The young man helped her to drag Sugreeva to safety. 'The chief has been flung by the bull. Get him too,' she ordered and after a moment's hesitation, the young man rushed in search of Riksarajas. Tara tore her dress and started cleaning Sugreeva's wounds. He was whispering something. She ignored it and tied his wounds, but the bleeding continued. He was whispering in panic. She put her ears to his mouth.

'Tara, I am dying. Tell me you love me, Tara. Tell me before I go. Please . . .'

She couldn't control her tears. He had given his life to save her. Whatever may be his faults, he truly loved her, perhaps more than Baali. But she loved Baali. His shivering fingers gripped hers.

'You won't say it even when I'm dying. Ha, I know. It doesn't matter. I love you as no man can ever love a woman,' Sugreeva said and passed out. She heard a roar from behind. She turned and saw Baali was down and the beast was attacking with renewed vigour. She had forgotten about Baali, she thought with shock. She freed herself of Sugreeva's grip. She saw Sugreeva's mace lying on the floor. She took it and rushed to Baali. He had managed to dodge the bull's thrust and was rolling on the floor. Dundubhi attempted to rip him apart with its horn. Sparks flew when its horns scraped the paved stones.

'Take your mace,' Tara cried.

Baali saw her. 'Get away,' he shouted as he dodged another thrust from the bull.

'Use the mace!' she shouted throwing the mace near Baali. It clanged on the stones and rolled. It distracted the bull and Baali was up on his feet in a flash.

'It is not fair,' Baali cried, 'I can't use a weapon against—'

'It has gored Sugreeva. Use the mace, you fool,' Tara cried, unable to control her frustration and anger. The bull saw her and charged towards her. She didn't know whether it was Sugreeva's injury or the fear that the bull would gore her that prompted Baali to fight 'unfairly'. He grabbed the mace and jumped high in the air. As the bull charged her, Tara saw Baali's mace break open the skull of the bull. She stood still as blood splattered over her face. The bull collapsed with a grunt, twitched for some time and then died. Baali stood panting, leaning on the mace. Tara went near him.

'I fought unfairly. The beast won, and I lost,' Baali mumbled. Tara shook his shoulders.

'Your brother is dying, and your father is injured, and you are bothered about unfairness of killing an animal.'

Baali stood as if in daze, mumbling over and over, 'I fought unfairly. I am worthless.'

Tara left him and rushed to Sugreeva. He lay consciousness. She screamed, and Baali walked towards them. He stood behind her. She heard his mace falling. Then an animal cry rose from Baali's throat. He crumbled on his knees.

'He is not dead, not yet,' Tara said.

Baali crawled to Sugreeva, 'Brother, brother, Sugreeva,' he called, slapping Sugreeva's face repeatedly. Sugreeva opened his eyes and saw Baali. 'Brother. Save me, Brother.' His voice was weak. Baali lifted his brother on his shoulders. He started walking towards the cave. Tara walked behind Baali, sobbing. A few in the crowd had seen the bull falling. They ran past Tara and Baali and started hacking the bull. Now that it was dead, they were free to show their bravery on its corpse. Tara ignored them and continued to walk.

She was a few feet behind Baali when the young man who she had sent to enquire about Riksarajas stopped her. Tara knew something was wrong from the demeanour of the young man.

'What . . . what happened?' she asked.

The young man didn't lift his head to face her. He said, 'The chief Riksarajas is dead.'

# Chapter 26

By the time Sushena came, Kishkinda had gone into mourning. The death of Riksarajas had cast a spell of gloom over the Vanaras. As he was dead, no one had anything bad to say about him. His failings were glossed over or indulgently laughed over, his virtues were exaggerated and often reiterated in the conversations. People huddled in the streets and talked about the event. More and more people arrived for the funeral of the slain chief. There were more than a dozen deaths in the stampede and the kin of those who had died lamented the departure of their loved ones.

Bards had already composed songs about the fight and the bull became a demon in disguise who had come to devour Kishkinda. The two brave Vanara brothers had valiantly fought the demon and vanquished it. Sugreeva was fighting for his life and bards were eagerly waiting for his death. It would make a good story if the prince died protecting his sister-in-law. The angry mob had hacked Dundubhi into pieces and taken the carcass out in a procession. They had strewn the pieces of its flesh wherever they pleased, and rumours floated around that some of the Vanaras had thrown the pieces of carcass into the Ashram of Rishi Matanga. The rishi had always treated Vana Naras well and had never bothered with their affairs. Now his Ashram lay desecrated by a few mischievous Vana Naras.

Elders feared a war or a riot; the younger generation was ready for a riot. Mobs of youngsters roamed around the city, shouting slogans about the Vana Nara pride. A Deva traveller who had come to see the city was killed by this mob. A few Asuras were almost beaten to death and some property was destroyed just because the mob felt like it. The majestic city and the great spectacle that bull-taming gave them made the young Vana Naras vain and proud of their identity. Bards sensed the trend and started making up stories that glorified the history of the Vana Naras. Soon, fantastic stories about ancient monkey men flying in winged chariots, Vana Nara geniuses who had invented weapons that could annihilate earth, sun, moon and a few hundred stars and many such absurd things were told by clever bards. Such songs became popular and Vana Naras, who had been slaves for many generations, began thinking that they once had the greatest civilization on earth. Anyone expressing the mildest of doubt were branded as enemies. With Baali in mourning and Sugreeva fighting for his life, Kishkinda slowly descended into chaos. Bards called it development and monkey men were proud of their patriotism.

Baali never left Sugreeva's bedside. All attempts by Tara to get him to rest turned futile. He kept repeating that it was his fault that Sugreeva got injured so gravely. 'I am not half a man as him. He tackled the bull bare handed, like a true warrior. I fought like a coward, cheated the poor beast by using a mace.'

When Tara had heard it for the hundredth time, she exploded with fury, 'Enough of this self-pity. You killed the beast to save me. Doesn't that mean anything to you?'

'I know. If it was not for you, I would have never used the mace. It is unfair.'

'What is unfair?' Tara tried to reason. 'The bull weighed ten times your weight and it had sword-like horns. It was using what God gave it—'

'No, Tara. It is unfair. The bull didn't seek the fight. It wasn't fighting for food, territory or mate. It was scared. It was doing what a bull would do. I should have fought fair and killed it with my bare hands. How will I face my people? They will think—'

'They think you are a hero.'

'He is the hero, Tara.' Baali kissed Sugreeva's forehead.

Tara wanted to say it was Sugreeva's fault to bring the bull to the city. He had stolen it. She knew why Sugreeva had made Baali fight it. The fact that Sugreeva got injured didn't change anything.

'I always loved him, Tara. Now my love has doubled, for he saved your life,' Baali said running his fingers through Sugreeva's hair.

'Your father got killed.'

'My fault, Tara. I couldn't save him too.'

'The bull-taming was a bad idea . . .'

Baali nodded his head. He remained silent for a long time. The room was oppressive. *This was supposed to be our bedroom*, Tara thought. She had been married for more than six months and yet they had not slept together so far. Sugreeva was always between them, either physically or as a thought. Sometimes she wished he would never wake up, he would die and set her free. Yet, his words after the bull had gored him haunted her. Even when he was sure he was dying, Sugreeva was professing his love for her. He had thrown himself between her and the raging bull. *Did that make him a hero as Baali claimed? Or the fact that he had planned to get Baali killed or injured made him a villain?* Tara had no answer. Her father came to the room to administer medicine to Sugreeva. When he had finished his job, he asked Tara to accompany him.

Tara was surprised to see Hanuman waiting for her at the entrance of the cave. Hanuman enquired about Sugreeva's health and Baali's condition. Then he briefed her about the grim situation in the city. Unless something was done, the monkey army would destroy everything the Vana Naras had dreamt of. Tare had no idea what she should do.

'Talk to the women. Call the mothers, sisters and wives of these men and address them. Make them understand that patriotism is not about hating others. They will tell their men when they are alone. It is the mob and the anonymity it provides that creates and fuels the problem. Convince the women of the futility of hatred.'

Tara nodded and Hanuman left after visiting Sugreeva and wishing him well. Tara was not very sure of the efficacy of Hanuman's advice. She knew that women were equally or more prejudiced. But the transformation of the city scared her. The vacuum that Riksarajas left was huge. His flippancy, sarcasm and the capability to turn any serious circumstance to something funny and irrelevant had led to the camaraderie of the people. Now, everyone was serious. Baali had withdrawn to serve his brother. Unless she did something, Kishkinda would become an impossible place to live in. Tara broached the subject to Baali, but his response shocked her.

'Tara, we had gone wrong from the beginning. My brother's selfless courage has taught me a great lesson. We were trying to imitate Devas and Asuras. We were competing to build a bigger city, a grander palace, a bigger arena. That is not how our ancestors had lived. They had hunted game or gathered fruits.'

'And they were captured by Devas and Asuras and made slaves,' Tara said.

Baali glared at her. 'They were captured because they didn't have a place to protect them. Kishkinda is that place. Here Vana Naras will live in peace. We will not allow any outsiders here. This is our land.'

'A city that closes itself will become stagnant,' Tara said.

'I am fed up of the so-called progress, Tara. See what happened to my brother, my father. Farming is against nature. Man can't go against nature. We were worried about others enslaving us. What are we doing now?'

'We don't have any slaves.'

'Tara, the cows, the bulls, aren't they our slaves? I have been thinking about this since my brother was injured. Farming is immoral, Tara. It is enslaving animals and making them do our bidding. And when the farm animals become too weak to be of any use to us, we kill them and eat them,' Baali said.

'That is the way of the world. Devas, Asuras and other races are racing ahead. They have huge farmlands. They are storing grains in the granary so that people don't die of hunger during the rains. They are trading so that they have money to sustain a huge army.'

'Money is evil, Tara. So is the army,'

'You aren't talking sense,' Tara retorted.

'See the animals, Tara. Do they have armies? Money? God? Temples? Traditions? Other people ridicule us by calling us Vanaras. Monkey men. Earlier, I used to feel offended. Now, I feel that it is the perfect name for us. We will embrace the name. Our flags will have the monkey totem. We will proudly say we are Vanaras.'

'There will be riots in the streets. Our men want us to raid Asura lands, Deva lands and build an empire,' Tara said.

'Ah, this Dandakaranya is our land. We will defend it, but never attack others. We shouldn't be doing what others did to us. I am banning money, God, army, farming, trade—we will live how our ancestors lived. We will hunt in our forest for food or collect fruits, but we will not enslave anybody, not even animals. There will be no King or chief. I am relinquishing my title. This cave will be open to all. Any Vanara can sleep here. This country belongs to all Vanaras. Foreigners are welcome if they follow our rules. No money, no God, no temples, no granaries, no farm lands, no industry, no fire—we live a free life, like that of animals.'

'Then destroy the city we built. Let's return to the forests. Let no one wear clothes, for that too is unnatural,' Tara fumed.

'I will do that too, but slowly. That is what I am aiming at, but people must be prepared.'

'You've gone crazy,' Tara cried.

'My city, my rules, Tara. If anyone wants to challenge me, they can duel me.'

'Baali, our dream—'

'This is my dream, Tara. I had taken the wrong path. My brother showed me the way. I fought the bull with a mace. I did something that was morally wrong. What is the difference between me and Ravana or Indra if I use such low tricks to win? My mace was made of bronze, and I hear Asuras have discovered a stronger metal called iron. Devas too are working on deadlier weapons like metal bows and arrows. They fight devastating wars and enslave poor people like Vana Naras or Kinnaras in their eagerness for dominance. They destroy forests and build cities. They torture animals for better clothes, better food, and better conveniences. They use horses and elephants in battle. They dam rivers. They destroy mountains and fill valleys. And they call themselves civilized. Ha, like a fool, the same madness had possessed me. I thought it was great to have an arena larger than the one in Trikota, or a palace that could rival that of Amaravati. Now I'm free. I am a Vanara, the monkey man.'

'Our people have become insane. They threw parts of the carcass of the slain bull on Rishi Matanga's Ashram. And you are proposing to make them wilder, Baali,' Tara sighed. There wasn't any way she was going to convince him. She had to speak to Hanuman.

'It wasn't because they were going wild that they threw the carcass. Our people had thrown the carcass of the poor bull I killed on the Ashram of Matanga to ridicule him. They were being arrogant about the strength of their leader. I went to apologize to him and the hermit was cursing me that my head will blow into pieces if I step into his Ashram. Poor old man. I have no rivalry with Matanga and no intention to hurt his beliefs. If he thinks cow is holy, I respect it. I don't believe in curses, yet I apologized to him and promised him that no Vana Nara would step in the Ashram premises. Animals are far better than us. My aim is to make us more animal like.'

'God has created us to be discerning and–'

Baali scoffed, 'I don't believe in God. No creature except man believes in God, Tara. The animals and birds believe in the power of their limbs, in the speed of their feet, in the strength of their wings. No God has punished any animal for not worshiping him or her. I'm Vanara, an animal and no God—if he exists—will punish me for being me, Tara.'

Tara decided it was wise to stop arguing. Baali was convinced he was right. He left her with Sugreeva and went out to announce his decision to the citizens. She looked at the sleeping figure of Sugreeva. Tara felt uneasy, being in a room with Sugreeva. She turned to leave when Sugreeva gripped her wrist. She gasped, and he freed her. Tara hurried out but stopped when she heard him call her.

'Tara . . .'

She stopped at the exit, where a curtain parted the chamber from the main hall of the cave.

'You never come to see me. You never sit with me, Tara. I expected you would be kind to me, after I saved–'

'I must go,'

'Just hold my hands, Tara. Just for a moment.'

His words pierced her heart. He had almost died for her. Reluctantly, she moved to him. He took her hand in his and caressed it. Tara struggled hard to suppress the thrill of tied up desires. She remained a virgin, despite being married for more than six months

'My brother has gone mad, Tara. Be mine and we shall rule Kishkinda the way you want.'

Tara was shaken by his words. She pulled her hand from his and ran out, her mind in turmoil. What Sugreeva suggested was treason. Even his injury hadn't changed him. If he is not freed of this obsession, Baali's life would be in danger. She toyed with the idea of telling Baali about Sugreeva stalking her, but in Baali's current state of mind, she was scared how he would react.

Tara ran to Kadalivana. As she hurried through the streets of Kishkinda, she found that the eternal fire had gone out. The fountains had stopped working. Baali had started implementing his madness. She reached Kadalivana and found Hanuman meditating. She didn't have the patience to wait until he woke up from his meditation. She fell at his feet and began sobbing. She told Hanuman about Baali's determination to reject civilization and go back to some assumed purity of the imaginary past.

Hanuman went to Kishkinda to meet Baali. Baali was drinking with his friends at that time. He was in a jovial mood and decided to indulge Hanuman. Tara stood by Baali's side, worrying how Baali would respond to Hanuman. He had come as per her request and she didn't want Baali insulting the mendicant. But Baali was becoming more and more unpredictable.

Hanuman said the wheels of progress cannot be reversed. There was some merit in Baali's thought. It would have been ideal had man remained an animal, but since he had already thrown away the simplicity for his greed, the greed only would remain the driving force of civilization. Those who don't change will be enslaved, exploited or eliminated by those who embrace change and master it. Vanaras had no choice other than to race other tribes likes Asuras or Devas if they wanted to be free. Else, they would end up as Dasas to the other races. The path Baali was proposing was perilous and the unrelenting chariot of progress would crush anyone who stood in its path. The only choice was to ride the chariot.

Baali heard Hanuman's speech and roared in laughter. Tara saw Hanuman's eyes flash with anger for a moment. Then the customary smile was back. Baali told Hanuman that when he needed advice he would ask for it. He had no respect for those who spent most of their lives in Deva land, studying their holy books called Vedas, wearing sacred threads like a Deva Brahmin and seeking something as illusionary as Brahman, which no one has seen, heard or touched. His drunken friends laughed at Baali's words. Hanuman folded his palms, said Namaste in the Deva style and walked away with his head held high. Tara felt miserable.

When she met him next time, she apologized profusely for her husband. Hanuman said he had forgotten about the incident the moment it was over. He went on to explain in detail why progress is inevitable and how Baali was wrong. Tara heard Hanuman politely, but she was more worried about her personal problems than the fate of human civilization or Vanara race. She wasn't sure whether she could confide in Hanuman about Sugreeva's passion for her. She needed someone to talk to, someone who she could trust. She decided to trust Hanuman and confessed to him about Sugreeva's obsession with her. Hanuman didn't reply for some time. He closed his eyes and started meditating. Tara waited impatiently, but when Haunman didn't speak, she lost hope and walked back to Kishkinda. She cursed herself for confiding in Hanuman about Sugreeva's obsession. She was scared whether the news would reach Baali.

Another month passed and Sugreeva had recovered his health. Her father stopped his frequent visits. Baali was busy curbing a few riots that broke out after he had started his reforms. A few young men challenged him for duels and he beat them without any difficulty. Surprisingly, Rishabha made peace with Baali and the council was formed again. They were enthusiastic about Baali's new reforms. Jambavan, Kesari and Rishabha lent their weight for Baali's plan of Vanara's shunning all vestiges of progress and going back to the pure, ancient Vana Nara lives. What they didn't approve was Baali's rejection of God, but no one dared to cross Baali. Some people left the city forever.

Tara visited a servant's home where she had secretly kept some fire burning. Cooking happened clandestinely, and Tara encouraged women to teach children new ways. She was desperate for a teacher who could teach her and other people to read and write. Most of the men and almost all women were illiterate and she had once dreamt of having a library full of books in her city. Now, Baali would laugh at such new things and would never permit it. She was fascinated by the thought that ideas could be frozen in words and retrieved again and again for later use. Books were magic. It was fascinating to think bards who had died thousands of years ago could speak to you through written words. She had seen books in Hanuman's humble ashram. Perhaps, he may be able to help her. She would learn the magic of words first and then spread it among other women. She slipped to Hanuman's ashram to enquire. Hanuman was amused by her request at first. Seeing her enthusiasm, he started teaching her the first letters. He knew the language of the Devas and the Asuras. He was trying to make a script for the Vana Nara language. Tara knew the risk Hanuman was taking. Baali had declared death to anyone who brought the polluting influence of other cultures. Books were alien to the Vana Naras. When she pointed out the risk to Hanuman, he said she was taking the same risk. Tara laughed and said she was sure Baali would never harm her. She broached the subject of Sugreeva's obsession with her many times and Hanuman evaded her questions. She lost hope and stopped talking about it. Meanwhile, Sugreeva continued to profess his love. She found tokens of his love at unexpected places. Living in the cave palace where Sugreeva lived was becoming unbearable for her.

One day when she reached Hanuman's ashram, he was not on his customary reed mat in the Veranda. She called out his name and waited for him in the courtyard. When Hanuman came out, there was an old man with him. She stood up, wondering who the old man was. He bowed to Tara and said, 'I don't know what deeds we have done in our previous lives for this fortune.'

Confused, Tara looked at Hanuman who was smiling at her.

'Ruma,' the old man called out, and a shy young girl came out and touched her feet. She looked beautiful with lovely eyes and honey-coloured skin.

'Daughter, ask Baali to seek an alliance for his brother to the girl's father as per custom,' Hanuman said to Tara.

Tara sighed with happiness. Here was a solution to all her problems. She went to Ruma who stood bashful near the rickety door of the Ashram. Tara lifted her chin and the girl looked at her with hazel eyes. *Innocent and pure*, Tara thought.

'Consider me your elder sister,' she told Ruma. The girl leaned to touch her feet. She picked her up by her shoulders and hugged her. A heavy weight had lifted from her heart. She thanked Hanuman and rushed back to the palace.

When she reached the palace, she found Baali busy discussing official matters with his counsel. Sugreeva was seated near him. She knew that Sugreeva would wriggle out of it if she broached the matter in private. He had to be caught unaware. She moved to the centre and Baali looked at her with impatient indulgence. The council of ministers had stopped their discussion and looked at her in surprise. It was unusual for the Maharani to interrupt their work.

Tara said, 'I have come with great news.'

'Yes, my dear,' Baali said, tapping his fingers on the armrest of the throne. Sugreeva frowned at her. She smiled heartily at Sugreeva and said, 'Isn't it the duty of a sister-in-law to find a suitable bride for her beloved brother-in-law?'

Sugreeva's face drained of blood and turned pale.

# Chapter 27

'I have found our Sugreeva a beautiful bride,' Tara said, smiling.

'No, no, I don't want to marry,' Sugreeva said, but Baali raised his hand, cutting off Sugreeva and addressed Tara. 'May I know who the lucky girl is?'

'Her name is Ruma and she is in the Ashram of Hanuman. In fact, he brought the alliance,' Tara said. She knew this was the riskiest part. She prayed Baali would support her.

'Hanuman, ha?' Sugreeva said with a derisive smile, 'I'm disappointed with you, Yata. That man insulted my brother. There are rumours that he does illegal things. And how rude was he speaking to my brother when he came to advise him about— huh—progress? How can you do this, Yata? You may not care for the prestige of my brother, but–'

Baali interrupted, 'No, brother. I was drunk that day. It was not his fault. I should have apologized that day itself, but my ego prevented me from doing so. My wise wife has provided me a chance to redeem myself. And if that apology can earn my beloved brother a good wife, should I not do that without delay? Tara, lead us there.'

'No, no, I don't want to marry,' Sugreeva was angry. 'I don't want to marry some unknown girl. I have not even met her.'

Baali put his hand on Sugreeva's shoulder, 'Alright, Sugreeva. Do you have any other girl in your heart? If so, your brother would be the first person to fulfil your wish.'

Tara was shocked. She was scared Sugreeva would point to her and all hell would break loose. She wished the earth would open up and swallow her.

'Is it so, my brother?'

She heard Sugreeva's frenzied tone. Her heart thudded in her ribcage.

'Anything for you brother, anything. You want the celestial nymph Rambha? Menaka? Thilothama? Your brother Baali will get all of them for you. You want to rule Kishkinda, I will abdicate now. Do you want to conquer the heaven? I will do it for you.'

'Shall I ask, brother? Do you give your word?'

'Ask, my brother. Ask for anything except my beloved Tara and it shall be yours before you could blink,' Baali said, looking at Tara.

Tara pressed her lips to prevent them from trembling. Her body was shivering. She looked at Sugreeva whose face had gone ashen. Did Baali know?

'I want nothing except my brother's love,' Sugreeva said in a cracked voice.

'That you shall always have, till my last breath,' Baali hugged Sugreeva.

The procession to the Ashram of Hanuman wound through the rocky outcrops of the hills. The huge boulders that abounded the hills around Kishkinda looked as if an unruly giant had played with colossal pebbles and left them scattered. Tara was walking beside Baali. Sugreeva walked a few feet behind, deep in thought. Tara took this respite to entwine her fingers with Baali's. Her husband held her close. She whispered in his ears, 'The girl seems to be from a poor family.'

'How does it matter? She should be of good character and love him with all her heart and remain faithful to him.' Baali said. That Sugreeva should remain faithful to Ruma was the bigger problem, but Tara didn't say it aloud.

As soon as they reached the Ashram, Baali wanted to apologize, but Hanuman was too big-hearted to care for such things. Sugreeva and Ruma saw each other briefly, but not in private. When Baali asked Sugreeva whether he liked her, he said he was ready to do whatever his brother commanded. No one sought Ruma's opinion. The date of the wedding was fixed by Tara on the same day the astrologer had given the auspicious day for consummation of their marriage. She could feel Sugreeva's hostility and helplessness, but she pushed her agenda with determination. It helped that Hanuman understood the situation and his words rendered weight to her cause. She knew Sugreeva was fuming inside, but consoled herself that once he was married he would forget about her. That thought strangely filled her with a sense of loss, but she determinedly pushed it away.

The next few days went past like a blaze, with Tara taking the responsibility of making arrangements for the wedding of her brother-in-law with all earnestness. She ensured that she was always surrounded by helpers and servants; she sent for her father and her friends and thwarted all efforts of Sugreeva to meet her in private even for a moment. Her father came with his old friends and it was a joyful fortnight for her. She was no longer a bashful bride in her new home, but the mistress of her home. She had assumed the role of Maharani earnestly. She ensured that her father and his poor friends were treated with utmost respect and taken care of. The joy and pride they derived from her prestige filled her heart.

Except her old father, Ruma had no one to call her own so Tara took charge of the wedding ceremonies and ensured that the celebrations after the rituals never got too out of hand. It was an important day in her married life too and she was excited for the night. She felt proud that she had solved such a thorny issue that had threatened to jeopardize her life. When it was time to go to the palmyra grove, Tara ensured both the couples went with their own procession. Just before Sugreeva and Ruma were about to leave, Ruma came to meet Tara.

'You gave me a good life, Tara. I shall always be indebted to you,' Ruma said, wiping the tears in her eyes.

Tara understood the girl was nervous and comforted her with a hug. 'I'm sure you will be a great life partner to Sugreeva and you

will bear him a dozen sons who will as be as strong and handsome
as their father.'

Tara saw Sugreeva standing at a distance. A torchlight was
blazing near him. There was no mistaking the gloom on his face.
It worried Tara a lot. She hoped Ruma would be able to make
him forget her. She watched them going away and felt something
snapping inside her. There was a numb pain in her guts. *No, I'm
not jealous, why should I be jealous, I'm not, I'm not*, she repeated in
her mind, but the pain kept growing. She was startled when she
felt a warm touch on her shoulders. Baali pressed his lips on her
neck. She turned and hugged him tight. She started weeping, with
guilt, with relief, with love.

'What happened Tara?' he asked, lifting her chin up.

'It has been so long,' she said.

Baali lifted her up and carried her outside. There were
musicians and drummers dozing at the steps. They scrambled up as
soon as they saw the couple and started playing their instruments.
Baali dismissed them and didn't allow anyone to follow them to
the grove.

Baali walked all the way to the palmyra grove, carrying Tara.
She had never felt so secure in her life. She drank in his smell,
her arms entwined his strong neck like snakes and she slept like
a baby in a cradle as Baali carried her uphill. When he gently lay
her down on the soft grass and kissed her eyes open, she saw there
were countless stars in the sky.

'My Apasara,' Baali whispered.

She smiled. A cool breeze caressed her face, but his touch
was gentler than that. The breeze made the palmyra fronds dance
above them and shook jasmine flowers off the creepers.

'The Heavens are showering celestial flowers on us, Tara,'
Baali said as he took a handful of jasmine flowers and sprinkled
it over her face. A flower got stuck on her forehead and he gently
took it off with his lips. She closed her eyes and held him close. It
was as sweet as a dream.

Tara woke up to birdsongs. Baali was sleeping near her. Golden rays of dawn filtered down through the canopy, drawing beautiful patterns on the grass. Dragonflies and honeybees buzzed around her. She stood up and stretched her limbs. It was a glorious dawn, a new beginning. She looked lovingly at her husband. Baali slept as if he had no worries in the world. She had an urge to hug him and lie on his chest. For a fleeting moment, she thought of Sugreeva, but hurriedly pushed away the thought. The river looked inviting. It was the colour of molten gold, as if the morning sun had melted in it. She walked towards the river.

Tara stopped in her tracks. Did she hear someone sobbing? She was not sure. She resumed walking and yet again she heard a sniffling sound. There was a tree leaning towards the river bank. She could discern someone sitting there. She approached gingerly, not sure who she would find. She stopped in her tracks.

'Ruma? What happened? Why're you crying?' She rushed to the girl.

Ruma glared at her. She had stopped crying. Her face was contorted with rage. Tara was confused.

'You cheated me,' Ruma said.

'What?!'

'He told me everything. I'm just a pawn for you. A front to continue your illicit affair. I trusted you, considered you my sister. You're a serpent.' Ruma broke down and turned away from her.

'Ruma, I don't know what you mean–'

'Get lost!'

# Chapter 28

Tara was livid. She had to confront Sugreeva. She stomped back to the groove, in search of her husband's brother. She wanted to tear him apart, limb to limb, with her bare hands. She found him sitting under a palmyra tree. She rushed to him. He had a vacant faraway look.

She shook him by his shoulders. 'I want to—'

'You betrayed me,' Sugreeva said in a heartbroken tone.

Tara was taken aback. 'What the hell are you talking about?'

'I didn't even touch Ruma, but you—'

'Sugreeva, don't talk nonsense.'

'I heard. I heard you two yesterday. You're so cruel, Tara.'

'Your brother is my husband,'

'I'm a fool, Tara. I thought you loved me.'

'I didn't ask you to think so.'

'Women are hypocrites. They can keep one man in their heart and give their body to another.'

'You're crossing all limits of decency, Sugreeva.'

'Ah, now I'm the villain? I, who in all my honesty, told everything to my wife.'

'You did what?'

'I opened my heart to Ruma. I told her how much I loved you. I told her there is no woman in my life other than you.'

'You're crazy!'

'Crazy for you, Tara.'

'Do you have any idea how cruel you're being to Ruma?'

'Do you have any idea how cruel you're to me, Tara?'

'For God's sake, she is your wife!'

'I didn't choose her. She was thrust on me.'

Tara had no answer for that. She was baffled. She didn't know how to unknot this tangle.

'Sugreeva, if you persist with this madness, I will have no option but to tell your brother.'

'Ah, would you do that? Would you do that please? I know him. He would understand. There is no one who understands me better than him. Tell him how much we love each other.'

Tara shook her head in dismay. She stood in silence, thinking of her options. It was better that she took the matter to Baali before it reached him through someone else. Tara turned back and came face to face with Ruma. She burst into tears and ran away. She had heard their conversation.

Tara rushed to Baali. She hated to wake him up and convey such news to him, but she had no choice. However, when she reached where they had slept, Baali was not there. She ran to the cave palace. She had to see him urgently. When she reached the palace, she found that he hadn't reached there too. She was getting scared. She waited for him at the threshold, praying that Ruma wouldn't reach him first.

She sat at the threshold, refusing breakfast, refusing lunch and anxiously waiting for Baali to come. It was almost evening when she saw him. He was walking fast, as if he was angry. She stood frozen, not knowing what to do. Had he heard it from Ruma before she could explain? Her knees were going weak.

Baali came like a storm and thundered, 'Tara. Is there any truth in what I have heard?'

Blood drained off Tara's face. Her throat went dry. 'I . . . I . . .'

'Why did you do this to me, Tara?'

Tara collapsed on her knees. She covered her face with her palms. 'I'm sorry. I'm sorry.' She didn't know why she was apologizing. Somehow, she was not able to face Baali. She was scared she had already committed some grave mistake. She was not pure, she didn't deserve Baali, she told herself. But no words came out. She kept sobbing.

She opened her eyes when she saw Baali laughing uproariously. He was clutching his belly. Tara glared at him. She saw Sugreeva standing with an impish smile.

'This idiot . . .' Baali sputtered between his laughter. 'This fool has played a prank on you, Tara. He told me that he is going to scare you and Ruma.'

'He . . . he–,' Tara could not control her rage. 'He is a bloody liar. He is fooling you.'

'He is a liar, Tara. A most lovable liar,' Baali reached out to Sugreeva and hugged him close. 'He is an eternal prankster. This rascal, this fool, my brother . . . oh God, what pranks you play. You got scared, Tara? You got scared! You will get used to his pranks. He is one affable devil,' Baali said, playfully punching his brother's chest.

'What did he tell you?' Tara glared at her husband

'Oh, he told me you're in love with him. Don't I know my brother? I knew it was a prank! I started laughing. Then he said, let us play this prank on you. Oh, it was fun!'

'It isn't funny at all.' Tara turned on her heels and rushed in, trying to control her rage and frustration. She didn't want to cry before them. She hated both the brothers. *Brutes*!

'Tara, Taaaaraaa . . .'

She could hear Baali running behind her. She went to a corner of the cave and stood panting. Baali scooped her off her feet. She struggled to be free. He showered her with kisses. She tried to push him away.

'I'm sorry if I hurt you, Tara,' Baali said between his kisses and Tara melted. But she was scared. She was sacred for Baali, she was scared for herself and for Kishkinda. Baali was too naïve. She had to protect him from himself and from his brother. She hugged him close and sobbed on his shoulders.

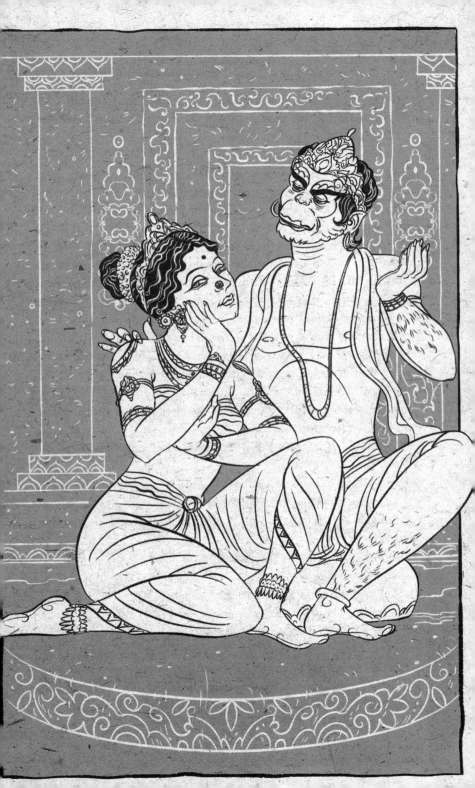

'Why are you crying, Tara? He is just a boy. He often plays such childish pranks. As his elders, is it not our duty to indulge him?'

'I'm scared.'

'Why Tara? Who can harm you when I'm here for you?' Tara didn't say a word. Baali whispered, 'I have brought you a gift.' Tara looked at his smiling face. A strand of curled hair had fallen on his forehead, giving him an impish look. She wanted to curl her fingers around it. She wanted to kiss him. He moved away, playfully, and ran. She stood, disappointed, waiting for him to come back. When he came back there was something soft in his hands. He asked her to close her eyes and she obliged. She almost dropped it when the 'gift' squealed. She opened her eyes to find a wriggling bundle of fur. *A puppy*!

'I found it in the grove. His mother and siblings are all dead, perhaps eaten by a leopard. This one was hiding inside a bush.' Baali stood grinning at her. The ball of fur opened its eyes and blinked at her. She felt a rush of affection. She was never fond of dogs, but this was a gift from Baali. She kissed it and smiled at the happiness of her husband.

'We need a name,' Baali whispered in her ears as he held her close to him.

She turned to kiss him on his lips. 'I did not know you love dogs.'

Baali took it from her hand and raised it high. Its black eyes twinkled, and it flicked a pink tongue. Its bushy tail was waving fervently.

'Not a puppy,' Baali laughed, 'A wolf cub.'

'A what?' Tara was shocked.

'He will grow into a fine wolf.'

'You can't have a wolf as a pet!'

'Pet? Who said it is a pet. He will be my friend,' Baali said, leaving the cub on the floor. It sniffed the ground and came to her. It put up its paw and tried to climb her legs. She stepped back.

'You didn't like it,' Baali's voice betrayed hurt. Tara didn't know what to say. She tried to smile, trying to push away the thought of having a wolf share their bedroom. The cub, perhaps, sensed her discomfort. It moved to Baali and sat with its ears perked up. Had she not known it was a wolf cub, she would have adored it. She watched Baali pick it up like a father would lift up a son. She wanted to give him a son and a daughter. She could see how wonderful a father he would be. He was cooing to the puppy, nay, the wolf cub. It cuddled in his broad chest and closed its eyes. He gently lay it on the bed. Tara watched him, her heart overflowing with love for Baali. She should learn to love the wolf too, if that made him happy.

'Sugreeva wanted me to kill it. "Wolves are wild," he said. I am also wild, I countered. I would trust anything wild rather than civilized,' Baali said. Unbidden, thoughts about Sugreeva came rushing to her. Her face grew dark. She was scared whether Sugreeva would continue to haunt her. Baali turned to her and caught her dark expression.

'Why are you looking worried? If you don't like it, I shall set him free in the jungle. He won't survive long though.'

'It . . . it is not that,' she said. 'I am scared for you. There are so many foes . . .'

'There is no warrior in Jambudweepa who can face me in a battle,' Baali said, standing up and embracing her. But such words didn't allay her fears. Neither did his loving kisses. Like spiders hiding in the crevices of the wall, fear lay hidden in the cracks of her mind. Fear started weaving webs, tangling her little joys, choking her innocence. Every time Baali went out, she was scared for him. The wolf cub started accompanying him wherever he went. He had named it Chemba, for its fur grew to a faded red. Chemba could always be seen by the side of Baali. It tolerated Tara but was ferociously loyal to Baali. Somehow, despite her reservations about the wolf that was growing bigger rapidly, she found her mind at peace when Chemba accompanied Baali. Sugreeva despised it. For Baali, Chemba had grown into another brother as dear to him as Sugreeva. Tara could sense Sugreeva's resentment. What made her more fearful was the manner in which Sugreeva acted as if he liked Chemba. The wolf sensed it and kept its distance from Sugreeva. She wished Baali would sense it too.

Sugreeva was always respectful towards Tara. He never mentioned his love again while Ruma avoided her. Sugreeva's behaviour confounded her. When she was alone, she found thoughts about Sugreeva's love bubbling up. Unbidden, his earnest pleading for her love came flooding back into her mind. She fought it with all her will. The thought that perhaps all his professing of love to her was a prank made her angry. And it scared her that she yearned for his attention. She tried to cling to Baali, who was always caring and loving to her. That made her feel guilty, for she thought she could never reciprocate his love with the same sincerity. She was scared she was going insane.

Hanuman was a solace, a Guru and a friend for Tara. She would often visit his Kadalivana, where the Brahmachari carefully nurtured a plantain garden. The thick red Kadali banana he served her were delicious. Hanuman would speak about the need for adopting farming and agriculture. His vision was in contrast with that of Baali. He would talk of how they could sustain by hunting and gathering. Baali was progressive when he started building the city, but he rejected the new ways of life after the killing of the bull Dundubji. Tara argued for her husband often, but in her heart, she knew Hanuman had a point. Hanuman would smile at her argument but would say farming taught man patience. One must wait for months before one can harvest and have the fruits of one's labour. A farmer understood life that depended on many factors, like the rains and sunshine, the birds and earthworm, the butterflies and bees, and countless other creatures. Hanuman's way of life was attracting many disciples. The Ashram had expanded much since Tara had first visited it. Baali never interfered in Hanuman's deeds or stopped anyone from joining the Ashram. Hanuman never interfered in Baali's Kishkinda nor did he visit it after Sugreeva's marriage. About Tara's frequent visits, Baali maintained a stoic silence. She suspected that Baali knew she had learned to read and write at least three languages and was teaching many women secretly, though he never mentioned it to her. Once she said to Hanuman that she wished Baali would learn to read.

'Whatever his faults, Tara, your husband is a man of integrity. He is one of the few I have met who lives as per his belief. There is no need to change him, nor do I think one can change anyone. Love him as he is, daughter.'

Hanuman made that day special for her in another way too. He took her to the edge of the river and smiled. Tara stood confused.

That day, when she was walking back, she pondered over Hanuman's words. Baali loved her as she was. He never tried to change her. In a way, her friend and her husband had more similarities than differences. She smiled at the thought.

In her arguments with Baali, she would often present Hanuman's views as her own. Baali would laugh and say, farming is unnatural. You prefer one kind of plant over all others. The farmer weeds out every plant other than what serves his selfish needs. Birds, animals, rodents, snakes and so many creatures, that are part of mother nature are killed or chased away, so that man can satiate his selfish needs. Then the farmer enslaves bulls, horses, asses, oxen or cows. He shows utmost cruelty to them when they have the strength to serve his purpose and eats them when they fall after a lifetime of service. The hunter hunts when he is hungry. His violence is only for his basic needs. He is truer to how nature intended any creature to be. There is no selfishness, except that of self-preservation in his deeds. When Tara argued with Baali, she felt he was right and when she argued with Hanuman, she felt Hanuman was right. She knew both men were not going to change their opinions. Once, when she was arguing with Baali, Sugreeva was present. She was curious to know what Sugreeva would say, but they were keeping away from each other, as much as two people who lived under the same roof could.

As if reading her mind, Baali asked Sugreeva what he thought about the relative merit of farming and hunting. Sugreeva said one should do whatever works, depending on the circumstances. Baali argued that it was hypocrisy and Sugreeva said, hypocrisy is natural to all creatures. The tiger crouches in the bush before pouncing on the unsuspecting deer. The chameleon changes colour as per the surroundings. Are these creatures not a part of nature? Spider weaves the web and waits for the prey. Nature is deception, nature is opportunistic. Hypocrisy is natural. So, if someone who is more powerful says farming is better, a wise man should not say otherwise. Baali asked whether Sugreeva was not disagreeing with the Vanara way of life because his elder brother was powerful. That led to more banter and mocking and each brother challenging the other to a duel.

As the brothers fought in a friendly way, cursing and mocking each other, Tara sat pondering over Sugreeva's words. Something about it made her uneasy. He hadn't bothered her after his marriage and Ruma never spoke to her after her initial outburst. When Baali gave his customary roar after defeating Sugreeva as usual, she looked at her brother-in-law who was squirming under her husband's feet. Was he the tiger crouching before pouncing on the prey?

Days passed, and dull monotony peppered with mild excitements, but the feeling of something ominous never left Tara. She learned to ignore Ruma's coldness and got busy with her work of spreading the light of reading to more women. Some of the women had managed to teach their children and men to read and write. Nala was a great help to her during these days. He admired her and was ready to do anything she asked of him. With no female friends after the departure of Prabha, she found happiness in the friendship she cherished with two men—Hanuman and Nala. Together, they were spreading the light of knowledge in the Vanara society.

Tara wished she could do the same at her home. Her attempts to teach Baali ended up in arguments and fights. Though he would use harsh words, he never used force to win an argument. Later, he would make up for his harshness by making passionate love to her. She was able to win small victories. She managed to get the eternal fire going and when she started cooking, he sulked for a few days but when he found she was determined to have her way, he acquiesced. Though he never admitted it in so many words, she knew he relished her cooking. Slowly, hearths returned to the humble abode of other Vanara homes. Nala helped building hearths in many homes.

For all such minor victories that gave her pleasure, one thought marred her contentment. She yearned for a child and often dreamt about it. Every month, she would be disappointed, but Baali never broached the subject. Tongues started wagging about her barrenness and she was scared whether Baali would marry another woman. On one occasion, when Baali saw her crying, he understood her fear without her putting it into words. He said he was her child and she his, and she cried more. He was baffled and tried to cajole her. He didn't know she was crying because she was so touched by his love. He was not good at reading such cues. He lay his head down on her lap and started cooing like a child. It was silly and ridiculous and had someone seen the great chief of Vanaras, it would have become a scandal. She loved him for such silliness, his ability to preserve the boyhood in him, this man who was built like a mountain and was feared and respected by many, the great Vanara King Baali. Tara thought the great God Ayyan was kind to her. Her life had found a rhythm. A child would have made her life perfect, she thought.

Ayyan, however, had other plans.

* * *

She was in Kadalivana, struggling with a poem written in Deva language, while Hanuman and Nala were pruning the leaves of the plantain when a messenger came. He had rushed from Kishkinda with some news. The Asura army led by the mighty Ravana was marching towards Kishkinda and Sugreeva had called for all able men to defend the city from Asura attack. Tara and her friends rushed to the city. They saw many hurrying to the safety of the fort. They met Baali standing at the gate, his body erect, his eyes looking far away and his mace on his shoulders. Beside him, stood Sugreeva, who appeared shaken and worried. A few feet ahead of them, Chemba sat, patiently waiting to pounce on any foe of his master. Tara rushed to her husband, but he gestured her to go inside the fort. Hanuman went to him and said, 'Baali, I shall organize and prepare our people for battle. I don't know how long we can stand against their army, but every Vanara will stand by you. We have to strengthen our defence . . .'

Baali looked straight. 'There will be no defence. I need no Vanara to fight the Asura.'

'Are you planning to surrender? It is . . .'

Baali stared at Hanuman. 'Surrender? I will fight Ravana and defeat him.'

'We need to raise an army . . .'

'I plan to defeat him alone. Either he kills me, or I kill him. There is no need for any war.'

'You are crazy, please come inside . . .' Tara held her husband's arms. He shook her away and gestured her to go inside the fort. Hanuman took Tara's hands and dragged her in. Sugreeva looked at her, helplessly. The fort gate closed behind her. She rushed to the rampart to see him standing. There were many people along the fort walls, but they made way for her. She could see dust rising from the horizon. Chemba was running around in circles, sniffing the air, barking, howling, darting to the river and back. The wolf was excited.

Tara felt dizzy. Despite the dry wind that blew from the east, she started sweating and felt parched. The army was growing, with thousands of men on horses, elephants and foot. Their armour gleamed in the summer sun and the lances bobbed up and down as they advanced towards Kishkinda. The dry riverbed was not going to be any barrier for the army. She could sense every Vanara was scared. She saw the pitiful face of Sugreeva, who was staring at his brother and then at the advancing army. The horses splashed through puddles of water. The sound of hoofs, the neighing of horses and the trumpet calls of war elephants rent the air. As they sighted the city, the Asura army captain on a black stallion cried, 'Har Har Shankara,' and judging from the defining response that rose in waves, Tara could imagine how big the invasion was. Someone called 'Ayya' and the Vanara men started chanting the great God's name. Tara was not sure who the God would prefer, for she knew both the armies were calling out to the same God.

'Surrender,' the captain of Asuras cried out as the first wave of horses set foot on Kishkinda soil. In response, Baali swirled his mace in the air and roared. His roar filled the air and silence descended except for his wild cry. Fear filled Tara and she thought she would faint. Hanuman's hands held her. She couldn't see clearly through her hazy eyes.

'Surrender,' the captain cried again. The wolf darted towards him. Baali whistled, and it darted back. It stood by Baali's side, baring its teeth and snarling.

'Ask your king to fight me like a man. Face-to-face,' Baali roared. The crowd gasped. The Asura army roared in anger. They clanged their maces to their iron shields. Chemba let out a blood-chilling growl, followed by a bark. The captain moved forward.

'Monkey, how dare you talk—'

His sound was buried in a thunderous clap from the sky. Trees swayed in torrential wind and dry leaves whirled up from the ground showering them with river sand. The Vana Naras watched in awe as a flying machine appeared in the horizon. It grew larger, with its massive sails fluttering in the wind. It hovered over Kishkinda for a moment, before descending on the riverbank before Baali. As the gigantic wooden fans slowed down, the sails shrunk, and a strikingly handsome man stepped out. He wore a diamond crusted crown and his broad chest was filled with pearl necklaces. The Asura army fell on their knees and bowed before him.

'Ravana, the emperor of Asuras, the king of Lanka'. Tara heard people whisper around her. Baali stood like a statue, unperturbed by the spectacular arrival of the great Asura king. Sugreeva took a step back and stood behind Baali. Chemba let out a low growl but as Ravana walked towards them, Tara saw the red wolf cower in fear and move behind Baali. It snarled and yelped from behind Baali's legs. Ravana's hand was on the hilt of his pearl crusted sword. He pulled it out in a fluid movement as he walked, and the glint of steal was blinding. Tara heard someone whisper the name Chandrahasa. She had heard the bards sing about the divine sword that Ravana possessed, a gift from the great God Shankara when Ravana had tried to lift the mount Kailasa. The bards' tales were often exaggerated, but the sword looked impressive even from a distance.

Ravana stood before Baali, assessing the Vana Nara with scorn. Here was the emperor who had crushed the Devas. Ravana's rise after his defeat at the hands of Karthyaveera Arjuna was phenomenal. He had conquered the entire Jambudweepa, destroying great cities of the Devas like Ayodhya and killing its king Anaranya. His son had brought Indra in chains to Lanka. The Asuras had achieved great technological advancement.

'I have come to know that one of your men has stolen the prized bull of my vassal King, Mayavi. If you don't want your city to be annihilated, your women to be enslaved and your men to be butchered, surrender—'

'Dare you fight me like a man?' Baali asked softly, looking at Ravana's eyes.

'I haven't come here for a fair. I have come to conquer,' Ravana scoffed.

'Fight me like a man,' Baali repeated.

'I have flying machines, I have steel, I have horses and elephants and thousands of men and—'

'You are a coward.'

A hush fell amongst the crowd. After a moment's silence, the Asura army roared and surged forward. Ravana stopped them with a snap of his fingers.

'Why should I wrestle with a monkey?' Ravana asked.

'Defeat me and Kishkinda is yours without shedding a drop of blood,' Baali said, shifting his mace from one hand to another. 'I am their chief. You vanquish me, and they are your slaves. You can use your arrows, elephants and horses for conquering some other kingdom. I have none of those. I have these hands and a mace. Dare to fight like a man? Let's match limb to limb, strength to strength and see whether the world-conquering Asura is a match for a forest dweller?'

Ravana stared at Baali. Tara felt she would faint. The Asura emperor was as well built as her husband. And Asuras were notorious for their skill in magic and the black arts. Ravana was reputed to be a great scholar, who knew various tricks and techniques in fighting. What chance did her illiterate and naïve husband have against the emperor of Asuras? Tara knew what Baali was trying to do. He was sacrificing himself to save his people from being butchered. The dream of the Vana Naras was ending. Baali wanted to go valiantly, fighting till his last breath before his people became slaves again. Just when her life was blossoming, fate had delivered a brutal blow.

'I accept your challenge, monkey man,' Ravana said with a smile that sent shivers down Tara's spine.

# Chapter 29

The duel was fixed for three days later and the Asura army was invited to Kishkinda. The city was overwhelmed by the Asura army. Every home had many Asuras as guests. Elephants and horses were tied by the streets or by the fort wall. Asuras and their elephants and horses frolicked in the fountain water. Streets were filled with horse shit and elephant dung. The monkey men and women strived hard to make the Asuras comfortable. The jungle people expended the food they had stored as monsoon reserve on their enemies. It didn't matter that the Asuras had come as invaders, ready to rape, pillage and loot. They were now guests and Vanaras would feed them even if they themselves starved. This was the code of honour, as old and unchanging as the hills.

The Asuras were surprised at the size of the city and the sophistication the seemingly uncivilized monkey men had achieved. The Asura emperor offered Nala a fortune for building a city in his Lanka, which Nala politely declined. Tara watched the camaraderie between Ravana and Baali with unease. She knew once Ravana defeated Baali, the friendship would vanish. It would be once again the bitter relationship between the victor and the vanquished. When Ravana said that he had seen Sugreeva somewhere, Baali laughed it off. Sugreeva denied having the fortune of meeting the Asura emperor before. Tara was watching Sugreeva when he said it. She was sure he was lying.

Many casks of toddy and gooseberry wines were consumed in the revelry that followed. Baali talked about Riksarajas and with pain, Tara realised that after the initial grief, the Vanaras barely talked about the eunuch. After his death, she had made Nala carve an umbrella stone, the customary memoir for Vana Naras over his grave by the river. For a few weeks she lit lamps, but her visits became infrequent as she got busy with her life. It stopped altogether in a few months and Riksarajas had gone into oblivion. She decided she would resume the practice of lighting a mud lamp by his grave. The conversation had moved from Riksarajas's antics to other matters.

The council elders stood sulking at the palace cave entrance. They could never approve the show of friendship between Asuras and Vanaras. Rishabha was vocal in his protest. To anyone who was willing to listen, he would complain that Baali was gambling with the future of Vana Naras. What right did Baali have to say that if he failed, the Vana Naras would be the slaves of Asuras? Tara was sure there were detractors among Asuras too.

The biggest victim of the Asura invasion was Chemba. The wolf was excited and angry at the intrusion and had to be chained to a corner of the palace. Chemba kept on barking and howling and became calm only when Baali found some time to pat him or sit with him. As the day neared, fear grew in Tara's mind and the wolf's continuous howling filled her with anxiety. She wished she could speak to Hanuman, but after Baali's decision to fight a duel instead of a battle, Hanuman had retreated to his ashram.

Baali was busy in his hospitality of the Asura emperor. Their talks bored Tara. Moreover, a man in the Asura group made her uncomfortable. The man's eyes never left her. He stood behind Ravana, but his roving eyes made her feel naked. She came to know that the man was Ravana's brother, Vibhishana. There was something evil about the man. To her dismay, Baali was friendly with him too. She saw him serving some foul looking liquor to Baali and her husband drinking it with relish. The man boasted that he brewed the best arrack in Lanka. He talked too much. Sugreeva appeared to have understood the man better than her husband. She could see the look of dislike in Sugreeva's face whenever the garrulous man talked. She avoided being with her husband and it irritated her that he appeared not to miss her. There was no need to show so much hospitality to an enemy who had come to invade his kingdom. But she didn't dare advise Baali and earn his displeasure. She fumed and fretted instead, taking out her irritation on the poor maids attending to her. Even Nala fell victim to her foul mood and kept his distance from her.

On the eve of the duel, she saw something that shook her. Tara had planned to visit Riksarajas's grave. As much as Ayyan, the ancestors too protected their wards. Baali had always considered Riksarajas as his father. Baali needed all possible prayers and help. Nala and Tara reached Riksarajas's grave. Nala had brought the materials for ancestor worship—freshly caught fish, a pot of toddy, some hibiscus flowers in a banana leaf and a lamp. As Nala was sweeping the dead leaves that had covered the grave, Tara thought she heard a giggle. Nala looked around in fear. Such places were often haunted. Tara looked around. The light was fading and the birds that had come to roost in the grove had become silent. The breeze carried a man's laughter from a bush nearby.

Tara started walking towards the bush, but her friend stopped her. 'It could be some Pisacha,' Nala said in a hushed voice. Tara pushed him out of her way and walked to the bush. She saw a couple entwined in each other's arms. The woman's bareback glistened with sweat. Tara gasped for she couldn't believe what she was seeing. The woman turned to look at her and with a cry, ran away, gathering her clothes and vanishing into the darkness. The man stared at her, not bothering to cover his nakedness. Nala came near Tara and the man tied his dhoti and started walking.

'Hey, Asura,' Nala called. The man continued walking. Nala ran behind the man and caught his shoulders. The Asura turned swiftly and knocked Nala down with a powerful punch. Nala fell hard on a bush. Tara recovered and ran to help her friend. Nala wanted to chase the man, but Tara restrained him. They finished the Puja in haste and walked back. Nala didn't stop cursing the man who had punched him. He wanted to murder all Asuras. He was sick of the duel that Baali had agreed to. He wanted war. How dare an Asura touch a Vana Nara girl? Tara had kept quiet all this while. When they reached the fort, Nala stopped in his tracks.

'Tara,' Nala said in a fearful voice. 'That girl... that girl . . . I think it was Ruma . . . Sugreeva's wife.'

Tara walked inside the fort without replying. She had seen the face of the woman clearly. As she entered the city, she saw the merriment going on in full vigour. She saw Baali sitting alongside Ravana. They were watching Sugreeva dance with a pot of toddy in his hand. Baali invited her to sit by his side. Sugreeva paused when he saw her. She turned her face away. She felt sorry for him. She sat through the performance, fearing the passing of time. Chemba was lying near Baali and her husband kept running his fingers through the red fur of the wolf.

Tara whispered in Baali's ears, 'Don't be overfriendly with the Asura. He is assessing your strength. You have foolishly let their army inside the fort. What if he plans an ambush?'

Baali was silent for a moment, as if contemplating her words. 'Had he wanted to kill me, he could have asked his army to finish me off. I stood no chance against an arrow shot by anyone from the rear of their army. There was no need for him to come before me and accept my challenge. I trust him.'

Tara had no answer for that. She hoped he would be right. She wondered whether she should tell him about Ruma, but decided against it. She had to talk to her first. Tara excused herself and went to the cave palace. It was dark as most of the lamps had gone off. The sounds of revelry at the eternal fire in the city's centre could be heard faintly. She stood at the entrance and looked back at the sprawling city below. There were fires burning here and there. Huddled before them would be soldiers from Asura and Vana Nara people. Everything may change tomorrow. Vanaras were fighting to protect their independence. What were the

Asuras fighting for? For more glory to their emperor? Tara sighed and entered the palace.

She found Ruma in her chamber. She was sleeping or perhaps pretending to sleep. Tara sat on the stone cot and gently woke her up. She refused to open her eyes and Tara was sure she was not asleep but pretending to be so. She sprinkled some water on Ruma's face and her sister-in-law sprang up, irritated.

'What do you want, Tara?'

'What're you doing?'

'Sleeping. Haven't you seen anyone sleeping?' Ruma said, gazing up at the roof.

'I saw you sleeping around. Why do–'

'Yes, I was f**** him,' Ruma's lips curved derisively.

The crudity of language shocked Tara. 'Is he . . . is he your lover?'

'I don't even know his name.'

'Ruma, he is an Asura,'

'I don't care. I will f**** whoever I please. I will f**** every man in Kishkinda. I will f**** Vanaras, Asuras, Devas, why I will f**** your husband too.'

Tara slapped her across her face, 'How dare you–'

Ruma started sobbing, 'I have no one. My Sugreeva hates me. He wants you. In his sleep, he whispers your name. Why don't you f****him once, b****? Maybe he will–'

Tara stormed out of the room. She had to tell Baali. There was no other choice. She waited restlessly in her chamber, waiting for Baali to come. When it was almost dawn, she heard approaching footsteps and rushed out. She came face to face with Sugreeva. Her eyes searched for Baali.

'Yata, I am sorry. He is drunk and has passed out.'

'Drunk? Tomorrow he must fight the duel,' Tara cried in alacrity.

'I tried Yata, but he wouldn't listen. May be that Asura has tricked him.'

Tara wasn't sure whether it was Ravana who tricked her husband or Sugreeva. She felt anger rising within her. Was he such a big fool, allowing her husband to get drunk and pass out on the most important day of his life?

'You left him alone?' Tara asked incredulously.

'That wolf is there with him. He isn't easy to carry, Yata.' Sugreeva grinned. She was about to rush out, when he grabbed her hand.

'Tara—'

She snapped out of his hand. 'Fool, your wife is waiting for you.'

'Be mine, Tara!'

'Fool,' Tara panted, 'Your wife is sleeping around with any willing male. Aren't you ashamed?'

'I know, Tara. I know what she does. Ruma wants to spite me. I have neither love nor hatred for her. Let her sleep with the whole world, I don't mind a bit. All I want is you.'

Tara spat in disgust and rushed out. She had to drive some sense into the thick head of her husband. As she reached the eternal fire place, she could see his crumpled figure lying prone on the street. *Maharaja of Vanara*s, she wanted to spit on his face. How dare he demean himself like this? He has gambled with the future of Vanara race and is behaving so irresponsibly. When she reached near him, the wolf jumped across her path and growled. When it saw her, it moved away to lie down by its master's feet. She ignored it and rushed to him. She tried to shake him awake. His toddy pot was lying half-drunk by his side. On an impulse she took it and smelt it. There was the faint smell of cannabis. Somebody had laced her husband's drink with drugs.

# Chapter 30

Sugreeva sat looking at the pale moon playing hide-and-seek with the puffy clouds. It was unusually cold. His head was bursting with pain. *I've had too many drinks*, he thought. He shouldn't have talked to Tara the way he did. He spat in disgust. *Fool, fool*, he chided himself. He was perched atop the hill above the royal cave. The embers in the campfire they had lit had died down and the air had an acrid, smoky smell. He wished he could flare up the fire again, but he dared not to. He rubbed his palms together to keep himself warm. The images of Ahalya being tied to the tree came flashing to his mind from nowhere. He blinked and Ahalya's face turned to that of Tara. They were dragging Indra out, naked. No, it wasn't Indra. It was he. They were dragging him naked through the Ashram. They were going to castrate him. He screamed in horror.

'Have this. Good for cold,' the man said, startling him. After a moment's hesitation, Sugreeva grabbed the pitcher and drank. The stinking liquid burned its path to his belly and he coughed. His companion chuckled.

'Too strong for your taste? This is Asura brew, brother. Now, what we need is a girl. It is cold like hell in this place. In our little island, it is always balmy and the sea breeze carries the fragrance of the Ashoka flowers. Ha, Ha! the sea does not have Ashoka trees. My brother's gardens do. A beautiful garden he has. Everything about him is beautiful, you know. He has a beautiful palace, beautiful city, beautiful wife, the bastard. Ha, Ha!'

Sugreeva didn't reply. The Asura's rant was making him anxious. He wished the Asura would stop talking and leave

212

him alone. The Asura filled Sugreeva's pitcher without asking. Sugreeva stared at it. He tried to push his thoughts away, but guilt weighed him down. He shouldn't have done what he had done.

'Brother, you don't worry. I know you hate your brother—'

Sugreeva flung the pitcher and stood up. The Asura stared at him in disbelief. The pitcher rolled down the hill and vanished into darkness.

'I don't hate my brother.'

The Asura chuckled and took a gulp from his pitcher. Sugreeva grabbed the Asura's shoulders and shook him, 'I don't hate my brother. I love him.'

The Asura smiled at Sugreeva and took another gulp. Sugreeva grabbed the Asura's pitcher and flung it down the valley.

'Now that was unnecessary, brother. You are wasting good arrack.'

Sugreeva turned away in disgust. *I shouldn't have come here. I shouldn't have listened to this sly Asura. I shouldn't have—*

'Now relax, Vanara. Relax. I know you are weighed down by guilt. Don't be guilty. It isn't a crime to covet the throne, even if it is the throne of a bloody, godforsaken monkey kingdom.'

Sugreeva turned in rage, 'How dare you—'

'Hey, don't glare at me like that. You look funny, monkey. You take me for a fool? I am the brother of Ravana. You came asking for cannabis. You aren't the cannabis type. Hell, you can't stand a pitcher of mild arrack. Who did you take it for? Eh? Hmm, let me guess. Your brother . . . eh?'

Sugreeva turned away. It was a mistake to come. He wanted to see his brother. He wanted to fall at Baali's feet and ask for his forgiveness. He was feeling giddy. He wiped beads of sweat that had formed on his brows despite the biting cold. His shoulders stooped. His eyes filled up with tears. He felt the cold damp hand of the Asura on his shoulders. It sent a shudder down his spine.

'If isn't the throne, what it is? A woman?'

Sugreeva didn't answer.

'You can't hide anything from me, brother. You can't hide anything from this Vibhishana. Let me guess. You love your sister-in-law and–'

Sugreeva started walking away. Vibhishana caught up with him. 'She is beautiful. Not as beautiful as my brother's wife. Mandodari. You should see her, brother. Oh, she is an Apsara–'

Sugreeva hurried down, but the Asura followed him, talking incessantly, 'I can understand how you feel, brother. We have more in common than you could imagine. Let me tell you a secret. I have an eye on Mandodari. Just like you have on your brother's beautiful bride.'

Sugreeva stopped in his tracks. The Asura had crossed all limits. 'You are drunk, Asura,' Sugreeva hissed.

'A drunken man always tells the truth, brother. Have no guilt. Love is a divine thing. Love for a beautiful woman is the most divine thing in the world.'

The Asura was holding a mirror to Sugreeva's soul, but irrationally it was the frequent use of the word beautiful that was riling Sugreeva's nerves. He thought of pushing Vibhishana down the cliff for a moment. The Asura had no plans to stop talking.

'Monkey man, listen to me. What you did is the right thing to do. I wish my life could be so beautiful. My problems could be solved so beautifully, and I would get my beautiful Mandodari. You should see her, brother. You would forget your monkey girl. Your monkey girl is also beautiful, but Mandodari is more beautiful.'

'Shut up.'

'Brother, oh this is an occasion to sing. Don't worry, brother. You did a beautiful thing. You have given me a beautiful idea. When the time comes, I would do what you did now. Until then, I would be the faithful brother to the great Ravana. The fool Ravana. One day he would die, just like your ugly brother, Baali will tomorrow.'

Sugreeva smacked Vibhishana across his face. The drunken Asura fell on his back. Sugreeva pounced upon him and punched him repeatedly. The Asura put up his hands, trying to ward off the blows.

'Hey, hey, monkey. Why are you angry? Oh, I get it. You are too good, Vanara. I should learn a trick or two from you. You are a born actor.'

Sugreeva beat him until his arms ached, but the drunken Asura kept laughing hysterically. Sugreeva left him in disgust and staggered down the path to the cave. When he reached his chamber, to his disgust, Ruma was sitting on the bed. She scrambled up when she saw him. She stared at his face. He looked away.

'Why are you crying?' Ruma asked.

'Out,' Sugreeva screamed and Ruma cowered. 'Nothing will happen to your brother,' Ruma said through tears.

Sugreeva grabbed her hair and dragged her out. He threw her on the floor outside his chamber. Ruma lay crying on the floor. When he turned, he saw Tara behind him with a bowl in her hand. He averted his eyes and stumbled to his chamber. He could feel her eyes boring his back. He collapsed on the floor and wept.

# Chapter 31

Since the bullfighting, where Baali had killed Dundubhi, the arena was full for the first time. Though it was only dawn, the gallery was overflowing with Asuras and Vana Naras. Many Vana Naras could be seen praying to the great God Ayyan. In the sacred grove of the seven palmyra trees, a special puja was done with fish and toddy to satiate Ayyan, his army of ghosts and the Vana Nara ancestors. Vana Naras, in their coarse clothes made of rough cotton, birch skin or deer skin sat with pounding hearts. Mothers were breastfeeding their babies, but their lips were chanting the name of Ayyan and his elephant faced son, Kari.

The other side of the arena was filled with Asuras in glittery clothes and helmets made of copper. Their ornaments caught the rays of the rising sun and gleamed. They mocked the poor Vanaras, passed coarse comments on the breast-feeding mothers and made fun of their black skin and thick lips of the Vana Nara people. They were sure of victory and argued over which Vana Nara woman each would take as slaves. They had every reason to cheer. The chief of Vanaras, the arrogant Baali, was sitting by the fountain on one corner of the arena. He appeared stoned. To add to the ridiculousness of the situation, the beautiful wife of the Vanara chief was trying to revive him. Tara was forcing him to drink some medicine. She was crying, but the Vanara king was refusing her treatment. Beside him, lay Chemba, the red wolf, surveying the gallery for anything that could endanger his master.

'Is your monkey husband meditating?' an Asura asked and the Asura side erupted with howls and laughter.

'Send that shaggy dog to fight. He looks sober.'

'Maybe the black monkey is doing Sandhya Vandhana, the prayer to the sun,' another Asura said, paying mock obeisance to the rising sun. There was more laughter and cat calls. The Vana Nara people sat with their head held low in shame. Tara could hear the elders making vitriolic comments about her husband. Rishabha was extolling the people to rebel. People were becoming edgy. Their freedom was at stake.

'Baali, Baali, please . . .' She tried to press the bowl of concoction to Baali's lips. He grabbed the bowl and threw it into the fountain. Fortunately, it didn't overturn. It floated over the ripples of the fountain. Baali looked at her with bloodshot eyes. The cat calls of Asuras were becoming unbearable. Any moment the King of Asuras would be in the arena to fight her husband. She needed help. She looked around, ignoring the raunchy comments about her wet clothes that clung to her body and saw Sugreeva. He was standing at a distance.

'You stand here watching the fun?' she asked him.

Sugreeva walked to her. 'Yata?'

'Hold his hands,' Tara said.

'What?'

'Hold his hands you fool.'

Sugreeva held Baali's hands and Baali struggled. Chemba started barking. Asuras roared with laughter. Rishabha cried, 'Enough of this mockery.'

Swallowing the insult and mockery, Tara entered the fountain. She was aware of the spectacle she was providing to the crass Asuras as water splashed over her body and had wet her clothes. She controlled her tears. She would bear any shame, even walk naked, if that would save her Baali. She retrieved the bowl of medicine. Sugreeva held a struggling Baali. Tara prised open Baali's mouth, and emptied the medicine into his mouth. He

tried to spit it out, but she held his mouth shut tight. Chemba bit
Sugreeva and tried to drag him away. Sugreeva cursed and kicked
the wolf. The Asuras were howling with laughter.

A sudden hush fell in the arena. Tara slowly left Baali's mouth.
Sugreeva somehow retrieved himself from the grips of Chemba.
The wolf ran to its master and started licking Baali's face.

'Devi, may I request you to kindly leave the arena.'

She looked up and saw Ravana, her husband's foe, the one
who may kill him in a few minutes. Ravana was standing with his
head bowed, his palms joined in Namaste. Sugreeva had walked
away. She stood before Ravana, wondering whether she should
plead with him to postpone the duel. She was tempted to plead for
her beloved's life. Then she looked around and saw the arrogance
of Asuras, the way they were mocking her husband, her people.
Baali would prefer to die as a warrior than a beggar. She turned
away, struggling to control the trembling of her lips, the immense
heaviness that was descending on her shoulders.

'Devi, you are wet. Please . . .' Ravana waved his shawl made
of the finest silk, embraided with gems and pearls, with the
fragrance of some exotic perfume. He was smiling at her. He was
being chivalrous, performing an act that his bards would sing in
his praise. Hatred bubbled up from her belly and made her gag.
Suppressing her urge to lash out at him, she returned his smile.
Then she threw back her head, matching his arrogance with
her pride and walked away with steady steps. She would watch
her dear Baali die in this charlatan's hands, but she would not
bow her head, take his help. She was Baali's wife. The monkey
woman.

Her gaze met that of Nala who was the middleman for the
duel. He turned away, suppressing his sob. She gave her friend's
hands a squeeze and smiled tearfully before taking her seat in the
gallery. Some woman kept her hand on her shoulders, as if to
pacify her. She snapped at the poor woman, saying she needed no
sympathy. She looked around and saw Ravana watching her with

a smile. He gave a bow. She couldn't help but notice how dashing he looked in his fine clothes. Baali was sitting by the fountain like a stone. Nothing could be more contrasting than the opponents. As Ravana's gaze fell on hers, he gave his exquisite shawl to Nala to hold. She saw her friend's eyes open in surprise. He was feeling the texture of the shawl, the richness of the weave and the pattern. He was smelling the pattern. She saw the derisive smile at the faces of Asuras and the bowed heads of her people. Her Baali's people. They were slaves since time immemorial. For a brief period, Baali had showed them a dream. The dream was ending. Something snapped in Tara's mind. She couldn't allow Ravana and his men to dazzle them with their wealth. Baali mustn't lose.

'Baali, my beloved,' Tara cried, forgetting propriety, forgetting shame. 'Finish the arrogance of this Asura.'

There was no response. Her people had raised their heads. But Baali sat like a stone. 'Kill him for me, Baali,' Tara cried pitifully. Baali sat without moving a muscle. She slumped on her seat. The Asuras roared in laughter. She could hear Chemba barking. Nala tried to pull the wolf away, but it snarled at him. Baali snapped his fingers and gestured it to move away. The red wolf walked to Tara, its tail behind its legs. It looked at her with pitiful eyes and curled down beside her feet. Nala blared the horn. Ravana waited at the centre of the arena, flexing his muscles. Tara could hear Vanara women whispering and admiring the Asura King. Nala blared his horn again. There was still no response from Baali.

'The monkey is still at his Sandhya Vandhana,' an Asura cried. A wave of laughter followed.

'Sandhya Vandhana? That is done by Brahmins,' another said. 'But this is a low-caste Monkey.' More laughter followed. Some Vanara young men rushed forward at this provocation but elders calmed them down.

Ravana laughed and walked to Baali. He tapped Baali's shoulders with a finger, as if he didn't want to dirty his hands by touching the monkey. Baali didn't move.

'What are the rules of duels? I can't be standing here the entire day watching my opponent dry in the sun,' Ravana said to Nala.

Nala explained to him that there are four fountains at the four corners of arena. Whoever flips the opponent to all the four fountains will be the winner. Ravana remarked that that made his task easy. Baali was already sunk half in the western fountain. Many found the remarks witty. The Asuras tittered.

Ravana tried to lift Baali by his armpit. Baali didn't budge. The entire episode was turning into a farce and the king of Asuras was enjoying it. Tara sat with her cheeks burning in shame. She could feel the sense of defeat among her people. A sudden gasp caught her attention. The crowd had gone silent. Baali had caught Ravana's head in his armpit. Ravana was still laughing, treating it as fun before he finishes off his opponent. Baali sat without moving. Only his bulging biceps betrayed his struggle. Ravana tried to free himself. His laugh had turned to a grunt. He started pummelling Baali's back with his free hand but Baali was choking him. The pummelling soon became weak. Baali stood up with a roar. Ravana was still at the crook of his arm. He jumped into the fountain, dragging his opponent. He dunked into water, taking Ravana with him. The crowd watched with trepidation. Baali sprang up, dripping wet but Ravana's head was still in his grip. He threw Ravana into water and walked out of the fountain. Behind him Ravana was struggling to get up. Baali stood at the edge of the water, beat his chest, threw back his head and roared.

The crowd erupted in a loud cheer. The Parai drums that were silent for so far, rolled in a frenzy. Many Vanaras were crying, hugging each other and Vanara women were ululating. Tara couldn't control her tears or her smile. Baali walked to the centre of the arena. The Asura crowd was dangerously silent. Baali stood with his clenched fists pressing his waist. Tara wanted to cry, Baali, watch out, for she saw Ravana had recovered and was rushing towards Baali. Ravana kicked Baali, sending him sprawling on the mud. The Asuras roared with cheer, but it was short-lived. Baali grasped Ravana from behind, his arms locking the Asura king's neck in a death grip. He dragged Ravana and threw him into the fountain on the east side of the arena. Baali let out his monkey roar again. Tara saw a few Asuras stand up. Their swords had come out of the sheath. Some were stringing their bows. The Vanara warriors on the other hand were busy cheering their chief. The moment Ravana was on his feet, Baali jumped into the fountain and caught Ravana by his long hair. He dragged the Asura king to the Southern fountain. The wild roar accompanied the pummelling of his chest. By now the Parai drummers had jumped to the arena and had started dancing. The drum rolls were deafening and the Vanaras were cheering in ecstasy. When Baali dunked Ravana in the Northern Fountain, the entire Vanara crowd rushed to the arena, erupting in joy. A monkey man had vanquished the mighty Asura emperor. The Asura crowd rose in anger, clanging their swords on their shield. They couldn't believe their king, the greatest of all warriors who had conquered the entire Jambudweepa, under whose armies the mighty armies of Devas crumbled, was defeated by a black-skinned, thick-lipped, monkey man. The great scholar of Vedas, musician, scholar, statesman, warrior and dashingly handsome Mahabrahmana Ravana was squirming under the feet of a crude, low-caste, untouchable, illiterate, ugly monkey. The Asuras couldn't digest the insult.

Tara screamed at her people to be alert. The Asuras were attacking against all rules of a duel. The Vanaras were busy celebrating their leader's victory. Even the three council members were cheering. The freedom and honour of Vanaras had been protected by Baali. The Asura army descended on the arena like a storm. They smashed everything on the way. A section of the arena caught fire, perhaps deliberately set. The terrified Vanaras were scattered. Some ran to Baali, while others pushed and shoved to get away from the chaos. Tara struggled her way to reach Baali. Sugreeva was brandishing his mace at the attacking crowd, shielding Baali. Chemba was snarling at anyone who dared to come near his master. Unmindful of the din, Baali was giving his victory roar. Tara broke through the crowd and ran to Baali. His gaze fell on her and he stopped his roar midway. The Asuras had circled him. If they kill him, she would die with him, she decided.

'Enough,' Tara heard Ravana speak. The Asura king stood up, dripping wet. There were gashes around his neck where Baali had gripped him. He steadied himself, holding Baali's shoulders.

'Back off,' Ravana commanded. The Asura army became still, but they were glaring at Baali and their arrows, spears, swords and lances pointed at her husband.

'We fought face to face, as any man of honour would do.' Ravana's voice was even. 'He won fair. I have no shame in admitting my defeat. That is the only honourable thing to do. And I am ready to die in his hands as per the rule of the duel. No Asura will raise even a whimper. If I have been a good leader, honour me at my time of death.'

The arena turned silent. Ravana knelt before Baali. He whispered, 'You won monkey. Now kill me. I assure you that no Asura would object to my death. That is my word. Don't be sacred. Do the honourable thing.'

'Why should I kill you?' Baali asked.

'The reward of defeat in a duel is death. Don't insult my honour, monkey. Make it fast.' For the first time in the day, Tara heard Ravana's voice shiver. The impending death was making him sound like an ordinary man. Tara wished her husband would finish the Asura king before Ravana lost his courage and nobility. The Asura army was fuming with the shame of a dishonourable defeat at the hands of those they considered barbarians.

'We are Vanaras, Ravana. The rules of humans don't apply to us. We fight only for food, territory or mate. The beast that gets defeated is spared unless the victor wants to eat the vanquished in our world. You are free to go. Never enter our territory again,' Baali said and walked away. Asuras parted to make way for the Vanara chief. The wolf trotted behind him.

'Baali,' Ravana called and Baali stopped in his track. 'In that case, won't you extend your hand to me in friendship.'

Tara watched Baali hesitate. She didn't want her husband to have any friendship with the Asura king. Disappointing her, Baali's face broadened into a smile. The two men who were fighting each other a few moments before ran into each other's embrace, sealing an eternal friendship between Vanaras and Asuras.

Later, they watched the Asura army leave and Ravana's flying machine whirled away and disappeared beyond the southern horizon. Tara asked Baali why he had accepted Ravana's friendship. They were lying side by side, on their backs, in the sacred grove, under the palmyra trees. Countless stars winked at their nakedness. They had made passionate love and had run out of entreaties to exchange. Baali supported his head on his left palm and smiled at her. Running a finger through her breasts, he said, 'Because he is an honourable man. He could have asked his army to finish us off, but he accepted his defeat and left. Such friendships are to be cherished.'

'But . . . but didn't he lace your drink?' Tara asked, pushing away his hand from her body.

'It was not Ravana who laced my drink, dear,' Baali said and before she could reply, he kissed her fully on her lips. Tara closed her eyes and they slipped into their own world where there were no invading Asuras or jealous kin. Chemba snored near them. The night was still young.

Tara was sleeping with her head resting on Baali's broad chest when a blood-curdling scream woke them up.

# Chapter 32

The scream was coming from the city. Baali and Tara scrambled up. It was yet to be dawn, but they could see from the grove that something grave was happening in the city. Had Ravana come back to launch a covert attack? Without waiting for Tara, Baali ran towards the city gates. Chemba dashed ahead of Baali. Tara ran behind him, trying to fight the panic that was gripping her. The screams got louder. They could see people running out of the fort gate. A man fell before Baali. In the flickering light of the torches from the fort gate, Tara saw that the man's head had an ugly gash. The man died in Baali's arms. More men were running out, with their limbs cut, face smashed, bleeding from everywhere. Chasing them, a hideous creature ran out of the fort, wielding an axe that was dripping with blood. Baali ran towards the monster. Tara screamed at Baali to stop, to be careful.

The monster swung its axe at Baali. He ducked, and Tara saw the axe had missed Baali's head by a whisker. Chemba sprang at the throat of monster and got stuck by the blunt end of the axe. It lay whimpering a few feet away. Tara rushed to the injured wolf. It was trying to get up, but its right hind leg seemed injured. Tara dragged away a struggling, growling Chemba from where Baali and the monster were fighting.

The monster attacked Baali with vigour. He dove away from the arc of the axe which smashed on the ground and got stuck for a moment. Baali sprang at the monster and slammed it to the ground. Its axe flew from its hand and clanged near Tara's feet. The monster tried to gouge Baali's eyes. Baali punched the monster in its face. They rolled on the ground, each trying to overpower the other. Tara took the axe but wasn't sure how to use it without hurting Baali. Despite her efforts, Chemba broke free and limbed around the duelling pair, trying to snap at the monster's throat. It growled and yelped and smacked the monster with its paws.

A hand took the axe from her. It was Sugreeva. She felt scared. Somehow the axe looked more dangerous in Sugreeva's hands than in the monster's. Sugreeva circled the fighting pair, carefully aiming his move. Tara stood terrified. Sugreeva found his gap and he jumped into fray. In a fluid move, he had caught the hair of the monster in his grip and the sharp edge of the axe was in its throat. Baali stood up, dusting his hands.

'Well done, brother,' Baali said smiling. The monster was panting and puffing. Sugreeva dragged the monster for a few feet and made it kneel on the floor. The axe was still in its throat. Chemba crouched before the monster, ready to spring if it moved. More people had gathered to see the captured monster. 'An Asura'- Tara heard people whispering.

'Who're you?' Baali asked, kneeling on one leg before the monster. The Asura spat on Baali's face. Baali smacked him across his ears.

'I'll kill you all, kill all Vanaras,' the Asura hissed.

'Ravana sent you?' Sugreeva asked.

The Asura spat again. 'Ravana, the cheat. He promised revenge for my Dundubhi's loss. I invited him to invade your bloody city. And he made friends with monkey men.'

Tara saw Sugreeva's face becoming pale.

'Dundubhi?' Baali asked.

'Dundubhi. He was my brother. My prized bull. You people stole him. You monkey killed him.'

'Stole?' Baali asked, confused. 'My brother won it in a competition at Asura Mayavi's place.'

'I am Mayavi. There was no competition-'

Tara saw Sugreeva raise the axe. She screamed, and it distracted Sugreeva. The axe missed Mayavi's head by a whisker and Sugreeva lost balance. Mayavi took off, screaming in fear. Sugreeva ran behind him, wielding the axe.

'Tara, I will come back with Mayavi. I'll catch him alive,' Baali said to her, as he ran behind Sugreeva. Chemba limped behind its master. She saw them vanish into darkness.

With trepidation, she waited for them to return. When they hadn't come back by noon, she became worried. She had to plan for the funeral of six men and a woman hacked to death by Mayavi. There were more than a dozen injured in his attack. Nala speculated that Mayavi might have come with Ravana's army and gained entrance to the fort. When Ravana went away after the truce, he might have stayed behind to take revenge. Tara regretted Baali's decision to allow all the Asuras inside the fort. She had advised him against it, but he had brushed her concerns away. By evening, Hanuman had come, and she broke down before him. It was difficult to face the family members of the slain men. The woman who died had a toddler and she found it impossible to face the bereaved husband. She felt they had failed as rulers. Hanuman pacified the mourning members with stories about how the soul never dies and death is like the soul changing the soiled clothes. Tare thought bitterly whether such advice would have satisfied her had her loved ones died. Even after nightfall, there was no sign of Baali and Sugreeva. Hanuman promised to go in search of them in the morning. Tara spent a sleepless night, worrying about her husband.

Two days passed and there was no news of Baali, Sugreeva or even Hanuman who had gone in search of them. Ruma kept cursing her misfortune about being married to the family. She blamed Tara for her husband's absence. She never said anything to Tara's face. She would talk to herself, ensuring that Tara was within earshot. Ruma was getting on the already strained nerves of Tara. In the absence of Baali and Sugreeva, the council members had started asserting their powers. A crisis was looming ahead as the food stock had vanished after extending hospitality to the invading Asura army. The wolves of hunger were at the gates of Kishkinda. Tara wanted to resume agriculture. The council objected saying Vana Nara faith was against farming. 'One should not hurt the mother earth,' they argued.

In the absence of Baali and Sugreeva, Tara was forced to call the meeting of the council. Rishabha rudely told Tara not to interfere in the governance of the city. His remark about woman's place being in the kitchen made Nala angry and led to a heated exchange of words between the young architect and Rishabha. They almost came to blows. Tara didn't want another crisis in the city when she had so much to worry about. She apologized to the council and chided Nala. She said she would abide by their decisions and she was trying to help them in absence of her husband and Sugreeva. She knew her limitations as a woman. That assuaged the bruised egos of the old men, but Nala stormed out of the council chamber. She was able to persuade them to get yam planted on the dry riverbed. In twenty-one days, they may get some harvest that would help feed old people and children at least. She was thankful to small victories and came out of the council chamber with some relief. She knew she had to sort out another problem. Nala would be sulking. She went in search of him and found him sitting alone near the sacred grove.

Tara's attempts to pacify him were met with a stoic silence. She knew he felt betrayed. He had fought for her and she had not stood by him, he told her when she coaxed him to speak. She took his hands in hers and said, 'We must hold the city together, friend. They won't want a woman ordering them around. We're still the people of forest. I'm worried for Baali. I don't want to fight with the elders for such petty things, at least not now. Nala, I thought you'd understand.'

Nala was embarrassed. He apologized and despite herself, Tara cried. She was feeling vulnerable and lonely. She missed Baali. Nala thought she was crying because she was hurt by the way he behaved. He kept on saying sorry repeatedly. She lost her temper and snapped at him, 'Donkey, I am not crying because you were playing the coy bride. I miss my husband. How can men be so thick?' Like a late blooming flower, a grin appeared on Nala's face. He started walking towards the river.

'Where're you going?' Tara asked.

'I'll come back only with Baali,' Nala said. She rushed to him and caught his wrist. 'I'll have to send someone to bring you back in a couple of days, if you go. Hanuman will bring my Baali back.'

Nala stared at her. 'You insulted me. I'm going.'

She caught him by his ears and brought him under the palmyara tree. 'You're going nowhere.'

'What'll I do here? Fight with you?' Nala smiled, rubbing his ears.

'You'll plant some yams. You'll make me equipment to till the soil. Do whatever you're good at, my sweet fool. You'll be lost in the jungle. And though you create more troubles than I can solve, I must admit you're my only friend left in Kishkinda,' Tara said.

'Admit you can't do anything without me,' Nala said as they walked back. He talked about his admiration for Baali and his great victory against the Asura king Ravana. There was no warrior in the world who could beat Baali and Nala wondered why he chose a fool like Tara when he could have had any princess or even Apsaras from the heaven. Tara said she was an Apsara and Baali himself had said it to her many times. Nala howled with laughter and said if Apsaras looked like Tara he would prefer a Rakshasi anytime. Tara wished him to be married to Soorpanakha, the sister of Ravana, who was notorious for her promiscuousness. They bantered and pulled each other's legs like old friends. Tara felt as if some weight had come off her heavy heart. What would she do without friends like Nala? As they reached the cave palace, Tara saw Hanuman waiting for them. She ran to him and as she reached, she tried to read his face. Hanuman remained calm and stoic. She stood before him, her heart pounding furiously in her ribs.

'Nothing to worry, daughter,' Hanuman said. 'I met Baali and Sugreeva. Mayavi has vanished somewhere. They are searching for him. Baali said he would come only with Mayavi.'

Tara sighed in relief. She smiled, though a drop of tear escaped her eyes and flowed down her cheeks. Hanuman said, 'You look tired.'

'The council members have been making her life tough,' Nala said.

'Why don't you go to your father's home, daughter? I'm sure Vaidya would be pleased to see his daughter.' Hanuman smiled. 'If you trust me, I shall take care of the affairs of the city for a few days.'

Tara pondered over the idea. She didn't want to stay in Kishkinda where everything reminded her of Baali. Besides, she missed her father. It had been a long time. She had never visited her home after the marriage. Hanuman's offer to take care of Kishkinda's affairs was a relief to her. She decided to visit her father.

By next dawn, she was ready to go to Sushena's hut and was excited about the prospect. She wished things would be the same and her childhood would remain preserved there, pristine and intact. As Hanuman was seeing her off, she asked him something that was nagging her, 'How were Baali and Sugreeva?'

'They were fine,' Hanuman answered, frowning.

'Were . . . were they friendly with each other?'

'Why do you ask?'

'No . . . nothing,' Tara said. She had started worrying when she saw the expression on Hanuman's face.

'As you guessed, I sensed some strain in their relationship. Baali was accusing Sugreeva of lying about Dundubhi and despite Sugreeva's repeated pleas, Baali was insisting that there would be a trial at Kishkinda once they were back. But I think there is nothing to worry. It happens in every home, between most siblings. Go in peace, daughter. They are happy. All three of them, including that red wolf.'

Tara took his blessings and started her journey. When she reached her home unannounced, her father was ecstatic. His happiness was a treat for her eyes. He enquired about her husband and when she said that Baali and Sugreeva had gone to hunt down an evil man, he remarked there was no need to hunt for evil, it resides in every heart just like God. Tara said philosophising was a sure sign of getting old. Sushena grinned and she noticed he was missing a few teeth. When she entered the hut, she was filled with guilt. The room looked unmade, there was dust in the corners and her father's clothes, a pair of dhotis and four angavastras, lay crumpled in a corner unwashed. Cobwebs hung from the ceiling. The thatch had withered and sunlight that filtered through the holes made curious patterns on the floor. She felt sad about how poor her father was. She was living in luxury, as a Maharani, and her father was living alone, in this hut that could collapse anytime. Trying to suppress the heavy feeling of guilt, she asked whether he had breakfast.

He stared at her as if not comprehending and she remembered they used to eat only once in a day. She went to the hearth in the corner, which she had got made through Nala at every home. The hearth looked unused. She frightened off a cat which was sleeping in the ashes that were months old.

'What do you eat, Appa?' she asked, suppressing a sob.

'Why? I eat tubers, honey, fruits, nuts, whatever I get. Whatever my patients can afford to give.' Sushena smiled. 'I've no use for your fancy equipment from the city, girl. I've seen sixty-five rains and lived well without cooking.'

Lived well, indeed, she wanted to say. If she said much, she was scared she would cry. She went out to find a broom to dust the floor. She didn't want to face her father. She worked through the day, cleaning the cobwebs, patching the cracked floor with cow dung, cleaning the windows. There was no latch on the door.

'You're staying alone and you've no latch on the door?' she asked him.

'Ah, I have the fortune of Kubera buried here for someone to steal,' Sushena guffawed.

There was no point arguing with the old man. When she was carrying his clothes to wash it in the river, he was sitting on the Veranda and chewing betel leaves. 'What is this new habit?' she asked in a stern tone. He smiled sheepishly. She thought of stopping him, then remembered these were his little pleasures. What right did she have to barge into his home—she paused. *Did she think of it as his home?* It is her home—no, it *was* her home. She sighed as she walked past him. How different would it have been had her mother been alive? Her father could have married again. He wouldn't have been this lonely. He hadn't for her sake and how had she repaid him. There were a few old women who were washing their clothes on the riverbank. They were surprised to see her. One of them remarked that the Maharani of Kishkinda was washing clothes like a common woman. She remarked it was her father's clothes. They watched her as if she was a creature from another universe. She felt she was showing off her false humility. The childhood she had dreamt about had vanished. She wished she hadn't married and remained the little daughter of her father. She wished she was that teenager, sitting with her ankles dipped into the cold waters of Pampa, and discussing boys with Prabha. Where was she now? Why did she go away?

When she was returning to her hut with the washed clothes, a few village children came running to her. They stood at a distance, watching her with awestruck eyes. She called them to the veranda and they approached her reluctantly. Tara spread out the savouries and treats she had brought from the palace. Her father distributed them among the village children. Old women came to enquire after her. Her father showed everyone the shawl Tara had gifted him. She had brought presents for everyone. The villagers overwhelmed her with their love. By the evening, her father's friends came with wild honey from the forest and gooseberry wine. It was delightful to watch the old men sitting

on the protruding rock that overlooked the falls and finding joy
in trivial things.

As the evening fell, she felt an inexplicable joy in the rustic
simplicity of her village. The pain she felt when she came had
withered away. She was getting used to the slow rhythm of village
life. The breeze was fragrant and the air rich. Even the moon looked
different, its light somehow felt purer. She sat on the veranda,
savouring her childhood. The bush where she used to hide during
the hide-and-seek game with Prabha had grown into a tree. The
courtyard looked smaller than she had imagined. Everything
looked different yet familiar, smaller yet more beautiful. If she
wished, she could perhaps lean and touch her younger self playing
hopscotch in the courtyard.

Her mind went to Baali. Where would he be? Would he miss
her as much as she missed him? Suddenly, the world swam before
her eyes. She tried to stand up and staggered. She tried to call out
for her father. Everything went blank and she collapsed on the
ground.

When she woke up, she was inside the hut. There were many
faces smiling at her. She tried to get up, trying to orient herself.
Her father gently pushed her down. He was grinning from ear to
ear.

'Daughter, take rest.'

'What happened to me?'

'Nothing. Take rest.'

'What illness do I have?'

The villagers burst into laughter. What was so funny about
it? An old woman came forward and said with a toothless grin,
'Sushena is soon going to be a grandfather.'

For a moment, she didn't comprehend what the old woman
had said. Then it stuck her with full force. She wanted to see Baali
now. 'Oh God, oh God, oh God,' she cried. She could not control
her tears. She held her father's wrinkled hands and laughed, then
cried. A huge cheer went through the villagers who had crowded

near her reed mat. The village women gently helped her to stand up. They led her to Veranda. There were many people waiting anxiously. The old woman announced the good news and an impromptu dance broke out. They made her sit on the veranda. They showered her with affection, sweets, the ones she had gifted them in the morning.

She was anxious to meet Baali and tell him the great news. Her father's home no longer appealed to her as it had sometime before. She wanted to be back in their chamber, in their carved stone bed. She wanted to lie on his chest and stare at his cragged face, feel the stubbles on his chin with her hand. She imagined his face when she told him that he was going to be a father. She spent a restless night, dreaming, in delicious anticipation, yearning for Baali's presence, dying for his words of endearment. She told her father she wanted to go back to Kishkinda the next day. Her father smiled sadly and blessed her.

She woke up with a searing headache and morning sickness. Her father was not in the hut and she fretted at the unexpected delay. Her father came, panting and puffing. He was covered in sweat. He sat on the veranda, fanning himself with his Uthariya.

'Where have you been?' she could not hide her irritation.

'I had to prepare for your departure,' he said with a smile.

'What preparation?' she asked puzzled and then it dawned on her. Her father might have begged and borrowed to give her gifts and savouries as per tradition.

'There was no need for all that, father,' she said.

'It's my duty, daughter. You're a Maharani. No one should speak ill of you in your in-law's home,' Sushena gave her an endearing smile. Her eyes misted.

'No, father. There is no one to speak ill or otherwise in my home. Baali is the last person to be bothered about such trivial things. I lack nothing.'

'That doesn't mean you will deny your father the pleasure,' Sushena said. 'That doesn't mean I can't buy new clothes for my son-in-law as per custom and that doesn't mean I should not present a few gold bangles to my daughter.'

There was no point arguing further. Soon, men and women arrived bearing gifts for her. Some were paid by her father, and some were gifted by the villagers on their own accord. She and her father started for Kishkinda by noon. They were trailed by a few men and women carrying gifts and presents.

When they reached Kishkinda, there was a crowd assembled near the palace. What was wrong? Tara felt uneasy as many stared at her. There were hushed whispers. Her heart started beating faster. Something was seriously wrong. No one was facing her. She ran to the palace and found the council of ministers huddled at the courtyard. Hanuman was there too.

'What happened?' she asked, and the men parted to let her pass. She saw Sugreeva sitting on the threshold with his head buried in his palms. She repeated the question. Hanuman came to her and stood without speaking. His eyes were brimming.

'Daughter, pray for strength.'

'What happened? Why're you looking at me like that? Please tell me.' No one answered. Sugreeva's shoulders heaved with emotion. He was sobbing.

'Will someone please tell me what happened?' she screamed in a shrill voice.

It was Hanuman who answered.

'Baali is dead.'

# Chapter 33

Tara laughed. She rushed to Sugreeva, 'It's your prank. Is it not? Tell me, it's your prank, right?' she laughed aloud and turned to the council of ministers. 'It's just a prank. He is a prankster. Baali can't be dead. Don't try to fool me.'

Sugreeva started sobbing.

'Sugreeva, enough of your acting. Nothing has happened to my Baali.' She laughed. Except for Sugreeva's sobbing, there was complete silence. A few dry leaves cartwheeled through the courtyard. No one spoke. Tara stopped laughing. She collapsed on the steps.

'Baali can't die, Baali won't die,' she kept mumbling. She could hear her father wailing loudly. The villagers who had accompanied her were beating their chests and crying aloud. Someone must have told them. She wanted to scream at them to stop. Baali can't die like that. Baali wouldn't leave her alone. He had to see his unborn child. How can he leave her like that? He had no right to do that. She hated him for it. He couldn't die.

Hanuman came near her. 'Daughter, no one can stop death when the time comes. That is the only certainty in life.'

'Baali isn't dead,' she repeated.

'He will always live in your memories and in those who admired and loved him. Only his physical form has changed. His soul is immortal.'

'Baali can't die,' she insisted.

'Anyone born will die, daughter. Baali had spotted Mayavi and the Rakshasa ran for his life. It was raining heavily in the

235

hills. Baali chased him. The Rakshasa entered a cave and Baali went in search of him. It was then the landslide happened, trapping both Mayavi and Baali inside the cave. The whole mountain caved in–'

Tara staggered towards Sugreeva. 'And you didn't do anything to help him?' she asked suspiciously.

Sugreeva stared helplessly at her and then at Hanuman. His eyes were red with grief.

'I did everything possible. I tried to remove the boulders with my bare hands. All the soldiers tried. But the entire mountain collapsed in the landslide.'

Tara withdrew to her room. She sat on the carved stone cot where they had spent countless hours in each other's arms. The chamber had Baali's smell. Every item in the room reminded her of him. She felt that any moment he would come in with his boyish grin and laugh at the prank he had played with her. The red wolf would come with him. Wolf . . . where was Chemba? Like a woman possessed, she ran down the steps of the cave palace. Hanuman and Sugreeva were huddled with the elders near the eternal fire. Their eyes widened in surprise when they saw her. Nala rushed to her. She pushed him away and went to Sugreeva.

'Where is Chemba? Where is the red wolf?' she cried holding his angavastra.

'The wolf . . .' Sugreeva fumbled. 'It was refusing to come with us. It is a wild animal. Without Baali it would have left to join its pack.'

'The wolf won't leave Baali.' Tara broke down. 'My Baali isn't dead. He can't die,' Tara repeated to everyone she saw. People nodded in sympathy. Nala accompanied her to the cave palace. Ruma was sympathetic for once. She tried to pacify her. Tara had ears for no one. She kept repeating that Baali can't be dead. Despite her protests, the arrangement for Baali's last rites were made. Her father tried to pacify her. She screamed at him to leave her alone. She watched him walk away with stooping shoulders.

She waited for Baali, refusing to talk to anyone. Ruma came with food and tried to talk to her. She sat like a stone, refusing to cry, refusing to believe that Baali was dead, refusing to eat anything. She wanted to be left alone with her grief and people respected it. Sugreeva avoided meeting her, but she cornered him once. 'He hadn't given up on you, when you were at the doors of death, Sugreeva. Why did you abandon him?' she screamed at him. He stood with his head bowed, not uttering a word in his defence. When she broke down, he left quietly.

There were no mortal remains of her husband to cremate and even if there were, Baali had no son to perform the rituals, at least not yet. No one asked Tara anything. She was left alone in her bereavement. Nala came and sat on the floor, not saying anything. His silent presence was soothing for her. A few women of her village tried to pacify her but were shoved away by Nala. Hanuman came and talked about the immortality of the soul. Tara kept repeating that Baali can't die.

When Hanuman brought Brahmins from Matanga's ashram to conduct the rituals, Tara stopped them and pleaded with them not to do the rituals. Everyone was sympathetic, but the rituals went on as per custom. Hanuman convinced the council to spare some money from the city administration. Cows were gifted to Brahmins, pindadan was done for the departed soul. Rituals were done by Sugreeva—as the younger brother, only he had the right to take the place of the son. Kishkinda mourned the death of a great warrior and king, a man who was generous to a fault. Magadhas and Sutas came to moan him. They made songs in his praise. Sugreeva gifted generous presents to everyone. Sugreeva's grief was heartbreaking for anyone who watched.

When the council met and decided that Sugreeva would be the king, he refused. He said no one could take the place of his brother. Hanuman and the others took almost a week to persuade him. Meanwhile, Tara mourned alone. Every rustle of leaf left her with an irrational excitement of perhaps seeing Baali, followed by heart-wrenching disappointment and grief. She wished she had seen the dead body of her beloved. She wished she could fall on him, hug his rigid body and weep so that the coldness of death would seep into her. She lived between hope and despair.

In moments of desperation, she hated the life growing in her womb that had brought her misfortune. It was followed by guilt for hating the only thing that Baali had left for her. She refused to see her father or anyone else. Finally, once all the rituals were over and it was time for her to enter the dreary life of a widow, Sugreeva once again refused the throne.

The council met for an emergency meeting. Sugreeva said that he couldn't bear to see his sister-in-law a widow. The shastras of Brahmins said a younger brother could marry his elder brother's widow. A few members who still followed the old tribal customs spoke against it, saying it was not as per Vanara tradition. However, the majority were for adopting the new Shastras. It was left to Hanuman to convey the news to Tara.

Hanuman met Tara to gently break the news. He said Tara had the right to refuse. However, he said it would be prudent to marry Sugreeva as it would render legitimacy to the child who would be born. If it was a son, perhaps he would inherit Kishkinda. For her unborn son's sake, she should agree to the marriage. Tara was livid at the suggestion. Though she didn't put it into words, she had a gnawing doubt that Sugreeva was responsible for Baali's death. Nala told her that it would be safe for the unborn child if she married Sugreeva. That set her mind ticking. She said she wanted to see the place where Baali had met his end.

Sushena tried to dissuade her from undertaking the arduous journey of fifteen days. However, she was adamant. Finally, a group of ministers along with Hanuman and Sugreeva decided to take Tara to the place where Baali and his foe, Mayavi had disappeared.

# Chapter 34

They reached the place after more than twenty days. Incessant rains had delayed their journey. The climb up to the hill was treacherous and slippery. She was determined to push herself to get there. When they reached the valley, Sugreeva pointed out the place where Baali had vanished. Her heart sank. Almost half of the hill had collapsed. Trees lay uprooted in a slushy mountain of mud. Water still gushed through the cracks of rocks and boulders were strewn around.

'The cave mouth had vanished,' Sugreeva said. His face was drained of blood. She uttered a cry of grief. The finality of everything broke her from within. She rushed up through knee-deep slush, fighting those who tried to restrain her. She wanted to try removing the huge boulder that lay over what could've been the cave mouth. It towered over her. She tried to push it, but it was like an ant trying to move a mountain. She banged her head on it and cried.

She heard a low growl. 'Chemba . . .' She called. The wolf came crawling from the debris. Its paws were thick with mud. Its nails had cracked. It came to her and stood, as if trying to convey something. Tara broke down when she saw her husband's companion. As if understanding her grief, it moved to her and licked her face. She hugged the beast and cried. Chemba wriggled out of her grip and ran, climbing the rocks. She watched it stand, staring at her, wagging its tail.

'Go, Chemba . . . you belong to him . . . be with him always,' she said through tears. The wolf lay down on the rock and watched her with mournful eyes.

Sugreeva and others stood at a respectful distance, allowing her to cry and overcome her grief. She talked to the boulder as if it was Baali. She said he was going to be a father. She whispered entreaties and asked him to come back. She chided him for playing this prank and threatened that she would leave him if he didn't come out fast. The boulder remained stone hearted. Finally, she collapsed and cried. No one dared to come near her. They waited for the storm to pass.

When the sun started dipping in the west, she stood up on her weak knees. She kissed the boulder and allowed the coldness of the rock to touch her. Then she whispered, 'Forgive me, Baali. Our son needs a father. I'm going to marry your beloved brother.'

She waited for some clue, some response. 'They say that souls are immortal, can't you give me a sign, Baali?' she pleaded. The rock stood solid, unmoving, uncaring. She sighed. Chemba was lying on the rock, as if he had been sculpted from it. Her gaze met the wild beasts' and she saw immense sadness in its eyes. The wolf's grief was heartbreaking to watch. She said a tearful goodbye to Baali's companion.

Tara had to pick up her shattered life and start living again. She told herself that it would be something her Baali would have approved of. She gave a parting kiss to the boulder and started climbing down with a heavy heart. The red wolf let out a mournful howl. From somewhere deep in the forests, the wild call was answered. Tara felt she was leaving her soul in the mountain. The others helped her tread the dangerous trek down the hill. When she reached the bottom, night had fallen and a full moon had risen above the mountain that had swallowed her beloved. She paused at the bottom of the valley and turned to look at the boulder. The wolf was silhouetted against the rising moon. She sighed. She wanted to say goodbye but she froze.

'Did you hear that? Did you hear him crying?' she screamed. She had heard him clearly. He had called her name. She rushed back, but Hanuman stopped her. He shook his head sadly. 'Daughter, your grief is making you imagine things.'

'Leave me, leave me. He is alive. My Baali is alive,' she cried. Hanuman left her. She took a few steps uphill, then came back. She wiped her tears. Hanuman was right. She was imagining things. They travelled back in silence. Everyone was respectful to her. Sugreeva was caring and deferential. On the third day of the journey, when they were resting by the sea shore where the Asura king Ravana had built a magnificent temple for Lord Shiva, they started talking again. Sugreeva talked about how he grew up under the protection of his elder brother. He talked about funny incidents that Baali had never shared with the others. He had a knack for making the most mundane things amusing. He had a gift for making her laugh and cry. She learnt more about Baali through his admiring words than she had ever known living with him. Baali grew in stature through Sugreeva's words. She saw how, despite his laughter and excitement while talking about Baali, Sugreeva ended up hoarse in his voice and misty in his eyes at the end of the story. His love for his elder brother was touching. She doubted whether she had loved Baali as much as Sugreeva did. The nagging suspicion of Sugreeva's hand in Baali's death melted away. The landslide was massive, and it was an accident. Sugreeva couldn't be responsible for it. It was her destiny. Sugreeva confessed to her that he had nightmares about a childhood incident. He told her about Ahalya and how Indra was castrated for his adultery. He said he was getting nightmares of someone castrating him. He pleaded that he was not seeking an adulterous relationship. He was honourably asking her to marry him. She had to learn to love Sugreeva for the sake of the life blossoming in her womb. Finally, under relentless pressure she agreed to marry him. She struggled to convince herself that she had never harboured any secret love for Sugreeva and she was doing it for the child in her womb.

The wedding was a simple affair. It had none of the gaiety of her marriage with Baali. Only a few were invited. Sugreeva wanted it that way. It was difficult for Tara to face Ruma. The woman never uttered a word of protest.

Sugreeva sat in the palmyra grove where they had come without uttering a word on the way. On the night of the wedding, Tara made a strange request to Sugreeva. She knew it was cruel, but she said that until she gave birth to Baali's child, she would not give herself to Sugreeva. The sky was overcast and there was the threat of a thunderstorm. The small lamp they had carried had gone off in the moisture-laden wind that howled around them.

'Alright, Tara. That is the least I can do for my brother,' Sugreeva said.

'Have you ever been a good husband to Ruma?' Tara asked. Sugreeva didn't reply. She repeated her question.

'My love for you doesn't allow me to do that, Tara,' Sugreeva said and walked away without waiting for her answer. Lightning split open the sky and a thunder cracked, shaking the earth. She watched him walking down the hill. The horrible doubt which she had suppressed so far started raising its hood in her mind again. A man, who was so madly in love with her to avoid his wife, wouldn't hesitate to murder for her. She steadied herself by holding the palmyra that was swaying in the wind. Oh God, oh God, let it not be true, she prayed. She hated herself for harbouring such a doubt. It seemed that the wind was carrying the distressed call of Baali to her from the hill where he had died. The howl of Chemba lingered in the air. *Or did he die? Was he trapped inside? Did someone trap him inside?* 'Oh God, why don't you allow me some peace? Why am I having such horrible thoughts?' she cried aloud. Lightning hit the ground ahead of her and the smell of burnt grass assaulted her. A deafening thunder clap followed a moment later. The vaults of heaven opened, and it started raining. She ran towards the palace. Behind her the seven palmyra trees danced wildly, their heads swinging like someone possessed, their fronds scratching the skies as the wind screamed murder.

Tara rushed to Sugreeva and blocked his path. He looked at her face and averted his gaze. Tara asked him, 'Did you kill my husband?'

Sugreeva's shoulders stooped. 'Do you suspect me, Tara? Do you think I am capable of such a crime? He was the one who brought me up. I loved him, Tara, more than anyone else in the world.'

'Remember the day before the duel with Ravana? Who laced Baali's drink?'

Sugreeva didn't raise his head. 'Answer me,' Tara said.

'Vibhishana. It was Vibhishana who brought the cannabis. It grows in Lanka,' Sugreeva mumbled.

Tara sighed. 'I . . . I suspected. I had seen them drinking together. But–'

'How could you suspect me, Tara? Do you think I am so mean?' Sugreeva's voice cracked. 'To . . . to kill my brother?'

'I . . . I am sorry,' Tara sobbed. She felt Sugreeva's hand embracing her. She pressed her face on his chest and cried. 'I miss him.'

'I miss him too,' he whispered. His hands caressed her hair soothingly. Suddenly, the image of his mother, Ahalya in the arms of Indra flashed in his mind. There was a boy standing at the door. He was watching them. There was a sparrow in his hand. A nest. The sparrow tweeted. Sugreeva shuddered. His hands went stiff and he stopped caressing Tara's hair. He started sweating.

They stood in silence. Then, she felt embarrassed. Guilty. She turned and hurried away. He stood watching her, his heart heavy.

Months passed, with one dreary day turning into another. Sugreeva enquired about her health every day and he sat with her often without speaking, like a prayer, but she never spoke a word to him. She knew he understood the change in her behaviour, yet he never complained. Like a chastised dog seeking its master, he came to her with touching devotion. No man would have cared for a woman like that, yet that filled her with a disturbing abhorrence.

Tara gave birth to a boy on an usually cold morning. She had refused to go to her father's home and her father had spent an awkward month anticipating her delivery in the palace. Sugreeva ordered for a great celebration and the entire city was decorated with marigold and jasmine. The priests came again to name the boy. When Sugreeva whispered Angada, his name in the boy's ears three times, Tara felt she would burst with grief. It should have been Baali who should have been doing it. She had dreaded the day Sugreeva would come to claim his rights as a husband. Now that Angada was born, she had no excuse to deny his conjugal rights.

Angada was showered with presents. Ruma came to her chamber for the first time after months. She stood awkwardly at the threshold, watching Tara feed the baby. Tara called her in and she sat at the edge of the bed, watching Angada surreptitiously. When Angada had finished his feeding and Tara had made him burp, she asked Ruma whether she would like to hold the baby. Ruma didn't reply but sat staring at her toes. Tara felt pity for the girl. For no fault of hers, she was suffering.

Tara placed Angada in Ruma's lap. She saw Ruma's eyes glisten with tears. She stared at the baby, her face displaying various emotions. Then she started cooing to the baby. The baby stared at Ruma with its bright eyes. Ruma kissed the baby's cheeks and Angada broke into a wail. Tara rushed to take the baby from Ruma, but before she could take him, Ruma started singing and Angada stopped crying. Tara did not know that Ruma's voice was so sweet. Her song filled the palace with a delicious melancholy and Angada slowly drifted to sleep. She gently placed the sleeping baby in the cradle, but the moment the baby touched the cushion, he started crying again. Ruma started singing another lullaby. Angada closed his eyes, as if in bliss. Tara wished she was blessed with such a voice. From that day, except for feeding, Ruma became the mother of Angada for all practical purposes. Sometimes, Tara felt jealous and possessive about her son, but she told herself that

Angada was the only pleasure poor Ruma had. She didn't have the heart to deny her that.

The day that Tara dreaded arrived sooner than she had anticipated. It was strange that when she was wedded to Baali, she used to secretly fancy the love of Sugreeva, but now, as his wife, she felt she was betraying Baali. Tara feared facing Ruma; the guilt that she had stolen the girl's husband hung like a stone on her neck. Ruma acted as if no one except Angada and herself existed in the world.

Tara prayed for rain so that the event may be postponed, but the evening was crisp and clear. It was as beautiful as poetry and as lyrical as a painting. And it filled her with an unfathomable longing for Baali.

As the sun was setting she was ushered to the room that had a balcony overlooking the river. The palace servants bathed her in milk and turmeric. They smoked her hair with fragrant incense and ushered her to the balcony. The sun was painting a magical vista over the hills and the river looked as if someone had toppled a cask of saffron into it. They made her sit facing the valley. She could see Ruma carrying Angada around. They were busy watching the birds that were coming to roost. Puffy clouds grazed like sheep in the sky. The maids pushed a table near her. It had various perfumes in it. They applied musk behind her ears. They braided her hair with jasmine flowers. A maid held a polished metal mirror for her to admire her beauty. The woman staring back at her from the mirror was a stranger to her. As the time approached, a numbness crept in from her toes and spread over her body. She had no ears for the naughty taunts of the maids.

Tara was shaken awake from her reminiscences by a commotion by the river. Why was everyone running towards the river? She stood up in confusion. She could see a mob coming towards the palace cave. The mob was growing larger as it approached. Was she having visions? She held the balustrade firm to steady herself. She blinked to reassure herself that she was not dreaming. She saw the wolf first. Behind the wolf was that familiar face she had pined for every moment. Baali was coming to the palace. She let out a cry of joy. She ran, toppling the table of perfumes. She rushed down the stairs, stumbling, half-falling, running down, pushing away the maids who were coming up with fruits. She ran through the palace hall, sobbing and laughing. She stood at the main door, panting.

'Sugreeva!' Baali's angry voice rose in the courtyard. He slammed his huge club on the lamp post and it broke into two. He screamed at the top of his voice, 'You bastard!'

Sugreeva came running from the palace. He pushed Tara out of his way and ran to Baali with open arms.

'Anna, Anna,' he cried, sobbing. Baali swung his club. It caught Sugreeva's chin, smashing his teeth. Tara screamed. Sugreeva cried in pain. He had fallen on his back. He folded his hand and pleaded, 'Anna, please, why're you–'

Baali kicked Sugreeva on his face. Ruma came running from the palace. She was carrying Angada. She was screaming at the top of her voice. She fell on Sugreeva and Baali stopped kicking his brother for a moment. Angada fell from her hand and started bawling.

'Your son?' Tara heard Baali asking Ruma. Tara rushed to pick Angada. She checked whether the baby was hurt.

'Tara . . .' Baali called in shock. He was staring at the baby and Sugreeva. Before she could say something, Baali grabbed Sugreeva by his hair and started dragging him down the steps. Ruma ran behind them, crying, pleading with Baali. Sugreeva's head bounced on the stone steps. He was begging for forgiveness from Baali.

'You trapped me, you bastard. You wanted my throne, you wanted my wife.' Baali was cursing Sugreeva who was pleading his innocence. He grabbed his brother's feet and cried, 'I thought you were dead. Believe me, brother–'

'You liar, you don't deserve to live.' Baali lifted his club and smashed Sugreeva's knees. Sugreeva screamed and writhed in pain, but he didn't try to defend himself. The wolf sat near the eternal fire and watched them with unforgiving eyes. Tara rushed back to the palace. On the way in, she shouted at the guards to fetch Hanuman before Baali murdered Sugreeva. The guards rushed to bring Hanuman.

By the time Hanuman came, Baali had beaten Sugreeva to a pulp. He was sitting by his side, watching Sugreeva writhe like a worm. Sugreeva kept pleading his innocence. Hanuman came like a storm. Tara heard a heated argument between Hanuman and Baali after which Hanuman lifted the injured Sugreeva on his shoulders and walked away. Baali kept screaming abuses, threatening to kill Sugreeva if he dared to step into Kishkinda again.

Then he turned towards the palace. Men moved away in fear. Tara hid behind the door, holding Angada close to her heart. This was not the reunion she had dreamed about. She caught herself thinking, *why did he come back*? When she saw his shadow, she rushed to her chamber. She sat on the cot. Angada had drifted to sleep. She dreaded the moment Baali would come to her. This wasn't the Baali she knew.

The pungent smell of the wolf came first. It came inside the chamber and growled. Baali followed with bloodshot eyes and dishevelled hair. He had become leaner and fitter. He stood before her. She waited for him to speak.

'You betrayed me, Tara,' he said softly.

She closed her eyes tight, but a drop of tear escaped and traced its path through her cheeks. She knew he had sat down beside her when the cot creaked, but she didn't dare to open her eyes.

'He looks exactly like Sugreeva,' she heard him say. That broke her restraint.

'Why should he look like Sugreeva?' All her pent-up rage exploded in that question.

'Is it wrong for a son to resemble his father?' Baali said in a derisive tone.

'So you've concluded everything,' Tara said bitterly.

'I expected you to wait for me, Tara,' Baali's voice sounded tired. That broke her. She bit her lips.

'I thought–' Tara didn't know how to complete the sentence.

'That I was dead,' Baali said with a sad smile. Tara leaned on the bedpost and sobbed.

'You forgot me so easily, Tara. Were you two waiting for me to die? Were you also involved in the conspiracy, Tara? You could've just told me about it. I would have happily given away the kingdom to him. I loved him with all my heart, perhaps more than I could ever love you. Yet, the two people I loved most, betrayed me, and . . . wanted me dead.'

'How easily you come to the conclusion? Every moment I have yearned for you. Every time I heard the rustle of footsteps outside, my heart would jump with joy, for I thought you would be coming for me.' Tara buried her face in her palms and sobbed.

'Then why did you leave me alone to die, Tara?' Baali asked with an edge in his tone. He was working himself to a rage. He stood up and came near her. He leaned towards her and she staggered back. He pointed a finger at her face and poked the air, 'Why did you leave?'

'I . . . I don't understand,' her teeth chattered in fear. *Oh God, it should not be that, it should not be that*, she prayed.

Baali slammed his fist on the bedpost. Angada woke up startled and cried. Baali ignored him and screamed, 'You don't understand . . . you don't know. I saw you, Tara. I saw you with him, when you came with him. He brought you to show you that he had done his job. You came to ensure I was dead. You had even the gall to say that you're going to marry him.'

'What– what–'

'STOP YOUR ACTING! You came to the hill. I was trapped behind the boulder. Through the crack between the boulder and the cave mouth, I could see you. I called you. I screamed for help. My leg was broken, my ribs had shattered. I was bleeding to death.

I thought you had come to help me, Tara. And then you left. You came to gloat that you two were getting married. I tried to stop you, Tara. I called you with all my strength. You even stopped, perhaps stuck by an iota of conscience that was left. Then my brother–' Baali spat, 'I can't call him my brother anymore. That scoundrel, he persuaded you to leave me.'

Tara stood up in shock. The scream she heard that day was true. It was not her grieved mind playing tricks. *Oh God, oh God, she had left him to die without knowing it!*

He caught her chin and turned her face towards the wolf. 'This animal never gave up on me. But you, Tara, the one who I loved with all my heart, the one I called my Apasara was waiting for my death.'

Tara sobbed.

'When you went away with him, I was determined to live. The anger gave me strength to live. I had killed Mayavi. I survived a few days, eating his flesh. You made me a cannibal, Tara! I found a source of water and I used to drag myself on my knees. What if you had given up on me, Tara. I learned a great lesson that day. Animals have better souls. This wolf, nay my brother . . . not brother . . . I hate the word brother . . . this Chemba, my friend, he dug through the debris. His paws broke, yet he wouldn't give up on me. Baali laughed bitterly. 'And I loved my brother perhaps more than I loved you and he wanted me dead. See this animal. What did I do for such love from this beast? For giving him a few crumbs from my food, he showed me so much devotion. I gave you my whole world, and you . . .'

Tara had lost the strength to cry. She wished Baali would stop.

'He managed to reach me in a few months by digging through the mountain. We hunted rats together. He would bring me food, raw meat from his kill. Slowly, everything healed except the wound in my heart. I could never crawl through the way he had burrowed. We dug for months, shoulder to shoulder. This wolf and I. He taught me the meaning of love. A good lesson to have, for I had thought what you had for me is called love. How mistaken was I? I wanted to know why you betrayed me, Tara. I wanted to know why, you, of all people would do this. It took me so many days, I have lost count of days and time, to find my way out of the cave. Then we started to walk. I begged for food. I hewed firewood for a living and ploughed like an oxen. Chemba would wait at the edge of the villages. He was a wolf and heartless men would have stoned him to death. They don't deserve him, so I kept him hidden. No one was ready to believe I was Baali, the Maharaja of Vanara. I preferred not telling anyone the same. I was collecting news. I heard you had married him. You had a son. You were living happily. I was not bitter about your happiness, Tara. I always wanted you to be happy, Sugreeva to be happy, but not by betraying me.'

'No one betrayed you. Not your brother, nor me.'

'Hmm, do you love him so much, Tara that you would even justify his villainy? Do you hate me so much Tara?'

'Oh God, how will I prove the truth?'

'What truth, Tara? The truth that you married him the moment you were sure I died? The truth that you gave birth to his son?'

'He is your son, Baali,' Tara said in anger. She was no longer sacred. Baali had crossed all limits.

'He looks like him, Tara.'

'And you look like Sugreeva,' Tara retorted.

Baali had no answer for that.

'I . . . I don't know, Tara. I want to believe you, I want to believe that he is my son, but I can't Tara.' Baali sat on the bed with a thud. He stared at Angada.

'Sugreeva hasn't even touched me,' she said in a flat voice, looking away. Baali looked at the tear glistening in her eyes and sighed.

'I know you won't believe me,' she scoffed at him. Baali looked away.

'Alright,' Tara said, 'I will prove it the way the women of Aryavartha prove their chastity. I will do Agnipariksha. If I have lied, the flames would consume me. If I'm pure—'

Baali stood up, 'Tara—'

'If that is the only way to prove—' She was unable to complete the sentence and she looked down.

'Tara, we're Vanaras. I don't need Agnipariksha to believe my wife, but . . .'

Tara looked at him, ready to face whatever he demands.

'But . . . can you vouch on your son that . . .'

'Our son . . .'

Baali stood speechless. He stared at Angada who was now playing with a rattle and cooing in the cradle. Baali took him up and the baby watched his face without blinking. A drop of tear ran down Baali's cheeks.

'What is his name?'

'Angada,' Tara said in a hoarse voice. She moved near Baali and his hand encircled her. 'I am a fool, Tara. Why can't I stop loving you?' Baali said. Later, after they had cried their heart out, after recounting their respective ordeals, Tara broached the subject of forgiving Sugreeva. That was a mistake. Baali's face darkened.

'No, I may forgive you, Tara, for he had fooled you. But he trapped me. That boulder didn't come there by itself. Someone must have pushed it to fit the cave mouth or nudged it down from the top. I was a fool to think that he was playing pranks when he did that drama of his—don't you remember—the one he played immediately after our marriage. He has always lusted after you, Tara. Now I can recall every incident with clarity. I was a fool not to see. I cannot pardon him. He doesn't deserve any mercy. I should have killed him . . .'

Before Tara could say anything, Baali stormed out of the room. Tara ran behind him and saw Baali's way was blocked by Ruma. Baali tried to sidestep her but Ruma threw out her hand, blocking his way.

'Marry me.' Ruma's tone was defiant. Baali recoiled at the abrupt request.

'What?'

'Marry me,' Ruma repeated.

'You're Sugreeva's wife.'

'Wife,' Ruma scoffed. 'I had never been his wife. For that . . .' she looked at Tara and her lips curled in a derisive smile.

Baali tried to go, but she grabbed him. 'You've defeated Sugreeva. As per our law, now I belong to you, just as your wife belonged to him when he had defeated you.'

'But . . . Ruma, you're my brother's wife, you're like a daughter to me—'

'Daughter?' Ruma's voice was shrill, 'Do I look like your daughter to you? Our tribe's rules are different. I belong to the strongest. You're a strong man. You defeated my husband and he ran away. Now I belong to you. Marry me!'

'Move away.'

'Marry me, marry me, marry me!'

Baali shoved her out of his way and hurried out. Ruma screamed at the top of her voice, 'Your brother hasn't touched me. He never wanted me. He lusted over your wife. I was a discarded rag. Unused yet dirty. Please . . . please don't go away. I have no one, I have no one. No one wants me. Am I so ugly? Am I so undesirable?' She broke down and sat on the floor. Her heart-wrenching sobs made Tara wince. She approached her gingerly.

'Ruma . . .'

Ruma stopped crying. She glared at her and then smiled. She wiped her tears with the back of her palm. Tara watched her go to Angada's cradle. Ruma picked up Angada, 'You're the only one for me. Would you also ask me to move out of your way one day, darling? Maybe you will, for you will grow up to be a man. Let you not grow up. Let you always be my son, my precious, my darling.'

Tara watched Ruma helplessly. She didn't know how she could help her. Ruma took the baby and went out of the room without even looking at Tara.

An uneasy equilibrium set inside the palace. She heard from Nala that Hanuman had hidden Sugreeva somewhere and they were waiting for Baali's wrath to cool down. In public, Ruma acted as if Baali had married her. Inside the palace, Baali ignored her despite her desperate attempts. It was pitiful to watch her demean herself. Her desperation made Tara almost wish she succeeded in getting her husband. After a few months, Ruma gave up trying, but she kept the act of being Baali's favourite wife in public. She spent so much time taking care of Angada that Tara started resenting it. Angada started calling both of them mother, but it was evident he preferred Ruma to Tara.

Sugreeva came to palace after three months with the hope that Baali's rage would have been spent by then. He walked into the Sabha when Baali was in discussion with the council and bowed low before his brother. Baali stared at him in disbelief.

# Chapter 35

'Stop there!' Baali roared. The wolf that was lying near the throne sprang up and growled. Sugreeva prostrated on the floor and begged for forgiveness before Baali. Men in the Sabha stood with bated breath. Tara saw Baali struggling with conflicting emotions of hatred and love. Unfortunately, hate won. He kicked Sugreeva on his face, toppling him over. He screamed abuses. Sugreeva pleaded innocence and said he would take any punishment.

Tara felt sorry for Sugreeva. His devotion to his brother was touching. No man would debase himself like this in the Sabha where he had been the King a few months before. Tara touched Baali's shoulders and he glared at her. She should have taken the hint, but she pressed on, 'Can't you forgive your brother?'

Tara recoiled as Baali's face contorted with unspeakable rage. He took his club and started beating Sugreeva with it. Tara caught Baali's hand and pleaded, 'Please, please, he is your brother.'

Baali glowered at her and in disgust, threw the club down. It bounced near Sugreeva's head and arced to rest near Tara's feet. She watched Baali storming away from the Sabha with tearful eyes. She tried to pick up Sugreeva, but he refused her help. He stood up slowly and turned to Baali.

'Baali!' he screamed, stopping his brother at the threshold. The members of Sabha sucked a collective breath. No one had heard Sugreeva calling Baali anything but 'Anna'. Baali turned back and stood with his legs spread wide and his muscled arms in his hips. Sugreeva, bleeding from his face, lips swollen and split, nose broken, and eyes blackened, staggered a few feet towards Baali. He pointed a trembling finger at his brother and said, 'You've lost all sense. I have demeaned myself like a dog in front of you. Every time I came, you kicked me, you beat me to pulp, yet I didn't raise my hand in protest. I was hoping that, as the brother who I loved and admired, you would understand me and forgive me for something I hadn't done.'

'If you don't shut your mouth, I will tear you into two!' Baali roared.

Sugreeva staggered forward, 'You're a brute, a beast. You can kill me now because I allowed you to kick me and beat me. Take pleasure in killing a fallen man. You coward! If you're a man—'

Baali bellowed and rushed towards his brother. Sugreeva stood unflinching, 'If you're a man, I challenge you to a duel.'

Baali stopped a few feet short of Sugreeva.

Sugreeva turned towards the members of Sabha, 'Hear me all, I'm going to kill this brute. I'm going to win this throne and everything that belongs to this man. You fix the dates, you fix the venue and I shall be ready for the duel.'

He walked past Baali with his head held high. Baali left the Sabha in great anger. Tara followed him. She stood by the bed as he sat on it, his rage still bubbling in his face.

'He is your brother. You should have—'

Baali grabbed Tara's chin and pushed her back. Her head banged on the wall. He leaned on her, his face a few inches from her face. She stared at her husband in fear. He said in a chilling voice, 'You b***. You would have wanted me dead so that you can sleep with him. You want me to die, you want me to die, you b***, tell me, tell me!'

'Kill me; kill everyone,' she managed to say.

Baali glared at her and slowly his grip loosened. She started crying. He collapsed on the bed and sat with his head bent down. She stood up to walk out.

'I'm sorry.' Tara heard him say. She continued walking.

'Tara,' he called. It was not the voice of a defiant and arrogant man. It was that of a man with a tortured soul, a man broken from within. She turned back and rushed to his arms. She hugged him tight.

'I loved him, Tara, more than you, more than myself. He shouldn't have done this to me, Tara.'

She didn't say anything. Tara knew that anything she said would only add fuel to the fire.

'He lusts over you, Tara.'

Tara stiffened.

'I'm sure of it. He is a charmer. He has a way with women. I know him better than anyone else. And I can't afford to lose you Tara. Not even for my brother. I would give away the kingdom, but not you . . .'

'I—'

'No, don't say a word. I don't want you to lie. I know in some corner of your heart, you love him too. I can see it in the way you look at him. No, don't deny it. I can see it in the way he looks at you too. Not that you don't love me. I know you're fighting your urge, but we don't have control over certain emotions. I can't control my rage, Tara just like you can't—' Baali smiled bitterly.

'Please don't talk like this—'

'I'm not afraid of the truth, Tara. I can understand why my brother betrayed me. He would have trapped me for you. Except his love for you, nothing would have made him do anything that would have harmed me. Maybe as you say, I was trapped due to a natural disaster, but the Sugreeva I know, the brother I had brought up, he would have moved heaven and earth to save me. He would have moved the mountain. Instead he walked away, leaving me to die, hoping that I died. He did it for you, Tara. I can understand his guilt too. It would have broken his heart. I can feel his pain. Yet, I'm sure he would do that again to me, for you. He is insanely in love with you Tara, just as I am. This will only end with the death of one of us.'

Tara said within her sobs, 'No, it's wrong to say so. I have loved only you.'

Baali scoffed but kept running his fingers through her hair.

'Kill him in the duel,' she said.

Baali stiffened. He slowly extracted himself from her hug and stared into her eyes. 'Tara, do you think I can do that? I can't kill him even for you. Maybe I don't love you as much as he does.'

Tara held her husband tight and wept on his shoulders. Baali continued to run his fingers through her hair.

The duel was a farce. Sugreeva was no match for Baali who roared like a lion after smashing his opponent to the ground. Sugreeva pleaded, this time not for forgiveness but for giving him a warrior's death. Baali walked away without even bothering to reply.

Sugreeva yelled at Baali, 'You will pay for this insult, Baali. I don't mind dying at your hands, but don't leave me like this. Kill me, kill me and allow me to die like a warrior.'

Hanuman stopped Baali and said that as a warrior, Baali should honour Sugreeva by killing him. It was the rule of the duel. Baali ignored him and walked back to his palace. Thousands hailed Baali and many mocked Sugreeva, leaving him fuming. Tara knew Baali had done a grave mistake, but she also knew he had no choice. He was incapable of killing Sugreeva.

What she had dreaded happened that day. Hanuman, her friend and Guru, spoke up, 'Baali, your fall is near. You are arrogant and vain. Your hatred for Sugreeva astounds me. No man should carry so much hatred. I warn you, if you don't mend your ways, God will punish you.'

Baali scoffed, 'God? Which God? The God that let Vanaras be enslaved for many generations? The God that had made this stupid world? I believe in no God. I believe in the strength of my arms, Hanuman. Ask your friend, the devil called Sugreeva, to defeat me in a duel. Ask him not to depend on non-existent gods.'

She had never seen Hanuman so angry. Hanuman stormed out of Kishkinda, carrying the injured Sugreeva with him. The loss of friendship hit Tara hard. But she couldn't even utter the name of Hanuman at her home in fear of Baali's wrath. And she was dealt with another blow. Baali ordered Nala not to step into Kishkinda for Baali's spies had seen Nala speaking to Hanuman. Tara didn't even get a chance to say goodbye to her dear friend.

# Chapter 36

Tara did not see Sugreeva or Hanuman for a long time. Nala, however risked death to meet her secretly. She heard from him that Sugreeva and a few of his supporters had taken refuge in the Rishyamukha Mountains where Rishi Matanga's ashram was situated. They were banking on Baali's promise that he would never disturb Matanga ashram. It came as a hope for her that they still believed her husband was a man of honour who wouldn't break his promise. She had no one to speak to, to share her burdens with. She missed Nala and Hanuman. She often spent time at Riksarajas's grave, pouring out her woes to the affectionate eunuch who had died saving her.

Tara could see the mountains to the east, half clad in mist from her balcony. Many a time, she would sit there and wonder about Sugreeva. Sometimes, she felt pity for him. Unsolicited, thoughts came about how different life would have been with Sugreeva. She would feel guilty for harbouring such thoughts. Baali was a caring husband and except for the irritant of Ruma who kept claiming that she shared Baali with her, life went on in its usual path. Angada grew up, more under Ruma's care than Tara's. Baali was as good a father as he was a husband. He taught his son the use of swords and clubs. Often, father and son wrestled in the courtyard and whenever she saw it, she could not help thinking that the same courtyard would have witnessed Baali affectionately teaching Sugreeva the art of wrestling. She knew Baali was also assaulted by such uncomfortable memories and the sweet pain of nostalgia, for he too appeared lost in thought. Tara avoided saying anything about Sugreeva and struggled to keep an indifferent face whenever the conversation in the Sabha veered towards Sugreeva.

Meanwhile, her father had grown old and his deteriorating health worried her. Two of her father's friends had died and the thoughts of her father's health always gnawed at her. She wanted him to come and stay with her, but the old man refused to leave his humble hut and familiar surroundings. When she tried to persuade him to shift to Kishkinda, he asked her who would take care of his poor patients. Would they come to Kishkinda, to the palace with their ailments? Won't they be intimidated? He wanted to serve his impoverished villagers till his last breath. He would continue in his humble hut and leaky roof, waiting for his patients who walked or were carried through the thick jungle with the hope that the Vaidya would save their lives, heal their illness. He couldn't be selfish and retire in the comfort of a palace, much as he wished to spend time with his grandchild. The sight of familiar faces from her village in the streets of Kishkinda filled her with dread for she thought they carried the inauspicious news of her father's death.

As years passed, Tara had another worry that occupied her thoughts more. She often fought with Angada for the boy had a streak of rebelliousness and she blamed Ruma for spoiling her son. Her son was a sprightly young lad of fourteen by now, yet he clung to Ruma and barely talked to Tara.

Meanwhile, travelling singers brought tales of Rama, the elder prince of some distant Kingdom of the North, called Ayodhya, who had abdicated his throne to respect his father's wish and how his wife Sita and his brother Lakshmana had followed him to the jungle. Sutas and Magadhas sung about the virtues of the prince who many claimed was the incarnation of the blue God Vishnu. Many evenings were spent hearing the stories of Rama and his greatness. Life went on in Kishkinda like it had from time immemorial. No one cared about what happened outside. The attack from the Rakshasa tribe had ceased after Baali killed

Mayavi. Ravana, the king of Lanka, who Baali had defeated in a duel long ago and who had become a close friend of Baali, provided protection from the south.

However, when the news about Soorpanakha's humiliation came, Tara started getting worried. Soorpanakha, Ravana's younger sister had found Rama and Lakshmana in the forest and was smitten by Rama. Asura women were free to choose their mate, so she had asked Rama to marry her. Rama might have been shocked by this unusual request as in Deva land such forwardness was considered indecent on the part of a woman. He pointed to Lakshmana, who neither had the patience nor the sense of humour of his brother. He insulted Soorpanakha and sent her back to Rama who promptly asked her to seek his brother's hand. Sita laughed at the predicament of this silly woman and her promiscuousness. An enraged Soorpanakha tried to fight with Sita. She might have thought like any other woman in her land, Sita would fight with her to keep her mate. She might have been shocked when Lakshmana caught her hand and chopped off her nose and breasts. Her teenaged son Shambhiri, who came to seek justice for his mother, was brutally killed by Lakshmana and so were her cousins, Khara and Dushana.

After losing her breasts and nose and her sons and cousins, she had gone wailing to her brother, the Lord of Lanka. When Tara heard about the incident, she was terrified of the man who could mete out such cruelty upon a woman. She hoped they would avoid Kishkinda in their wanderings. Like Rakshasas, Vanara women were also free to choose their mate and if it were such a big crime from where this prince came and if he went on chopping breasts and nose, Tara could not fathom how Baali would react. After that, for many days there was no news. Then she heard that the King of Lanka had kidnapped Rama's wife Sita to avenge the humiliation of his sister. She also heard rumours that Rama's wife Sita was Ravana's long lost daughter. Tara could not understand why mutilating a woman or kidnapping another became the mark of manliness. That was not how her Baali would have dealt with it. He didn't chop off the breast of Ruma when she asked him to marry her. But Baali was a monkey man, an uncivilized Malecha. Maybe in the civilized world they dealt with such delicate things in a different way.

When the news of the death of the holy eagle Jatayu at the hands of Ravana came, the old timers were terrified. It was a harbinger of misfortune for the Vanara race, they claimed. The bird had got caught in the giant fans of Ravana's flying machine in which he was kidnapping Sita and was chopped into pieces. Baali laughed off such rumours. He had almost killed its twin in his childhood. A bird is a bird and there was nothing holy about it, Baali said to the consternation of the elders.

And then she heard the news that Rama and Lakshmana had entered the forests of Kishkinda. That filled her with dread. She knew Sugreeva was desperate for a victory over Baali and he may seek the help of the Northern Princes. When she mentioned it to Baali, he laughed the threat off.

'What can two princes do to me, Tara?'

'They say, the elder one is an incarnation of Lord Vishnu.'

'Ha, you started believing the stories that Magadhas sing. They say I'm the son of Indra and my brother the son of Surya. They say you came out of the ocean of milk. Have you heard the story where Hanuman got his cleft lips because he jumped to eat the sun and my father, Indra was scared about the sun being gobbled up and hit him with his Vajrayudha. There is no end to their imagination,' Baali laughed.

'I'm scared,' Tara said.

'You think I won't be a match for some unknown prince, Tara? I defeated Ravana,' Baali said twirling his moustache. She didn't have the courage to tell him how scared she felt.

# Chapter 37

When Hanuman came with the news about the two Princes from the North roaming around in the forest, Sugreeva didn't bother much. If they went through the forest without any mischief, it was good for them. Else, his crazy brother would deal with them. Sugreeva had lost all hopes. It seemed there was no one who could defeat Baali. Hiding in the hills of Rishyamukha, every day brought more gloom than the previous. The sage in whose Ashram he was living had forbidden the consumption of the arrack of gooseberry wine on his premises. He had to travel surreptitiously to the villages far away, leaving the safety of the Ashram to get his drink. Baali had promised the old saint that there would be no violence on the hill where the Ashram stood; this was the only thing that ensured Sugreeva's safety. It hurt his ego to be indebted for his life to a promise made by his brother. When he had some money left, Sugreeva had paid some singers to spread the rumour that Baali didn't step on the hill premises for fear of the sage's curse. If Baali stepped on the hill, Baali's head would burst into smithereens, Sugreeva's paid singers sung through the villages.

Baali got the tongues of a few singers plucked out, but such acts only added weight to the rumour. That was the only form of victory Sugreeva achieved over his brother. Hanuman had chided Sugreeva for the act. Hanuman was sure Baali would appear one day at Rishimukha hills just to lay rest to the rumours and Sugreeva would be left with no other place to escape to. However, Sugreeva knew his brother better. Balli would never break his promise even

262

at the cost of his reputation. He was safe as long as he never left the hill.

As the years passed, Sugreeva ran out of things he could sell. He had sold all his ornaments, copper, silver and gold. He had sold the fine silk dhoti which he was proud of and had gone back to wearing deer skin. Without liquor, without the luxuries he was used to, Sugreeva suffered his confinement, pining for Tara. Many a time, he felt he should fall at his brother's feet and beg for pardon. He tried a few times to meet his brother to work out a truce, but Baali was adamant. Sugreeva had never cared for Ruma, but he complained to anyone who cared to listen that his brother had taken his wife. Hanuman stood with Sugreeva because he thought Baali had done grave injustice to Sugreeva by forcefully taking Ruma. Sugreeva fuelled the anger in Hanuman by crying for Ruma. Sugreeva drew Ruma's picture on a rock and kept staring at it, imagining it to be Tara. He was desperate and that was the only way to keep Hanuman on his side. There were not many followers he could call his own.

A few weeks passed before Sugreeva agreed to meet the princes from the North. Hanuman took him to the hut of an old woman called Shabari where the princes were living. Sugreeva was uneasy as he had stepped out of the Rishimukha hills in broad daylight for the first time despite Hanuman's assurance that not even Baali would dare to harm Sugreeva when the princes were there. Sugreeva was sceptical as he had seen even Ravana defeated by Baali. When they reached the hut, he saw a fair man polishing his arrows. Hanuman whispered, 'That is the younger prince, Lakshmana. He is totally devoted to his brother.'

Sugreeva nodded. He too was once devoted to his brother. Then Tara came in between. Sugreeva sighed. Memories of Tara brought on a dull heartache. Lakshmana looked at Hanuman and scowled. Hanuman bowed to him and nudged Sugreeva to do the same.

'Brother is meditating,' Lakshmana said and resumed polishing his arrows. Hanuman and Sugreeva waited in the sun.

Hanuman sat on his haunches and invited Sugreeva to do the same. Sugreeva felt miserable. He had been the chief of Vanaras a few years before. Now he was standing as a supplicant before some unknown princes from faraway lands. He was not impressed with the slight built of Lakshmana. He had firm muscles and perhaps a good aim with his arrows, but what good that would do in a duel? If his elder brother was of Lakshmana's size, he had wasted a day and demeaned himself for no good.

'Don't worry, Sugreeva. Rama will help you. He knows the pain of losing one's wife.'

Sugreeva didn't reply.

'Besides, he is staying in an untouchable's home. He doesn't consider people as high or low.' Hanuman's voice was filled with admiration. 'How many would do that, especially from Deva land? You will love him, Sugreeva. He is such a noble man. They say the old woman Shabari had given him mangoes after biting them to test for their ripeness and he ate them without any hesitation. Have you heard of Ahalya?'

The name sent a shiver down Sugreeva's spine. He wanted to go back. He felt he was doing something sinful. Tara's smiling face flashed in his mind and Baali's words came, scathing his soul. His brother had told him, 'Sugreeva, your sister-in-law is like your mother. Never forget that.' He had no idea why Baali told him that. Was it a warning? Did his brother know he had coveted his wife? Those casual words had spoilt his fantasy about Tara forever. Whenever he thought about Tara, his adopted mother Ahalya's face came to his mind. He fought such thoughts. And to make matters worse, he felt that the pull of desire towards Tara didn't abate. Guilt made his love even more thrilling.

'The poor woman was chained for she had sinned. Chained to a rock for so many years. Rama freed her. He gave redemption to a fallen woman. A person with a divine soul can only do such courageous deeds.'

Sugreeva shifted on his haunches uneasily. What would Rama want in return? And how was he going to kill . . . nay . . . convince Baali to take him back?

A tall dark man appeared, and Hanuman stood up with alacrity. Lakshmana also stood up and Sugreeva got up reluctantly. His heart sank upon seeing Rama. Though muscular, he was no match for Baali if it came to a duel. Rama saw Hanuman and his face lit up with a smile. He rushed to Hanuman and hugged him. Sugreeva stood awkwardly, watching them. He saw Hanuman's eyes fill up with tears. Up close, Rama looked tired. His eyes were puffy, like someone who cried a lot secretly. Maybe he missed his wife who the Asura King Ravana had kidnapped.

'This is Sugreeva,' Hanuman introduced and Sugreeva gave a nod to Rama. He had wasted his day. This man was no match for his brother. He barely came up to Sugreeva's shoulders and Baali towered over Sugreeva.

Rama grasped Sugreeva's palms and said, 'I can understand your pain, Sugreeva. I am suffering the same loss. My Sita . . .'

Sugreeva looked away, embarrassed. Perhaps, the man may not like anyone else seeing his grief. Rama's eyes had filled up and so had Hanuman's. Lakshmana had come near them. His face was contorted with suppressed rage.

'I will help you win your wife from your evil brother. I hope you and your people will help me in finding mine,' Rama said softly.

Sugreeva nodded, though he was sure Baali would snap this young man into two like a twig if it came to a duel. 'I will,' he mumbled. His doubt would have reflected on his face. Rama took the bow and arrow from Lakhsmana and started walking. Without a word, Sugreeva and Hanuman followed. They reached a clearing. From their they could see the seven palmyaras in the holy grove. The river beside was simmering in the sun.

Sugreeva saw Rama notching an arrow in his bow. The tip of the arrow caught the sun and glittered. The twang of the bowstring startled Sugreeva and with a whoosh, the arrow flew past his ears. The arrow vanished among the palmyra trees. Sugreeva looked at Rama. What was he trying to prove? Then he heard a distant rumbling and turned towards the grove. The first palmyara tree swayed and with a crack that came a tad later after he saw it, its canopy crashed down. In the next blink of eye, one by one, the canopy of the other six trees tumbled down. Involuntarily, Sugreeva sucked in his breath. That was impressive. This man could shoot. But how was it going to help in a hand-to-hand combat? Baali was sure to laugh at such tricks. He would say arrows are for cowards where you shot from a distance. Men fought face-to-face. Would Rama take up that challenge, especially when his body weight was not even equal to half of Baali's?

Rama patted him on his back and left without a word. Hanuman looked at him with admiring eyes. Lakshmana said, 'Don't worry Vanara. My brother will get you your wife.'

Sugreeva's eyes flashed with anger. How dare this prince call him a monkey. Before he could react, Lakshmana had followed Rama.

Hanuman was about to follow him, when Sugreeva grasped his wrist. He hissed, 'They don't respect us.'

Hanuman looked faraway, 'Sugreeva. Your brother has sinned. He has forcefully taken your wife.'

'That may be true. But I am Baali's brother. No one calls us monkeys. We are Vana Naras.'

'Baali called himself a Vanara.'

'No one calls me a monkey and gets away with it.'

Hanuman put his hand on Sugreeva's shoulders, 'Sugreeva, don't you understand? Only if you are a monkey, can they help.'

'How does–' Then it hit Sugreeva with a great force.

'They are going to hunt my brother like an animal. Is . . . is it fair?' Sugreeva asked.

'Do you know any other way to regain your wife? Do you know anyone who could fight Baali and defeat him in a duel?'

Sugreeva looked down. He had no answer.

'I know it appears wrong, but there is no other way. We can't allow a strong man to get away with evil actions. He took your wife which is an evil thing to do. Killing him by any means is the right thing to do. It breaks my heart to say so, but there is no other way Sugreeva. You think Rama is happy about it? But there is no other way. Your brother, you, me—all of us are monkeys. Vanaras. A king can hunt animals. That is their dharma.'

'But . . . but—'

'Forget your wife then.'

Sugreeva didn't want to say he cared nothing for his wife. He wanted Tara. But if he said that, he would lose Hanuman. His friend might even kill him. There was no choice. He had to do it. He would do anything for Tara. Once the deed was done, he would love her like no other man could. He would shower her with more love than his brute of a brother was ever capable of. He ran to catch up with Rama. He fell at Rama's feet.

'Swami, only you can help me. Please act on your dharma. Please help me regain my wife.' Sugreeva hugged Rama's feet and wept. Rama's compassionate hands lifted him up. Rama hugged him close to his heart. Sugreeva wept for the monkey brother he had once adored and loved.

# Chapter 38

Tara's worst fears were confirmed when Sugreeva came to the palace gate and started hurling abuses at Baali. The Sabha was on at the time. Baali heard the commotion and jumped down from his throne. Swinging his club, he rushed out. Tara ran behind him to stop him. She threw her hands across the door blocking his way and cried, 'Something is wrong. If the enemy who has been dormant for years has suddenly become bold, it means he has got help from someone powerful. Ignore him, please don't go out.'

'You want me to hide under my cot like a scared kitten? He has challenged me and as per our custom, the king who doesn't accept the challenge has to abdicate. Move away, Tara. Let me teach him a lesson.'

'Please, don't go.'

Baali pushed her out of his way and rushed out, screaming at Sugreeva. Tara watched him approaching Sugreeva and when he reached near, Sugreeva took off. Baali chased him, swinging his club. Something was wrong. She ran out, pleading Baali to come back. She saw Baali and Sugreeva circling, with their clubs in their hands, facing each other like fighting cocks. Why did Sugreeva choose this place? If he wanted to fight, he should have done it at the courtyard of the palace where everyone would have seen him either beating Baali or getting beaten by him. That would have lent him weight in his claim of kingship had he defeated Baali. Why did he run like a hare and then choose to fight away from the eyes of everyone? Chemba was growling at the tree. What was the wolf seeing that her eyes couldn't see? Tara looked carefully,

and her heart stopped beating. She gasped. Someone was hiding behind a tree.

An arrow peeped out, pointing at the fighting warriors. She screamed to alert the warriors. Sugreeva looked at her and at that moment, Baali hit him across his chest. Sugreeva fell down and Baali was on him like a typhoon on a rickety ship in the sea. Baali beat him mercilessly until Sugreeva somehow found his chance to flee. He vanished behind the bushes and Baali laughed uproariously.

'Fool, whenever you want to get beaten up, please drop by,' he roared. Tara walked to the tree. She had to find out who was hiding there. But when she reached there, no one was around. Baali came near her and grabbed her by her waist. He was covered in sweat. He lifted her up and swirled her. He was enjoying his victory. When he placed her down, and when her head stopped spinning, she said, 'Someone was waiting here. He was trying to shoot you.'

Baali looked around and remarked, 'Who will do such a cowardly thing, Tara? No one was here.'

Tara was sure she had seen someone. She observed Chemba was nervous and was sniffing around. But Baali's footsteps had erased any proofs. She pointed to the wolf and said he could smell someone. Baali laughed it off and whistled the wolf to him. It came reluctantly, looking back over its shoulders. Tara was filled with dread. They walked in silence, back to their cave palace.

'Look,' Tara gripped Baali's wrist and pointed to the palmyra grove. She was shocked beyond belief. The seven palmyras appeared headless, as if someone had chopped them off with a powerful arrow. They ran to the grove. Tara found footprints all around. There were arrow marks on the palmyra. Someone was using it for target practice. The image of the arrow that peeped out flashed across her mind. Jasmine creepers had started wilting. The grove lay in disarray. The grove which hid a thousand secret memories now emanated a sense of brooding, a premonition of something sinister. Tara felt that the air was thick with conspiracy. Something evil had been conceived here. Her nails dug into Baali's wrist.

'I saw death lurking at you. Be careful, please, be careful.' She cried. Her face had gone white as a sheet.

Baali frowned. He could not deny the evidence that was staring him in his face. He walked to the palace, lost in his thoughts. She walked quietly behind him. She was feeling feverish. By evening, Baali had regained his cheerfulness. He played with Angada and father and son wrestled in the courtyard as the sun set over River Pampa.

The night was deliciously cold. Tara was lying in the arms of her beloved. She was unable to sleep. To keep her mind away from the scary thoughts, she tried to think about the days when she was happy and free. She tried to recollect the magic of first love. She moved closer to Baali and put her arms across his chest. Through the cracks in the cave roof, moonlight dripped inside, painting faint circles on the damp floor. She could hear the wind ruffling the leaves outside. Sometimes, the breeze carried the fragrance of Champaka flowers. She could hear the babble of the brook if she cared to listen.

Tara lay her head on Baali's chest. It always filled her heart with joy to feel the rhythm of his heartbeat. For a shy moment, she thought it whispered her name. She raised her head and looked at his face. He was fast asleep. Only someone who had no deceit in his mind could sleep so soundly. Everything about Baali was straight, except for his impossibly curly hair and beard. She ran her fingers through his hair. He murmured something in his sleep. She kept her ears close to his lips. It was her name. She smiled. Her fears slowly started melting away. She put her head back on his chest and closed her eyes in contentment. Everything was going to be alright.

Some fireflies had entered the cave, painting everything inside with a faint green light. A firefly danced around Baali's face. She could see the bruises on his strong shoulders. Blood had clotted like leeches where Sugreeva's club had hit him. For a fleeting moment, Tara thought about Sugreeva. Then she pulled her mind back to the dimly-lit cave. In every nook and corner, monkey men and women were perched. Most of them were fast asleep. Others, who were awake, talked in soft whispers so that the sleep of their king wasn't disturbed. They were her husband's loyal subjects. For them, he was God. For fourteen years, he had ruled them well and made the city prosperous. He was a just ruler.

From the other side of the cave, she heard a soft whimper. Angada might be awake. He was running a fever. The boy hadn't been sleeping properly for quite some days. He had been haunted by nightmares. She had wanted to put him beside her and tend to him, but Baali would hear nothing of it. A Vanara boy can't be tugging along his mother's tail always, Baali used to say. Angada was only fourteen years old, but Baali treated him like an equal. He wanted Angada to grow up to be a better warrior than he was and in the name of training, Baali showed no mercy to him. She often pitied Angada for being her husband's son. It was tough to live up to the reputation that his father had built with his legendary deeds.

Angada whined again. She sighed and disentangled herself from Baali's grip. She rushed to where her son was sleeping. She frowned when she saw him. He was hugging Ruma. A pang of jealousy ran through her heart. This woman had no right over her son. She snarled at her.

'Nightmares as usual,' Ruma said. Tara shook her son awake. Angada looked at her and then at Ruma.

'Come and sleep beside us,' Tara snapped at her son.

'I will sleep here,' Angada turned away.

Tara yanked Angada's hands. 'You're not a small child, get up, hurry.'

'Let him be here, sister. Our son is scared. He is getting nightmares about our husband being dead.' Ruma tried to intervene.

Tara despised this woman. Our son indeed! Angada was born in her womb. He had drunk her milk. Ruma had no right over her. Wily woman! Tara was sure that Ruma didn't care much for Angada. She was simply trying to ascertain her right over her husband.

'He is neither your son nor is Baali your husband,' Tara hissed.

'Oh, sister, why're you so angry? I was once Sugreeva's wife, but since Baali defeated him, I became his. Just like how you used to be Sugreeva's wife when Baali was thought to be dead.' Ruma smiled at her. Tara's lips trembled in anger. She wanted to pronounce a scathing retort, but she could not think of any.

'Baali doesn't care for you. You're just the spoils of war,' Tara managed to say as she turned back. She had never spoken harshly to Ruma in sixteen years of their life together. But tonight, she felt she had the right to do so. She didn't like the way Ruma had been behaving since she had heard about the duel between Sugreeva and Baali. She was unusually aggressive. It was as if she knew something. It was as if she was waiting in anticipation of something.

'That is the rule of the jungle, sister. The one who wins gets the mate and the kingdom. Tomorrow, if Baali is defeated, you too will be a spoil of war.' Ruma's laugh scalded her ears.

Tara wanted to retort that Baali was never going to be defeated, but she didn't want to tempt fate. She dragged Angada to where she was sleeping and ordered him to sleep in her bed. Angada looked at her confused. His father's strict demeanour often scared him. She shoved her son down. The boy lay down, gingerly, unsure of himself. Baali turned in his sleep and put a protective hand over his son. She saw Angada eye his sleeping father with surprise. When he looked at her, she smiled and nodded her head. Angada hugged his father back. Baali didn't move, but his embracing hands never left Angada. Tara's eyes grew misty. She put her hand over her family, holding them close. Baali's hands sought hers and their finger's entwined. She felt like crying. This was too precious to lose. She tried to push away the evil premonitions she was feeling, but they came like waves, sometimes ebbing, sometimes cresting, but relentless. *Oh, mother of the forest, let us be happy like this always*, she prayed. Fireflies danced around them, giving an ethereal glow to the cave. She felt uneasy. She hugged her family closer and tried to sleep.

Sleep refused to be coaxed and kept away from her like a petulant lover. With a sigh, she sat up. There were snoring noises from dark corners of the caves. The wolf slept in the corner of the chamber. Her heart went for Chemba. Her husband's precious friend. She went to caress its red coat and it wagged its tail without opening its eyes. She felt a rush of affection for the beast.

There were many Vanaras sleeping on the floor. She treaded carefully, so as not to step on them and wake them from their sound sleep. She was jealous of the Vanaras who never worried about the future or the past. She wished she had that skill. Maybe she was an Apsara as Baali used to say and not an ordinary Vanara woman. That thought brought a smile to her lips. She came out of the cave mouth and stood at the edge of the cliff.

It was breathtakingly beautiful outside. A sliver of a moon floated in the sky sprinkled with thousands of stars. River Pampa glittered like a silver necklace as it snaked its way through the rocky valley of Kishkinda. A crisp wind played with her hair carrying the fragrance of Ankola flowers from the hills above. The smell brought back a thousand memories. She wished she was still the carefree young girl she used to be. She wanted to relive the movements when the first love flowered in her heart. She wanted to laugh the same way and feel the pangs of yearning. She closed her eyes, and everything rushed back with the same joy and pain. A delicious, numbing, exhilarating pain. The pain of first love. And she shuddered at the thought she was having. She was betraying Baali by such thoughts. She was scared. Baali had won again the previous evening. Why was she having such dreaded thoughts? Why did the fear refuse to go away?

# Chapter 39

When dawn broke, Baali was surprised to see her still standing on the balcony. He came and encircled her narrow waist with his hands. He pressed her close to him and looked into her eyes. 'Tara,' he whispered softly and kissed her forehead.

She could not withhold herself. She sniffled. 'Be careful,' she whispered in his ears.

They were shocked from their dream-like moment by a bone-chilling roar at the gate. Sugreeva had come back. He was wearing a garland of hibiscus around his neck. It looked so incongruous and dandy on him. He was screaming abuses. Baali cursed and was about to rush down when Tara hugged him tight.

'Don't go.'

Baali sighed. He gently said in her ears, 'Tara, you know I can't stay here like a cuckold. I have to go and fight.'

'An enemy who was beaten yesterday has come back in the morning, full of confidence. He has powerful friends. He is laying a trap.'

'Sugreeva is a fool. He will never learn however much I beat him. It's his fate. Had it been some other enemy, I would have killed him long ago. I can neither bring myself to kill the boy who I brought up, nor will he grow up strong enough to kill me. This joke will continue.' Baali laughed.

'Sugreeva is powerful. He may win this time. Please–'

Chemba came running to the balcony. His ears were straight. He let out a low growl.

'Tara,' Baali's frowned, 'Are you supporting him? Do you think he can beat me? Do you secretly wish that?'

'Why do you talk like that?'

'A good wife will encourage her warrior husband to win. She wouldn't sap his confidence with her tears and fears.'

'I'm a bad wife. It's alright. I can accept that tag. But please don't go. I saw the enemy hiding behind the tree yesterday.'

'Who? That Rama? I don't think he would do that, Tara. No warrior would do that. I have fought warriors of all tribes—Rakshasas, Vanaras, Asuras, Yakshas, Gandharvas—I have fought mean men, uncouth barbarians, cannibals. I have fought beasts. They might have been evil or noble, but they fought face-to-face with me.'

Tara cried, 'He was hiding there. If not for killing you, why should he hide with a loaded bow?'

'Tara, when even the most evil of tribes like Rakshasas chose to fight me face to face, I can't believe a Prince, who the bards claim to be an Avatar of God, would do such a thing. No, Tara, he can't do that. He wouldn't do that. And even if he does that, what choice do I have Tara? I don't know to hide and shoot. I know only to fight face-to-face like a man. And I'm sure, even if Rama wants to do that, my Sugreeva wouldn't allow that. It was not how I had brought him up. So there is nothing to worry. And if Rama comes to fight me, face-to-face, like what I believe him to do once I defeat Sugreeva, I would fight him too. If he is a better warrior, let him kill me. That would be an honour for me. So don't stop me, Tara.'

Baali turned to go but Chemba stood in his way.

'Move' Baali said to Chemba but the wolf refused to give way. Baali scratched behind its ears and patted its head. He asked the wolf to stay quiet. Chemba whimpered and wagged its tail. Tara watched helplessly as Baali walked away with deliberate steps. She watched him with tearful eyes when he crossed the gate of the palace and vanished. Chemba started whining.

Sugreeva had run away like the previous day. Tara knew what was in store. She didn't share the naïvety of Baali. She knew men who could brutally chop the breast and nose of a woman wouldn't play by the rules that a rustic like Baali cherished. She walked to the riverbank, dreading every moment, fearing her every step that took her near the place where Baali's death could be waiting. Chemba ran ahead of her, growling, whining and occasionally howling. The behaviour of the red wolf filled her mind with horrible premonitions.

The sky was overcast and heavy, pregnant with rain. The humidity was unbearable. Not even a leaf stirred. Dark clouds swirled above her head. When she reached there, Baali had thrown Sugreeva on the ground. Baali placed his right leg on Sugreeva's chest and roared. Chemba was growling at a tree that lay about twenty feet away. The wolf's ears were alert, eyes squinted in concentration and tail straight. Tara looked to see whether someone was hiding behind the tree like previous day. No one was there. Tara sighed in relief. Baali roared in victory. He was alive. She could not control her tears. All her fears were unfounded. She felt guilty that she had suspected Rama to be someone who was capable of shooting in sly. She said a word of prayer.

At that moment, an arrow whooshed through the air. She turned in surprise to see a dark young man ducking behind the tree. She watched in horror as the arrow pierced Baali's chest. She screamed, but no sound came out. She ran to her husband. Chemba reached first. Baali fell like a huge tree struck by lightning. She went near him, beating her head, crying, but she had lost her voice. Baali saw her with pity-filled eyes. She collapsed near him and took his head on her lap. Chemba whined piteously. It kept its head on Baali's heaving chest and stared at his face with all the sorrow in the world.

'As usual, you were right, Tara.' Baali gave a sad smile and blood bubbled out through his mouth.

'Don't go, Baali, don't go,' she wanted to say, but no sound came out. She was feeling cold. She shivered. He was dying in her arms. Sugreeva had got up and he watched his brother dying. He collapsed on his knees and buried his head in his palms.

Rama and his brother came near them. Baali saw the man who had hidden behind a tree to shoot him dead. Chemba stood up and bared his teeth. Baali patted the wolf to calm it down. It placed its head on his chest. Baali folded his hands to greet the uninvited guests. There was a derisive smile on Baali's lips.

'Welcome, Rama.'

Tara saw the dark man shifting his eyes, nervous, uneasy. Beside him stood a man with an angry scowl.

'You're unique, Rama,' Baali said.

Rama stood watching Baali die. Lakshmana's lips curved into a derisive smile.

'May I know why you shot me slyly instead of facing me like a man, Lord Rama?' Baali asked. His voice was getting weak.

'You had done injustice to your brother.'

'You could've faced me like a man,' Baali said.

'You stole his wife,' Rama declared.

'You could've faced me like a man,' Baali laughed.

'You're evil and my dharma is to eliminate evil,' Rama said.

'You could've fought evil like a man.' Baali laughed and vomited blood. Ignoring it, he laughed again.

'I'm a Kshatriya and my duty is to vanquish evil,' Rama said.

'You could've faced me like a man,' Baali said again.

'It's the Dharma of a Kshatriya to hunt animals. You're not human. You're a Vanara. I can hunt you and kill. It's Kshatriya dharma.'

'Ah, we're animals. Vanaras. Now I understand, my lord. Our lives don't matter. We're mere animals. Yes, my lord, we belong to the forest. We aren't familiar with the noble ways of civilized men. In the jungle, the tiger hunts its prey by stalking, like how you did, Rama. But the tiger does it because it's hungry. What are you hungry for, Rama?' Baali scoffed. Rama stood without a reply.

Baali turned to Tara. 'Don't cry, my dear. I have been killed by a God. The rules of men don't apply to them. As the Brahmins say, maybe I will get moksha. I don't know what that is. All I wanted was to live. Who can question gods, Tara? So bid me goodbye, dear,' Baali turned to his brother, 'Sugreeva . . .'

Sugreeva crawled near him. Baali's hands were shivering. Life was ebbing out of him. 'Son, I'm sorry I stood in your way. I know you love her. I was a selfish man. I mean a selfish animal. A mere Vanara. What do I know about nobility, son? I don't blame you, Sugreeva, my dear brother.'

Sugreeva broke into sobs. He hugged his brother and cried, 'I'm sorry. I'm a sinner.'

Baali touched the garland Sugreeva was wearing. 'It doesn't look good on you, brother. Garlands are for gods. We're animals, brother. We eat, love, fight and die. Our lives hold no value for anyone except us. Don't cry my brother. You might have promised something in return for the favour Rama did for you. Do it with all your heart. And take care of my . . . I mean . . . your Tara. She is a wise woman. She had warned me, but I was a fool. Don't ignore her advice. And take care of our Angada. And be nice to Ruma. The heaven for animals is waiting for me. Or do they allow animals into heaven? Don't bother. I'm not going to leave my forest. I will be the breeze, I will be the butterfly, I will be the grass . . . ah, I'm blabbering. My time is nearing. Tara, my love . . .'

Baali tried to kiss Tara, but lost his strength midway. His hand kept caressing the wolf on his chest. His strength ebbed away and he collapsed and died in the arms of two people he loved most. Chemba let out a heart-wrenching howl that fell on Kishkinda like a curse.

It started raining, first as a drizzle but soon copiously, as if Indra, the God of rain and thunder had lost all his restraint and was weeping unabashedly at the injustice done to his son. Tara watched in shock and disbelief. Memories rushed like torrents. She felt numb. She placed Baali gently on the ground and turned away, unable to see the blood that had pooled below him being washed away. Rain was washing away even the stains of Baali's blood from her clothes. The wolf lay on its paws, staring at the face of his master, waiting for his call, for a gentle pat on its head.

Tara tried to stand up but her head reeled. She gathered all her will and stood up on her weak legs. Rain lashed at her face like a whip. She stood drenched, gathering herself. Her fists curled and nails dug into her palms. She lifted her head and stared at Rama. He averted his eyes. She said in an even voice, 'I don't know whether you're God or a man. For me, you're just my husband's killer. I curse you. Though I'm not sure whether an animal's curse will have any effect on the gods, that is all a poor widow can do. I curse you. For whatever purpose you had killed my husband, let it be futile. I heard you're going to fight for reclaiming your wife. I curse you that you will never know happiness with her, even if you manage to win.'

She didn't wait for Rama's reply. She walked away, leaving Sugreeva to grieve over her husband's body. Hanuman ran after her, calling out her name loudly. She didn't bother to stop for her friend. He managed to catch up with her near the eternal fire and stood before her, panting. He was about to console her with wise words, but when he looked at her distraught face, he became incapable of saying anything. He folded his hands, seeking forgiveness.

'I have to plan for my Baali's funeral', she said softly. Hanuman stood with his head bowed, tears streaming down his cheeks. 'Sugreeva is in no state to plan anything. I have to arrange the funeral', she said, looking far away. Her wise friend stood like a statue. She walked away, repeating she had to make arrangements for the funeral, had to make arrangements, had to make arrangements for funeral befitting a King.

The wolf continued to howl, piercing the conscience of all who boasted one. For others, gods were there.

# Chapter 40

Later, when the funeral was over and when wise men had consoled her with words like the soul doesn't die and it discards bodies like old clothes, the kind of words which one can afford to say when the death has occurred not in one's own family, and she had given courage to Angada and Sugreeva, she went home to grieve alone. Her father didn't say anything. It wasn't needed. She just wanted to get away from the memories of Baali. She had failed miserably. Sugreeva came seeking her and begging her forgiveness. She was indifferent to him initially.

Slowly, her zest for life started asserting. Hadn't Baali himself asked her to live with Sugreeva? She was tormented by the thought of whether she was justifying her wish. Was she using Baali's words as an excuse? What will people say if she lived with the killer of her husband? Angada was devastated by the loss. Did she not have a duty to Angada? But every time she tried to convince herself that Baali had gone irrevocably from her life, she felt guilty. He had cheated death once, would he do that again? Would all this turn out to be a nightmare, perhaps a prank played by Sugreeva?

The rains were torrential that year as if mother earth needed more water to wash away the stain of Baali's brutal murder. She walked to the place where Baali's ashes were buried. To her surprise, she found Chemba lying over the umbrella stone paved over Baali's grave. The wolf let out a low bark and ran to her. All the courage and restraint of Tara broke at the sight of the beast. It ran to the stone and attempted to dig the stone with its paws. After a few attempts, it laid down panting. It had not given up hope. It had not given up on the one it loved. Once again, the animal's love was proving stronger than hers. She wished she could share the same hope and faith. She went near the wolf and found there were cracks between its nails. Chemba might have been desperately trying to save its master as it had once done. The wolf whined when she touched the blisters. She dragged the wolf to the river and washed its paws. Then she applied a paste of herbs. The moment she left it, Chemba ran to the grave and attempted to dig the stone with its bruised paws.

She put her cheeks on the grave with a faint hope that he would talk to her. Perhaps, he might be waiting there with his charming smile. He would call her Apsara. She broke down at the thought, gathered herself and walked to the cave palace. Behind her, the wolf continued its futile attempt to dig the stone, whining as its blisters broke, yet not giving up.

Tara continued walking in the slush. River Pampa had swelled up in the monsoon and had overrun its banks. She could not find the place where Baali had fallen. With a heavy heart, she walked to the overgrown palmyra grove. The headless palmyras stood as a reminder of man's wanton cruelty to nature. Moss had started growing in their barks. Mushrooms sprouted from their roots which had started putrefying. She stood amid the headless palmyras and whispered, 'Speak to me, dear.'

She waited for an answer. Did she hear a faint laugh? A whiff of breath at the back of her neck? She turned back. Nothing. 'You're here. I can feel you,' she said. She was scared whether she was going insane. She heard the rustle of leaves and turned. It was Chemba. The wolf came to her side and waited. 'He is here,' Tara mumbled. My Baali has cheated death again, she reassured herself.

'My Apsara,' the wind whispered. She bit her lips, trying to muffle a sob that threatened to overcome her.

'Dear, go to my brother. He is in trouble.'

She was angry. She hand't come here to talk about his brother. She wanted to talk about herself. She wanted him back in her hands. Now. 'Please come back,' she screamed.

'Only you can save him now.'

'Talk to me. Did you mean it when you said I can—' she didn't want to complete the sentence. She didn't have the heart to ask him whether he had meant it when he said she should marry Sugreeva.

She waited but the wind was just howling now. For a moment, she thought it was Baali who was crying in pain. He was too brave to cry, she chided herself. 'Talk to me!' she screamed into the wind. The wolf trotted back to the grave and resumed its pointless work.

She remembered his request. She ran to the palace. As she neared the cave palace, she sensed something was wrong. Many men were huddled in the courtyard. Tara rushed inside the palace. What she saw chilled her heart. Sugreeva was sloshed. He sat on the throne blabbering something. Pots of palmyra toddy lay strewn or broken on the floor around him. Ruma was wailing at the top of her voice. And with his foot on the handrest of the throne, Lakshmana was towering over Sugreeva.

# Chapter 41

'I will chop your head off, you good-for-nothing monkey!' Lakshmana screamed, waving his sword menacingly over the head of the Vanara king. 'You promised my brother that you would send your monkey army to fight the King of Lanka. And here you are—drunk and having fun with your ugly wife, not bothering about the promise you made to my brother, Rama, the best of all men and Avatara of Vishnu. Uncivilized barbarians!'

Tara was enraged by the arrogance of Lakshmana. Had Baali been sitting on the throne, would this man dare to talk like this? Was this the way to treat the chief of the Vanara tribe? Are we slaves? She wanted to drag him out of the palace. Then she paused. Lakshmana was a dangerous man. This was the same man who had chopped Soorpanakha's breasts and nose. It was wise to be diplomatic. She was angry that no one tried to stop Lakshmana. Why were they in such awe of the two brothers? Or were they being prudent?

'Your brother killed my brother.'

Tara heard Sugreeva's sloshed voice above the din. Sugreeva was not being prudent at all. Lakhsmana grabbed Sugreeva by his uthariya and yanked him down from the throne. He caught Sugreeva's hair and raised the sword.

'Ugly monkey, he did it because you requested him to do that. What did my brother gain by that act except the ignominy of someone who hides behind a tree and shoots his enemies?'

'Your brother cheated my brother and shot him on the sly. He didn't have the courage to face my brother.' Sugreeva looked at Lakshmana defiantly.

284

'Thankless Vanara. My brother, in his infinite kindness, did such an act for you and now you blame him!'

Tara knew Sugreeva would be dead if she didn't do something. She rushed to Lakshmana with folded hands and pleaded with him. 'Swami, my husband is drunk. He doesn't know what he is saying. We're mere Vanaras. We don't know what is right and wrong, Swami. We're like children. We're your Dasas, your slaves. Is it not the duty of the master to correct us when we go wrong? Forgive him, Swami. Your brother made me a widow once, please don't make me a widow again. I will ensure that once he comes back to senses, he will put the entire Vanara army under your brother's command so that he can reclaim his wife.'

Lakshmana glowered at her. Tara waited nervously. Lakshmana was unpredictable. She relaxed when Lakshmana threw Sugreeva down and put his sword in his scabbard.

'You're reputed to be wise. Make him see reason,' Lakshmana said with surprising calmness and walked away. All the Vanaras rushed to their fallen king once Lakshmana had left the palace. Tara and Ruma helped Sugreeva back to his throne and he sat listlessly. Tara was not sure whether he would remember what had happened in his Sabha when he came to his senses.

'Send for Hanuman. Send for every Vanara.' Tara commanded her ministers. 'The King is going to war.'

Soon the entire Vanara army assembled in the courtyard. Tara looked at them with a heavy heart. Outside the fort stood many women and children, scared and worried. They had never known of war except through the stories that bards brought them. Disputes were settled by duels and their King used to take care of that. They were unaware of a war where their men would leave them and go to distant lands with no guarantee of their return. Fear was writ large on the faces of everyone. Tara had no idea what she would tell them. She wished Baali was there to handle this crisis and then laughed at her folly. Had he been there, such a situation wouldn't have risen at all. *Give me courage*, she prayed, for she was sending

many innocent men to their deaths for a cause that had not a thing
to do with them. She wondered how she was going to face the
widows who would lose their husbands, the children who would
lose their fathers and mothers who would lose their sons. She took
a deep breath and closed her eyes, trying to gather strength. *Baali,
I want you beside me*, she prayed. She gripped the balustrade of the
balcony for strength and started her address.

'Your king is going to war. So far, we have fought only for
food or mates. So, war may be an unknown concept for you. War
is the way in which civilized people butcher each other.'

There was an angry murmur among the crowd. She pressed
on.

'You might be wondering what us Vanaras, who were living
peacefully with our little fights and friendships, who were minding
our own business and bothering no one, living in what we call the
animalistic, primitive way, have to do with this war of so-called
civilized men? We were born free, we lived free. We even fought
free and died free. We fought only for food and mates. Now you
will be fighting against the Asuras who have never bothered us and
have no enmity with us. You will be killing strangers with whom
you had no quarrel. That is the price you pay when you involve an
outsider in a quarrel between brothers.'

Tara paused. She saw that her people were confused. She had
no intention of sending her men without making them understand
what they were getting into.

'I have never seen war and I'm sure most of you also wouldn't
have seen any. War, I have heard, is a dirty business. It follows no
rules of the duel. Cunningness is valued over bravery and all is fair
in war. But we're yet to be civilized. We're uncouth, uncultured
Vanaras who speak in a strange tongue. Strange for others, but
that doesn't matter. We don't matter. We may consider ourselves
just one among many tribes that populate this Jambudweepa, a
strand in the rich tapestry, but others may not consider us so. They
would want us to adapt to their ways, adapt to their tongues, adapt

to their gods, adapt their views of right and wrong. Maybe they're right, for we're few and they're more in number.'

The crowd was getting restive. She wanted to say what she felt, for she was not sure whether she would be able to say them again.

'Beloved Vanaras, we used to believe our dark skin and thick tongues are signs of beauty, but now we're being told they're ugly. We have now also begun to believe it is the truth. We loved our language and respected others, we believed like the myriad flowers of the jungle, each is a part of the jungle, each is beautiful in its own way. Those days are gone. Now, we're like crops in a farm. Each must be exactly same as the other, with no diversity allowed. Anything different would be considered a weed and destroyed without delay. Unlike in the forest, where nothing belongs to anyone and everything belongs to everyone, in a farm, each plant belongs to the master. When the master needs, he will mow you down, he will thresh you, pound you, grain you, chaff you, ground you and even burn you. There are benefits of course, for your master will feed you water and give you manure. He will sit with a stick to protect you from being eaten by hungry beasts. He is cultivating you for a harvest that fills only his belly. Maybe he is right, for he has won, and we have lost. The time has come for every one of us to be a clone of the other, with no independent thoughts, no different language, customs, cultures or beliefs. So, mow down your enemy, or who your master shows you as the enemy and don't think much. Be a part of the mob and rejoice in violence. Be a bhakta, a devotee, and wait for the good times. Maybe that is the future. Therein may lie the glory.'

She paused to see the reaction of her subjects. She licked her dry lips, took a deep breath and plunged again.

'No one should say that the Vanara king isn't a man of his word. So, you all will be fight a war which isn't yours. We're being dragged to a fight where one prince has mutilated a woman and another man has kidnapped a woman in revenge. When you invite an outsider to meddle in a fight between brothers, the best you can hope for is slavery. Be good slaves for the new master, for you have no other choice now. But even when you fight, try to keep the values that we have cherished since the dawn of our race. Face your enemies like men and fight till your last breath. Leave the people who aren't a part of the war alone. That means no children, women, old men and invalids should be harmed by Vanaras. The cities or towns should be left alone, no looting or burning down homes of innocents. Even if you can't bring glory to your King, don't bring him shame. Even if you lose, you will lose doing the right things.'

The crowd was agitated. They were shifting their feet. She could understand their dilemma. They were worried about their families once they left to fight the war; who would tend their meagre farms, who would provide for their little ones and old parents? Even Tara had no idea, but she had to try her best to send these poor men with some consolation. Most of them may never come back, but they should not leave with a heavy heart. They were the subjects of her beloved Baali.

Tara's eyes were getting misty. She could feel their pain. She could sense their fear. She could see hundreds of children standing far away, staring at her.

'My dear brothers, worry not, for I shall be there with your women. I shall ensure your family is taken care of.' Tara's voice had gone hoarse. She addressed the women, young and old who were huddled at the far end of the courtyard, 'My sisters, my mothers. Can we not overcome this together?'

After a moment's silence, the women shrilled, 'Yes!'

'Can't we farm ourselves? I shall be with you. Can we not bring up our children together, even if your men don't come back. Are we not sisters?'

'We shall!' the women cried back.

'My son Angada will accompany the King in this war.'

Tara said. It burned her heart to part with Angada, with no guarantee that she would ever see him again. But if she kept him safe, and allowed other women's children to perish, how would she face herself. She gestured to Angada to come near her. The crowd was getting emotional now. Some were crying. Tara hugged her son and showered him with kisses.

'Angada, you will uphold the honour of your father, the great King Baali. You will come back victorious.'

When Angada bowed to touch her feet, her restraint broke and she broke down into sobs. She didn't hear the thousand voices hailing her and her deceased husband Baali. She stood at the balcony, gripping the balustrade with her eyes closed. The pain she felt was excruciating. Her pain was multiplied by the pain felt by every mother who was bidding goodbye to her son, for she was the queen. She watched people assembling.

Rama and Lakshmana were assembling the army of the ragtag Vanaras, some carrying clubs, some stones, some kitchen knives, to take on the might of the most powerful king in the world. Sugreeva came to say goodbye to her. The parting was quite formal, stiff and forced. Sugreeva asked her not to worry about Angada. The boy would come back as a man and it was an honour to fight for dharma, a privilege to be on the side of good that was sure to vanquish evil. He would learn what was right and what was wrong.

She saw her father straining to climb the steps to her palace and rushed to him. When he saw her, he smiled showing his toothless gum. He ran his fingers through her hair and said, 'I too am going, daughter.'

'Where?' she cried.

'To war,' the old man chuckled. 'I can't fight anyone. But they will need a Vaidya. Both sides. How can I sleep peacefully in my home when our people need me the most?'

Before she could find words to reply, her father was gone, alone with the army of Vanaras to fight someone else's war. The army carried her son Angada too to a war to be fought on a distant island, against a man who his father had defeated in a war in which men had fought like men, face-to-face. Tara wasn't sure how this war for vanquishing evil would be fought in distant Lanka.

# Chapter 42

The next monsoon passed without any incidents. No one attacked Kishkinda for the word had spread that all men had gone away, and the country was ruled by women. All Rakshasa, Asura, Naga, Yaksha and other tribes kept away from them for it would have been dishonourable to take advantage of another tribe's misfortune. That was the unwritten law of tribes in the forest. In fact, some Yakshas were willing to send help but Tara politely declined. She wanted her women to gain confidence, to make them learn to live with the sweat of their brows and the strength of their arms instead of depending on their men. This was a God-given opportunity. She was determined to take full advantage of the misfortune. Surprizingly, with no Sugreeva to fight over, Ruma had become herself again and was most enthusiastic in helping Tara achieve her dream.

When it was time for the next harvest, she looked at the fields that had turned golden, the sheep that had multiplied and her heart swelled with pride. Petty fights broke out among women initially as everyone was edgy and sick with worry, but slowly even those died down and the easy camaraderie that developed started knocking down the walls of caste that had been creeping into the society of Vanaras after Baali's death They were going back to the egalitarian tribal way of life that they had cherished for eons before the slow poisoning of Varna and Jati were brought in by the Brahmins after Sugreeva took over as the King.

Tara noticed that no one sat around idle, looking within oneself, in the name of trying to know the unknown. Such were the luxuries of men who had stuffed their bellies with sufficient food. No woman who had been once a daughter, sister, wife or mother could deny the truth of the world and go in search of a mirage. There was no time to waste searching for the unknown. And no seeker of the so-called ultimate truth had told them what one would do after knowing what is ultimate. What was beyond that? What use was it to know about something that one could never change or own or destroy? No wonder women were exempted from being the seekers of this 'truth' and so were the so-called lower castes. No one closed their eyes to the beauty of life and the reality of the world. They missed their loved ones often and discussions turned to the war that was being fought in some distant southern island, but they found solace in work and friendship. Being women, they worried even about the women of Lanka and wondered whether they felt the same pain they felt. And in their prayers, they wished them luck and even if their logic told them that both sides could not win, their hearts wished everyone well. They hoped that Rama and Ravana fought each other in a duel in the manner the Vanaras and other forest tribes used to settle disputes instead of the civilized way of burning down cities and butchering thousands and the winning side calling it a victory of good over evil.

One day, she received news that Rishabha wasn't well. Rishabha was one of the few Vanaras who hadn't soured his relations with Sugreeva. Tara visited his hut and found that the old man had suffered a stroke. He was lying down on the floor on a torn mat. He had no one to call his own. When she entered his dwelling, the strong and unpleasant stench of stale urine and pus made her gag. She wanted to run out, but she couldn't leave the old man alone. The village women peeped in through the cracks in the wall and crowded at the window and door. Tara was livid. How could they leave him to die like this? Rishabha's vacant eyes stared at the roof. She went near him and touched his shoulders. Slowly, he turned his eyes towards her. She saw them shining with tears. She remembered the fights she had had with him and the meanness he had shown to her. For a moment, she thought that fate was punishing him, but she was immediately overwhelmed by guilt for thinking so. She was the daughter of Sushena, the widow of Baali—she couldn't have such thoughts. She wiped her tears with the back of her hands and smiled at him. The old man started sobbing. His face was partially paralysed, and his mouth slanted at a grotesque angle when he tried to talk. He was trying to say something. She put her ears near his mouth. She was shocked when she deciphered what he told her with great difficulty. He was calling her a b**** who conspired with Sugreeva to kill Baali. She trembled with anger and disgust. *He deserves to die like a worm*, she thought.

She looked at the frail figure of Rishabha and sighed. The poor man was embarrassed that he had to depend on a woman. He was trying to assuage whatever little pride he had. It was an old man's babble, a sign of senility perhaps. She wasn't going to lose her sanity for his sake. She called for help to lift the old man up. She made him sit and started cleaning his bedsores. The old man continued to curse her. Later, she had him transferred to the cave palace. She knew there was no recovery and death would be a blessing for Rishabha. She learned to ignore his frequent screams in the night, accusing her of killing Baali.

Travelling minstrels brought news from the South. Unexpectedly, she received a message from her long-lost friend. A kinnara had brought her the leaf. It was a letter from Prabha. She had met the Vanaras under Sugreeva. In her characteristic style, it started abruptly:

'Tara, I met him after a long time and he hasn't changed much. I am sorry I never tried to contact you. I wanted to run away from everything after Sugreeva rejected me. I wanted to die but never had the courage. I love life too much, Tara. I have travelled in all directions, without any aim. I saw life, Tara. I was a lone woman travelling without a male companion. I was loved, hated, chased away, welcomed, ignored, accepted, raped, molested, protected—ha, everything has happened to me. Somewhere, sometime, I learned to forget Sugreeva. I thought I had gotten over everything. But when I met him, I knew nothing has changed for me. They were in search of some Deva woman, the wife of some prince. I don't know why they were bothered about some prince and his wife. Vana Naras will never learn, will they? To think that they are helping the man who killed your Baali. How foolish of me. I am sorry, Tara. I am hearing many dark rumours. What happened to Baali? I heard someone killed him on the sly. I even heard it was one of the two princes. I don't believe that rumour at all. If it was one of those princes, Sugreeva wouldn't be helping them. Would he? I asked him about it, but he was uneasy. Poor man. He loved his brother too much. How inconsiderate of me. I am sorry, Tara. Despite all my learning, I am your foolish Prabha. You were lucky to have a man like Baali in your life, dear. You are also lucky to have someone like Sugreeva. I know it is cruel, but I sometimes wish I were in your place. But my destiny is to be a mendicant. No regrets in life. That is what we say, isn't it? Even if I am, do I stand a chance? I know Sugreeva is your husband now and he loves you deeply. Don't worry about me. I am not going to be your rival. You did the right thing by marrying him, Tara. Angada is such a charming boy. I met him too. He looks like Baali, no, Sugreeva. Ha, ha, they were so similar, no? The men we fell in love with in the prime of our youth. I wish those days would come back. How is your father? I feel like visiting you. I want to be the same old Prabha again, looking out for handsome boys, swimming in the river, swinging and playing hopscotch. Alas, I am a mendicant now, in search of the ultimate truth, though I have no idea what it is. Such is life. Why did we become old, Tara?'

The letter ended as abruptly as it had begun. Tara smiled through her tears. Her mind became heavy with memories. Why did they become old, she repeated the stupid question of Prabha and laughed. She tore the letter to pieces and flung it up. She watched the wind carry away the pieces of her friend's letter and deposit them in the river. The river would take them to the sea and it would dissolve one day, never to be seen again. Why did they grow up? She asked the breeze. She wished she could hold Prabha's hand and run through the dry riverbank, their faces in the howling wind. She knew those days would never come back, neither would her friend.

It was after another two months that she heard from a traveling minstrel that Hanuman had gone to Lanka and had been captured by Ravana's son. Tara was sitting with the women's council when the minstrel came with the news. The women crowded around him, anxious to know the whereabouts of their loved ones. When the singer said Hanuman had burned down Lanka in revenge, they booed him and called him a liar. For they were sure that no one would arrest a messenger and set him on fire and no messenger would set a city of innocent people on fire for the rancour he felt for their King. Tara could never believe her gentle friend would do such things. They had never heard any such thing in their lives and they could not conceive such things could ever happen. They lamented about the exaggerations of the poets and their propensity to lie. And this soon became a joke among Vanara women, and the word poet became a synonym for liar. Only Tara felt uneasy, for she knew the definitions of right and wrong were changing and the Vanaras were too naïve to grasp the rapidity of change. She tried to prepare them for the new world, but it was difficult to make her people understand the complexities of the civilizational progress that was advancing towards them like wildfire.

Tara learned about the wonderful bridge that Nala built over the sea and her heart filled with pride for her friend. When the news came that Ravana was betrayed by his brother and was killed by Rama, the women of Kishkinda rejoiced. Their men would be home soon, and celebrations broke out. No one spoke about the secret dread that all women harboured about their men not being there in the victorious army that would soon return. There were hushed discussions about the strange news of Rama asking his wife to enter the fire and prove her chastity. This was unconceivable for ordinary folks of Kishkinda. They could not believe Rama would drag so many people to the battlefield if he suspected she was unchaste. And they wondered what the big deal was about being chaste, for among Vanaras, the man who won the duel always kept the woman. That was the rule among all beasts of the forest. Sometimes even women fought duels over men. They could understand such fights but not the chastity angle and how fire could prove or disprove it. After many discussions and gossips, they concluded that it was another lie by a poet. Tara was not so sure, for she had heard of such tests from the Brahmins who came often to do sacrifices in palaces during Baali's time. She remembered when she had offered to enter the fire after she had argued with Baali when he came back and how he had scoffed at the idea. He had taken her word for the truth despite his anger and jealousy towards Sugreeva at that time. He had trusted her to be honest and had he not, she would have never agreed to stay with him despite her heart-wrenching love for him.

Kishkinda waited for the return of the heroes. Every dawn, women would look longingly towards the south, expecting them to burst forth from the horizon and come rushing with victorious yells and slogans. The war was over, and they would be here soon. Old men worried whether they would die before they could see their sons one more time. Mothers made the favourite dishes every morning and wives dressed in the finest dresses. Children discussed what their fathers would bring and sisters yearned to once again argue and fight with their brothers. If only they would come soon. Rishabha died on a full moon day and Tara buried him near the grave of Riksarajas. They were rivals, but death erases all rivalry and friendship. Sometimes, she thought she heard Rishabha cursing her even from the grave. She never understood what she had done for him to hate her so much except for being a woman. She had forgiven him long ago.

The winter had set in and trees had started losing their leaves when the first news about the heroes' arrival reached Kishkinda. A few shepherds had seen them coming; they were a boisterous lot, halting in every village on the way and tasting the finest toddy in every tavern. Kishkinda was decorated with pontoons and mango leaves; marigold flowers were hung on every tree on the dusty village route. Near the village wells and tanks, by the river ghats and market places, conversation centred on the imminent arrival of the sons of Kishkinda.

They came one evening, a huge procession of unwashed, unkempt, war-weary men in their dusty dresses and matted hair, wild and rapturous in their victory—marching towards Kishkinda. As they waddled through the knee-deep waters of Pampa, any resemblance of order broke down and they started running, howling, shrieking, and raising dust to the skies. The women ran to meet them halfway. There were hugs and kisses and touching reunions. Children were tossed up by unshaven men high in the air and caught mid-way. Dogs yelped and danced around their long-lost masters, wagging their tails like fans. Shy brides forgot their bashfulness and kissed their husbands with gay abandon, almost choking the laughing men in their bear-like embrace. Mothers fussed over the lean bodies of their young sons, daughters cosied up with their fathers. Sisters teased their brothers and old men who were bent with age, suddenly found strength in their spines and stood erect and proud, grinning with their toothless smiles, watching the women of their families fuss around with their sons and grandsons, wishing they could show their affections and pride in the same way as women.

Many women returned beating their breasts, for their men had died and were never going to set foot in Kishkinda again. They waited until the last of the men had climbed ashore. Friends who had seen their husbands or sons or brothers die, came to break the news to them and tried to soften the blow by saying how bravely they had fought in the war. No words of consolation lessened the pain made bitter by the gaiety of the ones who had survived. It didn't matter that their loved ones had died for a God in his war against a demon—the death felt cruel and the finality of its devastation, just the same.

Tara waited at the gates of Kishkinda fort, eager to meet her son. She tried to push away the thoughts that he might have perhaps become a cripple or may be affected by a fatal injury. Near her, Ruma stood chattering incoherently, crying and laughing at the same time. They saw a group of Vanaras coming towards the fort. It was a riotous, boisterous gang carrying two men on their shoulders. They were dancing wildly as the group rushed through the narrow path leading to the gate. Clubs and swords were thrown up in the air and caught unfailingly. The victory cries from a thousand throats shook the foundations of the fort. Drummers and singers had joined the procession, and each played to their wish, with no respect to tune or rhythm. It all added to the cacophony and the air was electric with frenzied energy.

As they neared, Sugreeva jumped down from the shoulders of men who were carrying him and ran to Tara. Ruma rushed forward with open arms. Tara watched with blurred eyes, her happiness knew no bounds. Sugreeva stopped before Ruma.

'How are you, Ruma?' Sugreeva asked.

Ruma broke down, her words became incoherent. She closed her mouth with the back of her palm and cried. Sugreeva smiled at her kindly and Ruma embraced him and wept on his shoulders. It broke Tara's heart to see that Sugreeva's hands didn't embrace Ruma back. He stood stiff and awkward, looking embarrassed. Sugreeva gestured with his eyes to the waiting maids and they came to gently separate Ruma from him.

Sugreeva walked to Tara with wide open hands, expecting her to rush to his embrace. He had become leaner and fitter and had grown a beard. He looked handsome and tough and resembled Baali more than ever. He came so near to her with his open hands that she could smell his muskiness, his lust, and his longing.

Tara looked straight at his eyes and asked, 'Where is Baali's son?'

His face fell, but he recovered fast. He smiled, reminding her of Baali again, and gestured with a sweeping hand. Angada stepped forward.

Tara staggered with shock. The man stooped to touch her feet. Angada had changed so much. He had become a man. He resembled a young Baali, the one she had met fresh after his arrival with Riksarajas, so long ago yet so fresh in her mind. She pressed him to her bosom and showered his forehead with kisses. His stubble that brushed her cheeks surprised and shocked her. She wished he was still the baby who she could carry in her arms and show the crows and cuckoos. She felt his face, his strong limbs and broad shoulders, felt proud of him and sad that she had grown so old. She hadn't noticed the traces of wrinkles that had started appearing on her hand until she had saw them contrasted with her son's smooth skin.

'You've grown so . . . so big,' she finally managed to say. She could feel the jealousy emanating from Ruma who was standing beside her. She wished he would talk to Ruma and chided herself in her mind. This was her son, there was no need for her to be so generous. Angada was Baali's son. It was alright to be a bit selfish when it came to one's son.

'Tara,' Sugreeva said softly. 'Do you know what our son did?'

Tara didn't miss how he said our son. She ignored it. She was eager to know his exploits, to learn about her son's heroism in war.

'Without Angada, we wouldn't have won the war,' Sugreeva said.

She looked at her son, drinking the raw confidence and power that emanated out of him. Her chest burst with pride. She wished they were inside her chamber and not in the street with thousands of eyes fixed on them. *Oh, how I wish to fuss over him, run my fingers through his unruly hair, how I wish to feed him his favourite dishes*, she thought.

'Tell me, tell me about my Angada,' she said and the crowd cheered.

Sugreeva said, 'Our son has become a man, Tara. I promised you that he would come back a hero. Behold your hero.'

'Won't you tell me, please. I'm dying to hear about my Angada's valour.'

Sugreeva put his hand on Angada's shoulder and pressed him close. He started narrating the valour of Angada.

'The war was at a crucial juncture. Ravana's army attacked relentlessly. Ravana's son Meghanada had even succeeded in critically wounding Lakshmana and it was only due to the timely action of Hanuman that he was saved. As we were discussing the ways to defeat the King of Lanka, we heard the news that Ravana was making a sacrifice. Astrologers predicted that if the demon king completed this yajna, Ravana would become invincible. We were worried. It was a war of Dharma against Adharma. The evil should not be allowed to be victorious. No one knew what had to be done to save the war for us.'

Sugreeva paused and looked at Angada with pride. Angada stood with swelled chest and a confident air. Sugreeva continued, 'And Tara, when we were worrying about the Yajna, do you know what our son did? Such a strategist, such a brilliant thinker and if I may add, a bit of impulsive too. But he is young and that is to be expected, but his planning and execution was meticulous and brilliant. Tara, I couldn't have come up with such a plan even to save my life!'

The crowd cheered. They hailed the young prince of Kishkinda. Tara waited impatiently for Sugreeva to reveal what action her son had done that merited so much praise. Baali, she thought, would have been proud.

'Angada sneaked into the palace of Lanka. It was a grave risk and had I known, I wouldn't have allowed him to do that. Imagine breaking into the palace of the most feared Asura king Ravana? That is what our son did, this brave young man. He sneaked into the palace and found that Ravana was busy doing the Yajna. The demon's face must have looked fearsome in the light of sacrificial fire. Anyone less brave would have fainted but not our brave son. He broke into the Antapura of Ravana and found his wife, Mandodari. She was asleep, and he grabbed her by her hair. The poor woman screamed in panic. Angada dragged her through the corridor and tore her clothes off.'

Tara was shocked! 'He did WHAT?' she asked in disbelief.

Sugreeva continued, 'That was a brilliant, strategic move, Tara. He let her cry. It was a grave risk to take as other Asuras could've come there. A few came too but were too shocked to find their queen in the grip of a Vanara. Two of them tried foolishly to save their queen, but Angada cut them down. Others ran to inform their king, but Angada didn't want to wait. He dragged the half-naked queen to the sacrificial altar. The soldiers of Ravana were standing nearby, too scared to disturb their King's prayers. They knew this Yajna would make him immortal and even the Maryadapurushottam, Rama, the epitome of virtue and avatar of Vishnu, would not be able to slay the demon after the Yajna. Mandodari cried loudly at her nakedness.'

The crowd laughed at that comment. A few of the men jeered and catcalls and whistles were heard. Tara stood rooted, not able to believe her ears.

'The queen of the great Ravana cried that her husband was a shameless man. He was more worried about his death than the honour of his wife. She compared him with Rama who was willing to fight a war for his wife whereas Ravana was busy saving his own. That riled the Asura King. He stopped the Yajna and opened his eyes. His face contorted in rage at the sight of his hapless wife in the arms of Angada. He took his famed sword, Chandrahasa, and rushed towards Angada, but our son ran away. The poor King was so busy consoling his wife that he didn't bother to chase Angada.'

'I would have killed that demon,' Angada said. 'I didn't want to run away, scared. I ran away because it wasn't right on my part to deny that honour of killing Ravana to Lord Rama. I had done my dharma, I had stopped the Yajna.'

'Brilliant!' Sugreeva said and the crowd cheered.

Tara moved forward. 'Angada,' she called in a tired voice.

'Yes, mother,' he beamed.

Tara slapped him hard. 'You did that to a woman? You tore the clothes off a woman? You dared to touch her without her consent? Is this what you have learned?' She kept slapping him as he cowered in anger and fear. She pummelled him, screaming and hitting him hard across his face, his chest, wherever she could lay her hands. She didn't care that others were trying to stop her. She didn't feel Sugreeva slapping her hard or her nose bleeding. She didn't hear people abusing her. She kept hitting her son, 'You good-for-nothing scoundrel. I sent you to make you a man and you've returned a monster. Is this the dharma you learned? You should have died there in Lanka itself.'

They pulled her away from a battered Angada with great difficulty. Sugreeva glowered at her. Tara stood panting, her hair dishevelled and her cheeks burning with anger. Ruma was consoling Angada. Tara saw him weeping on Ruma's shoulders and her anger boiled again. She rushed to beat him again, but Sugreeva stopped her.

'Tara, have you gone mad?' he asked.

She stared at him and then without another word, she started walking away from them. The crowd parted to give her way. Some commented on her sanity, some called her a witch who didn't know how to honour a hero. Some threw expletives at her. It wasn't the Kishkinda she knew. War had changed their men. She walked through the crowd who were pushing and shoving to enter the palace premises. A celebration was being planned and she wanted to get as far away from it as possible.

Tara walked without any purpose. It was getting dark. She was awash with an empty feeling. She wished she could cry. Shadows thickened, and the river turned dark by the time she reached the overgrown palmyra grove. She sat on the grass and waited. Chemba came to her, parting the bushes. The wolf had gone old and weak. Its paws were filled with sores and blisters. It limped painfully to Tara and lay down beside her. She broke down upon seeing her husband's dear friend, who was still working without losing hope. She knew her love was worthless before that of the wolf's. *Man strived to be God when he couldn't even match animals*, she thought.

Tara didn't know for whom and what she was waiting for. Countless memories swirled in her mind, but they had lost their colours. They faded to different shades of grey, blurring, snapping and entwining. She desperately tried to clutch them, but they were fast losing their meaning.

A dull moon rose above the distant hills and earth appeared weary and old. Not a leaf stirred and silence thickened. She sat with her back to the stub of a palmyra tree, listlessly watching the grey clouds that crawled in the sky. She could hear the gaieties from the palace.

'Tara . . .'

She was not surprised when she heard it for she had been waiting to hear it. The wolf stood up on its legs. It let out a happy yelp.

She said, 'Here is your Chemba, your friend.' She felt the breeze caress the wolf's fur. The wolf shivered and emitted a mournful whine. It wagged its tail furiously and jumped up and down, excited. She watched the joy of the dumb beast with a tearful smile.

'I knew you would come,' Tara whispered to the wind.

'I knew it too.'

Baali's voice was kind and soft and that made her break down. She cried her heart out. She was grateful that he didn't try to pacify her. When she had cried her full, she smiled.

'I miss you a lot,' Tara said.

'I haven't gone anywhere. I have always been with you, Tara.'

'I–' she was too choked by her tears to speak. 'Why do you love me so much, Baali? I don't deserve your love. I've failed in everything I have done. Even when I was married to you, I was sometimes unfaithful—at least in my thoughts. And when I was married to your brother, I thought about you. I'm not worth half of this faithful Chemba.'

'In love, there are no *whys*, Tara.'

Tara's eyes filled. 'I want to see you, I want to touch you, I want to feel you in my arms. Come back, Baali.'

She was terrified of the silence that followed.

'Are you there?' she asked.

There was no answer.

'Baali, talk to me. Please don't go away. Please . . . I will never express such a wish. Please keep talking to me.'

Silence.

'I have failed you, Baali. I could not bring up our son to be worthy of you,' she cried into the wilderness. She waited for an answer. The silence was a damning indictment.

'You too have started hating me. I don't want to live anymore,' Tara screamed. Something scurried away in the bushes startled by her outburst. She collapsed on the grass and started weeping.

'Tara . . .'

She was alarmed to hear his voice. She looked around. It was frighteningly dark. The grey clouds had succeeded in silently sneaking up and and trapping the moon in their claws.

'Times are changing, Tara. A Baali doesn't have any place in this new world. I would have been a misfit. A new era is dawning and men like Angada will inherit it. A new world is dawning where convoluted justifications will take the place of the simple sense of right and wrong. Dwarfs will be made into giants and praised by blind followers who will attack like a pack of wolves and devour any dissenters. But don't give up, Tara. In the era of darkness, be a lamp. Your people need you. Don't give up on life.'

Tara didn't raise her head, but her tears had stopped. She waited for him to speak more. She felt a whiff of air on her cheek and stood up startled. Was that his parting kiss? She felt pain ripping her guts to shreds. The wolf disappeared into the bushes.

'Baali . . . please . . . come back . . . come back . . .' she cried. There was no response. Baali had said everything he had to say. She roamed around in the palmyra grove, frantically looking for Baali. She didn't see the night bleeding to death and dawn breaking out. She kept on walking as if in a frenzy.

'There she is . . .'

She heard someone cry, followed by the sound of many men running towards her. She was soon surrounded by a mob. They stood leaning on long sticks and swords. She watched them with curiosity. She felt no fear. They were drunk, and the pungent smell of sour toddy made her wince.

'We were searching for you, b****. How dare you insult our hero? Don't you know we fought a holy war? Don't you know it was done for dharma?' one of the men yelled at her.

She started laughing. The men looked at each other in confusion. They had expected her to fall on her knees and beg for mercy.

'Stop laughing. We're going to lynch you,' another man warned her. She laughed aloud, clutching her belly. They stood stunned. She pushed one man away and ran towards the palmyra grove. They chased her. When they neared her, she stopped in her tracks, turned towards them and started laughing again.

'She has gone mad,' one of the men whispered.

'Let us finish her off,' another man suggested.

They approached her, warily. She stood looking at them and as they approached, she called out at the top of her voice, 'Baali'. She turned to the grove and screamed Baali's name again. She caught the nearest man's wrist and cried, 'Baali, come fast, I have caught a scoundrel.'

Other men had taken to their heels. The man Tara had caught struggled to get free. She held him in a vice-like grip, 'Where are you running, O warrior of dharma. Fight with my husband and show your valour. Fight your king Baali,' she laughed. The man was on the verge of tears. He was terrified.

'The king is coming,' she whispered and that sent him into convulsions of fear. She felt pity for the coward and let him go just as suddenly. He fell back, scrambled up and ran away as fast as his legs would take him. She laughed aloud. She took a stone and flung it at him. 'Cowards! You're brave only when you're in a mob.'

By the evening, Sugreeva came with Ruma. They tried to persuade her to return to the palace. She searched for Angada among the people who had come to visit her. He was not there. She smiled bitterly. Sugreeva apologized for everything, but she knew he meant nothing. The war had changed everyone. She refused to go to the palace. She could see a a sense of relief on Ruma's face. Tara felt happy for her. The poor girl was going to have her husband for herself for the first time in her life.

They left by nightfall, having failed to persuade her. Later, a guard came with food, placed it far away from the grove and called out to her. When she appeared, he ran away in fear. For a few days, Sugreeva came with food for her. She shared it with the birds and soon many little animals started moving around in the grove without the fear of humans. She never failed to take some food to the wolf that kept digging the stone grave of Baali. She would watch it devour the food as fast it could, so that it could resume its work.

Sugreeva would often come and sit with her. They would sit in silence. They had nothing to say to each other. Slowly, the frequency of his visits dwindled and soon he stopped visiting altogether. The food also stopped coming from the palace and she went hungry for a few days. It resumed when Ruma herself came with the food. Tara wondered how old Ruma had become and laughed when Ruma said the same thing about her. Time was flowing fast like River Pampa. Ruma said Sugreeva was not keeping well and it filled Tara with immense melancholy. Age was catching up with all of them, but both women were worried about Sugreeva's health.

One day, the news of Ruma's death came unexpectedly. Tara wept silently in the grove and for the first time in many years, she prayed. She wept for Angada too, for the boy had considered Ruma, his mother. She could feel his pain. She wished she could see her son one more time. She heard Sugreeva had taken ill and Angada had become the king. She hoped against hope that he would come to take her blessings before he ascended the throne. After a few days, she lost that hope. She heard about the death of her father and saw a massive crowd going for the funeral. Vaidya Sushena had died poor but had more people at the funeral than any King. Such were the ironies of life and she had learned to laugh at them. Hanuman and Nala had become devotees of Rama and had migrated to Ayodhya. She missed her dear friends sometimes but was also happy not to meet them. With their blind devotion to their master, she might not have even recognized them had she met them. There was no news of Prabha. Some traveling singer said she had gone to Himalayas in search of the inner truth. That amused Tara a lot. If she had to climb an icy mountain to find herself, she would have preferred to be lost.

The food supply from the palace stopped altogether and she knew Sugreeva too had vanished into the folds of time. She felt numb when she heard the news. Her tumultuous youth and the crazy love she had for both the brothers made her smile and wished she could live her life one more time and commit the same mistakes again.

One day she had found a young couple burying their child. She watched them from a distance, her heart heavy with the grief of a bereaved mother. There were a few men at the funeral, some of whom she recognized. Then she saw the young father. It was the man who had tried to lynch her. She felt sorry for him. They were about to bury the child when something caught her eye. The child was not dead. Without thinking, she rushed to the funeral, shouting at them. Men scattered in fear, except the young mother. Tara took the child in her arms and rushed to her sleeping place in the grove. She hurriedly prepared her herbs and dripped it into its nose. After a tense moment, the child bawled. She rushed back to the grave yard and placed the child in the mother's hand. The mother showered the child with kisses and men rushed to see the miracle. Without a word, Tara withdrew to the grove and stood watching the ecstasy of the mother and the happiness of the father who had got their child back from the clutches of death. Tara said a silent prayer to her father, Vaidya Sushena, and thanked him for teaching her well. She went back to her makeshift bed with a full heart. She had to tell Baali how she had saved a life. He would be so proud of her.

She went hungry for a week after the incident but was pleasantly surprised to find food placed in a plantain leaf near the lamp lit at the entrance of the grove. Soon she found out that the men who had tried to lynch her were the ones who came with the offerings. They called her Devi. She was amused that the men who wanted to kill her had now elevated her to the status of a Goddess. Village women came to pray before her and unwind their worries. Men had changed after war and they always expected their women to serve them. The easy and egalitarian family life of Kishkinda had become a thing of the past. Men guarded women like they guarded their cattle and property and dictated how women should dress, speak, laugh and cry. This often led to family stifes which were settled by men with their fists. Earlier, the honour of a man depended on his honesty, now it was tied to the way their women dressed or spoke. The men were in awe of the Agnipariksha and how fire proved the chastity and many women perished in flames to the eternal shame of their family members. Men had lost the capability to treat women as their partners, friends and equals— now they were either to be despised, lusted over or won as a prize.

And if they were inaccessible, to be either shamed as a whore or revered like a Goddess.

Tara was disturbed by what she heard and saw. Poverty was stalking Kiskhinda as the society got divided into many sections. Soon many volunteered to be slaves. This was the destiny of Vanaras as per the holy books of Devas. If some Baali arose, well, they could be shot down and the equilibrium of dharma would be restored. She often wondered about the brimming barns the women had produced during the war years and wondered how with so many men around, hunger never left the homes of the poor. Earlier, everyone used to lend a hand in the fields, now it was the dharma of one specific caste only.

Tara often remembered Baali's words which reminded her that she should try to be a lamp in the sea of darkness. As time passed, she became a revered figure, a mother Goddess to entire Kishkinda and beyond. She would often sit by the palmyra tree and hold her court. Here, poor men and simple village women came with their problems. These were the dregs of the society, who were now banished from walking on streets without a pot tied to their necks to catch their saliva from falling and defiling the holy feet of the rich. Many had to tie a broom to their backs so that their footsteps were rubbed off from the path of the Brahmins. The world of Vanaras had turned a full circle. Simple gods who could be propitiated with a share of food and lived under trees, open to elements and accessible to all people, had grown powerless. Many gods had retreated to the inner forests, along with people who were unwanted by the society. Grand temples had come up where the majority of the people weren't allowed. The new gods craved for gold and ornaments. They weren't the ones to be satisfied with a bunch of bananas or a loaf of meat and a pot of toddy. They needed elaborate rituals. They demanded gold caparisoned elephants or carved chariots to visit their devotees, which they did once a year, condescendingly. They heard the prayers only if they were told in an unknown tongue and mumbled by a priest.

For many Kishkinda people who were too poor and impure of birth to be considered by the great Gods, Tara was a solace. Tara was a simple God. She had no powers to take avatars and vanquish evil. She didn't believe in evil or good. She believed in life. She didn't offer miracles, but pointed to those who had lost hope that life itself was a miracle. Her grove became a refuge to all forms of life. Soon, Kings came visiting to seek her advice and sat with commoners. At least in her presence, all were the same. She sat with the wolf lying at her feet in her lap and gave discourses. People heard her in awe and forgot whatever she had said the moment they left the grove.

But when everyone left after the sunset, she would often try to converse with Baali. She never got a reply. But the old wolf Chemba would come to her, often crawling because now he was too old to walk. He had never given up in his attempt to bring back Baali. Tara often wished she had the wolf's forbearance. The old wolf would lick her arms often and she would feel as if her Baali was kissing her. Baali had vanished after that eventful night. Yet, she lived with the hope that one day he would come back, cheating death yet again. When he returns, she promised herself, she would be as selfless as Baali's dearest wolf and love him as much as the old wolf did.